This bo ned on or before

The Siege of Krishnapur

The Siege of Krishnapur

a novel by

J. G. Farrell

Weidenfeld and Nicolson
London

ISBN 0 297 76580 9

Printed in Great Britain by
REDWOOD BURN LIMITED
Trowbridge & Esher

For W. F. F.

Part One

Anyone who has never before visited Krishnapur, and who approaches from the east, is likely to think he has reached the end of his journey a few miles sooner than he expected. While still some distance from Krishnapur he begins to ascend a shallow ridge. From here he will see what appears to be a town in the heat-distorted distance. He will see the white glitter of walls and roofs and a handsome grove of trees, perhaps even the dome of what might be a temple. Round about there will be the unending plain still, exactly as it has been for many miles back, a dreary ocean of bald earth, in the immensity of which an occasional field of sugar cane or mustard is utterly lost.

The surprising thing is that this plain is not quite deserted, as one might expect. As he crosses it towards the white walls in the distance the traveller may notice an occasional figure way out somewhere between the road and the horizon, a man walking with a burden on his head in one direction or another ... even though, at least to the eye of a stranger, within the limit of the horizon there does not appear to be anywhere worth walking to, unless perhaps to that distant town he has spotted; one part looks quite as good as another. But if you look closely and shield your eyes from the glare you will make out tiny villages here and there, difficult to see because they are made of the same mud as the plain they came from; and no doubt they melt back into it again during the rainy season, for there is no lime in these parts, no clay or shale that you can burn into bricks, no substance hard enough to resist the seasons over the years.

Sometimes the village crouches in a grove of bamboo and possesses a frightful pond with a water-buffalo or two; more often there is just a well to be worked from dawn till dusk by the same two men and two bullocks every single day in their lives. But whether there is a pond or not hardly matters to a traveller; in either case there is no comfort here, nothing that a European might recognize as civilization. All the more reason for him to press on, therefore, towards those distant white walls which are clearly made of bricks. Bricks are undoubtedly an essential ingredient of civilization; one gets nowhere at all without them.

But as he approaches he will see that this supposed town is utterly deserted; it is merely a melancholy cluster of white domes and planes surrounded by a few trees. There are no people to be seen. Everything lies perfectly still. Nearer again, of course, he will see that it is not a town at all, but one of those ancient cemeteries that are called "Cities of the Silent", which one occasionally comes across in northern India. Perhaps a rare traveller will turn off the road to rest in the shade of a mango grove which separates the white tombs from a dilapidated mosque; sometimes one may find incense left smouldering in an earthenware saucer by an unseen hand. But otherwise there is no life here; even the rustling leaves have a dead sound.

Krishnapur itself had once been the centre of civil administration for a large district. At that time European bungalows had been built there on a lavish scale, even small palaces standing in grounds of several acres to house the Company representatives of the day who lived in magnificent style and sometimes even, in imitation of the native princes, kept tigers and mistresses and heaven knows what else. But then the importance of Krishnapur declined and these magnificent officials moved elsewhere. Their splendid bungalows were left shuttered and empty; their gardens ran wild during the rainy season and for the rest of the year dried up into deserts, over whose baked earth whirlwinds of dust glided back and forth like ghostly dancers.

Now with the creaking of loose shutters and the sighing of the wind in the tall grass, the cantonment has the air of a place you might see in a melancholy dream; a visitor might well find himself reminded of the "City of the Silent" he had passed on his way to Krishnapur.

The first sign of trouble at Krishnapur came with a mysterious distribution of chapatis, made of coarse flour and about the

4

size and thickness of a biscuit; towards the end of February 1857, they swept the countryside like an epidemic.

One evening, in the room he used as a study the Collector, Mr Hopkins, opened a despatch box and, instead of the documents he had expected, found four chapatis. After a moment's surprise and annoyance he called the *khansamah*, an elderly man who had been in his service for several years and whom he trusted. He showed him the open despatch box and the chapatis inside. The *khansamah*'s normally impassive face displayed shock. He was clearly no less taken aback than the Collector himself. He stared at the purple despatch box for some moments before picking the chapatis out of it respectfully, as if the box had a personal dignity of its own that might have been offended. The Collector with a frown gestured to him to remove the wretched things. A little later he overheard the *khansamah* shouting at the bearers, evidently convinced that they were responsible for a reckless practical joke.

The Collector was busy at that time. In addition to his official duties, which had been swollen and complicated by the illness of the Joint Magistrate, he had a number of domestic matters on his mind; his wife, too, had been in poor health for the past few months and must now be sent home before the hot weather.

It is unlikely, given his other preoccupations, that the Collector would even have noticed the second pile of chapatis had his eye not been led towards them by a column of ants; the ants were issuing from a crevice between two flagstones and their thin column passed within a few inches of his shoes on its way to the chapatis. The chapatis had a grimy and scorched appearance; again there were four of them and they had been left on the top step of the brick portico which provided the main entrance to the Residency. The Collector had stepped out on to the portico for a breath of air. He hesitated for a moment, on the point of calling the *khansamah* again, but then he noticed the sweeper working not far away; he watched for a while as the man progressed, sitting on his heels and sweeping rather indiscriminately, with a bundle of twigs as a broom. No doubt the chapatis on the portico were the property of the sweeper. The Collector went inside again, dismissing the matter from his mind.

The following afternoon, however, he found four more chapatis. This time they were not in his study but on the desk in his office, neatly arranged beside some papers. Though there was still nothing very menacing about them, as soon as he saw them he knew beyond doubt that there was going to be trouble. He examined them carefully but this told him nothing, except that they were rather dirty.

The Collector was a large and handsome man. He wore low side-whiskers which he kept carefully trimmed but which nevertheless sprouted out stiffly like the ruff of a cat. He dressed fastidiously: the high collars which he habitually wore were sufficiently unusual in a country station like Krishnapur to make a deep impression on all who saw him. He was a man of considerable dignity, too, with a keen, but erratic, sense of social proprieties. Not surprisingly, he was held in awe by the European community; no doubt this was partly because they could not see his faults very clearly. In private he was inclined to be moody and overbearing with his family, and sometimes careless over matters which others might regard as of great importance . . . for example although he had seven children, and was living in a country of high mortality for Europeans, he had not yet brought himself to make a will; an unfortunate lapse of his usually powerful sense of duty.

At that moment he happened to be alone in the office, one of a number of rooms in a part of the Residency set aside for Government business. He was not fond of this room; its bleak, official aspect displeased him and usually he preferred to work in his study, situated in a more domestic part of the building. The office contained only a few overloaded shelves, a couple of wooden chairs for those rare visitors whose rank entitled them to be seated in his presence, and his own desk, untidily strewn with papers and despatch boxes; the person who had placed the offending chapatis on it had had to clear a space for them. On one of the lateral walls was a portrait of the young Queen with rather bulging blue eyes and a vigorous appearance.

Disturbed, and having now forgotten the reason he had gone to his office in the first place, he made his way slowly back towards the hall of the Residency, wondering whether certain measures might be taken to palliate the effects of this approaching, but still hypothetical, trouble, or even to avoid it altogether. "Just supposing that serious trouble should break out in Krishnapur ... an insurrection, for instance, ... where could we find shelter? Could the Residency, merely as a matter of interest, of course, be defended?"

As he stood in the hall pondering this question the Collector experienced a sensation of coolness and great tranquillity. During the daytime the light here came from a great distance; it came between the low arches of the verandah, across cool flagstones, through the green louvred windows known as "jilmils" let into the immensely thick walls, and, at last, in the form of a pleasant, reflected twilight, to where he was standing. One felt very safe here. The walls, which were built of enormous numbers of the pink, wafer-like bricks of British India, were so very thick ... you could see yourself how thick they were.

The Residency was more or less in the shape of a church, that is, if you can imagine a church which one entered by stepping over the altar. The transept, as you stand on the altar looking in, was formed by, on the left, a library well furnished with everything but books, of which there was only a meagre supply, some having been borrowed and not returned, some eaten by the ubiquitous ants, and some having simply vanished nobody knew where; yet others, imprisoned, glumly pressed their spines against the glass of cabinets whose keys had been lost ... and on the right, a drawing-room, lofty, spacious and gracious. Immediately facing you in the nave was a magnificent marble staircase, a relic of the important days of Krishnapur when things were still done properly. Behind the staircase the dining-room, together with a number of other rooms having to do in some way with eating or with European servants or with children, ran along the rest of the nave which was flanked on each side by deep verandahs. The building was of two storeys, if you discount the twin towers which rose somewhat higher. From one of these towers the Union Jack fluttered from dawn till dusk; on the other the Collector sometimes set up a telescope when the mood took him to scrutinize the heavens.

The Collector, whose mind had returned to browse on chapatis, gave a start as a man's voice issued loudly from the open door of the drawing-room nearby. "The mind is furnished," declared the voice in a tone which did not invite debate, "with a vast apparatus of mental organs for enabling it to manifest its energies. Thus, when aided by optical and auditory nerves, the mind sees and hears; when assisted by an organ of cautiousness it feels fear, by an organ of causality it reasons."

"What nonsense!" muttered the Collector, who had recognized the voice as belonging to the Magistrate and had now remembered that he himself should be sitting in the drawing-room at this moment for the fortnightly meeting of the Krishnapur Poetry Society was due to begin ... indeed, had already begun, since the Magistrate was holding forth, though not apparently about poetry.

"Dr Gall of Vienna, who discovered this remarkable science, happened to notice while still at school that those of his fellow students who were good at learning by heart tended to have bulging eyes. By degrees he also found external characteristics which indicated a disposition for painting, music, and the mechanical arts ..."

"I really must go in," thought the Collector, and reflecting that, after all, as President of the Society it was his duty, he took a few firm steps towards the door, but again he hesitated, this time standing in the open doorway itself. From here he could see a dozen ladies of the cantonment sitting apprehensively on chairs facing the Magistrate. Many of these ladies held sheaves of paper densely covered with verse of their own devising, and it was the sight of all this verse which had caused the Collector to hesitate involuntarily at the very last moment. Behind the ladies his four older children, aged from four to sixteen, all girls, (the two boys were at school in England) sat in a despairing row. They took no part in these proceedings but he considered it healthy to expose them to artistic endeavour. Only the youngest, still a baby, was excused attendance.

Unaware that the President of their Society was lingering at the door, the ladies stared at the Magistrate as if hypnotized, but very likely they did not hear a single word he said; they would be in far too great anxiety as to the fate of their verses to listen to him discoursing on phrenology, a subject in which only he found any interest. Soon the moment would come when they would read their works and the Magistrate would pronounce sentence on them, a moment which they both desired and dreaded. The Collector, however, only dreaded it. This was not because of the low standard of the verse, but because the Magistrate's judgements were invariably pitiless, and even, at times when he became excited, verged on the insulting. Why the ladies put up with it and still returned week after week for their poems to be subjected to such indignities was more than the Collector could fathom.

Yet it was the Collector himself who was responsible for this fortnightly torment since it was he who had founded the Society. He had done so partly because he was a believer in the ennobling powers of literature, and partly because he was sorry for the ladies of the cantonment who had, particularly during the hot season, so little to occupy them. At first he had been pleased with the ladies' enthusiasm and had considered the plan a success ... but then he had made the mistake of inviting Tom Willoughby, the Magistrate. The Magistrate suffered from the disability of a free-thinking turn of mind and from a life that was barren and dreary to match. To make things worse, he was married, but in the celibate manner of so many English "civilians". The Collector had eyed the Magistrate's marriage with complacent pity: his wife, imported from England, had stayed two or three years in India until driven home by the heat, the boredom and a fortuitous pregnancy. Ah, the Collector had witnessed this sad story so often during his time in India! And now, though later than most, it seemed that his own marriage, which had survived so long in this arduous climate, must suffer a similar fate, for his wife, Caroline, sitting nervously in the front row with her own sheaf of poems, would soon be sailing from Calcutta. Such was the reward for complacency, he reflected, not without a certain stern satisfaction at the justice of this retribution.

"Oh, there's Mr Hopkins," said the Magistrate, ending his discourse abruptly as he caught sight of the Collector lurking in the doorway. And the Collector was obliged to step forward smiling, as if in anticipation of the poetry that would soon be gratifying his ears

An empty chair had been placed beside the Magistrate, who was somewhat younger than the Collector and had the red hair and ginger whiskers of the born atheist; his face wore a constant expression of cynical surprise, one eyebrow raised and the corner of his mouth compressed, as far as one could make out beneath the growth of whiskers which here varied from ginger to cinnamon. It was said in the cantonment that he even slept with one eyebrow raised; the Collector did not know if there was any truth in this.

At one time everyone had sat in a circle and every member of the Society had been willing to voice an opinion on the poem which had just been read. Those were the days when every single poem had bristled with good qualities like a hedgehog and had glutted itself with praise like a jackal, the happy days before the Magistrate had been invited. Soon after his arrival the circle had begun to disintegrate, the ladies had progressively dropped away from each side of him until, soon, they faced him in a semi-circle, and now, at last, directly, as if in the dock. The Collector had bravely installed himself at the Magistrate's side in order to plead mitigating circumstances.

By this time the poetry reading had begun and Mrs Worseley, wife of one of the railway engineers, had faltered to the end of a sonnet about an erl-king. Everyone, including the Collector, was now watching the Magistrate in dismay, waiting for his verdict; although sure about most things, the Collector lacked confidence in his own judgement when it came to poetry and was obliged to defer to the Magistrate, but not without the private suspicion that his own judgement might be superior after all.

"Mrs Worseley, I found your poem defective in metre, rhyme, and invention. And to be quite honest I consider that we've had far too many erl-kings in recent weeks, though I can assure you that even one erl-king would be more than enough for me." Mrs Worseley hung her head, but looked quite relieved, thinking that she had got off lightly.

Mrs Adams, a senior lady, the wife of a recently retired judge, now read in a commanding voice a long poem of which the Collector could make neither head nor tail, though it seemed to have something to do with Nature, serpents, and the fall of Troy. He allowed his mind to wander and, as his eyes came to rest on his wife, he thought that if there should indeed be trouble at Krishnapur it was just as well that she would not be there to see it; perhaps he should have insisted that the children go home with her; he would have done so but he had feared that the fuss, even if the *ayah* went too, would be too much for her nerves . . . Never mind, he had almost decided to retire in a year's time, at the end of the next cold season. He did not have to worry, as did the poor Magistrate, about securing a pension. He had a glorious and interesting life awaiting him in England whenever he considered that his duty in India was done.

But still those chapatis lodged in his mind, undissolved. In this room it was even harder to believe in trouble than it had been in the hall, indeed, it was hard to believe that one was in India at all, except for the punkahs. His eyes roamed with satisfaction over the walls, thickly armoured with paintings in oil and water-colour, with mirrors and glass cases containing stuffed birds and other wonders, over chairs and sofas upholstered in plum cretonne, over showcases of minerals and a cobra floating in a bottle of bluish alcohol, over occasional tables draped to the floor with heavy tablecloths on which stood statuettes in electro-metal of great men of literature, of Dr Johnson, of Molière, Keats, Voltaire and, of course, Shakespeare . . . but now he was obliged to return his attention to the proceedings.

Miss Carpenter had begun to read a poem in praise of the Great Exhibition; the Collector groaned inwardly, not because he found the subject unsuitable, but because it had so evidently been chosen as homage to himself; poems about the Exhibition recurred every few weeks and seldom failed to excite the Magistrate's most cutting remarks. This was undoubtedly because his own interest in the Exhibition was as well-known to the Magistrate as to the ladies; indeed, it was more than an interest for he had been a prominent member of the selection committee for the Bengal Presidency and, having taken his furlough in 1851, had attended the Exhibition in an official capacity. It was generally held in the cantonment that the Magistrate resented the fact that the Collector should be in with all the "big dogs" in the Company simply because he was in the habit of collecting artistic and scientific bric à brac.

"Power, like the trunk of Afric's wondrous brute,
Had, on that stage, its double triumph found,
To lift the forest monarch .by the root,
Or pick a quivering needle from the ground."

Although it was usually considered unwise to offer explanations to the Magistrate as you went along, Miss Carpenter was
unable to prevent herself explaining that this image of the
Exhibition was a reference to the versatile talent of Edmund
Burke. But as the air of interrogation among her fellow
poetesses only deepened as a result of this explanation she was
obliged to add an explanation to her explanation, to the effect
that this talent of Burke's had been compared to an elephant's
trunk, which could uproot an oak or pick up a needle. The
ladies shifted their terrified eyes to the Magistrate to see how he
was responding; his face remained ominously impassive, however, beneath its ginger growth. Miss Carpenter bravely proceeded:

"Whilst they, the Royal Founders of the scene,
Through ranks of gazing myriads calmly move,
And Britons throng to proffer to their Queen
The willing dues of loyalty and love."

"Really, this is not at all bad," thought the Collector in spite
of his alarm on her behalf; he was fond of Miss Carpenter, who
was serious and pretty, and anxious to please.

"Pebbles and shells which little children find
Of rainbow-tinted hues, on ocean's shore;
Though full of learning to the thoughtful mind,
Themselves how vain, how shortly seen no more!"

"How excellent, how serious! The girl has a remarkable gift."
The Collector was surprised to find himself responding to a
poem composed by one of the ladies; hitherto he had considered
the poems of value only for their therapeutic properties. Alas,
Miss Carpenter had been unable to resist appending yet another
explanation: that this last verse was a reference to Newton's
description of himself as "only a child picking up pebbles on
the shore of the great ocean of truth". This was altogether too
much for the Magistrate. "Half of this poem appears to have

been copied from books, Miss Carpenter, and the other half is plainly rubbish. It's entirely beyond my understanding why you should feel you have to say 'Afric's wondrous brute' instead of 'elephant' like everyone else, and 'forest monarch' instead of 'tree'. Nobody in his right mind goes about calling trees 'forest monarchs' . . . I've really never heard such nonsense!"

The ladies gasped at this frontal attack, not just on poor Miss Carpenter, but on poetry itself. If you can't call an elephant "Afric's wondrous brute" what *can* you call it? Why write poetry at all? Miss Carpenter's eyes filled with tears.

"Look here, Tom, that's very extreme," grumbled the Collector, displeased. "I found it a very fine poem indeed. One of the best we've heard, I should think. Mind you," he added as his confidence once more deserted him, "the subject of the Exhibition, as you know, is one that holds a particular interest for me."

Miss Carpenter coloured prettily at this speech and appeared not to hear the Magistrate's derisive: "Ha!" "The fellow is quite impossible!" mused the Collector crossly.

Not everyone, the Collector was aware, is improved by the job he does in life; some people are visibly disimproved. The Magistrate had performed his duties for the Company conscientiously but they had not had a good effect on him: they had made him cynical, fatalistic, and too enamoured of the rational. His interest in phrenology, too, had had a bad effect; it had reinforced the determinism which had sapped his ideals, for he evidently believed that all one's acts were limited by the shape of one's skull. Given the swelling above and behind the ear on each side of his skull (he had once insinuated) there was not very much the Collector could do to remedy his inability to make rapid decisions ... Though, of course, one could not be "absolutely sure" without making exact measurements. He had also begun to say something about a bump on each side of the Collector's crown which signified "love of approbation", but noticing, at last, how badly the Collector was responding to this opportunity for self-knowledge he had desisted with a sigh.

"By the way, Tom," said the Collector as the meeting broke up, "I found something odd on my desk in the office just now.

Four chapatis, to be exact. And yesterday I found some in a despatch box. What d'you make of it?"

"That's strange. I found some too." The two men looked at each other, surprised.

Presently they heard that chapatis were turning up all over Krishnapur. The Padre had found some on the steps of the Church and had assumed that they were some sort of superstitious offering. Mr Barlow, who worked in the Salt Agency, had been brought some by his watchman. Mr Rayne who, in addition to his official duties at the opium factory, was the Honorary Secretary of the Krishnapur Mutton Club and of the Ice Club, was shown chapatis by the watchmen employed in the protection of both these institutions. It soon became clear that it was chiefly among the watchmen that the chapatis were circulating; they had been given them by watchmen from other districts, without apparently knowing for what purpose, and told to bake more and then pass them on again to watchmen of yet other districts. The Collector discovered by questioning his own watchman that it was he who had left the chapatis on the desk in his office. Although he had baked twelve more chapatis and passed them on, as he had been instructed, he had felt it his duty to inform the Collector Sahib and so had left them on his desk. He denied any knowledge of those in the despatch box and on the portico. Where these came from the Collector never discovered.

In due course an even more curious fact emerged. The chapatis were appearing not just in Krishnapur but in stations all over northern India. Not only the Collector found this disturbing; for a while no one in Krishnapur could talk of anything else. Again and again the watchmen were interrogated, but they seemed genuinely to have no idea what the purpose of it had been. Some said they had passed on the chapatis because they believed it to be the order of the Government, that the purpose had been to see how quickly messages could be passed on.

In Calcutta the Government held an enquiry, but no reason for the phenomenon came to light and the excitement it caused died down within a few days. It was suggested that it might be a superstitious attempt to avert an epidemic of cholera. Only the Collector remained convinced that trouble was coming. He half remembered having heard of a similar distribution of chapatis on some other occasion. Surely there had been something of the kind before the mutiny at Vellore? He asked everyone he met whether they had heard of it, but no one had.

Before leaving Krishnapur to escort his wife to Calcutta, where she was to embark for England, the Collector took a strange decision. He ordered the digging of a deep trench combined with a thick wall of earth "for drainage during the monsoon" all the way round the perimeter of the Residency compound.

"The Collector's weakness appears to have found him," observed the Magistrate lightly to Mr Ford, one of the railway engineers, as they smilingly surveyed the progress of this work.

2

It was during this winter that George Fleury arrived in Calcutta with his sister and first set eyes on Louise Dunstaple. It was hoped that something might come of this meeting for Fleury was not married and Louise, though not quite his social equal, was considered to be at the very height of her beauty ... indeed, she was being talked of everywhere in Calcutta as the beauty of the cold season. She was very fair and pale and a little remote; one or two people thought her "insipid", which is a danger blonde people sometimes run. She was remote, at least, in Fleury's presence, but once he glimpsed her at the race-course, flirting chastely with some young officers.

Dr Dunstaple in those days was the civil surgeon at Krishnapur. But somehow he had managed to get himself and his family to Calcutta for the cold season, leaving the Krishnapur civilians to the tender mercies of Dr McNab, who had taken over as regimental surgeon and who was known to be in favour of some of the most alarmingly direct methods known to civilized medicine.

The Doctor had left his son Harry behind in Krishnapur, however. Thanks to the help of a friend in Fort William young Harry had been posted as an ensign to one of the native infantry regiments stationed at Krishnapur (or rather at Captainganj, five miles away) where his parents could keep an eye on him and see that he did not get into debt. Harry, who by now was a lieutenant, was quite content to be left behind when his family, which included little Fanny, aged twelve, went away to enjoy themselves in Calcutta; being "military" he tended these days to look with condescension upon civilians, and Calcutta was undoubtedly riddled with the fellows.

Nor was Mrs Dunstaple displeased that her son should stay in Krishnapur, though this meant that he would be away from her side. Harry was at a vulnerable age and Calcutta swarmed with ambitious mammas anxious to expose young officers like

Harry to the charms of their daughters. Alas, Mrs Dunstaple well knew that India was full of young lieutenants who had ruined their careers at the outset by disastrous marriages. All the same, this consideration, as applied to Harry, did not prevent her from hoping to be able to show off the charms of Louise before suitable young men. In the East the roses in a girl's cheeks fly away so quickly, so very quickly (though, strictly speaking, this did not apply to Louise whose beauty was of the pale sort).

The Season had been unusually successful, and not only for Louise (who had shown herself hard to please, however, in the matter of proposals). There had been many splendid balls and an unusual number of weddings and other entertainments. Moreover, the Turf, which had fallen into a decline in recent years had revived wonderfully. Of course, you would be likely to see the same mounts in the Planters' Handicap as in the Merchants' Plate or the Bengal Club Cup but it was a season of remarkable horses, for this was the era of Legerdemain, Mercury, and of the great mare, Beeswing. But the cold season was nearing its end by the time Fleury and his sister, Miriam, arrived and new faces like theirs were longed for in Calcutta drawing-rooms; (by this time all the old faces were so familiar that they could hardly be looked at any more). Besides, it was known that their father was a Director, with all the social standing which that implied in the Company's India. It was also rumoured that young Fleury had scarcely been half an hour in India before Lord Canning had offered him a cigar. No wonder the news of his arrival caused some excitement in the Dunstaples' house in Alipore.

In spite of the very different ranks they now occupied in society Dr Dunstaple and Fleury's father had been at school together forty years earlier and still, after all this time, exchanged a gruff little letter on sporting matters once or twice a year, as between schoolboys. The Doctor had reason to be glad of this friendship for it was thanks to Sir Herbert Fleury that young Harry had been awarded a cadetship at Addiscombe, the Company's military college; these cadetships were in the gift of Directors.

In the course of their correspondence the elder Fleury had often mentioned his own son, George, in amongst the grouse, the pheasants and the foxes ... George was going to Oxford and perhaps in due course would come out to India. But the years had gone by without any sign of young Fleury. Nor was he mentioned in his father's letters any more. Divining some domestic tragedy the Doctor had tactfully confined his own letters to pig-sticking and ortolans. Another two or three years had gone by and now, suddenly, when the Doctor was no longer expecting it, young Fleury had popped up again among the foxes. It seemed that he was coming to India to visit his mother's grave (twenty years earlier when Sir Herbert himself had been in India his young wife had died, leaving him with two small children); at the same time he had been commissioned by the Court of Directors to compose a small volume describing the advances that civilization had made in India under the Company rule. But those were only the ostensible reasons for his visit ... the real reason that young Fleury was coming was the need to divert his recently widowed sister, Miriam, whose husband, Captain Lang, had been killed before Sebastopol.

Now George Fleury and his sister had arrived in Calcutta and Mrs Dunstaple had heard that he was making quite an impression. Even his clothes, said to be the last word in fashion, had become the talk of the city. It seemed that Fleury had been seen wearing what was positively the first "Tweedside" lounging jacket to make its appearance in the Bengal Presidency; this garment, daringly unwaisted, hung as straight as a sack of potatoes and was arousing the envy of every beau on the Chowringhee. At his wife's behest the Doctor sat down immediately and penned a warm invitation to Fleury and Miriam to join the Dunstaples on a family picnic they were planning to take in the Botanical Gardens. But even as he sealed his letter he could not help wondering whether Fleury would turn out to be quite what his wife expected. The fact was that Harry, while at Addiscombe, had once spent a few days with the Fleurys in the country and had later told his father about it. He had seen very little of George during his stay but one night, as he was going to bed, pleasantly tired after a day spent hunting with the elder Fleury, he had opened his window to the whirring, moonlit night and heard, very faintly, the strains of a violin. He was certain that it must have been George. Next morning he had come upon this violin, some leaves of music damp with dew on a music-stand, and a tall medieval candelabrum . . . all this was in a "ruined" pagoda at the end of the rose garden.

To the Doctor it seemed like evidence of the domestic tragedy he had feared for his friend. Perhaps George was insane? It certainly seemed disturbing that he had not gone hunting with Harry. And then, playing a violin to the owls that swooped across the starlit heavens, well, that did not seem very normal either.

The ladies were discreetly watching from an upstairs window the following morning when a rather grimy *gharry* stopped in front of the Dunstaples' house in Alipore. Even Louise was watching, though she denied being in the least interested in the sort of creature that might emerge. If she happened to be standing at the window it was simply because Fanny was standing there too and she was trying to comb Fanny's hair.

"Oh dear, you mustn't let him see you or whatever will he think!" moaned Mrs Dunstaple. "Do be careful." But she herself was peering out more eagerly than anyone.

"Here he is!" cried Fanny as a rather rumpled looking young man scrambled out of the gharry and looked around in a dazed fashion. "Look how fat he is!"

"Fanny!" scolded Mrs Dunstaple, but in a halfhearted way for it was perfectly true, he did look rather fat; but his sister looked beautiful and made the ladies gasp by the simple elegance of her clothing.

If the ladies were a little disappointed by their first glimpse of Fleury, the Doctor was definitely cheered. His misgivings had increased overnight so that when Fleury turned out to be a relatively normal young man, the doctor prepared himself to take a cautiously optimistic view of his friend's son. But in no time caution gave way to outright satisfaction, and so pleased and confident did he become, so grateful that Fleury was not the effeminate individual he had been expecting, that he even began to hint to Fleury about the manly pleasures he might find in Calcutta . . . Young men have wild oats to sow, as he very well knew from having sown a few himself in his day . . . and he began to count off the pleasures of the city: the racecourse, the balls, the pretty women, the dinner parties and good fellowship and other entertainments. He himself, he hinted, forgetting that Fleury's sister was a widow, as a younger man, had spent many a happy hour in the company of vivacious young widows and suchlike.

"But no native women," he added in a lower voice. "Not even as a youngster, never touched 'em."

Taken aback to find his father's friend personified in this jovial libertine, Fleury did his best to respond but secretly wished that Miriam were there to keep the conversation on more general topics. Miriam was being received by the ladies upstairs. They were still dressing, it seemed.

The Doctor was explaining, as they strolled up and down the drawing-room, that, alas, he and his family would soon be leaving for Krishnapur . . . though, actually, this was more a cause of despair to the ladies than to himself, for the pig-sticking season had been under way since February and would only last till July . . . indeed, the best of it was already over, because soon it would become too hot to lift a finger. Besides, he had to get back to save the cantonment from the attentions of a newfangled doctor called McNab who had recently been imposed on the military cantonment at Captainganj. His face darkened a little at the thought of McNab and he began to crack his knuckles in an absentminded sort of way. "As for Louise and her prospects," he added confidentially, forgetting that Fleury had been numbered amongst them, "if she's so hard to please she can try again another year." Fleury found himself somewhat embarrassed by this information and to avoid further domestic confidences he enquired if there were many white ants in Calcutta.

"White ants?" The Doctor suffered a moment's alarm, remembering the violin and the owls. "No, I don't think so. At least, I suppose there may be, somewhere . . ."

"I've brought a lot of books. I just wondered whether I should take measures to protect them.'

"Oh, I see what you mean," exclaimed the Doctor with relief. "I don't think you need worry about that. In Krishnapur, perhaps, but not here." He had given himself a fright about nothing! He could hardly have been more rattled if Fleury had asked him outright for some white ants steamed in a pie! What

20

an old fool he was becoming, to be sure.

Now at last the ladies could be heard descending and the Doctor and Fleury moved towards the door to greet them. As they did so, the Doctor's sleeve brushed a vase standing on a small table and it shattered on the floor. The ladies entered with cries of grief and alarm to find the two gentlemen picking up the pieces.

"My dear fellow," the Doctor was saying consolingly to Fleury. "Please don't apologize. It wasn't in the least your fault and, besides, it was an object of small value." And he smiled benignly at Fleury, who stared back at him in amazement. What on earth did the Doctor mean? Of course, it was not his fault. How could it have been?

This accident to the vase would not have particularly mattered, Mrs Dunstaple explained rather stiffly to Fleury, if it had been theirs; unfortunately, it happened to belong to the people who had let the house to them. However, there was no point in worrying about it now.

"I'm frightfully sorry," murmured Fleury, in spite of himself. He was painfully conscious of the loveliness of Louise who had come forward to watch this regrettable scene.

"Really, Dobbin!" said Miriam crossly. "You're so clumsy. Why don't you look what you're doing?" Fleury blushed and glared at his sister; he had told her a hundred times not to call him "Dobbin". And this was the worst possible moment for her to forget, with the lovely, slightly disdainful Louise standing there. But perhaps Louise had failed to notice.

The slight feeling of awkwardness which attended Fleury's clumsiness was soon forgotten, however, in the news that Mr Hopkins, the Collector of Krishnapur, and Mrs Hopkins had just then called to pay their respects and to allow Mrs Hopkins to say farewell to her dear friends, the Dunstaples, before embarking for England. Close on the heels of this announcement came Mrs Hopkins herself, and both Fleury and Miriam were concerned to see how harrowed and grief-stricken she looked. She was already sobbing as she advanced to embrace Louise and Mrs Dunstaple.

"Carrie, dear, you must not upset yourself. I shall have to take you away if you continue." The Collector had followed his wife into the drawing-room with such a silent tread that Fleury jumped at these words, spoken without warning at his elbow. He turned to see a man who looked like a massive cat standing beside him; a faint perfume of verbena drifted from his impressive whiskers.

Mrs Hopkins stood away weakly from Mrs Dunstaple, still weeping but attempting to dry her eyes. Ignoring the introductions that the Doctor was trying to effect, she said to Miriam: "I'm so sorry, you must forgive me ... My nerves are very poor, you see, my youngest child, a boy, died just six months ago during the hot weather ... ever since then I find that the least thing will upset me. He was just a baby, you see ... and when we buried him all we could think of was to put a daguerrotype of his father and myself in his little arms ... It was made by one of the native gentlemen and we had been meaning to send it home to England but we decided it would be better to put it in the baby's coffin with some roses ... You know, perhaps you will think me foolish but I feel just as sad to be leaving the country where his grave lies as I am to be leaving all my dearest friends ..."

Fleury had the feeling that Mrs Hopkins might have continued for some time in this vein had not the Collector said rather sharply: "Caroline, you must not think about it or you'll make yourself unwell again. I feel sure that Mrs Lang would prefer to hear of something more cheerful."

"On the contrary, Mrs Hopkins has my deepest sympathy ... and all the more so as I have myself only recently lost someone very dear to me."

The Collector's brows gathered up; he looked moody and displeased, but he said nothing further.

Although he generally liked sad things, such as autumn, death, ruins and unhappy love affairs, Fleury was nevertheless dismayed by the morbid turn the conversation had taken. Besides, this was the very thing that he had brought Miriam to India to avoid. But Mrs Hopkins had composed herself and Mrs Dunstaple, too, had dried her eyes, for she was easily affected by the tears of others and only the thought of making her eyes red had prevented her from shedding them as copiously as her friend. As for Louise, although she had allowed herself to be tearfully embraced, she was more self-possessed than her mother and her own eyes had not moistened.

In any case, there was no time left for crying. Large quantities of news had to be exchanged for the Dunstaples had left Krishnapur in October and a great deal had happened since then. And they wanted to know so many things . . . how was the Padre? and the Magistrate? and had Dr McNab despatched anyone yet? In turn Mrs Dunstaple had to explain everything which had occurred in Calcutta. She would have liked to detail the various suitors who had been attending Louise but she did not like to, in Fleury's presence, lest he should become discouraged. Moreover, Louise tended to be bad tempered if there was open discussion of her prospects. But while Fleury and Miriam were talking to the Collector Mrs Dunstaple just had time to intimate to Mrs Hopkins that there was one prospect, a certain Lieutenant Stapleton, nephew of a General, who looked very promising indeed.

The Collector was not in a good temper. He found leave-takings harrowing at the best of times and he was concerned for his wife, who had been overtired by the long and arduous journey by *dak gharry* from Krishnapur to the rail-head; but he was also worried as to what might be happening in Krishnapur during his absence, for his presentiment of approaching disaster grew every day more powerful. In addition, he felt himself to have been ill-used just now by Miriam, who had seemed to rebuke him for lack of feeling. "She cannot know how I myself suffered for the death of the baby! And how was I to know she had lost a husband in the Crimea?" (for the Doctor had enlightened him in a whisper) . . . "How like a woman to take an unfair advantage like that, dragging in a dead husband to put one in the wrong!" And the Collector stroked his side-whiskers against the grain, releasing a further cloud of lemon verbena into the air. "What was that phrase of Tennyson's? ' . . . the soft and milky rabble of woman-kind . . .!' "

But the Collector admired pretty women and could not feel hostile to them for very long. If they were pretty he swiftly found other virtues in them which he would not have noticed had they been ugly. Soon he began to find Miriam sensible and mature, which was only to say that he liked her grey eyes and her smile. "She has a mind of her own," he decided. "Why can't all women be widows?"

Fleury and Miriam sat opposite the elder Dunstaples in the carriage, beside little Fanny. Their space was confined because the ladies' crinolines ballooned against each other leaving very little room for a gentleman to stretch his legs with discretion. Even Fanny's slender legs were lost in mounds of snowy, tiered petticoats.

"How pleasant it is to be ashore again after those five interminable months at sea! How one misses the trees, the fields, the green grass! But, of course, Miss Dunstaple, you yourself must have experienced this very same ordeal by water and here I am speaking as if I were the only person ever to have come out from England!"

Fleury had regarded this as the beginning of a pleasant conversation but somehow his words were not well received. Louise's lips barely moved in reply and her mother looked quite put out. Had he made a blunder? It surely could not be that Louise was "country born" and had thus never been to England, a condition that he had heard was much misprised in Indian society. But alas, this seemed to be the case.

The carriage had slowed down to pass through a densely populated bazaar. Fleury gazed out at a sea of brown faces, mortified by his mistake. A few inches away two men sat cross-legged in a cupboard, one shaving the skull of the other from a cup of dirty water. A cage containing a hundred tiny trembling birds with black feathers and red beaks crept past. To Fleury India was a mixture of the exotic and the intensely boring, which made it, because of his admiration for Chateaubriand, irresistible. Now there was shouting. They had arrived at the *ghat*.

The boat which the Doctor had engaged turned out to be a very dubious prospect indeed; a mass of leaky, rotting timbers roughly oblong in shape, manned by Dravidian cut-throats. But never mind, it was not far across the Hooghly; over the water the soaring trees of the Botanical Gardens could be seen.

"Look, there's Nigel!" cried Louise, just as they were going on board, and clapped her hands with pleasure. A scarlet uniform could be seen glimmering in and out of the white muslin of the crowd and presently a young officer on horseback with a barefoot groom running along beside him clattered up to the *ghat*. He dismounted hastily and leaving the *sais* to cope with the horse scrambled on board, saying breathlessly: "Fearfully sorry to be late!"

Mrs Dunstaple greeted him a little coldly. Evidently Louise had not told her that she intended to invite Lieutenant Stapleton and she was not altogether glad to see him. Out of the corner of his eye Fleury saw Mrs Dunstaple frowning at her daughter and nodding surreptitiously in his direction. He remembered then what the Doctor had said about Louise and her prospects. So that was it! Mrs Dunstaple was afraid lest one of these eligible young men should become discouraged by the presence of the other. Fleury was pained to see Louise glance in his direction and then toss her head and look away, as if to say: "Why should I care whether he's discouraged or not?" Although discouraged, Fleury stared at the river, pretending to admire the view. Lieutenant Stapleton, who had evidently expected to be the only young male on the expedition, seemed himself rather taken aback; when the two young men were introduced he merely mumbled wearily and eyed Fleury's crumpled but well-cut clothes with sullen envy.

No sooner had they reached the mud banks on the other side than a commotion ensued; the ladies discovered that while sitting in the boat the hems of their dresses had sopped up a certain amount of bilge water. With many moans and complaints they retired to a glade at a discreet distance with a maidservant to wring them out. When at last they returned, the party moved off, trailing a crowd of grinning servants. The gardens displayed few flowers but many enormous trees and shrubs. Their way led past the Great Banyan and Fleury was filled with awe at the sight of its many trunks joined together by branches into a series of spectacular gothic arches. He had never seen a banyan tree before.

"It's like a ruined church made by Nature!" he exclaimed with excitement as they passed by; but the Dunstaples failed to respond to this insight and, while they were all trying to decide on a suitable place for their picnic, he thought he saw Louise and Lieutenant Stapleton exchanging a sly smile.

From time to time, as they progressed through the trees, they crossed green glades where young officers were already picnicking with their ladies; but when at last they found a glade that was uninhabited Mrs Dunstaple declared it to be too sunny. In the next glade there was yet another party of young officers drinking Moselle cup with what the Doctor clearly took to be vivacious young widows. Fleury saw him look at them wistfully as he prepared to pass on with his own party . . . but the young officers hailed him, laughing, and asked did he not recognize them? And it turned out that they were not only acquaintances but even the best of friends, for these young men were normally stationed at Captainganj; they had been to the musketry school at Barrackpur to learn about the new Enfield rifles that were making the sepoys so cross, and had taken the opportunity of visiting Calcutta for a bit of civilization, and were naturally delighted at bumping into Dr and Mrs Dunstaple and, of course, Miss Louise, and what about that young rotter Lieutenant Harry Dunstaple who had faithfully promised to write but had not put pen to paper? They would deal with the rascal when they got back to Krishnapur in a few days . . . and nothing would suit them but that the Dunstaples' party should join them.

Their ladies, it turned out, were not vivacious young widows at all, but girls of the most respectable kind, the sisters of one or other of the officers; so everything was taking place with the utmost propriety.

The officers had already made several dashing assaults on their own hamper, a converted linen basket which seemed to contain nothing but Moselle cup in a variety of bottles and jars. The Dunstaples had brought several hampers, more than one of which bore the proud label of Wilson's "Hall of All Nations" (purveyors by appointment to the Rt. Honourable Viscount Canning), for the Doctor obviously believed in doing things properly. The young men could hardly restrain themselves as the Dunstaples' bearers unpacked before their eyes a real York ham, as smooth and pink as little Fanny's cheeks, oysters, pickles, mutton pies, Cheddar cheese, ox tongue, cold chickens, chocolate, candied and crystallized fruits, and biscuits of all kinds made from the finest fresh Cape flour: Abernethy's crackers, Tops and Bottoms, spice nuts and every other delicious biscuit you could imagine.

With his hands palpitating his coat tails the Doctor surveyed his bearers at work and pretended to be unaware of the young men's interest, waiting until the last moment before declaring with mock diffidence: "I'm sure you young fellows don't feel like a bite to eat, but if you do . . ." at which a mighty cheer rang out, causing Mrs Dunstaple to look round in case they were drawing attention to themselves, but similar gay sounds were echoing from the glades around them; only a few ragged-looking natives had made an appearance and were sitting on their heels at the edge of the clearing, gazing at the white sahibs.

The young officers, in return, insisted that everyone should share their Moselle, of which they had an over-supply; indeed, sufficient to render themselves and their ladies insensible several times over. Soon a general merriment prevailed.

As for Louise, she looked quite ethereal in the dappled sunlight and shade, but it made Fleury sad to see her surrounded by gluttony and laughter; she was holding up the thigh of a duck one end of which had been wrapped in a napkin, not to be nibbled at by herself but to be wolfed at in an exaggerated and droll manner by the heavily mustached lips and somewhat yellow teeth of one of the officers, whose name was Lieutenant Cutter and who had been one of her particular favourites the year before in Krishnapur, it seemed. And not content with having everyone helpless with laughter by this behaviour Lieutenant Cutter became more droll than ever and threw back his head to howl like a wolf between bites.

Meanwhile, the Doctor was asking Captain Hudson about something which had been on his mind for a few days: namely, what was all this about there having been trouble with the sepoys at Barrackpur in January? Had he and the other officers been there at the time?

"No, that had all quietened down by the time we got there. But it didn't amount to much in any case . . . one or two fires set in the native lines and some rumours spread about defilement from the new cartridges. But General Hearsey handled things pretty skilfully, even though some people thought he should have been more severe."

Here Mrs Dunstaple cried out petulantly that she wanted an explanation, because nobody ever explained to her about things like defilement and cartridges; she could remain as ignorant as a maidservant for all anyone cared, and she smiled to indicate that she was being more coquettish than cross. So Hudson kindly set himself to explain. "As you know, we load a gun by pouring a charge of powder down the barrel into the powder chamber and after that we ram a ball down on top of it. Well, the powder comes in a little paper packet which we call a cartridge . . . in order to get at the powder we have to tear the end off and in army drill we teach the men to do this with their teeth."

"And so the natives feel themselves defiled . . . well, good gracious!"

"No, not by that, Mrs Dunstaple, but by the grease on the cartridges . . . it's only on balled cartridges of course . . . that is, a cartridge with a ball in it. You empty in the powder and then instead of throwing it away you ram the rest of the cartridge in on top of it. But because it's rather a tight fit you have to grease it, otherwise the ball would get stuck. With the new Enfield rifles, which have grooves in the barrel, the balled cartridge would certainly get stuck if it wasn't greased."

"Bless my soul, so it was the grease!"

"Of course it was, that's what worried Jack Sepoy! Somehow he got the idea that the grease comes from pork or beef tallow and he didn't like it touching his lips because it's against his religion. That's why there was trouble at Barrackpur. But now Major Bontein has suggested a change of drill . . . in future, instead of biting off the end we'll simply tear it off. That way the sepoys won't have to worry what the grease is made of. As it is, the stuff smells disgusting enough to start an epidemic, let alone a mutiny."

Hudson added that there had been yet another spot of bother on the twenty-seventh of February, at Berhampur, a hundred miles to the north where the 19th Bengal Infantry had refused to take percussion caps on parade; the absence of any European regiment had made it impossible to deal with this mutinous act on the spot . . . Now the defaulting regiment was slowly being marched down to Barrackpur for disbandment. But there was no cause for alarm and, besides, now that everyone had finished eating, a game of blind man's buff was being called for.

Everyone cried that this was a splendid idea and in no time the bearers had cleared the hampers to one side (and then been cleared away themselves) and the game was ready to begin. One of the ladies, a plump girl who was already rather hot

28

from laughing so much, had duly been blindfolded and now she was being turned round three times while everyone chanted a rhyme that one of the officers, who had decided as a pastime to study the natives, had learned from the native children:

"Attah of roses and mustard-oil,
The cat's a-crying, the pot's a-boil,
Look out and fly! The Rajah's thief
will catch you!"

With that they all darted away and the young lady blundered about shrieking with laughter until at last her brother, who was afraid that she might have hysterics, allowed himself to be caught.

This brother was none other than Lieutenant Cutter, a very amusing fellow indeed. As he lunged here and there he kept up a gruff and frightening commentary to the effect that he was a big bear and that if he caught some pretty lass he would give her a terrible hug . . . and the ladies were so alarmed and delighted that they could not help giving away their positions by their squeals, and they kept only just escaping in the nick of time.

But soon it became evident that there was something rather peculiar about Lieutenant Cutter's blunderings. How did it happen that far from blundering impartially as one would have expected of a blindfolded man, time and again he ignored his brother officers and made his frightening gallops in the direction of a flock of ladies? Perhaps it was simply that he could locate them by their squeals. But how was it that he so frequently galloped towards the prettiest of all, that is to say, towards Louise Dunstaple, and finally caught the poor moaning, breathless creature and gave her the terrible bear-hug he had threatened (and how was it, Fleury wondered, that he had so plainly become animally aroused by this innocent game?) Lieutenant Cutter had been cheating, the rascal! He had somehow or other opened a little window in the folds of the silk handkerchief over his eyes and all this time he had only been simulating blindness!

And so the merriment continued. What a wonderful time everyone was having . . . even the ragged natives watching from the edge of the clearing were probably enjoying the spectacle ... and how delightful the weather was! The Indian winter is the perfect climate, sunny and cool. It was only later that evening that Fleury remembered that he had wanted to ask Captain Hudson, who had looked an intelligent fellow, if he thought any more trouble was to be expected ... Because naturally it would be foolish for himself and Miriam to visit the Dunstaples in Krishnapur, as they intended, if there was to be unrest in the country.

The Collector had been astonished, on hearing of the mutiny of the 19th at Berhampur, at the lack of alarm in official circles over this development. Later he heard that General Hearsey had been obliged to address the sepoys at Barrackpur to reassure them that there was no intention of forcibly converting them to Christianity, as they suspected. The English, Hearsey had explained to them, were "Christians of the Book", which meant that nobody could become a Christian without first reading and understanding the Book and voluntarily choosing to become a Christian. It was believed in Calcutta, though not by the Collector, that this speech, delivered in their own language in strong, manly tones by an officer they trusted, had had a beneficial effect on the sepoys. The Collector, in the meantime, had arrived at a painful decision. In spite of his anxiety to return to Krishnapur after his wife's departure he had decided that it was his duty to stay in Calcutta for a few more days to warn people of the danger that he himself had first perceived in those ominous chapatis he had found on his desk.

Fleury had only met the Collector on one occasion and at the time, unfortunately, he had not realized that he was meeting someone who would soon provide an interesting topic of conversation for despairing drawing-rooms. During the two years the Collector had spent in England at the beginning of the decade he had been an active member of numerous committees and societies: the Magdalen Hospital for reclaiming prostitutes, for example, and the aristocratic Mendicity Society for relieving beggars, not to mention any number of literary, zoological, antiquarian and statistical societies. That, of course, was entirely as it should be; anyone of his private means would have done the same. But Hopkins had gone further. Not only had he returned to India full of ideas about hygiene, crop rotation, and drainage, he had devoted a substantial part of his fortune to bringing out to India examples of European art and science in the belief that he was doing as once the Romans had done in Britain. Those who had seen it said that the Residency at Krishnapur was full of statues, paintings and machines. Perhaps it was only to be expected that the Collector's efforts to bring civilization to the natives would be laughed at in Calcutta; but now here he was again, almost as entertaining, in the role of a prophet of doom.

In no time he became a familiar figure in Calcutta as he traversed the city paying calls on various dignitaries. If someone happened to see him making his way along Chowringhee he would say to himself: "There goes Hopkins. I wonder who he's going to warn this time." The Collector's foretelling of the wrath to come, based largely, people said, on his actually having *eaten* the chapatis he had found soon became a great source of amusement. Fleury, among others, followed his progress with amazement and relish. It even became something of a vogue in Government circles to be called on by the Collector and more than one host entertained his dinner guests with an account of how the Collector had buttonholed somebody or other to predict disaster. And when he visited you he would launch into a confused harangue about the need for civilization to be brought nearer to the native, or something like that, mixed up with gloomy predictions as usual. But as the days went by and people continued to see him driving here or there in Calcutta or stalking with lonely dignity across the no longer very green expanse of the *maidan* or even standing deep in thought beside the river at about the place where the great Howrah Bridge looms today, there came a time when they scarcely noticed him any more.

Gradually, as the weather grew hotter and the list of dignitaries whom he evidently believed it unwise not to warn grew no shorter, the Collector began to take on a frayed appearance, even though his shirt remained as white and his morning coat as carefully pressed. Then, in April, another story about the Collector went the rounds, though where it originated was a mystery. It was said that although he was still to be seen crisscrossing the city, he was no longer paying calls on anyone. During those first few days after his wife's departure everyone Fleury came across, if they had not been visited themselves, at least had a friend, or a friend of a friend, whom the Collector had visited "to draw his attention to the grave state of unrest in which the native finds himself". But now, if you asked in any of the drawing-rooms you frequented, there would be plenty of people who had seen the Collector on the road but nobody would have heard of him having reached a destination.

Moreover, now that the sun was scorching hot during the middle of the day the Collector was frequently to be seen (you would have seen him yourself if you had been out and about in Calcutta at that time) standing at the roadside in the shade of a tree, he would be standing there lost in thought (thinking, people chuckled, of a way to get a new civilization to advance with the railways into the Mofussil to soothe the natives) like a man waiting for the end of a shower, though, of course, there was not a cloud in sight. But whatever the reason for these long pauses under trees they certainly fostered the belief that the Collector had given up paying warning visits to people. But why, in that case, he should not simply have remained at home, no one could explain.

Of course, there was another explanation that nobody suggested. Now that it was no longer considered to be the height of fashion to be called on and warned by the Collector (indeed, it was thought to be rather ridiculous, for if he had waited this long before coming you were clearly not very high on his list of influential people) a number of those he visited were no doubt declining to see him on the grounds that they were too busy.

And then, one day, quite suddenly, he had disappeared. Evidently he had decided to leave Calcutta to its ignorance and had returned to Krishnapur to take up his duties. For a time nothing more was heard of him.

The cemetery where Fleury's mother was buried is still to be seen in Calcutta, in Park Street, a short distance from the *maidan*. Nowadays it is an astonishing and lonely place, untended and overgrown. Many of the more ambitious Victorian tombs tilt unevenly, others have collapsed or have been deliberately smashed. Very often, too, the lead letters have been picked out of the inscriptions, a small tax imposed by the living on the dead. Near the gate a couple of destitute families huddle uneasily in huts they have built of sticks and rags; no wonder they are so ill at ease, for even to a Christian the atmosphere here is ominous.

In Fleury's day, however, the grass was cut and the graves well cared for. Besides, as you might expect, he was fond of graveyards; he enjoyed brooding in them and letting his heart respond to the abbreviated biographies he found engraved in their stones . . . so eloquent, so succinct! All the same, once he had spent an hour or two pondering by his mother's grave he decided to call it a day because, after all, one does not want to overdo the lurking in graveyards.

This decision was not a very sudden one. From the age of sixteen when he had first become interested in books, much to the distress of his father, he had paid little heed to physical and sporting matters. He had been of a melancholy and listless cast of mind, the victim of the beauty and sadness of the universe. In the course of the last two or three years, however, he had noticed that his sombre and tubercular manner was no longer having quite the effect it had once had, particularly on young ladies. They no longer found his pallor so interesting, they tended to become impatient with his melancholy. The effect, or lack of it, that you have on the opposite sex is important because it tells you whether or not you are in touch with the spirit of the times, of which the opposite sex is invariably the custodian. The truth was that the tide of sensitivity to beauty, of gentleness and melancholy, had gradually ebbed leaving Fleury floundering on a sandbank. Young ladies these days were more interested in the qualities of Tennyson's "great, broad-shouldered, genial Englishman" than they were in pallid poets, as Fleury was dimly beginning to perceive. Louise Dunstaple's preference for romping with jolly officers which had dismayed him on the day of the picnic had by no means been the first rebuff of this kind. Even Miriam sometimes asked him aloud why he was looking "hangdog" when once she would have remained silent, thinking "soulful".

All the same, one cannot change one's character overnight simply to suit the fashion, even if one wants to. Some obstinate people in Fleury's predicament prefer to retain the one they started with, and are content to regard their own era as philistine, or effeminate, or whatever it is that they themselves are not. It only becomes a real problem if you fall in love like Fleury and want to seem attractive.

For a day or two Fleury became quite active. He had his book about the advance of civilization in India to consider and this was one reason why he had taken an interest in the behaviour of the Collector. He asked a great number of questions and even bought a notebook to record pertinent information.

"Why, if the Indian people are happier under our rule," he asked a Treasury official, "do they not emigrate from those native states like Hyderabad which are so dreadfully misgoverned and come and live in British India?"

"The apathy of the native is well known," replied the official stiffly. "He is not enterprising." Fleury wrote down "apathy" in a flowery hand and then, after a moment's hesitation, added "not enterprising". Unfortunately, this burst of energy did not survive the leaden facts which he was given to illustrate the Company's beneficial effect. When told of the spectacular increases in Customs, Opium and Salt revenues he fell into a stupor and not long after was to be seen stretched listlessly on a sofa once more, deep in a book of poems.

Dr Dunstaple had been prevailed upon by Louise and by Mrs Dunstaple to let them delay their departure for Krishnapur until the last ball of the cold season had been held. Louise could then be bridesmaid at the wedding of a friend that very same evening in St Paul's Cathedral. The Doctor sighed. Another few lucky pigs had escaped his spear. He was not fond of dancing.

In the town hall the temperature was well over ninety degrees, the high windows stood open, and punkahs flapped like wounded birds above the dancers. Although Fleury could not imagine how one could dance in such a heat Louise had filled her card in no time at all; by the time he came to make an application to his dismay there remained nothing but the *galloppe*. He passed the back of his hand across his brow and it came away glistening, as if brushed with olive oil. Nor could the ladies look cool; no amount of rice powder could dull the glint of their features, no amount of padding could prevent damp stains from spreading at their armpits.

34

Pointing out one marvel after another, the musicians, the magnificently liveried servants, the delightful buffet amid the flowers and chandeliers and potted palms, the Doctor strongly recommended Fleury not to ignore this elegant scene when it came to choosing examples of civilized behaviour for his book. This was civilization of a sort, it was true, agreed Fleury, but somehow he believed that what was required was a completely different aspect of it . . . its spiritual, its mystical side, the side of the heart! "Civilization as it is now denatures man. Think of the mills and the furnaces . . . Besides, Doctor, everyone I talk to in Calcutta about my book tells me to look at this or that . . . a canal that has been dug, or some cruel practice like infanticide or suttee which has been stopped . . . And these are certainly improvements of course, but they are only symptoms, as it were, of what should be a great, beneficial disease . . . The trouble is, you see, that although the symptoms are there, the disease itself is missing!"

"A beneficial disease!" thought the Doctor, glancing with dismay at Fleury's flushed countenance.

"Hm, that's all very well but . . . Here, have one of these." The Doctor proffered Fleury his cigar-case, adding, by way of a subtle compliment: "I'm afraid they're not as good as Lord Canning's though." He watched Fleury anxiously. He had heard, though it might be only a rumour, that Fleury had cornered some poor devil in the Bengal Club and read him a long poem about some people climbing a symbolical mountain.

Perplexed by this reference to Lord Canning, Fleury took a cigar and ran his nose along it thoughtfully. His eye came to rest on two lovely, perspiring girls nearby as one of them exclaimed: "I hate men who hop in the polka!" At any London ball he might have over-heard the same remark. Moreover, he had heard that wealthy Indian gentlemen also gave balls in Calcutta in the civilized European manner, even though at the same time they despised English ladies for dancing with men as if they were 'nautch' girls, something they would certainly never have permitted to their own wives. There seemed to be a contradiction in this. It was all very difficult.

The Doctor had taken Fleury by the elbow and was guiding him towards the buffet. And where was Mrs Lang this evening? Fleury explained that Miriam had refused to come with him,

not because she was still in mourning but because she considered it too hot to dance. Miriam had a mind of her own, he
grumbled.

"What a sensible young woman!" cried the Doctor enviously, wishing that his own ladies had minds of their own which
told them when it was too hot to dance.

They passed a row of flushed chaperones alongside the floor;
the incessant movement of fans gave a fluttering effect to these
ladies, as of birds preening themselves. Their eyes, starting out
of the pallor of heavily powdered faces, followed Fleury expressionlessly as he strolled by; he thought: "How true that
English ladies do not prosper in the Indian climate! The flesh
subsides and melts away, leaving only strings and fibres and
wrinkles."

Now there was a stir in the ballroom as the word went
round: General Hearsey had arrived! The throng at the edge
of the floor was so great that the Doctor and Fleury could see
nothing, so they mounted a few steps of the white marble
staircase. There they managed to catch a glimpse of the General
and the Doctor could not help glancing at Fleury and wishing
that his son Harry was there in his stead. Harry would have
given anything to set eyes on the brave General whereas
Fleury, his brain poached by theories about civilization, could
surely not appreciate the worth of the man now making his
slow way through the guests, many of whom came forward to
greet him; others who had not made his acquaintance rose out
of respect and bowed as he passed.

But the Doctor was doing Fleury an injustice for Fleury was
no less stirred than he was himself. Fleury suspected himself of
being a coward and here he was in the presence of the man
who, in front of a sepoy quarter guard trembling on the brink
of revolt, had ridden fearlessly up to the rebel who had just shot
the adjutant. To the warning of a fellow officer that his musket
was loaded the General had replied in words already famous
all over Calcutta: "Damn his musket!" And the sepoy, overpowered by the General's moral presence, had been unable to
squeeze the trigger. No wonder that, for the moment, Fleury
had forgotten about his theories and was feasting his eyes on
the elderly soldier below, on the General's thick white hair
and mustache, on the manly bearing that made you forget he

was sixty-six years old. And as the General, who was talking calmly to some friend, but whose face nevertheless wore a tired and strained look, lifted his eyes and rested them on Fleury for a moment, Fleury's heart thudded as if he had been a hussar instead of a poet.

Refreshed by this glimpse of courage personified Fleury and the Doctor continued up the marble staircase to the galleries. Here a number of people were comfortably seated in alcoves, separated from each other by ferns and red plush screens, in a good position to survey the floor below. There was a good deal of coming and going between these alcoves as social calls were paid and it was here that one might discuss the hard facts of marriage while the young people took care of the sentimental aspects downstairs. Mrs Dunstaple had found herself a sofa beneath a punkah and was talking to another lady who also had a nubile daughter, though rather more plain than Louise. At the sight of Fleury approaching with her husband Mrs Dunstaple was unable to stifle a groan of pleasure for she had just been boasting to her companion of the attentions which Fleury was paying to Louise and had had the disagreeable impression of not being altogether believed.

Fleury bowed as he was introduced and then sat down, dazed by the heat. The red plush screens surrounding him gave him the feeling that he was sitting in a furnace. He took out a handkerchief and mopped his oily brow. On the floor below, the dancers were coming to the end of a waltz and soon it would be time for the *galloppe*. Presently Louise appeared, escorted by Lieutenants Cutter and Stapleton who both stared insolently at Fleury and evidently found themselves unequal to the task of recognizing him.

Fleury gazed in admiration at Louise; he understood she had been a bridesmaid at the wedding of a childhood friend earlier in the evening. The two girls had grown up together and now, after they had told each other so many times: "Oh no, you'll be first!", the other girl *had* been first, because Louise was taking such a long time making up her mind.

Fleury could see that Louise had been moved by this experience of being her friend's bridesmaid; her face had become vulnerable, as if she were close to laughter or tears. He found this vulnerability strangely disarming.

37

And now that Louise had been keyed up in this way, small wonder if for a few hours at least, she should look at every young man she met, even Fleury, and see him momentarily as her future husband. Mrs Dunstaple looked at her daughter and then looked at Fleury, who was covertly grinding his teeth and scratching his knuckles, which had just been bitten by a mosquito. How quickly life goes by! She sighed. The rather plain daughter of her companion was suffering from "prickly heat", she was being informed. What a shame! She bent a sympathetic ear.

It was time for the *galloppe*. As they took up their positions on the floor Louise raised her eyes and gazed at Fleury in an enquiring sort of way. But Fleury was wool-gathering, he was thinking complacently that in London one would not still have seen gentlemen wearing brown evening dress coats as one did here, and he was thinking of civilization, of how it must be something more than the fashions and customs of one country imported into another, of how it must be *a superior view of mankind*, and of how he was suffocated in his own black evening dress coat, and of what a strong smell of sweat there was down here on the floor, and of whether he could possibly survive the coming dance. Then, at last, the orchestra struck up with a lively air and set the dancers' feet in motion, among them Louise's white satin shoes and Fleury's patent leather boots, charging and wheeling rhythmically as if all this were taking place not in India but in some temperate land far away.

3

Towards the end of April the *dak gharry* which carried the
English mail inland every fortnight made its laborious way as
usual across the vast plain towards Krishnapur. It dragged behind it a curtain of dust which climbed to an immense height
and hung in the air for several miles back like a rain cloud. As
well as the mail the *gharry* also contained Miriam, Fleury,
Lieutenant Harry Dunstaple, and a spaniel called Chloë, who
had spent a good deal of the journey with her head out of the
window watching with amazement the dust that billowed from
beneath the wheels.

"What I should like to know, Harry, is whether it's a Moslem
or a Hindu cemetery?"

"The Hindus don't bury their dead so it must be Mohammedan."

"Of course it must, what a fool I am!" Fleury glanced at
Harry for the signs of derision that newcomers to India, in-
sultingly termed "griffins", had to expect from old hands. But
Harry's pleasant face registered only polite lack of interest in
the burial habits of the natives.

Fleury and Miriam had come across Harry at the last *dak*
bungalow; he had very decently ridden out to greet them, in
spite of the fact that his left arm was in a sling; he had sprained
his wrist pig-sticking. Not content with riding out he had sent
his horse back with the *sais* and had joined the travellers in
the discomfort of the *gharry*, a carriage which bore a close
resemblance to an oblong wooden box on four wheels without
springs; they had now spent almost two days in this convey-
ance and their soft bodies cried out for comfort. Miriam had
spent most of the journey with her nose buried in a handkerchief and her eyes leaking muddy tears, not because she had
suffered a renewal of grief for Captain Lang but because of the
stifling dust which irritated her eyeballs. As for Fleury, his
excitement at the prospect of seeing Louise again was muted

by misgivings as to what sort of place Krishnapur might turn out to be. This arid plain they were crossing was scarcely promising. Very likely there would be discomfort and snakes. In such circumstances he feared that he would not shine.

Harry had greeted him with friendliness mixed with caution and they had spent a little time searching hopefully, but so far in vain, for an interest in common. The Joint Magistrate had been taken ill and had gone to the hills for a cure from which it was feared he would not return, Harry had explained, so it had been arranged that they should take over his bungalow while he was away.

Chloë, overcome by the heat, had thrown herself panting on to Fleury's lap and had fallen asleep there. He tried to shove her away, but a dog that does not want to be moved can make herself very heavy indeed, and so he was obliged to let her stay. Fleury did not himself particularly care for dogs, but he knew that young ladies did, as a rule. He had bought Chloë, whose golden tresses had reminded him of Louise, from a young officer who had ruined himself at the race-course. At the time he had thought of Chloë as a subtle gift; the golden tresses had blended in his mind with the idea of canine fidelity and devotion. He would use Chloë as a first salvo aimed at Louise's affections. But in the meantime he found her only a nuisance.

As they approached Krishnapur they saw a few travellers on the road, including some sepoys who looked very fine in their red coats and black trousers. As they passed, the sepoys saluted the pallor of the faces they glimpsed in the dim interior of the carriage (not to mention Chloë's gilt curls). Only Harry noticed with a frown that one or two of them had saluted with their left hands; if he had been alone he would have stopped and rebuked them for such a deliberate lack of respect; as it was he had to pretend not to have noticed. They crept ponderously past a camel harnessed to a cart and Fleury stared dubiously at the belt around the great balloon of its stomach . . . all these strange sights made him feel melancholy again, a lone wanderer on the face of the earth. Old men sat on their heels against the wall of a nabob's house and beside them sat a dusty lion chained to the wall. Next they passed a mosque, empty except for lamps of coloured glass, and rattled over an iron bridge. A family of yellow-green monkeys stared up at him with hostility, their eyes like lumps of polished jade.

And then they had plunged into the bazaar, crowded with people dressed in white muslin. Where could they all possibly live? An incongruous picture came into Fleury's mind of a hundred and fifty people squatting on the floor of his aunt's drawing-room in Torquay. The *gharry* lurched suddenly and turned into some gates. They had arrived. His heart sank.

They had not arrived. Harry had climbed down and was arguing with a man who had been scrambling along beside the carriage shouting and had caused them to turn into these gates which, it turned out, belonged to the *dak* bungalow. Harry seemed quite angry; this was not at all where he wanted to stop. A laborious parley was taking place, Harry's grasp of the language being limited to a few simple commands, domestic and military. He was becoming exasperated and beginning to shout; soldiers are notorious for reacting badly when their will is opposed. Yet though the man flinched slightly at every fresh outburst, he stood his ground. They might have continued like this for some time, Harry shouting, the native flinching, but for the appearance of another man, elderly and very fat, who hurried up from the direction of the bungalow. When he opened his mouth to speak, Fleury saw that it was stained an astonishing orange-red from the chewing of betel. Hypnotized he stared into this glowing cavern from which English was emerging, though not of a sort he was able to understand. This man was the *khansamah* from the *dak* bungalow, Harry interpreted for Fleury's benefit, and what he wanted to say was . . . wait!

A look of alarm appeared on Harry's face and without waiting to hear any more he sprinted towards the bungalow, up the steps, and vanished inside. Fleury would have followed had not Chloë chosen this moment to wrench herself from his grip and bolt into the enticing green jungle of the compound. Ignoring his shouts she careered away at high speed with her nose to the ground. He pursued her despairingly and after a long search found her experimentally licking the brown stomach of a baby she had come across playing in the mud by the servants' huts some distance away. He dragged her back, slapping and scolding. Harry had returned.

"What was all that about?"

"I thought you heard. The *khansamah* said a woman was trying to kill herself." Harry paused, looking shaken. "She appears to be . . . well, I suppose one would say 'drunk', not to put too fine a point on it."

"A Hindu?" ventured Fleury with medium confidence. He had remembered that Mohammedans do not drink.

"Well, that's the whole thing. She appears to be English, I'm afraid. That is, I mean to say, she definitely *is* English. I'd heard something about her before, actually. It seems . . ." Harry cleared his throat artificially. His already pink cheeks grew pinker and he threw an embarrassed glance in the direction of Miriam. "It seems some officer took away her virtue. He left her then, of course, or he'd have got into trouble with his colonel. She's done this before, you know. I mean, tried to kill herself. One really doesn't know quite what to do."

The sun was setting by the time Fleury and Miriam found their way to the Joint Magistrate's bungalow. It turned out to be a yellow-plastered building surrounded by a verandah and thatched for coolness. Bearers appeared out of the twilight to wrestle with their boxes while they peered inside. Two bedrooms, each with a bathroom attached, and two other rooms, divided from each other by pieces of red cotton cloth instead of doors. Saying she was tired, Miriam swiftly vanished into the emptiest bedroom with her boxes, leaving Fleury to his own devices. Fleury felt resentful towards her for so suddenly deserting him in this unfamiliar place; she had become like this since the death of her husband.

Melancholy overwhelmed him at the thought of the lonely evening ahead. Although the Joint Magistrate had gone away to die in the hills he had not seen fit to take his belongings with him. One of the rooms had been used as an office; paper was heaped everywhere. Fleury stirred a pile of documents with the toe of his boot and it toppled over gently on to the floor, exhaling dust; the light was just bright enough for him to see that it was a collection of salt-reports tied in bundles with the frail, faded red tape of India's official business. There were also blue-books, codes, and countless letters, some filed, some heaped at random. It seemed inevitable that no one would ever return from the hills to sort out this mass of official paper. From the wall the head of a very small tiger stared at him with dislike; at least, he supposed it must be a tiger, though it looked more like an ordinary household cat.

By now most of the baggage had been moved into his bedroom and was being unpacked under the eye of the *khansamah*, who in turn was being supervised by Harry, who had helpfully reappeared, bringing with him an invitation to supper at the Residency. Gradually the contents of his boxes were emptied out: books and clothes, Havanas, Brown Windsor soap, jams and conserves in miraculously unbroken jars, a cask of brandy, seidlitz powders, candles, a tin footbath, bound volumes of Bell's Life, more candles, boots in trees, and an ingenious piece of furniture designed to serve, in dire domestic situations which Fleury hoped never to experience, as both wash-stand and writing table. After a rapid discussion in Hindustani the books were placed on top of this table and its legs were stood in earthenware saucers filled with water. It was to protect them against ants, Harry explained. Fleury nodded calmly but a terrible thought occurred to him: what if snakes came to drink from these saucers while he was asleep in bed? Something warned him, however, not to mention this fear to Harry. Harry would not understand. Then, peering around in the gathering darkness, Fleury noticed that not only the legs of the table but also of the cupboards and even of the bed itself were standing in saucers brimming with water.

By the time Fleury reached the Residency it was much too dark for him to see the apoplectic snap-dragons that guarded the beds beside the drive, but he could smell the heavy scent of the roses ... the smell disturbed him; like the smell of incense it was more powerful than an Englishman is accustomed to. At that moment, tired and dispirited, he would have given a great deal to smell the fresh breeze off the Sussex downs. He said as much to Harry Dunstaple.

"Yes, I see what you mean," agreed Harry cautiously.

"I say, what's all this?"

Two looming banks of earth had rolled out of the darkness to engulf them like a tidal wave as they approached the gates.

"Drains," said Harry stiffly.

"Drains!"

43

"Well, actually, they're not really drains. They're fortifications in case the Residency has to be defended. It's the Collector's idea, you know." Harry's tone was disapproving. The military at Captainganj took a dim view of the Collector's earthworks, a view which Harry shared. Some people, Harry knew, would have put it more bluntly and said that the Collector had gone mad. Everybody at Captainganj believed that there was no danger at all, of course, but that what danger there *was*, would be maximized by the Collector's display of trepidation. All the same, the Collector wielded the supreme authority in Krishnapur, an authority even higher than that of General Jackson. The General could do what he liked at Captainganj but that was the limit of his estate; his authority was cushioned all around by that of the Collector whose empire ran to the horizon in every direction. In Harry's view, the Collector's authority resembled in many ways that of a Roman emperor; however fallible a Collector might be as a human being, as a representative of the Company he commanded respect. It was in the nature of things that sometimes a Roman emperor, or a Collector, would go mad, insist on promoting his horse to be a general, and would have to be humoured; such a danger exists in every rigid hierarchy. But the feeling at Captainganj was that it could not have happened at a worse time; the military were being made to look ridiculous. Word of the Collector's behaviour in Calcutta had already come back to the barracks, together with mocking comments from brother officers at other stations. Nobody likes ridicule, even when undeserved, but to a soldier it is like a bed of fiery coals. The Residency was not their province, but people would think, or pretend to think, that it was; people would say they were "croaking"! The Collector's timorous behaviour would rub off on *them*.

And yet, although Harry thought all this, he could not bring himself to say it ... at least, not to Fleury; in private with a brother officer, perhaps, he might allow himself to rant against the Collector, but with a stranger, even one who was almost a cousin, it would have offended his sense of honour. So the most he could permit himself about the drains was a tone of disapproval ... but in any case, by now they had left them behind and their boots were clattering on the steps of the portico.

The Residency was lamplit at this time of night. The marble staircase which faced Fleury as he entered gave him the delicious sensation of entering a familiar and civilized house; his eyes, which had been starved of such nourishment since he had left Calcutta, greedily followed the swerve of its bannister until it curled into itself like a ram's horn at the bottom. Other Europeans besides Fleury had feasted their eyes on this staircase; in Calcutta one might not have noticed it particularly, but here in the Krishnapur cantonment all the other houses were of one storey; to be able to go upstairs was a luxury available only to the Collector and his guests. Indeed, the only other dwelling in the neighbourhood which could boast a staircase was the palace of the Maharajah of Krishnapur; not that this was much use to the English community, because, although he had a fine son who had been educated in Calcutta by English tutors, the old Maharajah himself was eccentric, libidinous, and spoke no English.

Two chandeliers hung over the long walnut dining table and their rainbow glints were reflected in its polished surface. Fleury's spirits had been instantly restored, thanks partly to the civilized atmosphere of the Residency, partly to the Collector's "drains" which had reminded him what an entertaining character his host was. He began to look around eagerly for further signs of eccentricity. At the same time he tried to sort out the names of all the people he had just been introduced to. He had been greeted warmly by Dr and Mrs Dunstaple, and inaudibly by Louise who was now standing a little way back from the table, fair and pale, her long golden curls flowing out like a bow-wave from the parting on top of her head, slender fingers resting absently on ... well, on what looked like a machine of some kind. "Hello, what have we here?" Fleury crowed inwardly, "A machine in the dining-room, how deuced peculiar!" He peered at it more closely, causing Louise to release it from her tender fingers and drift away, ignoring him. It was a rectangular metal box with a funnel at one end and cog-wheels on both sides. A faint fragrance of lemon verbena stole up behind him. He turned to find the Collector watching him moodily.

"It's a gorse bruiser," he declared heavily, before Fleury had a chance to enquire. "What's it for? It's to enable gorse to be

45

fed to cattle. The idea is to soften the hard points of the prickles where the nutritive juices are contained. They say that once gorse has been passed through this machine any herbivore will eat it with avidity."

Fleury surveyed the engine with a polite and studious expression, aware that the Collector was watching him.

"Ah, now here's the Padre to say Grace."

No sooner had the meal begun than conversation of the most civilized sort began to flow around the table. Fleury appeared to join in this conversation: he nodded sagely, frowned, smiled, and stroked his chin thoughtfully at intervals, but he was so hungry that his mind could think of nothing but the dishes which followed each other over the table . . . the fried fish in batter that glowed like barley sugar, the curried fowl seasoned with lime juice, coriander, cumin and garlic, the tender roast kid and mint sauce. As these dishes were placed before him, occasional disjointed snatches of conversation loomed up at him through the fog of his gluttony, stared at him like strangers, and vanished again.

"*Humani generis progressus* . . . I quote the official catalogue of the Exhibition," came the Collector's voice eerily. "But I fear I must translate, Doctor, for this son of yours who has paid more attention to guns and horses than to his books . . . 'The progress of the human race, resulting from the labour of all men, ought to be the final object of the exertion of each individual.' "

But Fleury's base nature whispered that there are times when a man must let the world's problems take care of themselves for a while until, refreshed, he is ready to spring into action again and deal with them. And so he ate on relentlessly.

Only when pudding, in the shape of a cool and creamy mango fool, was placed before him did the fumes of gluttony begin to clear from Fleury's brain and permit him to hear what was being said about "progress". This was not a topic to interest everyone, however. Harry, for instance, had hardly said a word; like his father at the other end of the table he was clearly not much of a one for abstract conversations. Poor Harry, it had probably never occurred to him that one could make an "adventurous" remark (as he, Fleury, frequently did) or have an "exciting" conversation. He looked rather pale at the moment, no doubt his sprained wrist was troubling him; he should probably not have ridden out to the *dak* bungalow to get that jolting on the way back.

Louise, too, remained silent. In Fleury's view she was quite right to sit there quietly and listen to what the gentlemen had to say, because speaking a great deal in company is not an attractive quality in a young lady. A young lady with strong opinions is even worse. What can be more distressing than to hear a member of the fair sex exclaiming: "In the first place, this . . . and in the second place, that . . ." while she chops the air with her fingers and divides whatever you have just been saying into categories? No, a woman's special skill is to listen quietly to what a fellow has to say and thereby create the sort of atmosphere in which good conversation can flourish. So thought Fleury, anyway.

Mrs Hampton, the Padre's wife, did occasionally venture an opinion, as her rank and maturity entitled her to . . . but she took advantage of her privilege only to support the views of her husband, which no one could object to. Of the other ladies two were remarkably garrulous, or would have been had they not been overawed by Mrs Hampton who kept them severely in check, cutting in firmly each time one of them tried to launch into a silly discourse. One of them, a pretty though rather vulgar person, was Mrs Rayne, the wife of the Opium Agent; the other, even more talkative, was her friend and companion, recently widowed, Mrs Ross.

Now that he had eaten, Fleury was merely waiting for a break in the conversation before voicing his own opinion on progress. It came almost immediately. "If there has been any progress in our century," he declared with confidence, "it has been less in material than in spiritual matters. Think of the progress from the cynicism and materialism of our grandparents . . . from a Gibbon to a Keats, from a Voltaire to a Lamartine!"

"I disagree," replied Mr Rayne with a smile. "It's only in practical matters that one may look for signs of progress. Ideas are always changing, certainly, but who's to say that one is better than another? It is in material things that progress can be clearly seen. I hope you'll forgive me if I mention opium but

47

really one has to go no farther to find progress exemplified. Opium, even more than salt, is a great source of revenue of our own creation and is now more productive than any except the land revenue. And who pays it? Why, John Chinaman ... who prefers our opium to any other. That's what I call progress."

The Collector had been behaving oddly; moody and expansive by turns, perhaps on account of tiredness or of the claret he had drunk, he now suddenly became expansive again. "My dear friends, there's no question at all of a division of importance between the spiritual and the practical. It is the one that imbues the other with purpose ... It's the other that provides an indispensable instrument for the one! Mr Rayne, you are perfectly right to mention this increase of revenue from opium but consider for a moment ... what is it all for ? It's not simply to acquire wealth, but to acquire *through* wealth, that superior way of life which we loosely term civilization and which includes so many things, both spiritual and practical ... and of the utmost diversity ... a system of administering justice impartially on the one hand, works of art unsurpassed in beauty since antique times on the other. The spreading of the Gospel on the one hand, the spreading of the railways on the other. And yet where shall be placed such a phenomenon as the gigantic iron steamship, the *Great Eastern*, which our revered compatriot, Mr Brunel, is at this moment building, and which is soon to subdue the seven seas of the world? For is this not at once a prodigious material triumph and an embodiment, by God's grace, of the spirit of mankind ? Mr Rayne, both the poet and the Opium Agent are necessary to our scheme of things. What d'you say, Padre? Am I right?"

Although lightly built, the Reverend Hampton had been a rowing man at Oxford and he retained from those days a healthy and unassuming manner, illuminated by an earnest simplicity of faith which shone through his every word and gesture. In the seething religious atmosphere of Oxford in the Padre's time a man did well to stick to rowing; the Tractarian onslaughts were enough to shake the strongest constitution; it was said that in Oxford even Dr Whateley, now the Archbishop of Dublin, had preached a sermon with one leg dangling out of the pulpit. All the same, the Padre sometimes had a worried look; this was because he was afraid that the duties to which the Lord had called him might prove too much for his strength.

"Mr Hopkins, as you know, I had the privilege like yourself of attending the Great Exhibition which opened in our homeland six years ago almost to this very day. To wander about in that vast building of glass, so immense that the elms it enclosed looked like Christmas trees, was to walk in a wonderland of beauty and of Man's ingenuity ... But of all the many marvels it contained there was one in the American section which made a particular impression on me because it seemed to combine so happily both the spiritual and the practical. I am referring to the Floating Church for Seamen from Philadelphia. This unusual construction floated on the twin hulls of two New York clipper ships and was entirely in the Gothic style, with a tower surmounted by a spire ... inside, it contained a bishop's chair; outside, it was painted to resemble brown stone. As I looked at it I thought of all the churches built by men throughout the ages and said to myself: 'There has surely never been a more consummate embodiment of Faith than this.' "

"A splendid example," agreed the Collector. "A very happy marriage of fact and spirit, of deed and ghost."

"But no, sir! But no, Padre!" cried Fleury, so vehemently as to startle awake those guests whose minds had wandered during the preceding discussion. All eyes turned towards him and even as he spoke he wondered whether he might not be ever so slightly drunk. "But no, with all respect, that's not it at all! Please consider, Padre, that a church is no more a church because it floats! Would a church be any more of a church if we could hoist it into the skies with a thousand balloons? Only the person capable of listening to the tenderest echoes of his own heart is capable of making that aerial ascent which will unite him with the Eternal. As for your most brilliant engineers, if they don't listen to the voice of their hearts, not a thousand, not a million balloons will be capable of lifting their leaden feet one inch from the earth ..." Fleury paused, catching sight of the consternation on the Doctor's face. He did not dare glance at Louise. Somehow he knew she would be displeased. He could have kicked himself now for having blurted out all that about "the tenderest echoes of the heart" . . . that was the very last line to take with a girl like Louise who enjoyed flirting with officers. He had *meant* to say none of that . . . he had meant to be blunt and manly and to smile a lot. What a fool he was! As he sat there a random, frightening thought occurred to him: tonight he would have to sleep in the midst of sipping snakes!

Meanwhile, the Padre was looking distinctly alarmed. This young man had started a theological hare which might prove difficult to seize if he let it get away. He thought back grimly to his undergraduate days where this sort of theological beagling had been very fashionable and had ended, alas, in more than one young man taking a fall and losing his Faith. And the Padre was already beset by worries enough; apart from the manifold problems of ministry in a heathen country, scarcely two hours had passed since he had had a painful interview with the fallen woman in the *dak* bungalow, and he had found her still so intoxicated as to be unavailable to the voice of her conscience. But he had an even greater worry than that, for with the English mail that had arrived in the *dak gharry* that very evening had come a copy of the *Illustrated London News* with a strong editorial against a danger of which he had not even been aware . . . a projected new translation of the Bible. It had not taken the editorial to make him realize the extent of this danger looming over the Christian world. The Bible was sacred and the Padre knew that one cannot change something that is sacred. Men were preparing to improve upon sacred words! In their folly and their pride they were setting themselves to edit the Divine Author.

Yet at the same time he could not understand why the Bible should have had to be translated at all, even in the first place . . . why it should have been written in Hebrew and Greek when English was the obvious language, for outside one remote corner of the world hardly anyone could understand Hebrew, whereas English was spoken in every corner of every continent. The Almighty had, it was true, subsequently permitted a magnificent translation, as if realizing His error . . . but, of course, the Almighty could not be in error, such an idea was an absurdity. Here the Padre was aware of intruding on matters of extraordinary theological complexity which blinded his brain. It was so hot and one must not allow oneself to get caught like a ram in a thicket of sophistry. He made an effort to rally himself and said, mildly but firmly: "I agree, Mr Fleury, that a church is a house of God whatever its design. With the Floating Church I was citing an instance of men dedicating ingenuity of the highest rank to God."

Poor Fleury, he had rashly advanced too far into the swamp of disputation. His pride was at stake and he could no longer retrace his steps. He could only go forward even though each sucking footstep he took must inevitably increase Louise's contempt.

"But I think that to dedicate is not enough. We calculate, we make deductions, we observe, we construct when we should *feel*! We do these things instead of feeling."

Harry Dunstaple stirred uncomfortably in his seat, looking paler than ever; he could not for the life of him see the point of so much talk about nothing.

The Collector's stern features had set into an expression of good-humoured impatience; while Fleury had been speaking he had sent one of the bearers to fetch something and presently he returned carrying three bound volumes. "This Universe of ours functions according to laws which in our humble ignorance we are scarcely able to perceive, let alone understand. But if the divine benevolence allows us to explore some few of its marvels it is clearly right that we should do so. No, Mr Fleury, every invention is a prayer to God. Every invention, however great, however small, is a humble emulation of the greatest invention of all, the Universe. Let me just quote at random from this catalogue of the Exhibition to which the Padre referred a moment ago, that Exhibition which I beg you to consider as a collective prayer of all the civilized nations . . . Let me see, Number 382: Instrument to teach the blind to write. Model of an aerial machine and of a navigable balloon. A fire annihilator by R. Weare of Plumstead Common. A domestic telegraph requiring only one bell for any number of rooms. An expanding pianoforte for yachts etc. Artificial teeth carved in hippopotamus ivory by Sinclair and Hockley of Soho. A universal drill for removing decay from teeth. A jaw-lever for keeping animals' mouths open. Improved double truss for hernia, invented by a labouring man . . . There seems to be no end to the ingenuity of mankind and I could continue indefinitely quoting examples of it. But I ask you only to consider these humble artefacts of man's God-given ability to observe and calculate as minute steps in the progress of mankind towards union with that Supreme Being in whom all knowledge *is*, and ever shall be."

"Amen," murmured the Padre automatically. But had a still, small voice just tried to whisper to him?

The Collector had spoken in a voice of authority which closed the discussion. For an instant Fleury was tempted to deliver a final, heated harangue ... but no, it was out of the question. Fleury was left mute, with a faint air of disgrace clinging to him.

It was already daylight when Fleury awoke. A deep and oppressive silence prevailed, as if the bungalow were deserted; above him, the punkah, which had been flapping rhythmically through the night, now hung motionless; in the stagnant air his nightshirt clung to his skin. But when he looked out on the verandah everything was normal. The punkah-wallah had simply fallen asleep; he squatted there on the verandah still holding the rope which led up to a hole high in the wall. Beside him the *khansamah* was buttering some toast for Fleury's breakfast with the greasy wing of a fowl; seeing Fleury he woke the punkah-wallah with a kick and without a word the man began again the rhythmic tugging at the rope which he had maintained throughout the night.

Fleury dressed rapidly, thankful not to have fallen a prey to the drinking snakes during the night, and then breakfasted with Miriam, who had already risen. They spent the morning together, until it was time for Miriam to dress for a visit to the Dunstaple ladies. The hours dragged by. Fleury found it too hot to go outside. He tried to read a book. Miriam had not returned by four o'clock when Rayne, the Opium Agent, sent one of his servants over to invite Fleury to tea. From the shade of the verandah Fleury watched Rayne's servant hastening up from the depths of the compound under a black umbrella; once on the verandah he shook it vigorously as if to shake off drops of sunlight.

Fleury had not taken to Rayne the previous evening but his boredom was so acute that he decided to accept. He set off, accompanied by Chloë who had been sleeping all day and was full of energy, under the servant's umbrella. Rayne's compound, it transpired, was only separated from that of the Joint Magistrate by the compounds of a couple of deserted bungalows. The two young officials had been firm friends and had been so used to paying each other informal visits without resorting to the road that a path had been worn through the jungle into which these neglected gardens had been allowed to grow ... not that it was much of a path for in places the foliage had already shrivelled in the heat and there was no sign of a path at all. Rayne's bearer led the way past an old, deserted bungalow with holes in its thatched roof and a sagging verandah; beside it, on a little mound, lay the worm-pocked skeleton of a flag-pole, while in front of it there spread a glaring, nightmarish growth of geraniums. As they moved away from the bungalow there came a sudden scuffling sound, then silence.

"What was that?"

"Jackal, Sahib."

They climbed over a low mud wall, through a mass of wild roses still in bloom and scrambled through a shadeless thicket. Suddenly Fleury stopped dead in his tracks, aware that someone was lurking close by in the thicket, watching him. It was a moment before he saw that there was a figure there, a small fat man with a black face and six arms. A path led up to him; it was a shrine. Fleury approached it, accompanied by the bearer holding the umbrella over his head. "Lord Bhairava," he explained.

Lord Bhairava's eyes were white in his black face and he appeared to be looking at Fleury with malice and amusement. One of his six arms held a trident, another a sword, another flourished a severed forearm, a fourth held a bowl, while a fifth held a handful of skulls by the hair: the faces of the skulls wore thin mustaches and expressions of surprise. The sixth hand, empty, held up its three middle fingers. Peering closer, Fleury saw that people had left coins and food in the bowl he was holding and more food had been smeared around his chuckling lips, which were also daubed with crimson, as if with blood. Fleury turned away quickly, chilled by this unexpected encounter and anxious to leave this sinister garden without delay.

As they proceeded, one sweet suffocating perfume gave way to another so that, bemused with the heat and exertion, he had the impression of floundering through a new and sensuous element. Presently, another deserted bungalow came into sight, this one even more forlorn than the last, almost roofless, with giant thistles growing up out of the windows. An emaciated cow, horns painted green, was browsing on a few tufts of parched grass that had once been a lawn. Then they stepped over another mud wall into an equally barren but more orderly compound. As they approached Rayne's bungalow the sound of voices and laughter could be heard in the stillness and heat of the late afternoon.

After the glare of the compound a midnight darkness seemed to prevail on the verandah. A figure advanced out of the gloom and shook Fleury's hand, welcoming him in loud tones which he recognized as belonging to Rayne. Another figure loomed up, bowed and clicked his heels nearby: this was Burlton who looked after the Treasury. He seemed to be a sensitive young man, anxious to please, and laughing excessively at everything Rayne said. Inside, there was another man, as yet only dimly perceived, who made a motion of bowing from his chair as he was introduced; at the same time he laughed sardonically; his name was Ford, one of the railway engineers. "Always glad to meet a griff," he drawled.

"We have Ford and his ilk but I'm hanged if the railway will ever reach Krishnapur," jeered Rayne, who was evidently somewhat drunk. "Where's that damned bearer. Ram, bring the Sahib a drink . . . *Simkin*! That means champagne, old man. We don't drink tea in this house."

Fleury groped his way to a chair and sat down. For a few moments Rayne lapsed into silence and the only sound was his rather heavy breathing. When the bearer returned with a glass of champagne for Fleury, Rayne said loudly: "We call this lad 'Ram'. That's not his real name. His real name is Akbar or Mohammed or something like that. We call him Ram because he looks like one. And this is Monkey," he added as another bearer came in carrying a plate of biscuits. Monkey did not raise his eyes. He had very long arms, it was true, and a rather simian appearance.

"Where are the mems?" Ford wanted to know, but there was no answer.

"Soon it will be cool enough to go for a canter."

"Why don't we play cards till then?"

But nobody made any move. Fleury sipped his champagne which had an unpleasant, sour taste. He could hear Chloë moaning on the verandah where she had been tied up by one of the servants. Presently another servant came in bearing a box of cheroots; he was elderly and dignified, but exceedingly small, almost a midget.

"What d'you call this blighter?" asked Burlton.

"Ant," said Rayne.

Burlton slapped his knee and abandoned himself to laughter.

"I'd like to know what Mr Fleury thinks of this Meerut business," said Ford. "What? Can you beat that! I'm damned if he's even heard of it! Where have you been all day?" And delighted, he set to work to give Fleury what seemed to be a largely imaginary account of some terrible uprising of sepoys, full of "plump young griffins, fellows about your age" being "hacked to pieces in their prime". Fleury could see that he was being made fun of, but was alarmed all the same.

"Don't worry," said Burlton condescendingly; he had been in India almost a year and thus was less of a griffin than Fleury. "Jack Sepoy may be able to cut down defenceless people but he can't stand up to real pluck."

"When did all this happen?"

"What day is today? Tuesday. It happened on Sunday night."

Ford had lost interest in Meerut by this time but Fleury managed to get some idea of what had happened from Burlton. Two native infantry regiments had shot down their officers and broken into open revolt; in due course they had been joined by the *badmashes* from the bazaar who had set to work plundering the British cantonment. The British troops had been on church parade when the trouble started. In the end they had managed to quell the outbreak but the mutineers had escaped with their firearms. The telegraph wires had been cut soon after the first word of the outbreak had come through, but all sorts of grim rumours were circulating. Krishnapur was almost five hundred miles from this trouble. All the same, news travel-

55

led fast in India even without the telegraph . . . one only had to think of the speed with which the chapatis had spread. What nobody knew was whether the sepoys at Captainganj would follow this example and attack the Krishnapur cantonment?

"Ant! Monkey! Bring *simkin* double quick!"

"Of course, they're bound to know of it already," said Burlton. "What beats me, Rayne, is how the blessed natives got to hear of it before I did. I overheard the babus chatting in the Magistrate's office about Meerut this morning. They were saying that the mutinous sepoys had marched on Delhi and that soon the Mogul Empire would be revived."

"A likely story. The people know when they're well off. They wouldn't stand for it."

"Well, *they* seemed to think it could happen. They wanted to know who were the fifty-two rajahs who would assemble to place the Emperor on the throne."

But Rayne and Ford were not interested in this fancy of Burlton's and Ford said crushingly: "The first thing one learns in India, Burlton, is not to listen to the damned nonsense the natives are always talking." And poor Burlton flushed with shame and avoided Fleury's eye.

Fleury had by now grown accustomed to the gloom and could see that Ford was a heavy-featured man of about forty; in spite of his inferior social status as an engineer, he clearly dominated Rayne and Burlton. Ford said unpleasantly: "Perhaps Mr Fleury will tell us what *he* thinks about it, since he has so many bosom friends among the 'big dogs' at Fort William."

"What I think is this," began Fleury . . . but what he thought was never revealed for at this moment his interlocutors sprang to their feet. Startled, Fleury jumped up too; all this talk of mutiny had set his nerves on edge. But it was only the two ladies entering the room.

"What a disgusting creature!" exclaimed Mrs Rayne, smiling prettily.

"I beg your pardon?"

"I say, Burlton. Would you mind telling that little beggar to bring more *simkin* for the ladies?"

"Haven't you heard, Mr Fleury, that there is an English-woman who has been behaving disgracefully at the *dak* bungalow? The Padre has been out to reason with her more than once, I hear."

"Could they not send the wretched girl away?" Mrs Ross wanted to know. "She can't live for ever in the *dak* bungalow. At the same time she has clearly forfeited the right to the company of virtuous women."

"Is it true then, Sophie," asked Ford teasingly,

" 'That every woe a tear can claim,
Except an erring sister's shame?' "

Ford had pulled his chair closer to that of Mrs Ross and had abandoned his lethargic manner.

"How I wish Florence had a piano," wailed Mrs Ross, changing the subject abruptly. "My fingers fairly ache to play. I fear that Mr Fleury will find but few of the comforts of civilization in Krishnapur, is that not so?" Opening her eyes very wide she gazed interrogatively at Fleury.

"Well," began Fleury, but once again he was forestalled, this time by the arrival of what seemed to be a tornado hitting the verandah and the wooden steps that led up to it. Such a crashing and banging shook the house that the gentlemen started up and made towards the folding louvred doors to see what was the matter. But before they could take more than a couple of steps the doors burst open and a young officer, whom Fleury instantly recognized as Lieutenant Cutter, rode into the room on horseback, wild-eyed, shouting and waving a sabre. The ladies clutched their breasts and did not know whether to shriek with fear or laughter as Cutter, his face as scarlet as his uniform, drove his reluctant horse forward into the room and put it at an empty sofa. Over it went, as clean as a circus pony, and landed, skidding, with a crash on the other side. Cutter then wheeled and flourishing his sabre, lopped the head off a geranium in a pot as he turned his horse to drive it once again at the sofa. But this time the animal refused and Cutter, his sabre still in his hand, slithered off its back on to the floor.

"Do you surrender, sir?" he bellowed at a cushion on the sofa, his arm drawn back for a thrust.

"Yes, it surrenders!" shrieked Mrs Rayne.

"No, it defies you," shouted Ford.

"Then die, sir!" cried Cutter and charging forward trans-fixed the cushion, at the same time tripping up in a rug in the process, with the result that he collapsed in a whirlwind of feathers on the floor.

"It's just a joke," explained Burlton to Fleury, who was amazed and shaken by this latest development. "He's always up to something. What a clown he is!"

"Who is this griffin?" shouted Cutter, fighting his way out of the rug with which his spurs had become entangled. "Who is this milk-sop? Do you surrender, sir?" And drawing back his sabre once again he seemed to be on the point of running Fleury through.

"Yes, he surrenders!" shouted everyone except Fleury, who merely stood there, too dazed to speak, with the point of the sabre patrolling the buttons of his waistcoat.

"Oh, very well then," said Cutter. "No thanks, Rayne, you can keep your Calcutta champagne. I only drink Todd and James, my horse drinks that rubbish. Monkey, bring brandy pawnee!" But Monkey was evidently familiar with Lieutenant Cutter's tastes for he was already hastening forward with a tray.

"Does Beeswing really drink *simkin*?" Mrs Rayne wanted to know, for it seemed that Cutter had given his horse the name of the celebrated Calcutta mare. At this, Cutter, who had sunk despondently on to the feather-strewn sofa with his boots and spurs dangling over the end, started up again with a roar and nothing would do but that Beeswing, who all this time had been standing patiently by the window and occasionally drop-ping his head to try and crop the Persian rug on which he was standing, should join the party too and drink his fill. Ram hur-ried in with another bottle and a bowl, but Cutter ignored the bowl and seized a solar topee from a side table; into this he splashed the contents of the bottle, guffawing and shouting encouragement to his horse. When the champagne was stuck under his nose Beeswing, who was thirsty from his canter in the late afternoon heat, began to lap it up with a will.

The sun was already low on the horizon and Fleury was anxious to return home to see if Miriam had returned and to find out if by any chance the Dunstaples wanted to invite him to supper. But such was the jollity surrounding Beeswing that he had the greatest difficulty attracting the attention of his host.

"What? Can you be off already?" exclaimed Rayne. "I haven't yet had a chance to talk to you . . . A talk about civilization, that's what I wanted to have! You ask Mrs Rayne if I didn't say to her: 'I'll ask him over and we'll have a serious chat about civilization.' My very words. And now you're showing a clean pair of heels."

"I'd be most happy . . . another time, perhaps. I wonder would you mind asking one of your bearers to accompany me?"

Rayne shouted a command, but then he had to return his attention to Cutter, because he and Ford had just concluded an extravagant wager: namely, a dozen of claret that he and Beeswing could not spring from the compound over the verandah and in through the drawing-room window in one great leap Fleury said goodbye to the ladies and hurried away with Chloë frisking ahead; he was by no means anxious to witness this reckless feat.

4

Dark circles had appeared round the Collector's eyes, and the eyes themselves stared more moodily than ever at other members of the congregation during evening service in the Church; at other times during the service he was seen to hold his head unnaturally still; it was as if his features were carved in rock, on which the only movement was the stirring of the whiskers in the breeze from the punkahs. It was evident that he was having trouble in sleeping for soon he ordered one of the bearers to seek a sleeping draught from the doctor. Dr Dunstaple happened to be away at the time so it was Dr McNab who found himself summoned to attend the Collector. He found him in his bedroom beside the open French window giving on to the verandah.

Dr McNab had only recently come to Krishnapur. His wife had died a couple of years earlier in some other Indian station; otherwise, not much was known about him, apart from what Dr Dunstaple supplied in the way of amusing anecdotes about his medical procedures. His manner was formal and reticent; although still quite young he had a middle-aged and melancholy air and, like many gloomy people, he looked discreet. He had never entered the Collector's bedroom before and was impressed by the elegance with which it was furnished: the thickness of the carpet, the polish of the tables and wardrobes, the grandeur of the Collector's four-poster bed, inherited from a previous Resident, which to a man grown accustomed to the humble *charpoy* appeared unusually impressive.

The Collector looked round briefly as Dr McNab entered, and invited him to come to the window, from where there was an excellent view to the south-west, over the stable yard, over the Cutcherry, to the recently built ramparts of dried mud baking in the afternoon glare.

"Well, McNab, d'you think they will keep out the sepoys if they attack us here as they did at Meerut?"

"I confess I know nothing about military matters, Mr Hopkins."

The Collector laughed, but in a humourless way. "That's a judicious reply, McNab. But perhaps you are better fitted to judge the state of mind of a man who builds a fortress in the middle of a peaceful countryside. Doctor, I'm well aware of what is being said about me in the cantonment on account of the mud ramparts down there."

Dr McNab frowned but remained silent. His eyes, which had been on the Collector's face, dropped to the fingers of his right hand which were too tightly clenched around the lapel of his frock coat in what would have been, otherwise, the calm and commanding posture of a statesman posing for his portrait.

"If no trouble develops in the end, Mr Hopkins, no doubt you will look a fool," he said, then added grimly: "But perhaps it is your duty."

The Collector looked surprised for a moment. "You're quite right, McNab. It's my duty. I have a duty towards the women and children under my protection. Besides, I myself am a family man ... I must think of protecting my own children. Perhaps you think that I give too little thought to my children? Perhaps you think that I don't have their welfare sufficiently at heart?" He stared at McNab suspiciously.

'Mr Hopkins, I know nothing of your personal life." This was almost true, but not quite. A short time earlier McNab had happened upon the Collector's children in a velvet brood being escorted by their *ayah* along one of the Residency corridors. And he had remembered hearing that it was by the Collector's order that these children continued to wear velvet, flannel and wool, while the other children in the cantonment were dressed in cotton or muslin for the hot weather. Even as children, it seemed, they had a position to keep up in the community. Only perhaps in the hottest period, when he chanced to notice how red-faced his offspring had become, might the Collector permit a change to summer clothing.

"I can assure you, Dr McNab, that I am as much loved by my children as any father was ever loved," said the Collector, as if reading his mind.

McNab shook his head soothingly, implying that it would never have occurred to him to think otherwise, but the Col-

lector paid no attention to him; instead, he snatched up a
leather-bound volume from the table and flourished it. "You
see, my daughters bring me their diaries to read so that I may
exercise supervision over their lives . . . I require them to do
so, as any right-thinking father would. Every Sunday evening I
read a sermon to them and to my other children, by Arnold or
Kingsley, just as any father would. Why, I even prepared my
manservant, Vokins, for confirmation by hearing his
catechism! I think that you can hardly accuse me of neglecting
my duty towards my household . . ."

"It would never occur to me to accuse you of this or anything else," said the Doctor quietly.

"What? What are you saying? No, of course you wouldn't
accuse me of such things. Why should you? But tell me, d'you
believe in God, McNab?"

"Aye, of course, Mr Hopkins."

"I wondered because I noticed that you do not attend the
Sacrament. No, please don't think that I mean to pry into your
beliefs. I was merely curious because I have here a book of my
wife's . . . I found it the other evening . . . I suppose she left it
purposely by my bedside. It's Keble's *The Christian Year*, a
series of poems on religious themes, perhaps you know it. . . ?
Here, let me read you some lines . . . Let me see, this will do:

'Lo, at Thy feet I fainting lie,
Mine eyes upon Thy wounds are bent,
Upon Thy streaming wounds my weary eyes
Wait like the parchéd earth on April skies.' "

He paused and stared interrogatively at McNab, who yet again
made no reply. Nor had he any idea what it was that he was
supposed to reply to.

"I have always considered myself to believe in God," pursued
the Collector after a moment, his dark-ringed eyes searching
McNab's face "but I find such enthusiasm offends me. Evidently there are those who believe in Him in a way quite different
from mine. And yet, perhaps they are right?"

"It's only possible for a man to believe in his own way, Mr
Hopkins. Surely nothing more can be asked of him. So it seems
to me, at any rate."

"Splendid, McNab. What a fine philosopher you are, to be

sure. 'In his own way', you say. Precisely. And now I shall let you return to your duties." And while he escorted McNab towards the door he laughed as if he were in the best of spirits.

At the door, however, there was a moment of confusion for as McNab approached it, it opened to admit the very brood of children whom he had seen earlier. Now scrubbed and combed, these children had been marshalled by their *ayah* in the corridor outside to be presented to their father while he took his tea. The Collector reached out his arms to the youngest of them, Henrietta, aged five, but she shrank back into the *ayah*'s skirts. As he took his leave, McNab had to pretend not to have noticed this small incident.

Everything had remained quiet in Krishnapur as the news of Meerut had spread, but there had been a number of small signs of unrest, nevertheless. While the Collector was discussing with the Magistrate whether the ladies should be brought into the safety of the Residency a message from Captainganj arrived to say that General Jackson would be calling later to discuss a cricket match that was due to take place between the Captainganj officers and the civilian officials. This message was brought by a havildar who had ridden ahead of the General and who also brought a more ominous piece of news: fires had broken out in the native lines the previous evening.

"The cricket match may be only a stratagem, a means of not arousing suspicion."

The Magistrate made no reply and the Collector wished that for once he would lower that sardonically raised eyebrow.

"I hope the old fellow hasn't begun to go at last."

Presently a thud of hooves alerted the two men to the General's arrival and they moved to the window to watch. General Jackson was escorted by half a dozen native cavalrymen, known as *sowars*, who had dismounted and were now helping him to the ground. As one might have expected in an Army where promotion strictly attended seniority, the General was an elderly man, well over seventy. Moreover, he was portly and small in stature so he could no longer leap in and out of the saddle as had once been his custom; getting him in and out of the saddle these days was no easy task. Distributed on each side of the General's horse, the *sowars* took a firm grip of his breeches and lifted him into the air, his legs kicking petulantly to free his boots from the stirrups. Once he had been lifted clear the horse was led forward and he was lowered to the ground. As he advanced stiffly towards the portico both men noticed with foreboding that instead of a walking stick the General was carrying a cricket bat. Knowing that his memory was no longer quite what it once had been, the General frequently carried some object as an aide-mémoire; thus, if he had come to discuss horses he might carry a riding-crop, if the topic was gunnery he might juggle a couple of musket balls in his pocket.

"There was a new rumour in the bazaar this morning," said the Magistrate as the General disappeared from view. "They say that because so many British were killed in the Crimea there's nobody left in England for the memsahibs to marry. And so they're going to be brought out here and forcibly married to the native landowners. Their children and the lands they own will thus become Christian."

The Collector frowned. "Let us pray that the General is no longer as sanguine as he was before Meerut."

As he finished speaking the General was announced and shown into the library where the Collector and the Magistrate were awaiting him. He flourished the cricket bat cheerfully as he stepped forward, saying: "Now Hopkins, about this cricket match. In my view it had better wait till after the monsoon . . . It's much too hot as it is. What d'you think? I know your fellows want their revenge but they'll just have to wait . . . "

The Magistrate could tell by the expression of distress that appeared fleetingly between the Collector's side-whiskers that they were both thinking the same thing: the General really *had* come to discuss a cricket match.

"Just at the moment, General, we're too concerned about the fires last night to think about cricket."

"Fires?"

"The fires in the native lines at Captainganj last night. We fear that they may be a sign of an impending outbreak."

"Ah yes, I know the ones you mean," said the General cautiously. "But you mustn't let that worry you . . . The work of some malcontent."

"But General, in the light of Meerut ..." The Collector wanted to discuss the prospect of disarming the native regiments. Even now this plan would be risky, he felt, but soon it would become impossible.

But the General reacted to this proposal, for which he could see no earthly reason, first with astonishment, then with scorn and indignation. He refused to accept that the fires indicated disaffection among the sepoys and said so, testily ... thinking, however, that Hopkins and Willoughby could hardly be blamed, in a way, because they were civilians and, like all civilians, spent their time either in pettifogging or in "croaking" ... Now here they were, decent fellows in many ways, croaking like ravens.

"Why should the sepoys attack their own billets if they were bent on mutiny?" he demanded. "They'd have set fire to the British bungalows if that's what they were up to. As for Meerut, that's a demmed long way from Captainganj, if you'll forgive m'language. Special circumstances, too, shouldn't be surprised. Can't worry here what happens in China! Now look here, Hopkins, provided you fellows here in Krishnapur remain as usual, showing no sign of fear, everything will be alright ... But it'll be the devil's own job for us to control our men at Captainganj if you start panickin' here and diggin' mud walls ..."

On his way to the Residency he had cast a contemptuous eye on the Collector's fortifications. "Raise extra police with Mohammedan recruits, if you like. They're more reliable than Hindus or native Christians, but don't start a panic."

The Collector flushed, stung by the General's scornful reference to "mud walls"; after a moment's hesitation he asked: "How many English troops have you at Captainganj apart from officers of native regiments?"

For a moment it looked as if the General might refuse to reply. "Odds'n'ends left from two or three companies on their way to Umballa ... perhaps forty or fifty men."

"General," said the Collector in a soothing tone, "I should like to know if you'd have any objection to the women and children being brought in?"

"My dear Hopkins, either we rely on a display of confidence that the natives will behave properly, or we all fortify ourselves. We can hardly do both." The General paused, exasperated. Normally, this discussion would have stimulated him to a fearful rage, but while walking up and down the library he had relinquished the cricket bat, which had become tiresome to carry, and at some stage his hand had closed over a book. This book caused him some distress because he was unable to remember whether it was in his hand to remind him of something or not. He had taken a surreptitious look at the title, which was *Missionary Heroes* and told him nothing.

"Provided the civilians at Krishnapur don't start showin' fear I can guarantee that m'men will remain loyal. I am in complete control of the situation," he declared, though with less certainty than before.

"All the same, General, we can't simply ignore the fires at Captainganj. To do so would be the height of folly."

"We will bring the culprit to book!" exclaimed the General suddenly, with such a burst of confidence that for a moment even the Collector looked encouraged.

A week of indecision passed. News came of a massacre at Delhi but still the Collector hesitated to give the order for women and children to be brought into the Residency; he could see that there was some truth in what the General had said about showing fear; on the other hand, he continued surreptitiously to collect powder and provisions to store in the Residency in spite of the General's disapproval. What he most needed were cannons and muskets or, even better, rifles ... but he could not ask Captainganj to supply them without risking a fatal breach with the old General.

Meanwhile, those in the cantonment who followed the General and had been advocating a "display of confidence" continued to recommend it ... what had gone wrong at Meerut, they declared, was undoubtedly that the Europeans had begun to "croak", had tried to make concessions. The Collector's defensive measures, besides being ridiculous and inadequate, could very well generate the very danger they were supposed to guard against! At the same time, another question was being asked in the cantonment by the opposite and more timorous faction: namely, what was the point in feigning a confidence that no one felt and that in the eyes of the natives must appear quite baseless?

But it is probable that the majority of people in the canton-ment could not make up their minds as to the best course to follow. While the "confident" party recommended calm and indifference, and the "nervous" party were all for bolting to the Residency, the majority voted now for one course, now for the other, and sometimes even for both at once ... a calm and confident bolting to the Residency.

Fleury himself was, in principle, all for bolting, if that was what everybody wanted to do ... but he knew so little about the country that he had no real way of knowing whether or not the time for bolting had come. He had no sensation of danger in the least. The result was that he tended, by default, to find himself in the "confident" camp ... though, at the same time, quite ready to leg it for the Residency at the first sign of trouble.

The Collector regretted the spirit of animosity that was developing in the cantonment between the two opposing fac-tions. "After all," he thought, "we both want the same thing: security for our lives and property ... Why on earth should we be at each other's throats? Why do people insist on defend-ing their ideas and opinions with such ferocity, as if defending honour itself? What could be easier to change than an idea?" The Collector himself, however, did not yield an inch in his conviction that the only ultimate refuge lay behind his mud walls. Feuds began to break out between the two factions, ex-acerbated by the steadily mounting heat of the sun. They accused each other of endangering the lives of the innocent, of women and children. While one party seldom missed an oppor-tunity of loitering unarmed and defenceless in the midst of the crowds that thronged the bazaar, the other never ventured a step from their bungalows unless clanking with weapons.

The Collector, in a first and last effort to lead the com-munity in a democratic manner, spent these days trying to devise measures which combined insouciance with defensive properties. In this spirit he had a number of heavy stone urns set up along one vulnerable stretch of the compound wall and planted with flowers, which promptly withered in the heat. Next, he declared that he wanted a stone wall along another weak section of the compound perimeter in order to shield the croquet lawn from the glare of the evening sun. While it was being built he showed a sudden flourish of paternal indulgence by doggedly knocking balls through hoops in the company of his swooning elder daughters. His daughters at the best of times were not good at croquet, but now, on this sweltering patch of sun-baked earth ... So the Collector won game after game, implacably, because it was his duty ... and his daughters lost game after game, inevitably, because they were weak.

5

The Maharajah had his own army which although forbidden by law to carry firearms could still prove useful with sabres and the iron-bound bamboo staves, known as *lâtees*, with which most disputes among rival *zemindars* were traditionally settled. If it came to a fight whose side would the Maharajah's troops be on? Of course they would be no match for the sepoys but they still might come in handy to frighten the *badmashes* in the bazaar. The Collector had to pay a routine visit to the opium factory some way out of Krishnapur and so it was decided that Fleury and Harry Dunstaple should accompany him for part of the way and pay a visit to the Maharajah's palace which was not far from the opium factory . . . in normal circumstances a newcomer like Fleury might be expected to pay a casual visit of courtesy to the Maharajah to collect some exotic items of local colour for his diary, subsequently perhaps to be published under the title *Highways and Byways of Hindustan*, or something of that sort. At the same time the two young men might be able to see how the land lay with respect to the troops. It was, of course, out of the question to ask openly for the Maharajah's support because such a question would imply a drastic lack of confidence. Besides, Harry, as a military man loyal to the General, could not have been expected to convey such a request. All the same, one never knew . . . perhaps the Maharajah's son, Hari, whom Harry had met several times and who was a great favourite of the Collector's might pledge this support without being asked.

At the last moment Fleury discovered that Miriam had been invited to accompany the party; it appeared that she had displayed a sudden interest in the workings of an opium factory and that the Collector had decided she should see one for herself. Fleury was obscurely displeased by this discovery.

"It may be perilous," he grumbled.

"It certainly won't be more perilous, dearest Dobbin, than

remaining by myself in a bungalow surrounded by native servants who are scarcely known to us," replied Miriam with a smile. "Besides, I shall be in the company of Mr Hopkins. Surely that is protection enough."

"In Calcutta you said he had taken leave of his senses."

"On the contrary, sir, it was *you* who said that."

Fleury had noticed before that his sister seemed to become more animated in the Collector's presence and he suspected her of some flirtatious design. While they were waiting for the Collector's carriage to call for them he noticed further that Miriam was wearing her favourite bonnet, which she seldom wore merely in his own company. His sense of propriety was offended, as indeed it often was, but more by Miriam's opinions than by her behaviour. Although adventurous in some respects, Fleury had rather strict ideas about how his elder sister should behave. But he could find nothing precisely to accuse her of. Regulating Miriam's behaviour was made even more difficult by the fact that she had, to a large extent, supervised his own childhood. "And don't call me 'Dobbin'," he added crossly as an afterthought.

Ahead, the sun was rising above the rim of the plain into the dust-laden atmosphere. The Collector was in an expansive mood again: the motion of the open landau, the coolness and beauty of the morning filled him with confidence. He set himself to explain to Fleury about the character of rich natives: their sons were brought up in an effeminate, luxurious manner. Their health was ruined by eating sickly sweetmeats and indulging in other weakening behaviour. Instead of learning to ride and take up manly sports they idled away their time girlishly flying kites. Everything was for show with your rich native ... he would travel the countryside with a splendid retinue while at home he lived in a pigsty. But fortunately, young Hari, the Maharajah's son, had been educated by English tutors and was a different kettle of fish. To this information Harry Dunstaple added gruffly: "You have to be careful thrashing a Hindu, George, because they have very weak chests and you can kill them ... Father says it's a thinness of the pericardium." Fleury murmured his thanks for this warning, indicating that he would do his best to hold himself back from the more fatal blows ... but he privately hoped that the situa-

70

tion would not arise. He was still having difficulty adapting himself to his new "broad-shouldered" character.

In due course they turned off their road on to another track which ran between fields of mustard, shining yellow and green. Ahead of them what looked like a mountain of dried mud shimmered over a scanty jungle of brush and peepul trees; the Collector uttered a grunt of pleasure: evidently the sight of so much mud reminded him of his own "mud walls". As they got nearer, the mountain of mud transformed itself into high, shabby walls, unevenly battlemented. The track led towards massive wooden gates, bound and studded in iron, set between square towers of mud and plaster. These towers were not solid, Fleury noticed as the landau passed between them, but hollow and three-sided with an open floor of rafters built halfway up. The hollowed-out space seethed with soldiers, some practically naked, others amazingly uniformed like Zouaves with blue tunics and baggy orange trousers and armed to the teeth with daggers and clubs. Many of the more naked of the soldiers were still reclining, however, on the straw mattresses which covered the floor.

"Rabble," said Harry with a superior smile. "Our Adjutant, Chambers, says they're no more use in a fight than the chorus at Covent Garden. Over there is where the so-called Prime Minister lives." The building indicated by Harry was in the French style with balconies and shuttered windows. It had an abandoned air.

They had passed into an outer courtyard, in the centre of which was a derelict fountain and a plot of grass where a hoopoe dug busily with its long beak. Pieces of wood, old mattresses and broken cartwheels lay around. To the left, between low buildings which might have been stables, stood another archway leading to the Maharajah's apartments. They proceeded through into the next courtyard and halted by some stone steps to allow the young men to alight. Then the landau turned in a wide circle and bore the two silhouetted heads, one wearing a pith helmet, the other a bonnet, back towards the arches, beneath which they presently vanished.

Fleury and Harry had promptly been surrounded by a swarm of servants in an extravagantly conceived but grimy livery; in the midst of this chattering throng they made their way along a stifling corridor, up another flight of steps and out on to a long stone verandah, where they at last felt a faint, refreshing breeze on their faces. Beside elaborately carved doors a guard in Zouave uniform dozed with his cheek against the shaft of a spear. Their host awaited them within, the servants explained, and they found themselves pushed forward in a gale of muffled giggles.

The room they were thus urged into proved to be a delightful place, with an atmosphere of coolness, light and space; three of its walls were of blood-coloured glass alternating with mirrors and arranged in flower-shaped wooden frames; outside, green louvred shutters deflected the sunlight. Chandeliers of Bohemian glass hung in a line across the middle of the room with himalayas of crystal climbing between the lipped candle-glasses. Along the fourth wall, which was solid rather than of glass, ran primitive portraits of several past maharajahs. These faces stared down at the two young Englishmen with arrogance and contempt . . . though really it was just one face, Fleury noticed, as he passed along, repeated again and again with varying skill and in varying head-dresses, composed of coal-black eyes which seemed to be all pupil, and fat, pale cheeks garnished with a wispy black beard and mustache.

Near a fireplace of marble inlaid with garnets, lapis lazuli and agate, the Maharajah's son sat on a chair constructed entirely of antlers, eating a boiled egg and reading *Blackwood's Magazine*. Beside the chair a large cushion on the floor still bore the impression of where he had been sitting a moment earlier; he preferred squatting on the floor to the discomfort of chairs but feared that his English visitors might regard this as backward.

"Hello there, Lieutenant Dunstaple," he exclaimed, springing to his feet and striding forward to greet them, "I see you've been kind enough to bring Mr Fleury along . . . How splendid! How kind!" And he continued to give the impression of striding forward by a simulated movement which, however, only carried him a matter of inches towards his visitors and was a compromise between his welcoming nature, which urged him to advance and shake people warmly by the hand, and his status as the Maharajah's heir, which obliged him to stand his ground and be approached. This mimed movement in the presence of inferiors entitled to some respect, which included all the British in India, had developed swiftly in the course of social contact with Europeans so that by now it had become not only quite unconscious, but also so perfect as utterly to destroy perspective. The result was that Fleury found himself having to advance a good deal further than he expected and arrived at his host somewhat off balance, his last few steps a succession of afterthoughts.

"Why did my dear friend Mr Hopkin not call to see me? I am hurt. You must tell him so. It's most very unkind of him. How's your wrist, Dunstaple?"

"A little better thank you," Harry said, rather stiffly, as they crossed a rich, dusty carpet scattered here and there with ragged tiger skins. Nearer at hand Fleury was startled to see that the face of their host exactly resembled that of the score of portraits on the wall; the same fat, pale cheeks and glittering black eyes surmounted a plump body clad, not in Mogul robes, but in an ill-cut frock coat. He had been watching Fleury intently and now, seeing that he was about to open his mouth, broke in hastily: "No, please don't call me 'Highness' or any of that nonsense. We don't stand on ceremony in this day and age . . . Leave that sort of thing to Father . . . Just call me Hari ... There are two Haris, eh? Well, never mind. How delightful. What a pleasure!"

Fleury said: "I hope we haven't interrupted your breakfast, but I fear that we have."

"Not in the least, old fellow. A boiled egg and *Blackwood's* is the best way to begin the day. Now, come and sit down. I say, are you alright, Dunstaple?" For Harry, stepping forward, had given a rather odd lurch and had almost plunged on to one of the ragged tiger skins. His face, now they came to look at it, was as white as milk, though given a superficial tinge of colour by the bloodstained glass of the windows.

"It's nothing. It's just the heat. I shall be alright in a moment. Damned silly!"

"Correct!" cried Hari. "It's nothing. You'll be alright in twinkling. Come and sit down while I get the bearer to bring refreshment. Where is he the wretched fellow?" And he hurried to the door shouting.

73

In response to their master's shouts more servants in grimy livery poured in, barefoot but in knee breeches, carrying two more chairs constructed of antlers; these they placed adjacent to Hari's and to a small table supported by rhinoceros feet on which Hari had abandoned his half-eaten boiled egg. Tea was brought, and three foaming glasses of iced sugar cane juice, a delightful shade of dark green. Harry Dunstaple, looking a little green himself, rejected this delicious drink, but Fleury who loved sweet things and had never noticed the filth and flies that surround the pressing of sugar cane, drank it down with the greatest pleasure, and then admired the empty glass which was embossed with the Maharajah's crest. Harry asked permission to undo the buttons of his tunic and with a shaking hand began to fumble with them.

"Sir, make yourself altogether as if in your home, I beg you! Bearer, bring more cushion."

Cushions were arranged on the floor and Harry was persuaded to lie down. "Damned silly. Alright in a moment," Fleury heard him mutter again, as he stretched out and closed his eyes.

"Bearer, bring tiger skin!" and a tiger skin was also stretched over Harry, but he kicked it aside petulantly. He was much too hot already without tiger skins. Fleury was very concerned by Harry's sudden debility (could it be cholera?) and wondered aloud whether he should not take him back promptly to the cantonment and put him under his father's care.

"Oh, Mr Fleury, it is much too damnably hot to travel now until evening."

"They make such a frightful fuss," muttered Harry without opening his eyes. "Just give me an hour or so and I shall be right as rain." He sounded quite cross.

"Mr Fleury, Dunstaple will have refreshing repose here and during this time I shall show you palace. I call Prime Minister to watch Dunstaple and tell us if condition worsen."

Harry's groan of irritation at this further intervention was ignored and the Prime Minister was summoned. They waited for him in silence. When he at last appeared he proved to be a stooped, elderly gentleman, also wearing a frock coat but without trousers or waistcoat; he wore instead a dhoti, sandals, and on his head a peaked cap covered in braid like that of a French infantry officer. He evidently spoke no English for he put his palms together and murmured *"Namaste"* in the direction of Fleury. He seemed unsurprised to find an English officer stretched on the floor.

There was a rapid exchange in Hindustani which ended in Hari gaily shouting: "Correct!" and taking Fleury by the arm; as they left the room the Prime Minister was sitting on the floor with his knees to his chin, staring introspectively at the supine Harry.

Once outside Hari brightened visibly. "Mr Fleury, dear sir, I am delighted to make your acquaintance. Collector, you know, Hopkin is my very good friend, most interested in advance of science. This English coat, sir, is it very costly? Forgive me asking but I admire the productions of your nation very strongly. May I feel the material? And this timepiece in pocket, a half hunter is it not called? English craftsmen are so skilled I am quite lost in admiration for, you see, here our poor productions are in no wise to be compared with them. Yes, I see you are looking at my coat which is also of English flannel, though bought in Calcutta, unfortunately, and cut by *durzie* from bazaar and not by your Savile Rows. Timepiece is purchased in London and not Calcutta also I think?"

"It was a present from my father."

"Correct! From your father, you say. I have heard that fathers most frequently give to the sons who leave home the Holy Bible, your very sacred scripture of Christian religion, is that not the case? Did your father give you also Holy Bible when you came to India?"

"As a matter of fact the only book he gave me was Bell's Life."

"Your father gave you Bell's Life? But is that not a sporting magazine? That is not sacred scripture? I do not understand why your father gave you this book instead of Holy Bible ... Sir, please explain this to me because I do not understand in the smallest amount." And Hari gazed at Fleury in bewilderment.

Meanwhile, they had moved on to an outer verandah overlooking the river and formed of the same mud battlements Fleury had noticed on the approach. It was the same river, too, which, after a few twists and turns, passed the lawn of the

75

Residency six or seven miles away. But it was no cooler here; a gust of hot air as from the opening of an oven door hit Fleury in the face as he stepped out ... the river, moreover, had shrunk away to a narrow, barely continuous stream on the far bank, leaving only a wide stretch of dry rubble to mark its course with here and there a few patches of wet mud. Half a dozen water buffaloes were attempting to cool themselves in this scanty supply of water.

"He didn't give it me *instead* of the Bible," explained Fleury, who had attempted the mildest of pleasantries and now regretted it. He added untruthfully, sensing that the situation required it: "He had already given me the Bible on a previous occasion."

"Correct! Bell's Life he gave you for pleasure. All is no longer 'as clear as mud'. The Holy Bible it must be a very beautiful work, very beautiful. Religion I do enjoy very greatly, Mr Fleury, do you not also? Oh, it is one of the best things in life beyond shadows of doubt." And Hari stared at Fleury with a smile of beatitude on his fat, pale cheeks. Fleury said: "Yes, how true! I'd never thought of it like that before. We should enjoy religion, of course, and 'lift up our hearts' ... of course we should." He was surprised and touched by this remark of Hari's and wondered why he had never thought of it himself. They were now pacing over a continuation of the verandah made of wooden planks, many of them loose, which spanned an interior courtyard ... below were a number of buildings that might have been *godowns* or servants' quarters; there was a well, too, and a man washing himself by it, and more servants in livery squatting with their backs to the mud wall of the palace. A peacock, feathers spread, was revolving slowly on the dilapidated roof of one of the buildings below and Hari, under a sudden impulse of warmth towards Fleury, pointed it out and said: "That is very holy bird in India because our God Kartikeya ride peacock. He was born in River Ganga as six little baby but Parvati, lady of Siva, she loved them all so very very dearly she embraced them so tight she squeezed into one person but with six face, twelve arm, twelve leg ... 'and so on and so forth', as my teacher used to say, Mr Barnes of Shrewsbury." Hari closed his eyes and smiled with an expression of deep contentment, whether at the thought of

76

Kartikeya or of Mr Barnes of Shrewsbury, it was impossible to say.

Fleury, however, glanced at him in dismay: he had forgotten for the moment just what sort of religion it was that Hari enjoyed . . . a mixture of superstition, fairy-tale, idolatry and obscenity, repellent to every decent Englishman in India. As if to underline this thought, the bearer who had served refreshments a little earlier suddenly appeared in the courtyard below. He held something in his hand as he laughed and exchanged a few words with the other servants and it flashed in the sunlight; he raised it, examined it casually, then dropped it on the flagstones where it shattered. Fleury was certain that it was the glass from which he himself had been drinking a little earlier.

They walked on, Fleury chilled by this trivial incident; how could one respond warmly to someone who regarded your touch as pollution? But Hari, on the other hand, had noticed nothing and was still thinking warmly of Fleury . . . how different he was from the stiff, punctilious Dunstaple! He could hardly bear to look at Dunstaple's face: there was something obscene about blue eyes . . . In fact, that had been the only real drawback to Mr Barnes, for he too had had blue eyes.

"And so on and so forth," he repeated with pleasure. "Mr Barnes has gone back to England. Perhaps you have made acquaintance with him? No? One year ago he wrote me letter from Shrewsbury. He is a very fine gentleman. I would like to ask special favour of you, Mr Fleury, sir. I would like to have pleasure of making daguerrotype of you, you see I am most very interested in science, sir. In Krishnapur I am only one who make daguerrotype and all who want picture come and see me. Mr and Mrs Hopkins, Collector and his bride, come to me, and many other married persons in cantonment I have made pictures to send to England for absent brides and love ones. You also have bride in England, sir, I think? No? How is that? Your bride is perhaps no longer 'in the land of the living'?" And Fleury was obliged to explain that so far he had not succeeded in capturing a bride . . . he had been unable to find one to suit his fancy. Hari's brow puckered at this, for it was evident that Fleury was impeded from choosing a bride by being unable to find one suited to some special requirements of his own, beyond the usual ones of birth and dowry ... but what these might possibly be he had not the faintest idea; in this matter Hari's incomprehension was shared by Fleury's own relations in Norfolk and Devon.

"Soon I make daguerrotype but first I show you my pater. Come with me please. At this hour when it is so very much hot he is usually to be found 'in arms of Morpheus' which means, I understand, that he is asleeping. It is best time to look at pater when he is asleeping ... Correct!" and Hari, laughing cheerfully, led the way.

As they walked on through breathless mud corridors and climbed narrow stone steps Fleury found himself thinking again of Kartikeya, what a charming story, after all! Six babies pressed by love into one, there was surely no harm in such a pleasant fairy story.

They were now progressing through windowless inner apartments, dimly lit by blazing rags soaked in linseed or mustard oil and stuck on five-pronged torches. In the distance an oil lamp of blue glass cast a sapphire glow over a small, fat gentleman sprawled on a bed and clad only in a loin cloth; above the bed an immense jewelled and tasselled punkah swept steadily back and forth. A bearer stood beside the bed holding an armful of small cushions.

"Father is asleeping," Hari explained softly. "He has blue light for asleeping, green light for awaking, red light for entertaining ladies, and so on and so forth. To make comfortable he has cushion under every joint of body ... bearer watch him to place cushion under joint when he move."

Hardly had Hari given this explanation when the Maharajah with a grunt kicked out one of his short, plump legs. Instantly cushions appeared under knee and ankle. Fleury could now see that the Maharajah's face was yet another copy of the portraits he had seen earlier and of Hari himself. As he watched, the Maharajah's mouth opened, stained red with betel, and he belched resonantly. "Father is breaking wind," commented Hari. "Now come with me please, my dear Mr Fleury, and I shall show you many wonderful things. First and foremost, you would like perhaps to see abominable pictures?"

"Well ..."

Hari spoke to one of the bearers who advanced with a cup

containing blazing, oil-soaked rags on the end of a long, silver pole. He held this close to the wall and a large and disgusting oil-painting sprang out of the gloom. But Fleury found that the picture was such an intricate mass of limbs that he was quite unable to fathom what it was all about (though it was clearly very lewd indeed).

"Sir, shall I show you more disgraceful pictures? Very disgraceful indeed?"

"No thank you," said Fleury, and then, not wanting to sound ungrateful, he added gruffly: "I'm afraid I'm not very well up in this sort of thing."

"Correct! For a gentleman 'well up' in science and progress it is not in the least rather interesting. Come, I show you many other things."

Suddenly there came what sounded like the lowing of a cow from the adjoining apartment; Hari frowned and spoke sharply to one of the servants, evidently to tell him to steer the animal in another direction, but already it was clattering towards them. "This is most backward," muttered Hari. "I am sorry you have witnessed such a thing, Mr Fleury. My father should not be permitting it. Always in India cow here, cow there, cow everywhere!" The cow, alarmed by the servants, hastened forward and was only diverted at the last moment from charging the sleeping Maharajah. An elderly servant hurried after it with a large silver bowl.

"To catch dropping," explained Hari as they moved on. "Here march of science is only just beginning, you understand."

They now found themselves in the armoury, which turned out to contain not only arms of every imaginable sort but many other things as well. But Fleury could only stare with indifference and wish they could discuss religion or science or some such topic. He had some spying to do, too, on the Maharajah's troops, better not forget that! He was unaware of Hari's sensitive and vulnerable eyes devouring his every reaction to the objects he was being shown.

"This is not rather interesting at all," apologized Hari with intensity. "This is spear-pistol. Shoot and stab one gentleman at the same time. When sharp point stabs gentleman breast, mechanism releases trigger, shoots gentleman also."

"Good heavens," said Fleury languidly.

"This big knife open out into four small knife, stab person four times."

"Well . . ."

"And here is brass cannon which can be mounted on camel saddle. This is rather very dull also, don't you think?" And Hari began to look rather annoyed.

"I think, Fleury, that you will not find this absorbing, too," he pursued relentlessly, indicating a rack of flint-lock guns with extraordinarily long barrels which could be re-loaded from horseback without dismounting, a sporting rifle by Adams with a revolving magazine, a cap in the shape of a cow pat with a feather of gold tinsel sprouting from it which had belonged to Hari's grandfather, and an ostrich egg.

Fleury stifled a yawn, which Hari unfortunately noticed but yet he continued as if unable to stop himself: "This is astrological clock, very complicated . . . The circle in centre shows zodiacal sign over which the sun pass once in year . . . From movement of this black needle which passes over circle in twenty-four hours the ascendant of horoscope can be ascertained. But I see that this miserable machine, which show also, I forget to add, phases of moon, sunrise and sunset, day of week, is not worthy of your attention also. Correct. It is all very humble and useless materials such as you do not have in London and Shrewsbury. Now, Fleury, I make daguerrotype."

As soon as the landau had arrived at the opium factory the Collector handed Miriam over to Mr Rayne and vanished about his business in the neighbourhood. Mr Rayne then handed her over in turn to one of his deputies, Mr Simmons, and instructed him to show her the process by which opium is refined. Mr Simmons was a little younger, Miriam found, than her brother; he was a nice young man whose freckled skin was peeling seriously in several places. Not many ladies visited the factory and Mr Simmons, in any case, was unused to their company. His manner was excessively deferential and he blushed frequently for no apparent reason. In addition, he was very zealous in his explanations and allowed few details of the preparation of opium to escape Miriam's notice. He conducted her round immense iron vats and invited her to peer at mysterious fermenting liquids ... mysterious because although Miriam was told all about them, she discovered that Mr Simmons's words slipped through her mind like fish through a sluice-gate the instant after he had spoken them ... this was embarrassing and she had to be careful that he did not notice. But gradually it became clear that although Mr Simmons was overwhelmed by the superior qualities of the gentler sex, to the extent that a too personal smile or frown from her would have crushed him as easily as a moth beneath the sole of her shoe, he did not include the possibility of intelligence among these qualities. He did not expect to be understood or remembered from one instant to the next.

Miriam was content, however. The drowsy scent of the poppy hung everywhere in the hot darkness of the warehouses and lulled her senses. She felt wonderfully at peace and was sorry when at last the tour came to an end and she was taken to watch the workmen making the finished opium into great balls, each as big as a man's head, which would be packed forty to a chest and auctioned in Calcutta. Each of these head-sized balls, explained Mr Simmons quietly but with the air of someone speaking his words into a high wind, would fetch about seventy-six shillings, while to the *ryot* and his family the Government paid a mere four shillings a pound. As he talked he nervously scratched his peeling wrists and brow while Miriam, diverted, sleepily tried to think of a sensible question and watched the falling flakes of skin drift to the ground.

When the Collector returned, Miriam smuggled a last yawn into her gloved hand, said goodbye to Mr Simmons and climbed back into the landau, which now had its hood raised against the sun. Mr Simmons blushed again and a few more flakes of skin drifted away. Miriam raised her gloved hand to wave and the yawn it was holding seemed to float away on the poppy-scented air. She would have liked to recommend a certain pomade to Mr Simmons but was afraid that in doing so she might crush him like a moth beneath her shoe. How sleepy she felt! If the Collector began to talk to her she would never be able to stay awake.

Before they had properly emerged from the jungle of scrub on to the road an incident occurred to revive her. A naked man suddenly stepped out on to the track they were following. He was tall and well built; in one hand he carried the trident of the devotee of Siva, in the other a brass pot containing smouldering embers. His hair and beard hung in untidy yellowish ropes over his bronzed body, almost as far as his male parts. In a moment the landau had creaked and swayed past him; the path was deeply rutted and they kept rising and falling, as if in a small boat breasting a succession of unexpected waves. The Collector could not help turning to Miriam sternly, shocked on her behalf . . . but Miriam's cheeks had only pinkened slightly and she said with a faint smile: "You must tell me why such men do not wear clothes, Mr Hopkins. In winter they must surely feel the cold."

"I believe that he must belong to a Hindu sect which has renounced the material world. Such men see their nakedness as a symbol of this renunciation and keep a fire constantly burning at their side to signify the burning up of earthly desires." He added reluctantly: "One can't help but admire the rigour with which they pursue their beliefs."

"Even though they follow an erroneous path?"

"One has to admit, Mrs Lang, that few Christians follow the true one with as much zeal. Indeed, this renders the conversion of the native very difficult for beside this ascetic fervour he sees the Christian priest living in a comfortable house with a wife and family . . . and I fear he's not impressed. Not only the clergyman but the whole Christian community must seem very dissolute to him, I'm afraid . . . What use is it if we bring the advantages of our civilization to India without also displaying a superior morality? I believe that we are all part of a society which by its communal efforts of faith and reason is gradually raising itself to a higher state . . . There are rules of morality to be followed if we are to advance, just as there are rules of scientific investigation . . . Mrs Lang, we are raising ourselves, however painfully, so that mankind may enjoy in the future a superior life which now we can hardly conceive! The foundations on which the new men will build their lives are Faith, Science, Respectability, Geology, Mechanical Invention, Ventilation and Rotation of Crops! . . ."

The Collector talked on and on but Miriam, soothed by the heat and the poppy fumes, cradled by the worn leather upholstery of the landau, found that her eyelids kept creeping down in spite of herself. Even when the Collector began to shout, as he presently did, about the progress of mankind, about the ventilation of populous quarters of cities, about the conquest of ignorance and prejudice by the glistening sabre of man's intelligence, she could not manage to keep her eyes properly open.

And so, as the landau creaked away into the distance, dust pouring back from the chimneys of its wheels, the Collector's shouts rang emptily over the Indian plain which stretched for hundreds of miles in every direction, and Miriam fell at last into a deep sleep.

In the meantime, although Fleury had not yet noticed it, Hari's good humour had deserted him. He continued to point things out to Fleury ... some embroidered rugs and parasols, and a collection of sea-shells, but he did so carelessly, as if it were of no importance to him whether or not Fleury found them of interest.

"You know also how to make daguerrotype, I suppose."

"I'm afraid not."

"Not? Ah? But I thought all advance people ..." Hari raised his eyebrows in surprise.

"Hari," said Fleury presently, and from his tone it was hard to tell whether he was breathless with excitement or was simply having trouble keeping up with his host, who was now bounding along a dim inner corridor at the greatest speed. "I say, I hope you don't mind me calling you Hari, but I feel that we understand each other so well ..."

The speed and gloom which attended their progress prevented Fleury from seeing Hari's frostily raised eyebrow.

"Would you mind if we went a little slower? It's fearfully hot." But Hari appeared not to hear this request.

"Do we understand each other? Sit here, please."

They had entered a whitewashed room giving on to the courtyard Fleury had seen earlier from above. No sooner had he stepped over the threshold than he was seized by a fit of coughing, for the air in here was laden with mercury vapour and a variety of other fumes no less toxic, emanating from crystals and solutions of chlorine, bromine, iodine, and potassium cyanide. On a table there was a mercury bath, a metal container in the shape of an inverted pyramid with a spirit lamp already burning beneath it. A camera box had been placed on an ornate metal stand, pointing at a chair by the window. Still coughing, Fleury was steered towards the chair and made to sit down; it had a rod at the back surmounted by an iron crescent for keeping the sitter's head still. Fleury's head was forced firmly back into it and some adjustments were made behind him, tightening two thin metal clamps which nestled in his hair above each ear.

"Of course we do, Hari," said Fleury warmly, though rather stiffly because of the immobility of his head. "I can see you feel the same about all those not very useful things you have just been showing me as I feel about the sort of junk the Collector has in the Residency. What you and I object to is the *emptiness of the life behind* all these objects, their materialism in other words. Objects are useless by themselves. How pathetic they are compared with noble feelings! What a poor and limited world they reveal beside the world of the eternal soul!" Fleury paused, guiltily aware that he was indulging "feelings" once more. "As you were walking along just now pointing out how uninteresting everything was, I suddenly realized that it makes no difference that I was born in England and that you were born in India . . . Your ancestors have been taking an interest in just the same sort of irrelevant rubbish as mine have. D'you see what I mean?"

It was hard to tell whether Hari saw what he meant or not, for he merely grunted and fished in the pocket of his waistcoat for his watch; this was a gold watch, as it happened, but one would not have thought so, because Hari had spent so much time in the mercury-laden atmosphere of this room that both watch and chain had become coated with a white amalgam. He was frowning now as he picked up a copper plate coated with silver and began to polish it with soft leather and pumice, using slow, deliberate strokes parallel to the edges of the plate, first in one direction, then in the other.

"A spear that shoots someone as well as stabbing him? Ludicrous! And all these other things you have shown me, collections of this and that, sea-shells and carved ivory, disgraceful pictures, chairs made of antlers and astronomical clocks, d'you know what they remind me of?"

"No," said Hari sullenly. He was now looking pale as well as angry, perhaps from his exertions or because he had inhaled too much mercury vapour ... He was still polishing the silvered copper plate but had exchanged the leather for a pad of silk.

"They remind me of the Great Exhibition!"

"They had disgraceful pictures in Great Exhibition, I did not know?", said Hari, curious in spite of himself and slightly mollified by this comparison.

"No, of course not. But what I mean is that the Great Exhibition was not, as everyone said it was, a landmark of civilization; it was for the most part a collection of irrelevant rubbish such as your ancestors might well have collected."

Hari winced at this reference to his ancestors and turned paler than ever; his polishing of the plate intensified. But Fleury did not notice. He was seething with excitement and would have sprung to his feet, gesticulating, had not his head been firmly wedged in the iron ring.

"Take the Indian Court in the Crystal Palace, it was full of useless objects. There were spears, a life-sized elephant with a double howdah, swords, umbrellas, jewels, and rich cloths ... the very things you have just been showing me. In fact, the whole Exhibition was composed merely of collections of this and that, utterly without significance ... There was an Observatory Hive . . . ah, the tedious comparisons that were made between mankind and the hive's 'quietly-employed inhabitants, those living emblems of industry and order.'!"

Hari, whose face remained stony and expressionless, had finished polishing; the plate no longer had a silver appearance but seemed black. He now had to focus the lens of the camera on Fleury.

"Take your hands off chest, Fleury," he ordered, for Fleury was gripping his lapels and the movement of his breathing would undoubtedly blur the image.

"I'm afraid I'm not making myself very clear," Fleury groaned; he had become carried away with his denunciation of materialism and was dizzy, moreover, with the heat and the fumes of chemicals and the pressure of the clamps on his skull. "What I mean is that collections of objects, whether weapons

85

or sea-shells or a life-sized stuffed elephant, are nothing but distractions for people who have been unable to make a real spiritual advance."

"And Science? Were there not many wonderful machines?"

"It's true that the Agricultural Court was often full of bushy-whiskered farmers staring at strange engines . . . But reflect, these engines were merely improved methods for doing the wrong thing."

"The wrong thing! I am sad, Fleury, that you should be so very backwards. These machines make more food, more money, save very much labour," said Hari coldly and vanished under a tent of dark muslin hung over a frame in one corner of the room. An instant later his head reappeared from beneath the draped muslin, black eyes glittering in his pale, flabby face. "And this that I am doing to you at the moment, perhaps this is not progress also!" he demanded angrily. His head vanished again.

Fleury gazed at the muslin tent bewildered. He could hear Hari muttering angrily to himself as he made the metal plate sensitive to light by passing it through his two wooden coating boxes, which between them were largely responsible for the toxic fumes which Fleury could feel assailing his powers of reason. Each box contained a blue-green glass jar: in one jar there was a small amount of iodine crystals, in the other, a mysterious substance called "quickstuff" which contained bromine and chlorine compounds and served to increase the sensitivity of the plate. By holding the plate over the evaporating iodine crystals for less than a minute Hari allowed a thin layer of light-sensitive iodide of silver to form over it; when it had turned orange-yellow he held it over the "quickstuff" until it turned deep pink, then back over the iodine for a few seconds. Then, grinding his teeth with rage, he slipped the sensitized plate into a wooden frame to protect it from light while it was not in the camera, and emerged trembling from his dark muslin tent.

"Perhaps this is not progress also?" he repeated, waving the boxed plate in front of Fleury's pinioned head in a threatening manner. "To make metal sensitive to light."

"Yes, it is progress, of course . . . but, well, only in the art of making pictures. Mind you, that is no doubt wonderful in its way. But the only *real* progress would be to make a man's heart sensitive to love, to Nature, to his fellow men, to the world of spiritual joy. My dear Hari, Plato did more for the human race than Monsieur Daguerre."

Hari put the plate in the camera and pulled out the protective slide. "I beg you not to insult any more my ancestors nor this very worthy gentleman, Mr Daguerre."

"Please don't think I mean to insult them," cried Fleury. "That's the very last thing I want to do. It's just that we must change the direction of our society before it's too late and we all become like these engines which will soon be galloping across India on railway lines. An engine has no heart!"

"Keep still!" Hari, watch in hand, snatched the cap off the lens and by the look on his face he might have been wishing it was the muzzle of a cannon that was pointing at Fleury.

"Oh dear!" thought Fleury, "I seem to have offended him somehow."

Hari counted off two minutes, replaced the lens cap, snatched out the plate and slipped it over the heated mercury bath. Fleury goggled at him, dismayed.

"I am very sad," declared Hari with frosty dignity, "that you, Fleury, should reveal yourself so frightfully backward."

He shook his head over the mercury bath with lofty distress. "This will be portrait of very backward man indeed, I am very much regretting to say."

A discouraged silence fell between the two young men as they waited for the fine mercury globules to settle on the parts of the plate which had been affected by light. When this process had been accomplished Hari picked the plate up with a pair of pliers and poured over it a solution of hyposulphite of soda to wash off the unchanged iodide and make the image permanent; then, still holding it with pliers he washed it with a solution of gold chloride to increase the brilliance of the image. All that now remained to be done was to wash the plate in water, dry it over the spirit lamp, and put it into a frame behind glass for the image was as delicate as the wing of a butterfly and as easily harmed. This done, Hari sighed and took it over to show Fleury, whose head was still clamped in the ring. Hari's anger had given way to sadness and disapproval.

"It looks as if it has been drawn by the brush of the fairy

queen Mab," said Fleury, hoping that this conceit would soothe Hari's wounded feelings.

"It is the portrait of a very backward man indeed," replied Hari severely. And with that he turned and trudged out of the room with heavy steps, leaving Fleury to free himself from the clamps as best he could.

6

The river which flowed, when there was any water in it, past the Maharajah's palace to wander here and there on the vast and empty plain passed alongside the cantonment and the now yellow lawns of the Residency, beneath the iron bridge, along the native town (which had been built, unlike the cantonment mainly on the western bank so that the devout would be facing the rising sun as they stood on the steps of the bathing *ghat*), past the burning *ghat*, and out on to the plain again, reaching at long last, some eight miles from Krishnapur, a stretch of half a mile where it ran between embankments. At this point the plain ceased to be quite flat. There was a slight depression in it of four or five miles in circumference, made by the footprint of one of the giant gods who had strode back and forth across India in prehistoric times settling their disputes and hurling pieces of the continent at one another. The land was particularly fertile here, either because it had been blessed by the footprint, as the Hindus believed, or, as the British believed, because it was regularly flooded and coated with a nourishing silt.

This flooding, though, was a nuisance and it grew worse every year because of the attrition of the embankments. Cattle were drowned and crops lost. To stop the flooding by reinforcing the embankments was the great ambition of both the Collector and the Magistrate. While the Collector had been visiting the opium factory the Magistrate, accompanied by his bearer, Abdallah, had ridden out of Krishnapur to visit the embankments and consult the landowners whose coolies would be needed for the work of reinforcement. Why go to so much trouble when the river could be persuaded not to flood by the sacrifice of a black goat on its banks, the landowners had wanted to know.

"But that doesn't work. You've tried it before. Every year the floods are worse."

The landowners remained silent out of polite amazement that anybody could be so stupid as to doubt the efficacy of a sacrifice when properly performed by Brahmins. They were torn between amusement and distress at such obtuseness.

"The *Sircar* will make you supply labour," declared the Magistrate at last, but he knew that the Government could do no such thing in the present state of the country, and the landowners knew that he knew. The hollowness of this threat embarrassed them. To spare the Magistrate's feelings they feigned expressions of sorrow, alarm, of despair at the prospect of this coercion ... but when the Magistrate had at last ridden away, though not before he was out of earshot, they shouted with laughter, held their sides, and even rolled in the dust in undignified glee. Their glee redoubled when soon after the Magistrate's departure they heard that there had been a massacre of the *feringhees* at Captainganj. Then an argument broke out which began playfully but soon became serious, involving prestige. The argument was this: would the Magistrate get back to Krishnapur alive or would he be killed on the way?

The Magistrate and Abdallah (who, although he enjoyed seeing Mr Willoughby discomfited, was saddened that it should be Hindus who gained an advantage over him) rode slowly back to the cantonment. The Magistrate ignored the heat of the sun which beat down on his pith helmet and touched off his blazing ginger whiskers. How he hated stupidity and ignorance! He hoped that the river, when it broke its banks again this year, would drown the stupid men he had just been talking to ... but he knew that this was not likely: when disasters occur it is only the poor who suffer. Abdallah wanted to cheer up the Magistrate by telling him a Mohammedan joke against the Hindus.

"Sahib, why are the crocodiles in Krishnapur so fat?" The Magistrate rode on without answering.

"Because they eat up all the sins which Hindus wash off in the river!" And Abdallah laughed loudly so that Mr Willoughby would know that it was a joke.

Later in the afternoon the Collector and the Magistrate sat together in the Collector's study and the Magistrate described the result of his journey. By now it was the late afternoon. When he had finished both men sat in discouraged silence. The Collector was thinking: "Even after all these years in India Willoughby doesn't understand the natives. He's too rational for them. He can't see things from their point of view because he has no heart. If I had been there they would have listened to me." Aloud he said: "The river will have to flood again this year then, Tom. But immediately the flooding is over we'll tackle the embankments before they have time to forget that their wretched black goat didn't work."

The study was the Collector's favourite room; it was panelled in teak and contained many beloved objects. The most important of these was undoubtedly *The Spirit of Science Conquers Ignorance and Prejudice*, a bas-relief in marble by the window; it was here that the angle of the light gave most life to the brutish expression of Ignorance at the moment of being disembowelled by Truth's sabre, and yet emphasised at the same time how hopelessly Prejudice, on the point of throwing a net over Truth, had become enmeshed in its own toils. There was another piece of sculpture beside his desk: *Innocence Protected by Fidelity* by Benzoni, representing a scantily clothed young girl, asleep with a garland of flowers in her lap; beside her a dog had its paw on the neck of a gagging snake which had been about to bite her.

Yet Art did not hold sway alone in the Collector's study for on one corner of the desk in front of him there stood a tribute to scientific invention; he had come across it during those ecstatic summer days, now as remote as a dream, which he had spent in the Crystal Palace. It was the model of a carriage which supplied its own railway, laying it down as it advanced and taking it up again after the wheels had passed over. So ingenious had this invention seemed to the Collector, such was the enthusiasm it had excited at the Exhibition, that he could not fathom why six years should have passed away without one seeing these machines crawling about everywhere.

Beside the model carriage stood another ingenious invention, a drinking glass with compartments for soda and acid following separate channels; the idea was that the junction of the two streams should come just at the moment of entering the mouth, causing effervescence. The Collector had only once attempted to use it; all the same, he admired its ingenuity and had grown fond of it, as an object. "The trouble with poor

Willoughby," he mused now, surreptitiously observing the face of his companion and noting, as far as the now cinnamon whiskers permitted, how it was raked, harrowed, even ploughed up by free-thinking and cynicism, "is that he's not a whole man, as I am ... For science and reason is not enough. A man must also have a heart and be capable of understanding the beauties of art and literature. What a narrow range the man has!" The Collector's mood of self-satisfaction, which had been brought on by his agreeable conversation with the pretty Mrs Lang, deepened as he strolled to the window and saw the mosque three or four hundred yards away, for the mosque was a perfect example of what was right with himself and wrong with the Magistrate.

The Magistrate had argued that if there was going to be trouble it could not be allowed to remain there ... its narrow windows commanded the Residency completely; beside it stood some mud hovels which were less of a problem: a few well-aimed shot should reduce them to powder which the next breeze would blow away. What the Magistrate in the blindness of his rationalism failed to appreciate was the spiritual importance of the mosque; the Mohammedans would be outraged if it were demolished and with every justification. The Collector could not afford to alienate the Mohammedans, who were generally considered to be the most loyal section of the native population, and besides, a member of a civilized society does not go around knocking down places of worship, even those belonging to a different faith from his own. The Collector frowned, annoyed with himself. He should have thought of the second reason first.

"He surely can't be paying us another visit already," grumbled the Magistrate, unaware of the unfavourable judgement which had been passed on his character a few moments earlier in the Collector's mind.

At the window they both listened to the familiar thud of hoofs and jingle of harness which announced the arrival of the General and his *sowars* from Captainganj.

"Damn the fellow!" sighed the Collector. "I expect he's come to sneer at my ramparts again." But even as he spoke he saw the cluster of riders rein up in front of the Residency and realized that something was amiss. The General, instead of waiting to be lifted, had plunged forward over the horse's head and slithered to the ground. And there he continued to lie until the *sowars* came to pick him up. But the glare even at this time of day was still so intense that the Collector, looking out from the semi-darkness of his study, could not be sure that he had actually seen what he had just seen ... The sudden shouting and commotion that echoed immediately afterwards from the hall left him in little doubt, however.

As he stepped outside on to the portico the light and heat smote him, causing him to falter and put a hand on the wrought-iron railing, which he snatched away instantly, his fingers seared. He waited at the top of the stairs and watched then, as the *sowars* came towards him carrying the General. Blood was running freely from the General's body and splashing audibly on to the baked earth. The *sowars* were evidently trying to stop the flowing of blood by holding him first one way, then another, as someone eating toast and honey might try, by vigilance and dexterity, to prevent it dripping. The General's blood continued to patter on the earth, however, and all the way up the steps and into the hall where he was laid down at last, after some hesitation, on a rather expensive carpet.

Even when he had at last succeeded in freeing himself from the metal clamps Fleury was by no means sure how to find his way back to the room where he had left Harry stretched on the floor. He started tentatively through a dim series of naked, malodorous chambers; his head was still singing from the combined effect of the clamps and the mercury fumes. Presently he came to the end of the connecting rooms and was faced with a crumbling staircase. He climbed it impatiently and found himself in another chamber as empty as the one he had just left. The air was better here, however, and there were a number of windows screened by intricately carved marble ... in one corner of the ceiling there was the bulging, basket-like growth of a bee's nest. Beyond the window was a verandah, part of which was shaded by lattice curtains and here a number of the Maharajah's servants were drowsing on charpoys in a long row like the Forty Thieves, their liveries piled untidily beside them. They paid no attention to Fleury as he passed.

The heat and glare were stupendous; the countryside lay motionless in the grip of heat and light and somehow it had taken on the appearance of an Arctic landscape. From where he stood there was nothing but white or grey to be seen: there was the same dim, lurid sky, beneath which clouds of dust resembled driving snow. Returning his eyes to the shade of the verandah Fleury continued to see a grove of leafless *sal* trees imprinted on his retina like the bars of a glowing furnace.

He heard the sound of rapid footsteps and turning the next corner almost collided with Harry Dunstaple who demanded: "Where on earth have you been? I've been looking for you everywhere. There's been a disturbance at Captainganj and Father sent his *sais* with a message to warn us . . . We must get back to the cantonment immediately."

Over Harry's shoulder Fleury saw the Prime Minister hastening towards them. In spite of the physical effort he was making his face still wore an expressionless, introverted look.

"The blighter's been following me everywhere," Harry muttered with exasperation. "I've no idea what he wants. *Go away!*" he added loudly as the Prime Minister scampered up.

"I think he was told to keep an eye on you in case your illness got worse. How are you feeling, by the way?"

"Oh, right as rain." But Harry's face was still pale and beaded with sweat, nevertheless. "Where's His Highness? We must leave immediately."

The sepoys had mutinied and attacked their officers on parade, Harry explained as they set off to find the courtyard where the *sais* was waiting with horses for them. Nobody knew yet how serious it was. "It's damnable," he added. "I came out here without a pistol." And Fleury realized from the tone of his voice that Harry, finding himself unarmed, was suffering not from fear but from disappointment. Here was a possibility of some action at last and he was going to miss it!

With Harry aggressively striding out in the lead they clattered rapidly through another series of chambers, empty except for an occasional servant asleep on the floor. There was no sign either of Hari or of the Maharajah, but the Prime Minister continued to dodge along introvertedly behind them. They came at last, by a stroke of luck, to the door by which they had originally entered the palace. Stepping outside, they were again struck by an oven-draught of hot air.

The *sais* who had come to warn them was now asleep in the shade of the wall and it took some moments to rouse him. The Prime Minister, his sacred thread just visible beneath his frock coat, squatted mutely on his heels at a distance and observed them in an impartial manner. He was still sitting there when at last they rode away. As the sun shone fully on Harry's scarlet tunic, which he had re-buttoned in readiness for any military engagements which might present themselves, its colour intensified until it was almost impossible to look at with the naked eye. Then they were cantering through the outer gates where the Maharajah's army, on which the Collector had earlier been pinning some hopes, still seemed to be in a state of repose, very much as it had been earlier.

7

Picture a map of India as big as a tennis court with two or three hedgehogs crawling over it ... each hedgehog might represent one of the dust-storms which during the summer wander aimlessly here and there over the Indian plains, whirling countless tons of dust into the atmosphere as they go ... until the monsoon rolls in and squashes them flat. Because there was a dust-storm in the vicinity it seemed, and was, much darker than usual. This darkness could not help but be associated with the terrible massacre at Captainganj; even the Collector, who had gone up on to the roof to be alone and had found the stars blotted out, caught himself thinking so.

Harry and Fleury had spent the late afternoon riding about the country warning indigo planters to come into the Residency. When they returned to the cantonment for the second time they found their way obstructed by abandoned carriages and hackeries; such a panic had taken place that the road to the Residency had become jammed with vehicles and people had been obliged to continue on foot, bringing what possessions they could with them or having them carried by coolies on their heads.

In the darkness of the Residency drive, which was lit only by a flaring torch on the portico, the silhouettes of men and horses thrashed and wrestled with boxes, bundles, and mysterious unnameable objects which they clung to with desperate tenacity; it was as if they were struggling up to their waists through a swamp of pitch towards the solitary, dancing flame of the Residency. Curiously enough, they struggled in almost total silence except for laboured breathing and an occasional strained whisper.

Those who managed to win through this slough of darkness and despair found themselves in the hall, which more resembled purgatory than Heaven, and was crowded with ladies and children who sat huddled on trunks and boxes. They stared about them with that wide-eyed, alert look which people have during emergencies but which is really the result of shock; if you spoke to one of these alert-looking ladies she would have difficulty understanding you.

Almost five hours had passed since the General had dived bleeding from his horse, thereby conceding the weakness of his arguments. During this time the Collector had hardly for a moment stopped giving orders. At first he had found it difficult because the refugees were stunned; even when he shouted no one paid any attention to him. So he had changed his tactics: he had assembled all the young lieutenants and ensigns who had managed to escape unhurt from Captainganj (for once the senior officers had borne the brunt of the slaughter) together with half a dozen civilian officials. With this retinue at his heels he had stalked about the Residency doing his best to impose order on chaos, organizing a skeleton defence for the "mud walls", allocating rooms for the women and children, sending out parties of loyal Sikhs to patrol the cantonment. All these orders he murmured to the dazed young men around him and, curiously enough, the quieter his tone, the more greedily his orders were swallowed and the more hastily executed. Soon he was barely whispering his commands.

Now, on the roof, all was quiet except for that laboured breathing, the crunching of gravel and the creaking of wheels, that filtered up from the struggling mass in the darkness below. The Collector cursed them silently. Why had they to bring their useless possessions? Already the rooms and corridors of the Residency were shrinking with the deposit of furniture, boxes, and bric à brac. He knew now that he should have forbidden everything except food and weapons ... but in their place, ah, could he have brought himself to leave behind his statues, his paintings, his inventions?

On his way to the roof he had looked into his bedroom. The General lay in a coma in the dressing-room; his whistling breath could be heard through the half open door and the Collector could just glimpse the nimbus of mosquito net which enveloped him. Miriam and Louise Dunstaple were watching together beside his cot now that Dr Dunstaple had gone to aid Dr McNab in treating the other wounded who had escaped from Captainganj.

97

Presently the stars began to appear and the night became brighter. Some time later, the Magistrate joined him on the roof.

"Thank heavens they got away with some cannons, Tom," said the Collector.

The Magistrate made no reply except to sigh and peer over the balustrade at the seething mass of men and possessions below. It was evident that he did not think that cannons would make any difference. Nevertheless, enough men had escaped from Captainganj to make a useful force. Two dozen British officers of native regiments, twice that number of English private soldiers, and the majority of the Sikh cavalry, numbering over eighty men; add to that at least a hundred European civilians, either Company officials or planters and, finally, a large but as yet undetermined number of Eurasians. Perhaps there would also be a handful of loyal sepoys. But all the same the Magistrate was right: against the vast numbers that the rebel sepoys were capable of marshalling the Residency force was insignificant.

Now the moon rose and other gentlemen began to appear on the roof. Among the first was Dr Dunstaple who seemed in surprisingly good spirits and was anxious to tell the Collector an amusing story about Dr McNab. An hour or two earlier, while the two doctors had been working together to sew up a young ensign, McNab had suddenly asked him if he had heard of the native way to staunch wounds . . . a way which he was, he said, eager to try out for himself. " 'And what's that, McNab?' says I. 'It's this,' says he . . ." and here, although McNab had barely a trace of Scottish accent, Dr Dunstaple set himself to imitate him in an exaggerated and amusing way. " 'Hae ye no hairrd o' burtunga ants, Dunstaple?' 'As a matter of fact, McNab,' says I, 'I cannot say that I have ever heard burtunga ants mentioned in the entire course of my existence.' 'Och, then, lesten to this, laddie,' says he. It seems that the little beggars have large and powerful jaws. What you have to do, he tells me, is to press together the lips of the wound and place the ants on it at intervals. They bite immediately. The necks are then snipped off and the bodies fall to the ground leaving the edges of the wound firmly held by the heads and jaws. 'Och, Dunstaple, I hae foond me a naist o' the wee baisties

98

and I shall see for maeself 'ere long.' " And Dr Dunstaple laughed heartily at the thought and repeated: "Hae ye no hairrd o' burtunga ants, Dunstaple?"

When Harry Dunstaple and Fleury came up on to the roof the Doctor, failing to notice that neither the Collector nor the Magistrate were enjoying it, insisted on repeating the anecdote about McNab, adding that all the time Ensign Smith had been listening with his face as grey as porridge, expecting McNab to produce his ants then and there. It was something for Fleury to put in his book about Progress, he chuckled ... the strides that medicine was making in India.

By this time Fleury and Harry, though each still considered himself privately to have nothing in common with the other, had become firm friends. It so happened that they had had an adventure together; they had had to ride all the way back to Krishnapur unarmed through mutinous countryside and then the Collector had sent them out again to warn indigo farmers ... and at one point they had heard what had sounded mighty like a musket shot which, although not *very* near, might or might not have been fired in their direction but, they decided, probably *had* been. Harry clung to this adventure, such as it was, all the more tenaciously when he found that because of his sprained wrist he had missed an adventure at Captainganj.

Those of his peers who had escaped with life and limb from the Captainganj parade ground did not seem to be thinking of it as an adventure, those who had managed to escape unhurt were now looking tired and shocked. And they seemed to be having trouble telling Harry what it had been like. Each of them simply had two or three terrible scenes printed on his mind: an Englishwoman trying to say something to him with her throat cut, or a comrade spinning down into a whirl-pool of hacking sepoys, something of that sort. To make things worse, one kept finding oneself about to say something to a friend who was not there to hear it any more. It was hard to make any sense out of what had happened, and after a while they gave up trying. Of the score of subalterns who had managed to escape, the majority had never seen a dead person before ... a dead English person, anyway ... one occasionally bumped into a dead native here and there but that was not quite the same. Strangely enough, they listened quite enviously to Harry talking about the musket shot which had "almost definitely" been fired at himself and Fleury. They wished they had had an adventure too, instead of their involuntary glimpse of the abattoir.

It was much cooler on the roof. The moon hung, soft and brilliant, above the cantonment trees and the dust in the atmosphere caused it to shine with a curious dream-like radiance which Fleury had never seen before outside India. In its light he could make out figures huddled on bedding, for a number of gentlemen had found it too hot to sleep without punkahs in the interior of the building and had come up here. Others were standing and talking together in low tones. Presently the Padre's voice rose above them, reciting the Prayer in Time of Wars and Tumults ... "Save and deliver us we humbly beseech thee, from the hands of our enemies; abate their pride, assuage their malice and confound their devices; that we, being armed with thy defence, may be preserved ever more from all perils, to glorify thee, who art the only giver of victory ..."

A weird, melancholy cry started up now, echoing over the moonlit hedges and tamarinds and spreading like a widening ripple over the dark cantonment. Beside Fleury, the Magistrate said: "Listen to the jackals ... The natives say that if you listen carefully you hear the leader calling '*Soopna men raja hooa* ...' which means 'I am the king in the night' ... and then the other jackals reply: '*Hooa! hooa! hooa!*' 'You are! you are! you are!' " Fleury could make out nothing at first, but later, as he was falling asleep it seemed to him that he could, after all, hear these very words. Below, the last refugees had now struggled out of the darkness with their burdens and all was quiet. At last Fleury fell asleep, and as he slept, a fiery beacon lit up the cantonment, and then another, and another.

The Collector awoke to a pleasant smell of wood-smoke, which for some reason reminded him of Northumberland where he had spent his childhood. He had slept in his clothes, of course, and had woken once or twice as people came through his bedroom to attend to the General. He had had a nightmare, too, in which he had found himself struggling to free himself from a stifling presence that had wrapped itself round him like a shroud. But he had slept well, on the whole, and felt refreshed. He had Miriam to thank for that because, while watching by the General's bedside she had made it her business politely to discourage all those who wanted to wake the Collector to tell him that the cantonment was burning, as if there was anything he could do about it. As soon as he was properly awake, however, she told him what the pleasant smell was.

In any case, it was by no means the whole cantonment which had burned; the watchers on the roof had only counted five or six different fires, and the majority of these were of already deserted bungalows, inhabited only by the ghosts of magnificent company officials. The other bungalows still for the most part had their servants to protect them, however tepidly. More important, the sepoys were still at Captainganj, arguing among themselves as to whether it would be best to sack the cantonment or to march straight to Delhi to restore the Emperor. It was said that the sepoys were also sending a horseman to Saint Petersburg to acquire the assistance of the King of Russia whom they believed would be sympathetic to their cause.

Before the morning grew too hot the Collector summoned the Magistrate to the roof to plan the defence of the enclave. The Residency was the most solid as well as the most imposing building in the cantonment. It stood, together with Dr Dunstaple's house, the Church and the Cutcherry, in a compound of several acres which was roughly three-sided. Against one of these three sides the native town abutted in the shape of a handful of not very substantial mud houses and, of course, of the mosque which the Magistrate, blinded by rationalism, had been so anxious to destroy.

"We'll establish a battery in the flowerbeds down there to protect us against attack from the native town," said the Collector. He saw the Magistrate shift his gaze to the mosque and knew what he was thinking. He himself, as it happened, was coming to see the mosque less as a sign of his own largeness of mind than as a source of trouble to the cannons in the flowerbeds. However, the Magistrate made no comment and together they crossed the roof. From here they could see the cantonment spread out in the shape of a fan, roughly bisected by the Mall, where in peaceful times Europeans took their evening stroll; anywhere else it was considered undignified to be seen on foot. The line of tamarinds which gave it shade came to an end on the far side of the cantonment at the old parade ground, long since abandoned, perhaps fortunately, for a better site at Captainganj.

"Tom, I want you to pick the men you need and establish a battery behind the Cutcherry rampart. You'll command it with Lieutenant Peterson to advise you. We'll need another battery in front of Dunstaple's house. I intend to put Lieutenant Cutter in charge there. At the ramparts in between the batteries we'll establish pickets every few yards with rifles and bayonets. In the meantime we must do what we can to build them up higher."

"What about the river?"

Again they crossed the roof. Below them the barren lawns stretched away towards the river; on its far bank lay melon beds, rich green contrasting pleasantly in that glaring landscape of whites and greys with the bright yellow of the melons. These melons, the Collector knew, were only eaten by the very poorest natives in Krishnapur and by one other person, namely the Magistrate himself who during the hot weather liked to scoop out the pips, pour in a bottle of claret, and then dip his ginger whiskers into the cool mixture of wine and juice. "A sad example," thought the Collector with pity, "of the eccentricity to which men living by themselves are subject. Thank heaven that I myself have been spared such peculiar habits."

Aloud he said "An attack from this direction isn't likely in my opinion. The ground beyond the ramparts is open for quite a distance. The only cover is the near bank of the river and that must be a good three hundred yards away. On the far bank the ground rises and they can't approach unobserved. But above all there's the banqueting hall. They'd be mad to attack that."

The banqueting hall stood on a rise in the ground which corresponded to the hill beyond the melon beds. It was a solid building, not much used any longer. In design it was an unhappy mixture of Greek and gothic; the six pillars of its façade were an echo of the six imposing pillars of its illustrious parent, East India House in Leadenhall Street. Inside there was wood panelling, a great baronial fireplace complete with inglenooks, and even a minstrel gallery. It possessed stained-glass windows, too, but perhaps the most surprising pieces of ornament were outside, the four giant marble busts of Greek philosophers which gazed out over the plain from each corner of the roof.

"They might attack there even so," said the Magistrate doubtfully.

"If they do, so much the better." Through modesty the Collector had failed to mention the final attribute which rendered the banqueting hall utterly impregnable, for it was here that he had allowed the books he was reading on fortification to influence the plan of his "mud walls". He had chosen the simple and traditional *tenaille* trace: a system of flanks and faces arranged something like the points of a star to cover each other so that, at least in theory, there was no angle at which the rampart might be attacked without the risk of cross-fire. Of course, once past the banqueting hall these elaborate fortifications petered out again into the same wandering line that followed the prickly pear of the compound wall and which might well be contemptuously dismissed by a military man as "mud walls".

"We'll put Major Hogan in charge to keep him quiet. And we'll give them a six-pounder, though I don't suppose they'll find much use for it. Now we'd better get down and set up those batteries while we still have the chance."

Major Hogan was a rather muddled and peppery old fellow who was generally considered to have been too long in the East. The garrison under his command was composed of Harry Dunstaple (relegated there until his wrist was properly mended), a couple of portly Sikhs, half a dozen very elderly native pensioners who had loyally presented themselves on hearing of the Company's difficulties, a taciturn man from the Salt Agency called Barlow and, lastly, Fleury. Major Hogan, as it happened, was the only officer over the rank of lieutenant to have survived the slaughter at Captainganj. He might have laid claim to the military command of the whole enclave but had not done so ... Years had passed since he had last taken any serious interest in his profession.

Although disappointed to be posted to the safest place inside the enclave, Harry swallowed his feelings and set to work to improve the Collector's fortifications. Soon Fleury was hard at work too, sitting in the shade of a Greek pillar and directing the native pensioners who came tottering up from the river bed with boulders where to put them. But Fleury had little stamina and presently this tedious job became too much for him; so he sauntered away in a rather unmilitary fashion. Harry would have reprimanded him, because one cannot have a soldier, even an amateur soldier like Fleury, leaving his post whenever he gets bored, but Harry had just received delivery of his six-pounder and could think of little else . . . it was made of brass and he had set his two Sikhs to polishing it. Brass cannons are lighter than iron but gunners who knew their business, like Harry, preferred them because they were less likely to burst. But brass does have a disadvantage, too. If a great number of shots are fired the muzzle becomes distorted into an ellipse from the shot constantly hammering upwards against its rim, and then loading becomes difficult or impossible. But several hundred shots would have to be fired before this happened, which would take weeks or months of siege warfare . . . and there was no question of the garrison at Krishnapur having to hold out for more than a few days, while help was sent from Barrackpur or Dinapur. So Harry had no need to worry about that.

Fleury had wandered over to the Residency hoping to find someone to have a chat with, perhaps even Louise if he were lucky . . . but everything was in turmoil. All the men were working in a frenzy to throw more earth on to the ramparts before the sepoys had a chance to attack . . . they did not even appear to *see* Fleury standing there amiably in his Tweedside lounging jacket. And where the women were, heaven only knew . . . though he would not have been surprised to learn that they were organizing something else, somewhere else. Fleury wandered away, feeling unwanted. At the Church, there was more feverish activity; a difference of opinion was taking place because the Collector had ordered food, powder and shot to be stored in the Church; the Padre and some members of his congregation were entertaining serious doubts about the propriety of this. But while the more spiritual were entertaining doubts, the military were shifting the stores. Fleury watched the great earthenware jars containing grain, rice, flour and sugar being carried into the Church and arranged in rows at the back.

When he returned to the banqueting hall he found Harry behaving rather oddly. He was gazing in a trance at the brass cannon and running his fingers over its soft, hairless, metal skin. It might have been a naked young girl the way Harry was looking at it. He gave a start when he heard Fleury approach, however, and slapped the chase in a more manly fashion.

"Look here, Harry, you must tell me all about cannons. To begin with, what's this thing like a door-knob on the end for?"

"That's the cascable," muttered Harry, taken aback. He could see that Fleury was not going to be such a success as he had hoped.

"Sometimes, Tom, I wonder that I am not an atheist myself!"

It was the Collector who had uttered this heartfelt cry. He and the Magistrate were standing in the vernacular record room of the Cutcherry; from outside there came the steady clinking of spades as a detachment of English private soldiers, the remainder of the General's "odds and ends" on their way to Umballa, threw gravel against the outer wall.

The Collector was displeased; he had just had to arbitrate a dispute over the graveyard between the Padre and the Roman Catholic chaplain, Father O'Hara. A small portion of the grave-yard had been reluctantly allotted to Father O'Hara by the Padre for his Romish rites in the event of any of the half dozen members of his Church succumbing during the present difficulties. But when Father O'Hara had asked for a bigger plot, the Padre had been furious; Father O'Hara already had enough room for six people, so he must be secretly hoping to convert some of the Padre's own flock to his Popish idolatry. The Collector had settled the dispute by saying with asperity: "In any case, nobody's dead yet. We'll talk about it again when you can show me the bodies."

The vernacular record room, which had a surprisingly cheerful appearance, was the very centre of the British administration in Krishnapur and as such was the object of the Magistrate's scientific scrutiny. He had come to see this room as an experimental greenhouse in which he watched with interest, but without emotion, as an occasional green shoot of intelligence was blighted by administrative stupidity, or by ignorance, or by the prejudices of the natives.

As a matter of fact, it even looked like a greenhouse. Its walls were lined from floor to ceiling with tier over tier of stone shelves; to protect the records from white ants they were tied up in bundles of cotton cloth brilliantly dyed in different colours for ease of reference ... and these bright colours gave the shelves the gay appearance of flower-beds. This cloth protection, however, was not always effective and sometimes when he opened a bundle the Magistrate would find himself looking, not at the document he required, but at a little heap of powdery earth. And then he would give a shout of bitter laughter which echoed across the compound and had more than once caused the Collector to raise his eyebrows, fearful for his sanity. In India all official proceedings, even the most trivial, were conducted in writing, and so the rapidity with which the piles of paper grew was alarming and ludicrous. The Magistrate was constantly having to order extensions to be made to his laboratory. Sometimes, when tired, he no longer saw it as an experimental greenhouse but instead as an animal of masonry that crept steadily forward over the earth, swallowing documents as it went.

The Collector, his splendid ruff of whiskers standing out clearly against a bank of yellow bundles, was looking at the Magistrate in a moody, persecuted sort of way. The Magistrate himself was standing with his head against a bank of cinnamon-coloured documents which so nearly matched the colour of his own hair and whiskers that for a moment it seemed as if his eyes, nose and ears were floating disembodied above the morning coat. He knew what the Collector was feeling persecuted about and could not resist persecuting him a little more, thinking with relish: "His high-mindedness could hardly be expected to survive the pressure of circumstances." He enquired innocently: "How about the mosque?"

The Collector winced. "The Engineers are going to knock it down presently. We have a *futwah*, of course, but one still doesn't like to have to do it."

A *futwah*, or judgement, had been obtained from the Cazee in Krishnapur after tedious negotiations by messenger and in return for a promise of future favours. It sanctioned the demolition of the mosque on the strength of a precedent of the Emperor Alumgire; that pious monarch, while at war with the Mahrattas, had pulled down a mosque which sheltered them from his artillery ... In that instance the doctors of the law had declared that the Almighty would pardon the removal of His temple for the destruction of His enemies. But at Krishnapur it was for the *protection*, not the destruction of unbelievers that the mosque was to be demolished. The Collector was not convinced by this precedent and doubted whether the Mohammedans would be very satisfied with it either, particularly as the Cazee was already letting it be known that the *futwah* had been extorted from him. Yet even the dire risk of arousing Mohammedan resentment was not at the heart of the Collector's disquiet, for beside the practical reason, the question of resentment, there lay its moral shadow, the fact that a civilized man does not countenance the destruction of places of worship.

They had moved out now and were standing at the door of the Cutcherry. Some distance away, squinting into the glare, the Magistrate could make out Lieutenant Dunstaple and young Fleury talking together in the shade of a peepul tree with the wonderful enthusiasm and sincerity of youth (but which, reflected the Magistrate, can be a bit sickening if you have too much of it). But the Magistrate was, in any case, not interested in youth for the moment ... he was more interested in the Collector's skull and character, and in the relationship between them. Indeed, he was perplexed. He had believed himself capable of reading that skull as easily as you or I would read a newspaper. But the fact remained that although the Collector's organ of Cautiousness seemed, according to his skull, to be unduly pronounced, he had not been behaving as if it were well developed at all. On the contrary, he had been behaving as if it were rudimentary, even atrophied. He had been making rapid decisions all day. It was very worrying.

The advance of science is not, the Magistrate knew, like a man crossing a river from one stepping-stone to another. It is much more like someone trying to grope his way forward through a London fog. Just occasionally, in a slight lifting of the fog, you can glimpse the truth, establish the location not only of where you are standing but also perhaps of the streets round about where the fog still persists. The wise scientist deliberately searches for such liftings of the fog because they allow him to fill in the map of his knowledge by confirming it. The Magistrate knew that to prove the truth of his phrenological beliefs he must find a person who, unlike the Collector, was subject to *one powerful propensity only*, which could then be verified beyond dispute by the development of the skull. The Collector was too difficult a case; the fog of ambiguity, of counter-active organs, clung too thickly round his head.

The sight of Harry not far away reminded the Collector of something as he stood at the Cutcherry door ... He must send young Dunstaple for the "fallen woman" in the *dak*. In all the fuss of the past twenty-four hours nobody had thought to warn her and bring her in. It was probable, however, that she knew of the danger but was too conscious of her shame to show herself at the Residency. Still, she could not possibly stay where she was; a terrible fate lay in store for an unprotected English-woman, he did not doubt. Admittedly, it would be a problem having her in the Residency with the other ladies but there was nothing to be done about that. She must come in, no matter how greatly she had sinned.

The Collector had heard a little about her and was inclined to be charitable. She had come out to India as someone's "niece", a rather remotely connected "niece", one gathered. Calcutta was full of such "nieces" ... girls who had come out from England sent by anyone who could scrape up an acquaintance with a respectable family in India, as members of "the fishing fleet" to find a husband. The war had taken such a toll of young men! Only in India was there still a plentiful supply to be found, because many young men had chosen India without necessarily intending to choose celibacy as well. Poor girl, it was probably not her fault. No doubt she would still make a good wife for some homesick young ensign willing to incur the disapproval of his colonel. He sighed. Now he must get back to work.

"We'll see what happens, in any case," he observed cryptically, and walked out into the sunlight. The Magistrate watched his head glow for a moment before a bearer sprang forward to protect it with the shade of a black umbrella. He too sighed. More than ever he longed to grasp the Collector's skull and make some exact measurements of it.

Now that the greatest heat of the day was over, the engineers were setting to work on the demolition of the mosque. Presently, the Collector found himself alone once more in his study. He stood near the window, one hand resting on the marble head of *Innocence Protected by Fidelity*. "It really wasn't altogether my fault," he suggested to himself hopefully.

A strange thing was happening to the mosque; a golden cloud had begun to spread outwards from its walls into the still air. Gradually the cloud darkened and spread into a thick cloak of dust that completely masked the building from the Collector's troubled eyes, as if to protect him from the evidence of his own barbarity.

While the Collector was observing the slow demolition of the mosque Harry Dunstaple, attended by Fleury and a couple of Sikh *sowars*, had gone to rescue the "fallen woman" from the *dak* bungalow . . . this was exactly the sort of daring and noble enterprise that appealed to the two young men's imaginations, rescuing girls at the gallop was very much their cup of tea, they thought.

The difficulty about the *dak* was that it had not been built, as it should have been, in the cantonment but in the middle of the native town, which made the expedition dangerous. To make matters worse the sun was setting; they had to hurry lest they be caught in the native town after nightfall. After the tranquillity of the cantonment the noisy crowds surging through the streets came as a shock to Fleury; as they penetrated deeper into the bazaar men shouted at them, words he could not understand, but they were plainly jeering. Their progress was constantly impeded by the crush; a perilously swaying cargo of Mohammedan women passed by on a camel, their masked heads turned towards Fleury; he felt himself stared at weirdly by their tiny, embroidered eye-holes.

'Sahib. Yih achcha jagah nahin!' one of the Sikhs said to him. "No good place, Sahib. Come quick." He was leading them towards a short cut which would take them away from the principal road through the bazaar.

They plunged into a wilderness of dark and stinking streets, so narrow that there was hardly room for two people to pass each other. Their way led down flights of twisting steps and past shadowy doorways redolent of smoke, excrement and incense; sometimes the street narrowed to a mere slit between houses and once a massive, comatose Brahmin bull stumbled past them. Then, abruptly, they emerged from the stifling darkness into light and air. The *dak* bungalow lay beside them. While Fleury waited at the gate with the Sikhs Harry darted inside for the "fallen woman".

After a few minutes Harry emerged alone, looking perturbed, to confer with Fleury. The "fallen woman", whose name was Miss Hughes, was refusing to come. What on earth should he do? They could not possibly leave her alone for a second night without protection ... And now, not content with refusing to come she was even thinking of killing herself again. Anyway, that is what she had *said* she was thinking of doing. She had implied that then he and all the others would not have to worry about her any longer. She might as well be dead, anyway, loathsome creature that she was, because *now* ... (Harry had blushed at that "now" knowing only too well what it referred to) ... because *now* she had nothing to live for. She had ruined herself.

"Nonsense!" Harry had declared gruffly. "You have a jolly great deal to live for."

"Just tell me one single thing!" And Miss Hughes had turned her tear-stained face, which was like that of a sensual little angel, towards Harry.

"Well ... Any amount of things."

"What things?"

But Harry had been unable to think of anything. This was not the sort of thing he was good at. So he had dashed out to see if Fleury had any ideas. All this time the light was fading. To remain here after dark would be to invite disaster. So there was no time to lose. The two young men stared at each other in dismay.

"Tell her ... tell her ..." But Fleury, too, found himself baffled by this unexpected development. And it was not that his mind had gone completely blank, as Harry's had ... because he could think of a number of ways for a dishonoured woman to spend the rest of her life ... becoming a nun, good works to achieve redemption, that sort of thing. The trouble was that these did not sound to him like the sort of lives one could recommend to someone who thought she had nothing to live for; they sounded too uncomfortable for that.

But this was getting them nowhere. The Sikhs were beginning to roll their eyes ironically, and the horses were becoming restive too.

"Look here, tell her what a joy it is just to be alive. You know, the smell of new-mown hay, crystal mountain streams, the beauty of the setting sun, the laughter of little children . . . or rather, no . . . never mind the children . . . And, of course, you might also bring in the woman taken in adultery, the casting of first stones, Our Lord loving sinners and so forth."

"Wouldn't it be better if I stayed here and *you* spoke to Miss Hughes?" pleaded Harry.

"Certainly not. She knows you."

So Harry again hurried inside, his lips moving silently as he rehearsed Fleury's reasons for life being worth living. Outside, meanwhile, Fleury had to pretend not to notice that the Sikhs, their irony verging on impertinence, were ostentatiously saying goodbye to each other.

So it was that when Harry again emerged, distressed and still without Miss Hughes, it was less the fear of death in the native town than of appearing foolish in the eyes of the Sikhs, which caused the two young men to ride back to the Residency, leaving Miss Hughes to her fate. But they did not feel very pleased with themselves.

8

Days passed and still the sepoys made no decision to attack the Krishnapur cantonment. They moved out once, but after only a mile they stopped, engaged in disputes, and then moved back to Captainganj again. This movement of retreat caused some of the Europeans to hope that the affair might pass away without further bloodshed, but neither the Collector nor the Magistrate shared this optimism. A strange calm prevailed.

By acting as if the Company still retained some authority in the region, by staging a pantomime of administrative government to an empty theatre, the Collector had done his best to keep everything going as usual. But he found that all business in the courts and offices had ceased, except for the opium-eaters who came for the drug at the usual hour. There was another sign of this ominous calm, too, for the native sub-officers out in the district reported that crime had ceased altogether. The Collector remembered something he had once read . . . a Sanskrit poem describing how, in an overwhelmingly hot season, the cobra lay under the peacock's wing and the frog reclined beneath the hood of the cobra. So it must be, he thought, in Krishnapur, where all personal antagonism had been forgotten in the general feeling of expectation.

At the same time, however, as this sudden absence of crime was noticed, there was evidence of unrest in the native town. Merchants had latticed up the fronts of their shops with bamboo hurdles to protect them against the looting which they evidently expected. The wealthier merchants had even hired small armies of mercenaries to protect their property. These men, armed with swords and *lâtees*, were to be seen swaggering about the streets in various uniforms of their own confection, shouting with laughter if they saw a European and boasting that they were now the masters.

The Collector was grateful for the days of respite. He knew that if the sepoys had attacked immediately after the mutiny at Captainganj they would have had little chance of defending themselves in the Residency. For the past few days everyone had been working to make the defences solid. It was true that some of the ladies were becoming bad-tempered and disconsolate from the heat, from the absence of active punkahs (the punkah-wallahs were vanishing one by one), and from the scarcity of *khus tatties*, the frames woven with fragrant grass over which water was thrown in order to cool the air during the hot weather. But on the whole the community had worked together, frantically and with a common purpose, until now order prevailed where there had only been confusion before. And the Collector thought admiringly of that observation hive of bees they had had in the Crystal Palace. What fine little beasts bees were!

He was standing in his bedroom with one elbow on the chimney piece as he mused on the qualities of bees. But suddenly it occurred to him that he could no longer hear the General's whistling breath from the adjoining dressing-room. This breath had grown daily less audible ... yet how tenaciously the old General had been fighting to survive! Dr Dunstaple proclaimed it a miracle that he should have lasted so long.

The Collector was moving towards the dressing-room where Louise was watching by the General's bedside, when he heard another noise coming from outside in the compound, a strange, resonant murmur, a humming sound which slowly grew in volume until it reverberated everywhere, and which sounded, by an odd coincidence with his reflections of a moment earlier, not unlike the sound of bees about to swarm. As he hesitated a bearer knocked and came in with a message from the Magistrate, asking him to come immediately to the Cutchery.

Outside the offices the Collector found the explanation for the resonant humming he had heard. A crowd of Eurasians and native Christians had assembled with bundles of bedding and other possessions loaded on to hackeries or balanced on their heads; the noise came from their humming, a sound like that made by the native infantry when striking camp, combined with a high-pitched wail of discontent.

The Magistrate, looking harassed, was sitting at his desk.

From the wall the portrait of the young Queen surveyed her two subjects with bulging blue eyes.

"What on earth is the matter with them?"

"They want to come into the enclave. They say they're loyal to the Company and that as Christians they'll certainly be murdered by the sepoys. They're probably right, at that." Noting the look of dismay on the Collector's face he added: "I know, but what can we possibly do? I suppose we could take in the Eurasians at a pinch but we can't possibly have any more native Christians . . . We have more than enough as it is. We haven't enough food."

"We can't just leave them out there to be massacred for Heaven's sake!" cried the Collector, who had turned pale and was groping for a chair. The Magistrate was taken aback by the Collector's show of emotion. He said: "I'm sorry, but we won't be able to stand a siege for any time at all if we have to feed such a crowd. Of course, it's up to you to decide, but I can't recommend you to take them in."

"Is there nothing we can do?"

"We'll take in the 'crannies', if you like . . . They would be the most in danger, anyway. All I can suggest for the native Christians is that we give each of them a certificate to say that they've been loyal to the Government, for when these difficulties are over. They can be rewarded afterwards."

"A fat lot of good a certificate will be!" groaned the Collector, but there was no alternative that he could see. He stayed for an hour in the Cutcherry helping the Magistrate to sign and issue the certificates. All the time he remained there the high-pitched, resonant humming did not cease for a moment.

It was only as he was walking back to the Residency that he remembered the General and summoned a bearer, telling him to go and enquire how the General was. The bearer, however, did not move. Instead, he replied quietly that it was unnecessary . . . He had just heard . . . he dropped his eyes and after a moment's hesitation, murmured . . . "*. . . is dunniah fänê sā rehlat keah*" (that his spirit had begun its march from this transitory world).

It was about noon that the General died. The humming of the native Christians was the only sound to break the silence. As

114

the afternoon wore on, the humming was silenced by the great heat; all living creatures were obliged to crawl into some shade in order to survive. For a while the silence now became profound at the Residency, as it did every afternoon. Besides, there was nothing further for the garrison to do; by now they had made their defences as secure as was possible in the circumstances. The ladies, having fought polite but ruthless battles for a place under those punkahs in the billiard room that were still moving (that is to say, those which still had a native attached to the other end), lay stretched out on charpoys and mattresses in their chemises and petticoats like arrangements of wilted flowers, their faces, necks, and arms shining with perspiration. Flies and mosquitoes tormented them and they longed for the evening which would bring, if not coolness, at least a fall in the temperature.

About three o'clock the deathly silence was broken by a terrible noise of banging and hammering which startled them awake. It was the native carpenters knocking together a coffin for the General. The Padre was to bury him that evening. Towards four o'clock, when the heat had at last begun to die down a little, the aggrieved humming started up again. This time it came from a little further away ... from outside the Residency gates, where the native Christians had been moved, each holding his certificate of loyalty to the Company.

The Padre, too, was distressed by this humming. He had complained to the Collector about the Christians being left outside, just as he had complained about the storing of great jars of grain and powder at the back of the Church, but it had done no good. The Collector had been polite and soothing, but he stubbornly continued to ignore the Padre's demands.

The Padre was dismayed that his authority, which ought to have increased at this time of danger, had instead melted away. Even on the day following the disaster at Captainganj when he had taken the Sunday evening service in the expectation, at such a critical time, of finding it full to capacity, he had found himself with a congregation of a mere half dozen, all ladies.

He had intended beforehand, picturing to himself a large and anxious congregation, to preach a comforting sermon on a text from the Psalms: "It is better to trust in the Lord than to put any confidence in man. It is better to trust in the Lord than to put any confidence in princes." But seeing that mere handful of worshippers in the empty, echoing Church, he had been seized by righteous anger and had preached instead on the theme: "Go ye into all the world, and preach the gospel to every creature."

He had heard, he declared, that there were those in the British community who blamed their present perilous situation on the missionary activity of the Church. They blamed a colonel of a regiment at Barrackpur who had been preaching Christianity in the bazaar. They blamed Mr Tucker, the Judge at Fatehpur, for the piety which had made him have the Ten Commandments translated into the vernacular and chiselled on stones to be placed by the roadside . . .

"They blame the pale-faced Christian knight with the great Excalibur of Truth in his hand, who is cleaving right through all the most cherished fictions of Brahmanism . . . the literature of Bacon and Milton that is exciting a new appetite for Truth and Beauty . . . the exact sciences of the West with their clear, demonstrable facts and inevitable deductions which are putting to shame the physical errors of Hinduism.

"They blame the pious men who have circulated this missionary address to the more educated natives in our Presidency," cried the Padre, flourishing a pamphlet in the pulpit, "demonstrating that our European civilization, which is rapidly uniting all the nations of the earth by means of railways, steam-vessels and the Electric Telegraph, is the fore-runner of an inevitable absorption of all other faiths into the One Faith of the white ruler. They blame these devoted men for daring to suggest such a thing! They blame Lord Canning for giving a donation to the Baptist college at Srirampur and Lady Canning for visiting the female schools of Calcutta! They blame our most saintly men of God . . . and I ask you, brethren, for what sin do they blame them? They blame them for buying little native orphans during famines in order to bring them up in the true Way. Is this a crime? No, it is the service of Our Lord!

"Brethren, if our little community is now in peril it is because of *Sin*. The bad lives that are led by many of the Christians among us are a cause of discontent to Him . . . and make Him, who is above all, withdraw His protection. *Sin* is the one thing above all others which grieves Him . . Sin is the thing which God most hates . . ."

The Padre paused. It had grown dark in the Church. On each side of the pulpit a wrought-iron bracket, raised like a skeletal arm, held a thick white candle. The two small flames from these candles suddenly furnished him with inspiration and he began to explain their significance . . . As the world grows darker, so the flame of truth grows brighter . . . just as these candles were slowly growing brighter as darkness fell outside. He was talking in a different tone, hurriedly, even incoherently. In spite of the wafting punkahs which made the candles flicker, it was stifling in the Church. He left the candles and returned to the subject of Sin. He felt there was something he had left unsaid, something that it was vital to explain to his congregation. No doubt they were suffering from weariness after the anxious night they had passed. But if they were tired, so was he. He had never felt more tired in his life, nor more suffocated by omnipresent Sin. The heat was appalling . . . but Sin dazed him even more.

As he continued to talk, somewhat at random, the conviction slowly gained on him that he was delivering his sermon not to the half dozen ladies in front of him but to the ranks of great earthenware jars at the back of the Church. They crouched there in their shadowy pews, perfectly motionless. He pleaded with them to listen to the Word of God, but they made no answer. Ignoring the ladies, who were becoming uneasy, he tried again and again to formulate the one elusive argument that would win over those dim, sinful ranks of jars. But they remained deaf to the exhortations which echoed round their stony ears.

Although Miss Hughes had not yet killed herself (she was reluctantly reserving this measure until Harry was satisfied that he had done justice to the cause of life) she had steadfastly maintained her refusal to move from the *dak* bungalow. Neither of the two young men had expected her to survive that first night. They were even more surprised when she continued to survive.

Fleury secretly believed that it was Harry's lack of eloquence which had caused Miss Hughes to stay where she was.

Unfortunately, when Fleury rather condescendingly agreed to accompany Harry on another mission to convince Miss Hughes, he found that he was quite unable to get into his stride. Miss Hughes appeared quite insensible to the wonders of the natural world, on which he had been counting. Worse, he soon discovered that the wonders of man's own creation (Shakespeare, and so on) meant no more to her than had "the golden glories of the morning", about which she had peremptorily cut him short, to ask him to kill a mosquito that had somehow become obsessed with her lovely naked arms. Harry and Fleury exchanged an uneasy glance.

"Oh, do look! I feel sure it's bitten me." Miss Hughes sulkily rubbed her arm, blinking like a child. The two young men peered dutifully at her smooth skin, which was of a delicate, transparent whiteness, showing here and there the faintest of duck egg blue veins. Fleury, forgetting for the moment that he was supposed to be looking for the place where the mosquito had had the good fortune to penetrate this lovely skin, gazed with frank admiration at Miss Hughes, thinking what a fair substance her sex was made of. What large, sad eyes she had! What glistening dark hair! Her features, though small, were perfectly sculpted: how delightful that tiny nose and delicate mouth! And he immediately began to consider a poem to celebrate her alabaster confection.

On account of the heat, and perhaps also on account of her despair as a "fallen woman", Miss Hughes had received the two young men in her chemise, reclining on her bed in a way so forlorn that no normally good-hearted gentleman, unless a man of granite principles, could have resisted an impulse to comfort her; beside her chemise she wore only her drawers and two or three cotton petticoats. The criteria of female beauty, as Fleury knew very well, tend to change from place to place and from generation to generation: now it is eyes that are important, now it is the slenderness of your hands; perhaps for your grandmother her bosom was crucial, for your daughter it may be her ankles or even (who can tell?) her absence of bosom. Fleury and Harry were particularly sensitive to necks. Louise Dunstaple, Fleury had already noticed, had a lovely neck, and so did Miss Hughes. There was something so defenceless about Miss Hughes's neck, it was so different from their own muscular, masculine necks that the two young men could hardly keep their eyes off it. Her dark hair was piled up into an untidy chignon beneath which a number of dark wisps had escaped; above the collar of her chemise, as she moved her head, delicate tendons played like the filaments of a spider's web. What a beautiful neck it was! And the fact that it could plainly have done with a good scrubbing somehow made it all the more attractive, all the more sensual, all the more *real*. That is what Fleury was thinking as he gazed at Miss Hughes.

Miss Hughes, who sensed that she was being found attractive, permitted herself to cheer up a little and asked the young men to call her Lucy. They needn't think though, that she was going to the Residency with them. She could not bear the shame of everyone knowing she had been ruined. The frankness with which she spoke of her "ruin" rather took one's breath away at first, but one soon got used to it. It was evident that she was still resolved to kill herself, if the sepoys did not do so first. And no matter how hard they tried to persuade her they were quite unable to make her yield on this point. The most that she was prepared to concede was that she might notify them once she had decided not to delay the fatal act any longer, to allow them "a last chance" (provided she did not get drunk again and kill herself spontaneously the way she almost had the other day) . . . it was purely out of friendship towards them that she agreed to this, and on condition that they did not bring the Padre.

"Oh, it's trying to bite me again!" she exclaimed. "You said you wouldn't let it!" And the rest of the visit passed pleasantly enough with Harry sitting on one side of her bed and Fleury on the other, each keeping a watch on one of her arms to prevent the mosquito from again ravishing the unfortunate girl.

Talking it over later, Fleury said: "Look here, we should be asking ourselves *why* Lucy won't come into the Residency . . . Instead of which we waste our time thinking of plans to kidnap her or reasons why life is worth living."

"She won't come because she's ashamed of what that cad did to her. I should like to give him a deuced good thrashing." Harry, lying on his mattress in the banqueting hall looked as if he would have given a great deal to have a horsewhip and the offending officer placed within reach.

"Precisely. She's ashamed. But above all it's the ladies who make her feel ashamed. I mean she doesn't seem to mind *us*. Now if we could get one of the ladies to go and visit her and act as if being seduced wasn't the end of the world ... D'you see what I'm getting at?"

"That sounds a good idea ... but who would go?"

"I'm sure Miriam would go willingly but she's got her migraine at the moment. You don't think we could ask Louise?"

"Oh, I say, she's my sister! And she doesn't know anything about ... you know, being seduced and all that rot. She wouldn't be any good at all at that sort of thing."

"But she doesn't have to know anything about it. She would just have to go along with us and ask her to come to the Residency."

"Oh no, George, steady on. You probably don't know how *gup* spreads in India. One has to think of her reputation, after all. She *is* my sister, you know."

And that seemed to be the end of the matter. But they both wondered whether one morning they would wake up to hear that Lucy had been found lifeless.

9

Fleury had been so busy with one thing and another that he had not had the chance of seeing very much of Louise. This was a pity because he still had not settled the question of the spaniel, Chloë. It was not a very suitable time to start giving people dogs. A dog must eat and perhaps food would soon be in short supply. On the other hand, although he did not care for dogs he had grown sentimental about the idea of Chloë as a gift for Louise: he wanted to see the golden ringlets of Chloë's ears beside Louise's golden tresses (afterwards, Chloë could be got rid of in some way or another).

At last, on the eighth day after the mutiny at Captainganj, Fleury found an opportunity for a private word with Louise. Harry, who was still busy reinforcing the banqueting hall, had sent Fleury to invite his sister to visit his battery, of which he was very proud. He found her attending the Sunday school which the Padre was holding in the vestry: it was her custom to bring little Fanny and then stay to soothe the smaller children if they became distressed by the Padre's explications. But hardly had Fleury delivered his message when Louise was obliged to hand him the baby she was holding in order to comfort another member of the Padre's audience. Fleury, who was unused to babies, was thus obliged to sit with the infant squirming on his lap and to listen to what was being said.

The Padre, who had decided, perhaps rashly, to address the children on the subject of the Great Exhibition, was telling them about the wonders to be found in the Palace of Glass: the machines, the jewels and the statues.

"And yet, children, all these wonderful things were only the natural products of the earth put into more useful and beautiful forms: trees into furniture, wool into garments and so on. Man is able to make these things but he isn't clever enough to make trees, flowers and animals. They must have been made by someone with far greater knowledge than us, in other words . . ."

"By God," piped up a little boy with a shining halo of curls.

"Precisely. Only God could produce something so complicated in its structure and workings. Everywhere in the world we see *design* and that, of course, plainly shows that there must have been a *designer* . . ."

"Oh Padre!" cried Fleury who had unfortunately heard these words and was unable to let them pass, "should we not rather speak to these little ones of the love of God we find in our hearts than about design, production and calculation? Only too soon the materialism of the adult world will smother these innocent little lambs!" And as he uttered the word "lambs" he picked up the baby from his lap and brandished it in his excitement. For a moment it looked as if the unfortunate infant he was wielding might slip from his grasp and dash out its little brains on the floor . . . but Louise swiftly darted forward and took it from him before the disaster could occur. Discountenanced by this removal of his evidence Fleury watched the Padre turn pale.

"Mr Fleury," he muttered. "I must ask you not to interrupt. I was merely proving the existence of God *by logical means* to these little ones, so that they might know that they are completely in His power . . . so that they might know that of themselves they are nothing but sinners who can only be washed clean by the Blood of our Lord." The Padre paused. Fleury had dropped his eyes and was shaking his head sadly, whether in penitence or disagreement it was impossible to say. The Padre was silent for a little while longer wondering what heretical assumption could have just shaken Fleury's head for him. Could it be that he did not believe in the Atonement?

But the children were waiting so he began cautiously to talk about the lighthouse he had seen at the Exhibition, a splendid lighthouse with a fixed light and moving prisms. What did it remind him of?

"Of God," piped up the little boy with glittering curls.

"Well, not exactly. It reminded me of the Bible. Why? Because I thought of the many lives it had saved the way a lighthouse saves men from shipwreck. The Bible is the lighthouse of the world. Those nations which are not governed by it are heathenish and idolatrous. Men without the Bible worship stars and stones. For example, ancient history gives an account of two hundred children being burned to death as a sacrifice to Saturn ... which is, of course, the Moloch of the Scriptures." The Padre surveyed the class. "You wouldn't like that, children, would you?" The children agreed that they would not care for it in the least.

Presently it was time for the Sunday school to disband. The Padre went to a cupboard and took out a large, flat wooden box. This box he brought over to the children and when he had opened it they uttered a gasp, for inside there nestled rows of crystallized fruit glowing amber, ruby and emerald. Some of the smaller children could not resist reaching out their tiny fingers to this box. But the Padre said: "I'm going to give you each a piece of sugar fruit, children, but you must not eat it yourselves, for we have been taught that it is better to give than to receive. Outside the gate you will see some poor Christian natives sitting on the ground ... I shall now go to the gate with you and there you must each give your piece of sugar fruit to one of these unfortunate men."

By this time there was only a handful of native Christians left. They sat in the dust with their backs to one or other of the tamarind trees which made an imposing crescent of shade around the gates. They were silent, too, for one cannot keep on wailing or humming indefinitely, and they looked as if they had given up hope of being offered protection. There were also one or two money-lenders, known as *bunniahs*, who had come along to buy up the "certificates of loyalty" as a speculative investment, at a price which varied between four and eight annas at first, but which soon dropped to nothing for a rumour was going about that now, at last, the sepoys were making a definite move to crush the *feringhees* in the Residency; that very evening they would advance from Captainganj and take up positions to attack at dawn. Apart from the *bunniahs* there were, of course, the inevitable bystanders one finds everywhere in India, idly looking on, wherever there is anything of interest happening (and even where there is nothing) because they are too poor to have anything better to do, and the least sign of activity or purpose, even symbolic (a railway station without trains, for example), exerts a magnetic influence over them which nothing in their own devastated lives can counter.

The ragged group of native Christians received the sugar fruit from their little benefactors expressionlessly and in silence. But when the children had gone back into the enclave they wasted no time in throwing it into the ditch for, although Christians, many of them considered themselves to be Hindus as well, indeed primarily, and had no intention of being defiled like the sepoys with their greased cartridges.

Fleury had contrived to walk back with Louise and Fanny to the Dunstaples' house. Because he was nervous of Louise he playfully tried to tease Fanny about what pretty dimples she had; but Fanny failed to respond and the teasing fell rather flat. To tell the truth, this was by no means the first time that Fanny had been used as a conversation piece by some lovesick suitor trying to get on a more relaxed footing with Louise, and she resented it. Presently she ran off, leaving Fleury feeling more awkward in Louise's company than ever.

Disconcerted, Fleury said humbly: "I'm afraid I must apologize, Miss Dunstaple, for that disturbance during Sunday school . . . and as for the baby which you so wisely took from me, to be honest I'd quite forgotten I had it in my hand."

"Really, Mr Fleury, there's no need to apologize because there was no harm done, after all, though I must say that I do wonder if there is anything achieved by sending such young children to Sunday school."

"I fear the Padre was angry with me for speaking out like that," Fleury said. The rolls of fair curls which escaped from beneath Louise's bonnet seemed to him so like a spaniel's ear that, for a moment, he was able to imagine that it was not Louise but Chloë who was walking along beside him. Something told him, however, that it would not be a good idea to give Chloë to Louise, at least for the immediate future.

Louise was surveying him with a gentle frown. "I'm sure you're right, Mr Fleury, to plead for love rather than calculation to order our lives but . . . forgive me if I speak frankly . . . should you not also give a thought to the distress you are causing the poor Padre Sahib with your views?"

"My dear Miss Louise! I should never for a moment wish to cause distress to the Padre Sahib. But think how important it is that we should find *the right way to lead our lives!* And it is only by argument that we *can* find the right way ... There is no other way to find the truth."

"Alas," said Louise, looking sad, "I sometimes wonder whether we shall ever find the right way. I wonder whether we shall ever live together in harmony, one class with another, one race with another ... Will not the labouring classes always be resentful of our privileges? Will not the natives always be ready to rise up against the 'pale-faced Christian knight with the Excalibur of Truth in his hand' as the Padre so picturesquely referred to him last week?"

Fleury was having trouble smothering his excitement; when he became excited he invariably began to sweat copiously and he did not want Louise to see him in such a disgusting state; it seemed unfair, the higher his spirit soared, the more his face, neck and armpits seeped ... but such is man's estate.

"Oh Louise," he exclaimed, "that is why it's so important that we bring to India a civilization of the heart, and not only to India but to the whole world ... rather than this sordid materialism. Only then will we have a chance of living together in harmony. Will there even be classes and races on that golden day in the future? No! For we shall all be brothers working not to take advantage of each other but for each other's good!"

Louise was perhaps looking a little taken aback by the excitement she had suddenly aroused in Fleury. She was certainly looking with curiosity at his vehement, perspiring features. But Fleury with an involuntary groan of ecstasy had whipped a folded paper from the pocket of his Tweedside lounging jacket.

"These are the words of a very dear friend of mine from Oxford, a poet (like myself), who is now working as an inspector of schools ..." And Fleury began to declaim in such ringing tones that a couple of native pensioners slumbering in the shade of one of the cannons started up, under the impression that they were being ordered to stand to arms.

"Children of the future, whose day has not yet dawned, you, when that day arrives, will hardly believe what obstructions were long suffered to prevent it coming! You who, with all your faults, have neither the avidity of aristocracies, nor

125

the narrowness of middle classes, you, whose power of simple enthusiasm is your great gift, will not comprehend how progress towards man's best perfection ... the adorning and ennobling of his spirit ... should have been reluctantly undertaken; how it should have been for years and years retarded by barren commonplaces, by worn out claptraps. You will know nothing of the doubts, fears, prejudices they had to dispel. But you, in your turn, with difficulties of your own, will then be mounting some new step in the arduous ladder whereby man climbs towards his perfection: towards that unattainable but irresistible lodestar, gazed after with earnest longing, and invoked with bitter tears; the longing of thousands of hearts, the tears of many generations."

Louise did not speak. Her eyes shone, as if with tears. She looked distressed, but perhaps it was simply the strain of listening to Fleury in such a heat. A pariah dog, half bald with mange, as thin as a greyhound, and with a lame back leg, which had been sniffing Fleury's shoes and had slunk away whining as he began to declaim, now cautiously came hopping back again to investigate. He aimed a kick at it.

"My brother has spoken to me of this poor girl in the *dak* bungalow," said Louise hurriedly after a silence. "I'm afraid Father is rather angry with you for suggesting that I should go to the *dak* to persuade her to come here. But please don't think that I'm angry too. I think it right that a woman should go to bring the poor sinful creature back into the Residency ... Isn't it punishment enough that she has been dishonoured? And no doubt it was more the man's fault than her own. And could it not be that she was more foolish than sinful? But, of course I know nothing of these matters as my dear brother is forever telling me."

Fleury was deeply touched by these sympathetic words; at the same time he was too overwhelmed by Louise's loveliness to be able to gaze directly at her face. Meanwhile, the pariah dog, which for some reason found him strangely exciting, had again come stealthily hopping back and was attempting to lean lovingly against his ankles.

Word of mutiny at the prison and Treasury reached the Residency an hour before dusk. Not long after five o'clock, when the streets of Krishnapur were most crowded, a strange clinking sound was heard. People wondered at first where it was coming from; it seemed to be all around them. As it grew louder they realized that among the familiar inhabitants of the town a number of strangers had appeared: they moved in long lines through the evening crowds, looking neither to right nor left, moving with a curious, rapid shuffle away from the middle of the town; presently, it became clear that the sound came from the ankle chains with which they were shackled. The prison guards had mutinied on a signal given by the sepoys at Captainganj and had freed their prisoners.

Soon afterwards came the news that the Treasury sepoys had also mutinied: a number of them had been seen hurrying through the now empty streets of Krishnapur from the direction of the Treasury. They wore *dhotis* instead of uniforms and carried heavy, oddly-shaped burdens on their shoulders and around their necks; they had broached a cart-load of silver rupees and filled the legs of their breeches with them. Now it seemed that they were staggering away with heavy, trunkless men on their shoulders.

As it was growing dark Lucy appeared at the Residency gates, accompanied by the Dunstaples' *khansamah* and a large amount of baggage. Harry and Fleury were beside themselves with astonishment and relief. What had caused Lucy to relent? Presently they learned that Louise had sent the *khansamah* with a letter, begging Lucy to accept her friendship and pleading with her to come into the Residency. Surprisingly enough, Lucy had agreed and now here she was. And not a moment too soon either. Behind her, just visible against the darkening sky, a pillar of smoke climbed from the *dak* bungalow. Then, as the thatched roof caught, the native town was brightly illuminated for a few moments before fading back into the darkness once again.

That night the entire cantonment burned. The Collector had expected that it would and consequently he at first showed no particular sign of alarm as people came to report, while he was at supper, that new fires had been sighted from the Residency roof. He continued eating placidly at the head of the table which had been set up in his bedroom and to which he

127

had invited a number of guests, just as he might have done in normal times downstairs.

The table, although smaller than that of the dining-room, was set no less elegantly with glistening silver and glass. It also held one of the Collector's favourite possessions, a centre-piece by Elkington and Mason of Birmingham in electro-silver and on which candle-holders in the shape of swans' necks alternated with winged cherubim holding dishes. It was not simply that this centre-piece was an object of remarkable beauty in itself, it was also a representative of a new and wonderful method of multiplying works of art.

This was yet another startling advance which had occurred in the Collector's lifetime. Indeed, not much more than a decade had passed since the first small medals, coated by the aid of electricity, had been shown as curiosities. Now articles of far greater complexity even than this elaborate centre-piece were being produced, not singly, but by the thousand. Perfect copies had been made by electric agency of the celebrated cup by Benvenuto Cellini in the British Museum. Who could doubt the benefits which would result from placing such articles within the means of all classes of society ... articles which could not fail to produce a love of the fine arts?

The Collector had several examples of electro-plating scattered about the Residency ... in particular a heavy-thighed "Eve" in electro-bronze leaning against a tree-trunk around which a snake had wound itself ("How popular snakes were with sculptors these days!" he mused parenthetically): this piece stood on the landing at the top of the stairs. He also had a smaller piece in his drawing-room made of an alloy of nickel, copper and zinc which very nearly approached the colour of silver ... this represented "Fame Scattering Rose Petals on Shakespeare's Grave". His wife, too, on her own account, possessed a number of electro-metallic dogs. Could anyone doubt, the Collector wondered, sitting slumped in his chair for he was very tired and watching absently the winking highlights of the electro-silver before his eyes, that this was another invention which would rapidly make mankind sensitive to Beauty? Yes, he remembered sadly, the Magistrate had doubted it, and had scoffed when he had suggested that one day electro-metallurgy would permit every working man to drink from a Cellini cup.

The other people at the table included the Magistrate, Miriam, Major Hogan, Dr McNab, Mr and Mrs Rayne, the pretty Misses O'Hanlon, and, at the far end of the table in the most inconspicuous places they could find, his two eldest daughters, for whom a meal in the presence of their authoritarian father was an ordeal almost as alarming as the prospect of the siege itself. They had all seen a shadow of despondency pass over the Collector's face and naturally assumed, as anyone would, that it had been caused by the news that several bungalows were in flames. Only Miriam guessed otherwise, for he would surely never allow himself to appear despondent in the face of their common danger ... moreover, in the past few days she had come to know him a little better and had noticed more than once that when he was tired his mind had a habit of slipping away from the urgent business it should have been attending to, and browsing on quite other matters. And she wondered what he might be thinking about now.

The atmosphere around the table was very strained. Since the Collector himself was saying nothing about their predicament none of his guests felt that it would be proper to introduce the subject, yet how could they possibly talk of anything else? The truth was that every single topic of conversation they attempted promptly fled back like a bolt of lightning to this predicament. Only the Magistrate seemed to be deriving any pleasure from the atmosphere of constraint which hung over the table, and he presently observed: "I wonder what the Apostles found to talk about during the Last Supper." But this remark, to put it mildly, was not found to be amusing, and was coldly received ... not that the Magistrate would mind about that.

What made things worse was that messages did not cease to arrive for the Collector. Whichever of the young officers it was who was in command of the sentinels posted around the enclave and on the Residency roof had no doubt been ordered to report the least new development, and he was performing his duties with punctiliousness. Every fresh beacon that sprang out of the darkness of the cantonment, in the view of this officer, constituted a new development. A verbal message was sent to the Collector and intercepted at the door of his bedroom by his English manservant, Vokins. Vokins then advanced, portentously discreet, to whisper it into the Collector's ear. The Collector's eyebrows would rise sadly, but he would listen without looking up, slumped in his chair and twirling the stem of his claret glass. Perhaps he would nod slowly, puffing out his cheeks in an odd and gloomy sort of way as he did so. The Collector's guests could not hear what was whispered in his ear, of course; the only person who knew the content of these messages was Vokins. Vokins, however, did not inspire confidence by his demeanour. He was a pale and haggard sort of individual at the best of times; now his pallor increased and the bones of his skull seemed to stand out more sharply, in a way which the Magistrate found interesting but which everyone else found sepulchral.

The trouble was that Vokins, as he made his solemn journeys from the door to the Collector's ear, did not understand that many of these messages were redundant (for, after all, once a cantonment has been set alight the number of bungalows blazing, more or less, is a matter of relative indifference). Vokins thought they were cumulative and progressive; Vokins lacked the broader view. He tended only to see the prospect of the Death of Vokins. Although some of the Collector's guests might have been hard put to it to think of what a man of Vokins's class had to lose, to Vokins it was very clear what he had to lose: namely his life. He was not at all anxious to leave his skin on the Indian plains; he wanted to take it back to the slums of Soho or wherever it came from.

By the time pudding was being served his expression had become tragic and he was uttering his messages in a muted gasp of terror . . . so that in the end even the Collector noticed and looked up enquiringly, as if to say: "Whatever is the matter with the fellow?" but then, evidently concluding that it was the heat, sank back into his own thoughts which were still following, in a meandering fashion, the theme of progress.

When the last of these messages was whispered funereally into his ear (five more bungalows adding warmth to the already stifling night) such a look of dismay came over the Collector's face that the two pretty Misses O'Hanlon could not resist a rapid intake of breath at the sight of it. But the Collector had merely been thinking of Prince Albert's Model Houses for the Labouring Classes and of another argument he had had with the Magistrate about them ... how shocked he had been at the Magistrate's attitude to these model houses!

On his way to the Crystal Palace a small block of houses had caught his eye not far from the south entrance to the Exhibition and a little to the west of the Barracks. He had paused, thinking how cheerful they were in their modest way. They had stood there, respectful but unabashed, without giving themselves airs amid the grander edifices round about. They were square and simple (like the British working man himself, as one of his colleagues of the Sculpture Jury had lyrically expressed it) with a large window upstairs and downstairs, and they were built in pairs with a modestly silhouetted coping stone above the entrance but no flamboyant decoration. They were not dour and sullen like so many of the houses in the populous districts; they were proud, but yet knew their places. In short, they were so delightful that for a moment one even had to envy the working man his luck to be able to live in them as one passed on one's way towards the Exhibition.

But when the Collector had grown eloquent about these charming little dwellings, for this was in the early days before he had realized that the Magistrate was impermeable to optimism where social improvements were concerned, the Magistrate had spoken with equal vehemence about the exploitation of the poorer classes, the appalling conditions in which they were expected to live and so on, dismissing Prince Albert's model houses as a sop to the royal conscience. The Collector had protested that he was certain that the Prince's houses had been prompted, in a genuine spirit of sympathy, by the reports published by the Board of Health's inspectors about the wretched home accommodation of the poorer classes, the utter lack of drainage, of water supply and ventilation.

"What prompted these trivial improvements, on the contrary," the Magistrate had replied, "was a fear of a cholera epidemic among the wealthier classes!"

Well, the Collector mused, it is impossible to argue with someone who ascribes generous motives to self-interest, and he looked up mournfully past the optimistic glints scattered by the electro-silver branches of the centre-piece to the fox-red growth that sprouted from the Magistrate's permanently contemptuous features. "What on earth is that?" he wondered

131

aloud, having noticed, beyond the Magistrate, through the open window a tinge of buttercup in the night sky. Then, he added: "Oh yes, I see," and got to his feet.

Downstairs in his study he lit a cheroot and shortly afterwards put it out again; instead he plucked his watch from its nest below his ribs. Once more he had to go upstairs; it was time for the last and most unpleasant task of the day. As he opened the door of his study he was confronted by a stuffed owl in a glass bell; one of its shoulders had long ago been eaten away by insects and it glared accusingly at the Collector with its glittering yellow eyes. But if the owl did not like the Collector, the Collector did not like the owl ... for this owl was one of a vast population of owls, and of other stuffed birds which had come to roost in the Residency, together with a million other useless possessions. The Collector had long ago realized that he should have ordered them to be left to their fate. Instead, these possessions were stacked all over the Residency, all over Dunstaple's house, and even in the banqueting hall. Only the Magistrate had refused to allow this useless but prized rubbish into the Cutcherry, which, of course, had meant more for everyone else. Now every room, every corridor, every staircase was occluded with the garrison's acquisitions. "But still, are not possessions important? Do they not show how far a man has progressed in society from abject and anti-social poverty towards respectability? Possessions are surely a *physical* high-water mark of the *moral* tide which has been flooding steadily for the past twenty years or more."

Amid the lumber of furniture, vases, crockery, musical instruments, and countless other objects, several more birds, motionless within their bubbles of glass, watched him wearily climb the stairs. He paused at the top, frowning. A ghostly voice had whispered in his ear: "The world is a bridge. Pass over it but do not build a house on it." Was that a Christian or a Hindu proverb? He could not remember.

To accommodate the new arrival the Collector had had to turn out an indigo planter and his wife who had lodged themselves, uninvited, in the only remaining room. They had made a disagreeable fuss and had left, still grumbling, to seek shelter from Dr Dunstaple. Now, in their place, Hari was sitting cross-legged on the floor with his elbows propped on his knees and a sullen expression on his face. The Collector was annoyed to see that the room was lit only by a single candle; he spoke sharply to the bearer waiting at the door and he hurried away to find an oil-lamp.

"My dear Hari, why ever did you not call for more light? How long have you been sitting in the dark like this?"

Hari shrugged his shoulders crossly, as if to indicate that lights were of no importance to him. In the shadows the Collector could make out the form of another seated figure, but the light of the solitary candle was too dim for him to see who it was.

"I left instructions that everything for your comfort ..."

"Oh, comfort ... You think that I worry anxiously about such a thing as comfort!"

"I should have come before this but you must understand, I've had so many things to see to." But not meaning to sound plaintive, he added firmly: "One's duty has to come first, of course." Hari shrugged again, but made no other reply.

The Collector was fond of Hari; it distressed him deeply that he should have to take advantage of him but he could see no alternative. He sighed and waited with impatience for the bearer to bring the lamp. To conduct this interview in semi-darkness seemed furtive and unmanly to him.

When the lamp came at last it illuminated not only Hari but also the other figure seated on the carpet, who turned out to be the Prime Minister. Of course, he had come too! And he could not help thinking ungratefully: "Another mouth to feed!" Not that the Prime Minister looked as if he ate very much, however, he was only a bundle of skin and bones. The Prime Minister, in any case, seemed indifferent to his fate; he was gazing incuriously at the carpet a few inches in front of the Collector's feet.

"I know that it must seem ungrateful of me to detain you here in the circumstances. I should like you to know that, personally speaking, it is the very last thing I should want to do. But I have to think of the safety of those under my protection ... hm ... a great number of women and children ..."

"I show loyalty ... You take advantage of loyalty. You give certificate to sweepers and send him away. Me you keep!"

Hari's voice rose in shrill indignation. "Me you keep prisoner and Prime Minister also! Very frankly, Mr Hopkin (although Hari correctly referred to 'Mr and Mrs Hopkins' he had a habit, distressing to the Collector, of reducing each separately to the singular), very frankly, it is all 'as clear as mud' to me. Please to explain these questions."

Humiliated, the Collector could only repeat what he had said before about the safety of women and children.

Hari and the Prime Minister had presented themselves at the gates towards the end of the afternoon; evidently Hari and his father, the Maharajah, had had a disagreement over the question of loyalty to the British. Hari, firmly on the side of Progress, had insisted on leading the Palace army to their defence. But the Maharajah had declined to let him do any such thing. The whole country was rising to put the *feringhees* and their vassals to the sword; his own power was certain to increase once the Company was destroyed. He did not want Progress ... he wanted money, jewels and naked girls, or rather, since he already had all of these things, he wanted more of them. Hari, like any reasonable person, found these desires (money, jewels, naked girls) incomprehensible. His father was prepared to connive at the destruction of the fount of knowledge ... the knowledge that had produced Shakespeare and would soon have railway trains galloping across the Indian continent! He had made a short speech on this topic, summoning the army and the Prime Minister to follow him to the side of the British to defend Progress. But in the end only the Prime Minister had followed him. The army, even if the circumstances had been more enticing, had long since lost its appetite for fighting. There was nothing left for Hari to do but to pledge his loyalty, obtain a certificate, and return to the Palace. The Collector, busy with other matters, had sent a message to ask him to stay. Hari had not wanted to. It is one thing to bring an army to defend one's friends, another thing to join them simply to be attacked and probably killed. But in the meantime the advantages of having Hari in the Residency had become only too clear to the Collector. Hari's presence might give the impression that the Maharajah supported the British. At the very least it would guarantee the neutrality of his army. Soon it became obvious to him that he could not let Hari go. Now, thinking about it again he became irritated. "It's not my fault. How could I have acted differently? It's unjust of Hari to treat me as if I'm personally responsible!"

"Come, Hari," he said after a long silence. "You must forgive me for treating you so badly. Let's go up on the roof and watch the cantonment burning. That's not a sight we see every day of the week."

From the roof it seemed as if a perfect semi-circle of fire stretched around the Residency enclave like some mysterious sign isolating a contagion from the dark countryside.

Part Two

Part Two

10

The Collector had intended to make a round of the defences in the hour before dawn in order to give encouragement to his men. But he was desperately tired and Vokins failed to wake him at the time he had requested. The result was that he overslept by a good forty-five minutes and he was still pulling on his clothes as the first shots were fired.

The Padre, however, was making a round of the defences on his own account and, in the circumstances, this was probably encouragement enough . . . for the Padre had become extremely worried by the dangerous situation that his Krishnapur flock now found itself in. It was not the dangerous situation itself, however, but rather its implications that were at the source of his anxiety. If they now found themselves in mortal danger it could only be that God was displeased with them and was preparing to punish them as he had punished the Cities of the Plain! And yet the Padre, in his blindness, had believed that he was having some success in ferreting out sin among his flock.

In the few days since they had all been gathered together into the enclave the Padre, becoming increasingly frantic, had not ceased hurrying from one group to another. Even the steady, hot wind which blew relentlessly all day had not deterred him . . . indeed, it drove him on, for it seemed like a foretaste of the breath of Hell. His feet continued to patter over the searing earth while his black habit drank up the heat of the sun. Sometimes he wondered whether he might not already be in Hell. One thing above all kept him going. This was the possibility that God, in the last resort, might stay His hand from the total destruction of the Krishnapur sinners . . . if they showed signs of penitence.

But Sin is hydra-headed; chop a sin off here and a dozen more are bristling in its place. Sometimes as he toiled about the glaring compound the Padre was obliged to stop for a cool drink of water in a shady place; he would have dropped from exhaustion, otherwise. And in these brief interludes of peace he found himself having to admire, in a perfectly objective way, the incredible ingenuity of the Lord's ways. He did not move in mysterious ways so much as in beatifically cunning ones. For at the same time as He had shown the Padre the path he must follow, the path had instantly sprouted new obstacles. Perhaps it would not have been such a difficult matter to isolate sin in the normal life of the cantonment and stamp it out, but now, with his flock herded together in extreme contiguity, many of them at the young age when temptation of the flesh and of the mind is most acute, his task together with occasions for sinful behaviour seemed to increase daily as by a system of compound interest. The closer together that people live the more they sin . . . in the Padre's experience such a proposition was axiomatic.

So the Padre had toiled on, trying to stem the tide. Sometimes he became dizzy with fatigue and suffered strange imaginings; the sinful jars in the Church, for example. But in a sense the Padre was not wrong about these jars for they were a concrete symbol of the material world that was constantly encroaching on the shrinking spiritual sandbank where the Christians of Krishnapur were standing. *Krishnapur!* Even the name of their community was that of a heathen deity.

Now, in the hour of darkness before dawn, the Padre stumbled on around the defences where men waited in silent huddled groups for the order to stand to arms. The darkness at this hour was at its most intense; frequently he tripped over unseen objects in his path, and more than once he fell, hurting himself badly. At each post he exhorted the huddled figures to penitence. He knew they were sinners, he told them; they must repent now before it was too late.

"Look down, we beseech thee," he pleaded, his voice echoing weirdly in the darkness, "and hear us calling out of the depth of misery, and out of the jaws of this death which is ready now to swallow us up: Save, Lord, or else we perish. The living, the living, shall praise thee . . ."

Did his exhortations move the hearts of those shadowy, motionless figures whom he could feel standing there in the darkness but whom he could not see? They remained as silent as the stone jars. He hurried on with the fear in his heart that he was failing.

"Stir up thy strength, O Lord, and come out and help us; for thou givest not alway the battle to the strong, but canst save by many or by few. O let not our sins now cry against us for vengeance . . ."

At each post he handed out a bundle of devotional tracts for the men to read as soon as it became light. Hands took them from him in silence; no word was spoken. He was afraid now that he would not be able to complete the circuit of the defences before dawn. It seemed to him that the darkness was becoming less opaque . . . and soon he realized why he was no longer stumbling: it was because he was becoming aware of objects in the darkness.

"O Almighty Lord," he intoned in such a high, weird voice that all the pariah dogs in the compound set up a howl and the Collector, at last awake and cursing himself as he fumbled for his clothes, said to himself: "The poor fellow has gone off his head with the strain."

". . . who art a most strong tower to all them that put their trust in thee . . ."

"Dammit, bring a light," shouted the Collector to the trembling, haggard Vokins, afraid that he might have to do battle with the sepoys in his nightshirt.

"Be now and evermore our defence; grant us victory if it be thy will; look in pity upon the wounded and the prisoners; cheer the anxious; comfort the bereaved; succour the dying . . ."

That high voice continued to echo eerily over the slowly brightening ramparts and batteries, over the still smouldering cantonment, to float over the sleeping town and lose itself in the vast silence of the Indian plain.

"For God's sake will someone tell the Padre to stop that noise," raged the Collector, his normal piety shattered by nerves.

". . . have mercy on the fallen; and hasten the time when war shall cease . . . in . . . all . . . the . . . world."

Hardly had the Padre's chanting died away when the first shots sounded from the outer darkness, gusts preceding the storm of fire and brimstone that was to fall on the enclave.

The Padre had not had time to visit the banqueting hall before the first fiery squalls dashed themselves against the Residency defences. Fleury and Harry would not have welcomed him anyway; they were beside themselves with excitement as the sky began to brighten and were finding it a torment to remain silent beside their six-pounder. Every time one caught the other's eye they would both almost swoon with repressed glee. They had spent the hours of darkness in whispered conversation over the silken brass skin of their cannon; so much was happening, never had they felt more wide awake! Thank heaven that Lucy was safe! This was, they agreed, a great load off their minds, though there were, of course, still problems which had to be sorted out with respect to Lucy. In spite of the harrowing circumstances the ladies were still refusing to have anything to do with her ... they had hissed with indignation at the suggestion that she should sleep in the billiard room where ladies of the better class had been installed. But where else could she sleep? The Collector's authority had been invoked in the end and she had duly been established there, but nobody was happy about the arrangement.

Now, in their excitement the young men had temporarily forgotten about Lucy. What was concerning them at the moment was the thought that, since the sepoys could not be expected to attack from their direction, they might have no chance to fire their cannon. There was an important question they had to resolve: would it be considered permissible, in the circumstances, to fire at *any* native who presented himself within range, as they might well not see any actual sepoys? Would it be sporting? What they concluded in the end was this: it all depended on the direction of the native's progress ... if the native was coming either directly towards them, or at an angle of anything up to forty-five degrees, it was fair to assume that his intentions were mischievous and they could blow him to smithereens (at any angle greater than forty-five degrees they would quickly review his case and then blow him to smithereens or not, as the case might be).

While they were settling this the darkness was slowly fading on the verandah where they waited; the forms of the old native pensioners began to appear out of the gloom, sitting there white-mustached and medalled with their knees to their ears.

Barlow, the taciturn man from the Salt Agency, who had spent the early hours eating Kabul grapes and dismally spitting the pips into a handkerchief which he afterwards replaced in his pocket, sat in a chair with his hands in his pockets breathing asthmatically. He had been allotted no specific job and his manner was disaffected. The two fat Sikhs chewed *pan*, aside, and spat at intervals. Faintly from within the banqueting hall came the sound of snores; Major Hogan had taken a quantity of brandy after dining with the Collector and had then made a corner for himself amid the lumber of "possessions"; there he had stretched out his bedding. He had left instructions that he was not to be disturbed unless the situation became critical.

It was Harry who had established the emplacement for the six-pounder on the verandah; he had had a couple of yards of the balustrade knocked away to increase the field of fire; at the same time he had had an excellent notion for protecting the gunners, which was to prise off two of the giant marble busts that crowned the roof and have them dragged into position on each side of the cannon. What a labour that had been! So heavy were these great lumps of marble that when they had fallen from the roof they had half buried themselves in the earthen surround. Harry and Fleury had become quite hoarse shouting at the doddering pensioners; in the end they had had to commandeer a pair of bullocks to aid the ropes and levers the pensioners were wielding so feebly. But now the giant heads of Plato and Socrates, each with an expression of penetrating wisdom carved on his white features surveyed the river and the melon beds beyond.

Sometimes, when you try to peer too intensely into the gloom, your eyes make you see things which do not exist; Harry and Fleury presently began to have just this experience. If they had not known that it was impossible they could have sworn that the distant melon beds were seething with moving shadows. Yet there was no question of an attack from that quarter across so much open ground. Their heads turned to each other uneasily, nevertheless; then they looked at the pensioners to see if they were noticing anything; they did not want to make fools of themselves in front of these veterans by ordering them to fire at shadows. But the pensioners sat there impassively; their eyes were too weak, in any case, to be much help in this situation. After some hesitation Harry, in a gruff and insecure tone, gave the order to light the portfire; the portfire, made of a mixture of brimstone, gunpowder and saltpetre, was sixteen inches long and would burn for fifteen minutes; that should be long enough to see them past this tricky twilight interval.

"What on earth is that?"

It was the Padre's voice floating eerily over the compound from the direction of the Cutcherry.

"When war shall cease ... in ... all ... the ... world ..." concluded the Padre amid such a lugubrious howling of pariah dogs that in spite of their excitement the two young men experienced a sudden dread.

"Look at the other bank!" Now that the sky had lightened one could distinguish silhouettes against it; for an instant it had seemed that a strong breeze was blowing through the melon-beds and setting them on the march, but the day's wind had not yet risen. Hardly had Fleury spoken when the rim of darkness beneath the horizon began to sparkle like a firework and immediately the air about them began to sing and howl with flying metal and chips of masonry ... then in a wave came the sound. Daubs of orange hopped at regular intervals from one end of the rim of darkness to the other. Suddenly, a shrapnel shell landed on the corner of the verandah and all was chaos.

Harry had been on the point of giving the order to fire but he had been plucked from Fleury's side and was grovelling somewhere in the darkness.

"Fire!" shouted Fleury, but the pensioner who was holding the portfire merely looked towards him apologetically and sank to the ground where he lay like an empty suit of clothes.

"How terrible!' muttered Fleury helplessly. The verandah was littered with dead pensioners, or what looked like bits of pensioners, it was hard to be sure in the gloom. The two Sikhs lolled against each other, stone dead, with what could have been blood but was probably only *pan* juice trickling from their mouths. Barlow, though he still had his hands in his pockets and was still looking disaffected, had been blown off his chair and was lying on his side. Hardly a minute of the engagement had elapsed and as far as Fleury could see only two pensioners were still alive, and they appeared to be the very oldest and most infirm of the contingent. And still they had managed to fire no shot. While Harry was still struggling in-effectually to get to his feet Fleury grasped the portfire stick and touched it to the vent of the cannon; a jet of flame issued from the muzzle and there was a crash that made the whole verandah quake and set a shower of stone chips and fragments of mortar dancing on the flagstones. In a second or two there appeared out of nowhere against the bright dawning sky a black ball sailing towards the dark rim of melon beds, into which it presently vanished with no visible effect whatsoever.

"Are you alright, Harry?"

"Just winded," grunted Harry, though in fact a flying brick had struck him a painful blow in the groin; for a moment he had thought his entire trunk had been sliced off, pictures of his dear mother and, less appropriately, of Lucy in her chemise, had crowded before his drowning eyes as he prepared to die; then he realized that no actual damage had been done; he was holding his genitals cupped in his hand for they were too pain-ful to massage.

"Almost everybody appears to be dead," shouted Fleury in a discouraged tone. The noise of musket fire from the ram-part on each side was so great that he could not hear Harry's reply but saw that he was pointing at Barlow. Barlow was alive and appeared uninjured. They picked him up and sat him on his chair again. Once more Harry's mouth began to move, this time with an expression of frenzied excitement on his face. Again he pointed, this time over the balustrade.

The day had brightened enough for them to pick out shadowy detail in the landscape. What they saw, six or seven hundred yards away, was more than enough to cause Harry's excitement. Sepoys were swarming through the melon beds and down towards the far bank of the river. But this was all wrong. The sepoys were not supposed to attack from the south. The south was the one cardinal point from which the Residency was defensible; from the others, all the sepoys had to do, prac-tically, was to step over a low wall and slit your throat. And yet the south was where they were coming from (what Harry and Fleury did not yet know was that they were coming from the other cardinal points as well). Without their British officers,

145

of course, the sepoys were likely to commit the most extraordinary follies, such as attacking impregnable positions (never mind for the moment the Redan at Sebastopol).

It was true that the banqueting hall was the most easily defensible corner of the enclave; all the same, it required men to defend it. There were a dozen indigo planters and Eurasian civilians scattered sparsely behind the low earthen wall on each side of the battery. If the native cavalry attacked here, and even if they did not, these men could be easily overrun by a moderately determined assault, in spite of the three hundred yards of open ground which the attacking infantry would have to cross.

One thing had become clear to Harry: the cannon was going to be crucial. It was the one factor that could compensate for the lack of rifles and bayonets. If that first, unlucky shell-burst had not obliterated so many of the pensioners at least they might have been able to serve the cannon adequately; but now there were only two pensioners left. They were making weak efforts to drag the bodies of their comrades back from the verandah and stack them against the lolling Sikhs. Harry ordered one of the remaining pensioners to take a message to the Collector asking for more men; he doddered away, attempting to whip his limbs into a gallop.

Fleury had not been paying attention when the cannon was loaded; the beginnings of an epic poem had been simmering in his brain. Although he did not know it he had just fired a round shot into the sepoy encampment which lay out of sight beyond the melon beds. A round shot is all very well for a steady artillery exchange or for reducing defences, but it is no good for stopping an infantry charge; it does not kill enough people simultaneously for that. What you need is canister or grape. Harry had no shortage of canister for the occasion. But what worried him was how they were going to fire it.

Nine men were needed to serve a cannon if you include those attending the limber and the ammunition wagon; it was difficult to serve without at least five men. But Harry, Fleury and the other elderly pensioner, Ram, set to work in a frenzy. Ram was very thin and tall, and his white mustaches drooped almost to the medals on his tunic; but fortunately he had

146

served in the artillery and knew what he was about. So they divided up the work as best they could, Harry commanding and laying the gun, Fleury spongeing, Ram loading and serving the ammunition; then Fleury or Harry would prime the vent and, after Ram had fired it, clear it with the drift.

They were very slow at first. Fleury did not know what he was doing and they had to keep shouting at him, and Ram was really too old to carry ammunition as well as load it. But then Harry remembered Barlow who was still sitting on his chair with his hands in his pockets. Now that it was daylight you could see that Barlow's face had turned a fearful grey, but somehow Harry got him on his feet and carrying ammunition. He only had to carry it a few yards, from the banqueting hall to the gun emplacement, but in these few yards there was no protection offered by the marble heads of Plato and Socrates, and musket balls kept droning by his nose and tugging at his garments.

Not only did Harry have to organize his amateurish team of gunners, he also had to direct his fire so that it had the most damaging effect; this involved a calculation of variables that could be extremely complicated: the weight of the powder charge, the degree of elevation of the gun, whether the shot to be fired was solid or powder-filled, all these considerations could make a crucial difference to where the shot landed. But Harry had practised this sort of thing so often he did not even have to calculate: he knew by instinct that with a two-pound charge and an elevation of one degree he could drop a shell in the river bed where the sepoys swarmed as thick as flies on a treacle pudding.

Fleury found himself looking at Harry, whom he had always condescended to think rather dull, with new eyes as he watched him making some delicate but fatal adjustment to the handles of the elevating screw. Fleury was confronted, as he toiled clumsily with the spongeing rod in the dust and smoke, with a simple fact about human nature which he had never considered before: nobody is *superior* to anyone else, he only may be better at doing a specific thing. Doubtless, Coleridge or Keats or Lamartine would have been as clumsy with the sponge as he was himself . . . but wait, had not Lamartine been a mili-

147

tary man? With French poets you could never tell. He stepped back, his ears ringing as the cannon crashed again. He could not remember.

"Fleury, for God's sake!" shouted Harry, who knew how desperate the situation was. Fleury did not know; he was in a daze from the noise and smoke which had tears streaming down his face, and the haze of dust which hung everywhere, very fine, lending the scene a "historical" quality because everything appeared faintly blurred, as in a Crimean daguerrotype. Fleury found himself appending captions to himself for the *Illustrated London News*. "This was the Banqueting Hall Redoubt in the Battle of Krishnapur. On the left, Mr Fleury, the poet, who conducted himself so gallantly throughout; on the right, Lieutenant Dunstaple, who commanded the Battery, and a faithful native, Ram."

"Fleury!" shouted Harry desperately. But Fleury's mind *would* keep wandering; the trouble was that being ignorant of military matters he only had a vague idea of what was going on; all he knew for certain was that he was spongeing a gun and, after a while, his stunned senses refused to find that very interesting. He skidded suddenly as he was dashing to clear the vent for Harry and sat down on the flagstones. Only then did he realize that he had skidded in a great lake of blood which had leaked out of the pile of bodies and spread over the verandah.

Harry knew that they needed a miracle ... that is, if the Collector did not send any more men with rifles and bayonets to reinforce the handful at the rampart. They needed another cannon, too, preferably a twelve-pounder, and a mortar to drop shells under the near bank of the river. What looked to Fleury like two or three hundred dim figures in a dust storm wandering aimlessly on the far bank a quarter of a mile away, had a precise meaning for Harry. He knew exactly what was happening: the sepoys were massing under the near bank be-fore making an attack. The only thing that puzzled him was why they were taking so long about it.

By this time the sun had risen and the hot wind was beginning to blow, but still the sepoys delayed their assault. While they waited for it Major Hogan suddenly reeled out on to the verandah and steadied himself with a hand on the door-frame.

He had had a terrible night, but the morning had been worse; every time the six-pounder fired it drove hot needles through his ears. Now he had got himself on to his feet, however, and was coming to take command of his men. He could see by the pile of bodies that they needed him.

Harry greeted Major Hogan's appearance with dismay; it was not simply that he himself was no longer in command; he knew Hogan to be incompetent. What slender chance they had of holding the position vanished with Hogan giving the orders.

Now Hogan, having rallied himself, opened his mouth to give his first order; his brown teeth parted, but as they did so a musket ball vanished between them into his open mouth; his eyes bulged, he appeared to swallow it, then he dropped conveniently near to the other bodies, the back of his skull shattered. Harry and Fleury exchanged a glance but said nothing.

It was nine o'clock and the heat was becoming unbearable; the chase of the cannon could not be touched; if a drop of water fell on it from Fleury's sponge it sizzled away in an instant. The flagstones shimmered and the lake of blood where Fleury had slipped had become a sticky brown marsh sucking at every footstep. Once Fleury trod on something which squashed beneath his foot and he thought with horror: "Someone's eye!" He hardly dared to look down. But it was merely one of the Kabul grapes which Barlow had been eating.

Harry could tell that Fleury and Ram would not be able to go on much longer without a break: Ram because he was old, Fleury because he was inexperienced. Fleury had begun to have a shattered look; he kept his eyes away from the sticky mass and wisps of steam rising from it, and from the bodies. The shock, aided by the noise and heat, was taking hold of him. So Harry gave the order to stop firing; in any case it was time they moved the bodies out of the sun.

While the others rested in the shade, Harry went out again with his telescope; he had considered dragging the gun from one position to another in order to give the impression that they had more than one cannon in the battery. But a brass six-pounder weighs seventeen hundredweight: the prospect of getting it off its trunnions and on to the limber, dragging it to a new position, unlimbering, firing, limbering up once more, and going through the whole process again, quickly enough, and in such heat, with only four men was simply too much to contemplate.

It seemed to him that he could see movement above the rim of the near bank of the river; a green flag was being swept slowly back and forth in the hot breeze and at the same time a faint beating of drums came to his ears. The attack was coming at last. As he turned to order the others back to the cannon, the pensioner whom he had sent to the Collector hurried towards him, saluted and told him that the Collector Sahib could send no men or guns at present. "Collector Sahib very sorry and send this gentleman, Sahib." Harry looked at the figure who had followed the pensioner diffidently out on to the verandah. It was the Collector's manservant, Vokins.

Vokins gazed at him unhappily for a moment, but then a spent musket ball came humming through the air, struck the brickwork beside him and rolled towards his feet. He recoiled as if it were a scorpion, and fled back into the darkness of the banqueting hall to cower in a pile of bedding. But as his eyes grew accustomed to the gloom he became aware that this pile of bedding was, in fact, a pile of bodies, the result of the morning's work. After a brief debate with himself he decided it was best to venture outside again among the living.

11

The Collector was certainly worried about the banqueting hall; if he had only sent Vokins it was not because he doubted that Lieutenant Dunstaple was in difficulties, it was because the other three batteries and every inch of the rampart were in difficulties too. At first he had considered sending men from the Residency; the firing from the direction of the native town had been weak at first. It had even seemed as if the sepoys might be short of ammunition because they had been firing nails, bits of ramrod, even stones. But the fire had grown heavier and a twelve-pounder had begun to send round shot crashing through the upper storeys; then the enemy infantry had advanced into the native houses of dried mud surrounding the site of the demolished mosque. He cursed himself for not having had them levelled too; what he had not realized was that earth makes better material for fortification than masonry, which shatters, cracks and sends out splinters like shrapnel.

Soon after nine o'clock the Collector set out for the Cutcherry to see how they were getting on there. He took a cane and a pith helmet; in the buttonhole of his coat he wore a pink rose which one of the ladies had given him the evening before. He was pleased with the rose; it helped him to appear calm and cheerful. Now that the defence of the Residency had begun his main function must be to keep up the morale of the garrison. With this in mind he walked over to the Cutcherry as if he were going for a morning stroll, paying no attention whatsoever to the musket balls which sometimes droned by. He even paused on the way to inspect the odd collection of animals that had gathered to shelter from the sun in the shadow of the Church.

They were dogs mainly, but there was also a mongoose or two and even a monkey with a bell round its neck and a sailor cap fastened to its head with elastic. The Collector thought he recognized one of the dogs as belonging to Dr Dunstaple from having seen it run against one of his own dogs (Towser, 1852–55, much loved but now dead and buried beside the sundial with a little gravestone all of his own, RIP) at a meeting of the North of India Coursing Club. This dog of the Doctor's, Towser's former adversary, was a brown mongrel ... although he had run remarkably fast and close, the Collector recalled, and had even jerked the hare, in the end he had let her go and she had escaped into a sugar-cane khet. So there had been no kill. But now he seemed to recognize the Collector for he sat up among the other somnolent dogs, amongst whom Chloë was dozing, and gave a little bark, staring up at him with intelligent brown eyes as he moved on.

A few yards away, still in the shadow of the Church, was another collection of dogs, uncivilized ones this time and dreadful to behold. In spite of the years he had spent in the East the Collector had never managed to get used to the appearance of the pariah dogs. Hideously thin, fur eaten away by mange to the raw skin, endlessly and uselessly scratching, timorous, vicious, and very often half crippled, they seemed like a parody of what Nature had intended. He had once, as it happened, on landing for the first time at Garden Reach in Calcutta, had the same thought about the human beggars who swarmed at the landing-stage; they, too, had seemed a parody. Yet when the Collector piously gave to the poor, it was to the English poor, by a fixed arrangement with his agent in London; he had accepted that the poverty of India was beyond redemption. The humans he had got used to, in time ... the dogs never.

A musket ball striking a puff of dust from the Church wall reminded him of his duties, however, and he passed on towards the Cutcherry with a dignified step, thinking that the pets, too, had been a mistake ... he should never have allowed them into the enclave. There was no ration for dogs ... nor, come to that, for monkeys or mongooses; they would all starve unless relief came soon ... or their masters would share their own food with them and all would starve together. It would have been better to have shot them all. But a civilized man does not shoot his dog ... his "best friend". Yes, but these were exceptional circumstances. Now there was even talk of shooting wives if the situation became hopeless, to spare them a worse fate at the hands of the sepoys.

The dogs, both pets and pariahs, slumbered on uneasily, tongues lolling in the great heat, while the Collector disappeared on his way towards the rattle of rifle fire and the crashing of artillery. A little later, if they had had the energy to lift their heads from their paws, they might have seen him coming back. He looked just the same, more or less, though now he was walking more quickly and did not pause to notice them. The pink rose he was wearing had withered in his buttonhole in the few minutes it had been exposed to the hot wind and sun.

He went straight to his study when he got back to the Residency, closed the door and drank off a glass of brandy. He had done what he had intended: he had made a confident tour of the Cutcherry buildings; he had spoken encouragingly to the men firing through the windows from behind stacks of records and documents (an excellent protection from musket fire); he had visited the half dozen wounded who had been removed to the Magistrate's office until they could be conveyed to the library in the Residency, where the hospital had been provisionally established; he had even gone outside to speak to the men at the rampart. But now he needed to marshal his courage again.

He was standing at his desk with the empty glass in his hand when a stray musket ball ricocheted off *"The Spirit of Science Conquers Ignorance and Prejudice"* by the window. He instantly dropped to the floor in fear. He could hear that musket ball droning about the room, lethally bisecting it again and again like a billiard ball going from one cushion to another. He remained crouching there for a long time before he was able to convince himself that it was quite impossible, physically speaking, scientifically speaking, for a musket ball to go on and on ricocheting like that in a rectangular room; it could only be his imagination. So he forced himself to stand up again and suffered no ill-effects; a small but significant triumph for the scientific way of looking at things. Presently he felt sufficiently restored to make another confident sortie, this time to encourage the men in Dunstaple's battery.

"Save, Lord, or else we perish. The living, the living, shall praise thee . . ."

At the banqueting hall the little garrison was standing to arms, waiting for the enemy assault. Loaded Enfield rifles had been propped against the balustrade and the cannon loaded with canister. While they waited Harry had been giving some elementary instruction in the use of the Enfield rifle to Fleury, Barlow and Vokins; he had explained that this rifle was the 1853 model, three grooves, with a cartridge of two and a half drams exploded by percussion cap. To hit a human figure at 100 yards you aim at the waist. At 150 yards raise the sliding bar, raise the sight and aim with the 200 yards point at the thigh. At 200 yards aim at the waist with the 200 yards point. At 300 yards aim at the waist with the three hundred yards point. Any questions? No, there did not seem to be any questions. Vokins's teeth were chattering in spite of the heat and he looked like someone in whose mind thighs and waists and percussion caps and sliding bars had become inextricably entangled. Fleury, his mind a hopeless jumble of figures, was wool-gathering again, though trying to look politely interested, and was vaguely trying out various poses in his mind for daguerrotypes to appear in the *Illustrated London News*. Only Barlow seemed to have been taking an intelligent interest.

"How do you judge distances?" asked Harry disagreeably. "I suppose you all must know since nobody had any questions." They all looked chastened so Harry explained. At 1300 yards good eyesight can distinguish infantry from cavalry. A single individual detached may be seen at 1000 yards but his head does not appear as a round ball until 700 yards, at which distance white cross-belts and white trousers may be seen. At 500 yards the face may be seen as a light coloured spot and limbs, uniform and firelocks can be made out. At 250 and 200 yards details of body and uniform are tolerably clear. "Or alternatively, Vokins, you multiply the number of seconds which elapse between the time of seeing the flash of the enemy's musket and hearing the report by 1100 and the product will be the distance in feet. Have you got that?"

"And the product will be the distance in feet," mumbled Vokins impressively, but with an air of complete incomprehension. He was spared any further inquisition by the sudden appearance of the Padre.

The Padre was looking more haggard and wild-eyed than ever. He had thought that he would never be able to reach the banqueting hall because he had had to cross the stretch of open lawn swept by musket fire and grape which lay between the Church and the hall and which he had thought of as the Slough of Despond. How naked one feels and how small! Crossing such a piece of land, like navigating the rocks, reefs and shoals of life, one feels that of oneself one is nothing. One's only protection is in the Lord. The living, the living, shall praise thee! The Lord had been like a strong shield to him and had covered his head in the day of battle.

The Padre explained all this and more to the little garrison. They were glad of prayers. They felt that the more prayers they heard the better. But they became a little impatient as the Padre rambled on about Sin. What he said was true, no doubt, but they had the enemy to think of . . . It was rather like having someone keep asking you the time when your house is on fire. They found it hard to give him their whole attention.

But something else was rankling in the Padre's mind. This was the thought that, if they were being punished now, as Sodom and Gomorrah had been punished, it might be because there was not only Sin but Heresy in their midst. And so he led Fleury into the banqueting hall, asked him to kneel while he said a prayer over the pile of bodies, and then asked him why he had objected to hearing God described as the designer of the world.

"Do you not think that God designed the world and everything that is in it?"

"Well," said Fleury, "it's not exactly that I don't believe it . . ." With the Padre's blue, unblinking eyes fixed on him he

155

found it hard to collect his thoughts. The Padre waited in silence for Fleury to continue. They had closed the doors and windows against the hot wind but the heat was no less intense. A cloud of flies surrounded each of them, battling constantly to land on their faces. They could hear the sound of boots on the flagstones outside and the occasional crack of a musket, but within even the flies were silent.

"If you believe, as you must, that God designed the world and everything in it, then why should you not proclaim it? Why should you not praise Him for these wonders He has created? I'm sure you read Paley at school."

"But I think," blurted Fleury suddenly, "that God has nothing to do with that sort of thing ... God is a movement of the heart, of the spirit, or conscience ... of every generous impulse, virtue and moral thought."

"Can you deny the indications of contrivance and design to be found in the works of nature ... contrivance and design which far surpasses anything we human beings are capable of? How d'you explain such indications? How d'you explain the subtle mechanism of the eye, infinitely more complex than the mere telescope that miserable humanity has been able to invent? How d'you explain the eel's eye, which might be damaged by burrowing into mud and stones and is therefore protected by a transparent horny covering? How is it that the iris of a fish's eye does not contract? Ah, poor, misguided youth, it is because the fish's eye has been designed by Him who is above all, to suit the dim light in which the fish makes his watery dwelling!"

A terrifying crash shook the building as a round shot struck the outside wall and brought down a shower of bricks, followed by a fine sprinkling of dust which sparkled in the thin beams of sunlight. But the Padre paid no attention to it.

"How d'you explain the Indian Hog?" he cried. "How d'you account for its two bent teeth, more than a yard long, growing upwards from its upper jaw?"

"To defend itself?"

"No, young man, it has two tusks for that purpose issuing from the lower jaw like those of a common boar ... No, the answer is that the animal sleeps standing up and, in order to support its head, it hooks its upper tusks on the branches of trees . . . for the Designer of the World has given thought even to the hog's slumbers!"

Hardly had the Padre's voice ceased to echo when Fleury heard a shout from outside and the sound of rifle fire from the rampart.

"Look here, I'm afraid I shall have to go!" shouted Fleury excitedly, dashing for the door. But the Padre sprang after him, crying: "Think of the stomach of the camel! Adapted to carry large quantities of water which it needs for the desert regions through which it frays its diurnal passage."

Blinded by the glare, Fleury groped for his sponge and took up his position at the cannon. The Padre, too, came out and stood there, as dazzled as a fish in bright light, muttering, as if to himself: "Think of the milk of the viviparous female!" Fleury pulled him down hurriedly into the protection of the philosophers; it occurred to him that the Padre had perhaps become delirious from heat and exhaustion.

But whether he was delirious or not, Harry needed practical as well as spiritual assistance from the Padre; so he dragged him to his feet again and set him to work with Vokins serving ammunition; Barlow and the second native pensioner, Mohammed, he ordered to take up positions on the verandah with rifles, while Fleury and Ram waited to take up sponge and ramrod once more. Now the rifle fire from the rampart to right and left of their position redoubled; the sepoys could be seen swarming over the near bank of the river as they began their assault. Harry and Fleury had laid their sabres beside them on the parapet; they had decided that should their defences be overrun they would sell their lives as dearly as possible, rather than trying to bolt for it . . . Fleury had succeeded (but only with difficulty) in overcoming certain qualms as to whether selling one's life as dearly as possible, or even putting it up for sale at all, was, in fact, the wisest course.

Although the enemy were now plainly in sight and advancing steadily over the open ground Harry held his fire. Canister shot consists of lead balls loosely packed into cylindrical tin canisters, whose tops are soldered on, and bottoms nailed to a wooden shoe to prevent "windage" (that is, the escape of the propellant gases around the shot); although very destructive from a hundred to two hundred yards, at a distance of more than three hundred the shot scatter so much as to be almost useless. Fleury did not know this and kept glancing at Harry, wondering what he was waiting for. He felt tired, lightheaded, thirsty, and wretched; now that he could see the glinting sabres of the sepoy cavalry he did not feel nearly as brave as he had expected. He was further unnerved by the Padre who in spite of their predicament, or even because of it, had not ceased to mutter urgent evidence of the Designer's telltale hand ... The instinct which causes butterflies to lay their eggs on cabbages which, not the butterfly itself, but the caterpillar from its egg, requires for nourishment. (But, wondered Fleury, distraught, why had the Designer not simply designed butterflies to eat cabbages too?).

The Padre's eyes searched Fleury's troubled countenance for signs that his resistance was beginning to weaken. For the Padre could not help imagining a situation where the combined Sin of the garrison hung in the balance against such virtue as they could muster made heavier by the Grace and Mercy of God. In this situation Fleury's refusal to acknowledge His patent could only displease the Inventor and would doubtless weigh very heavy indeed on the side of Sin. If the Padre could shift that weight, perhaps, who could say? the scales might tip against the sepoys.

"Think how the middle claw of the heron and cormorant is notched like a saw! Why? Because these birds live by catching fish and the serrated edges help them to hold their slippery prey!"

Now a stomach-turning howl rose from the advancing natives; the *sowars* spurred forward, the infantry broke into a trot, bayonets at the ready; behind them a curtain of yellow dust climbed into the heat-distorted air. At two hundred yards Harry gave Ram the order to fire; once again there was a crash that sent the debris dancing on the flagstones; but this time there was no round shot or shrapnel shell to be seen sailing towards the river ... only a solid-looking ball of smoke driven from the muzzle by a jet of flame. Yet now they saw the dreadful effect as the oncoming men and horses were sprayed with the invisible lead balls. The fierce cry became swollen with the shrieks of the wounded ... The charge faltered, then continued as the wave of dust rolled forward and swallowed up the scene of carnage.

They worked desperately to re-load the cannon. Fleury sponged and then primed the vent with a shaking hand that scattered powder everywhere, while the Padre, his puny ecclesiastical arms scarcely able to heft such a burden, handed the morbid canister to Ram, and Harry spun the elevating screw until it marked point blank.

But how few seconds it takes a galloping horseman to cover two hundred yards! Already, by the time Harry, grabbing the portfire in his excitement, had touched it to the vent, the leading *sowars* had ridden under the muzzle and were spurring along the rampart lopping the heads off Eurasians and planters as if they had been dandelions. But again the gun vomited its metal meal into the faces of the advancing sepoys, this time into the very midst of their cavalry. Men and horses melted into the ground like wax at the touch of its searing breath. Death, whirring on its great pinions high above, plummeted down to seize its prey.

Again they wrenched and prodded and fumbled to load the six-pounder. Fleury's hand was now shaking so much that he seemed to spray priming powder everywhere but in the vent and Harry prayed that there would be enough to fire the charge, for if it failed there would be no second chance. He could now see the silhouettes of the sepoy infantry as they plunged through the veil of dust with sparkling bayonets.

"Even among insects God has not left himself without witness," wailed the Padre. "Is not the proboscis of the bee designed for drawing nectar from flowers?"

Harry touched the portfire to the vent and in front of the rampart the advancing infantry, like the legs of a monstrous millipede whose body was hidden in the dust cloud above them, collapsed all together, writhed, and lay still. The men behind who were still on their feet hesitated, unable to see what lay ahead of them in the dust. All they could see was the looming shape of the banqueting hall and, startling in their clarity, two vast, white faces, calmly gazing towards them with expressions of perfect wisdom, understanding and compassion.

The sepoys quailed at the sight of such invincible superiority.

"Come on," shouted Harry, and grasping their sabres he and Fleury blundered through the dark banqueting hall and out into the light again. Here they were met with a terrible sight, two *sowars* were in the act of cleaving the skull of the last of the Eurasian defenders. Harry grasped a riderless horse, swung himself into the saddle and charged headlong as the two *sowars* turned away from their fatal business; but they were both ready for him and both cut at him simultaneously as he was sent flying by the momentum with which his horse came into contact with theirs. One cut missed, the other laid open his tunic at the breast. He lay still and the *sowars* turned away, leaving him for dead. Meanwhile, in unmilitary fashion, Fleury had come hareing up behind them on tiptoe and now he dealt the nearest a blow in the face which dropped him from his horse. The other *sowar* promptly spurred after Fleury with his lance, driving his horse up the steps of the banqueting hall, chasing him in and out of the "Greek" pillars and then down the steps again, so close that Fleury could feel the horse's nostrils hot on his neck. On the bottom step Fleury stumbled opportunely as the man drove forward with his lance; at the same time he managed to grasp the lance and drag the man out of the saddle. His head and shoulder hit the ground with such force that his collar-bone snapped and he was dragged away screaming over the rampart by the stirrups to vanish into the cloud of dust.

Fleury now was gasping for breath, but ready to congratulate himself. He sat down on the bottom step with his head between his knees trying to recover. Looking up, however, he found a giant, bearded sepoy standing a yard in front of him, his sabre already raised to despatch him . . . somehow he managed to parry the blow and struck at the sepoy, but the sepoy turned his sabre with ease, twisted it out of his hand and threw it away, grinning. Fleury unhopefully punched at the bearded face with his bare fists, an attack which unfortunately passed unnoticed by the sepoy who was busy preparing to deal a death blow with his own sabre. Fleury, too weak to run, watched his adversary fascinated. The sepoy seemed to swell as he drew back his sword; he grew larger and larger until it seemed that his tunic, on which Fleury could see the unfaded marks left from where he had ripped the insignia of his rank in the Company's army, must burst; his face grew redder and redder, as he raised his sabre in both hands, as if his motive were not merely to kill Fleury but to chop him in two, length-wise, with one stroke. But the stroke was never delivered. Instead, he removed his eyes from Fleury's terrified face and dropped them to his own stomach, for a bright tip of metal had suddenly sprung out of it, a little to the right of his belly button. Both he and Fleury stared at it in astonishment. And then the sepoy stopped swelling and began to shrivel. Soon he was normal size again. But he continued to shrivel until, sud-denly, he dropped out of sight revealing Harry's rather earnest features peering at Fleury to see if he was alright.

"I think we've got rid of them all for the time being," he said, putting a foot in the small of the sepoy's back to withdraw his sabre. "The infantry turned, thank Heaven!"

"Think how apt fins are to water, wings to air, how well the earth suits its inhabitants!" exclaimed the Padre, suddenly appearing at Fleury's side as if conjured up by this reference to Heaven. "In everything on earth we see evidence of design. Turn from your blindness, I beg you in His name. Everything, from fish's eye, to caterpillar's food, to bird's wing and gizzard, bears manifest evidence of the Supreme Design. What other explanation can you find for them in your darkness?"

Fleury stared at the Padre, too harrowed and exhausted to speak. Could it not be, he wondered vaguely, trembling on the brink of an idea that would have made him famous, that some-how or other fish designed their own eyes?

But no, that was, of course, quite impossible. So he sub-mitted to the Padre. But although the evidence of Divine Design could not seriously be questioned, he still thought ... well, it was more a matter of feeling really ... But the Padre was too overjoyed that Fleury's ears should have at last been opened to the truth to listen to his equivocations about feelings and emo-tions. He sank down, his knees using the chest of the bearded sepoy as a hassock, and gave thanks, for the sepoys had been repulsed at every quarter.

"We gat not this by our own sword," he sang in explanation, "neither was it our own arm that saved us: but thy right hand, and thine arm, and the light of thy countenance, because thou hadst a favour unto us."

13

The Collector had risen a little before dawn. While eating breakfast in the company of his two eldest daughters he made one or two brief, factual entries in his diary under the heading of the previous day, Thursday, 11 June. Breakfast was the main meal of the day and consisted of roast mutton, chapatis, rice and jam. As it stood, the ration of meat, bone included, was sixteen ounces for the men and twelve for the ladies and children, together with an allowance of rice, flour and *dal* for those, now the majority, who had no provisions of their own. Under the date of 12 June, which was today, the Collector recorded his intention to consult Mr Rayne, who was in charge of the Commissariat, about a possible further reduction of the ration. He was coming to realize that in the end it might be hunger rather than the sepoy cannons which proved their undoing. Leaderless, the various contingents of sepoys were finding it increasingly difficult to mount concerted attacks. "Settle trouble among the ladies," he added beneath the note about rations.

With ladies still in his mind he went through into the dressing-room to comb his mustache and pour oil on the stormy sea of his side-whiskers. By this time it was broad daylight and the hot wind which made the day unbearable was already sighing through the rooms and corridors of the Residency; from the window of the dressing-room he could see the horses of the Sikh cavalry, tethered in the lee of the verandah to protect them from sun and shot beginning to stamp restlessly as the first gusts swirled round them. "Poor beasts. This is none of their quarrel."

He tied his cravat with care, plumping it out with his fingers and fastening it with a Madras pearl; as he did so he remembered with displeasure that Vokins was not there to brush his coat and help him on with it. His displeasure increased as he passed through again into the bedroom and caught sight of his daughters, Eliza and Margaret, with whom he had just taken breakfast, already looking alarmed on his behalf, for they had come to dread his daily tours of the ramparts which now took up the whole day and very often did not finish until after dark. He noticed with irritation that the brass telescope with which they kept an anxious watch for him from the window as he made his rounds had been laid on the table in readiness for the day.

As he went to the chest in which he had ordered their personal store of food to be kept, he thought, baffled, that it was absurd, all this emotion! Although, of course, it was right that they should love and respect him as their father, what did they really know of him? His real self was a perfect stranger to them. "May I always accept Papa's decisions with a good heart, without seeking to oppose them with my own will," one of them (it was a symptom of his difficulty that he could not remember which) had written piously in her diary. This dutiful phrase had surprised him. It had never occurred to him that either of the girls had a will which might in any circumstances wish to oppose itself to his own. He often thought that he would have liked to understand them better, but how could he? "Is it my fault that they never reveal themselves to me?"

The Collector strode along the wide verandah towards the billiard room carrying a parcel and with the twin devotions of his daughters clinging to him like limpets. The billiard room was long enough to contain two tables end to end and still leave ample room for the players to move about without getting in each other's way; indeed, it would have been possible to fit a third table in without discomfort. At each end there was a tall window, for the room spanned the Residency, breadthways; the ceiling, very high for the sake of coolness, bore elaborate plaster mouldings of foliage in the English fashion. This had once been one of his favourite rooms but now he dreaded to enter. Indeed, he had to pause a moment to compose himself for the inevitable assault on his senses.

Even before he had stepped over the threshold the first of his senses had come under attack. The noise in this room was deafening, especially if you compared it, as the Collector did, with how it used to be in the days when it had been reserved for billiards. Ah, then it had been like some gentle rustic scene

... the green meadows of the tables, the brown leather of the chairs, and the gentlemen peacefully browsing amongst them. Then there had been no other sound but the occasional click of billiard balls or the scrape of someone chalking his cue. Above the green pastures the billowing blue clouds of cigar smoke had drifted gently by beneath the ceiling like the sky of a summer's day. But now, alas, the ears were rowelled by high-pitched voices raised in dispute or emphasis; the competition here was extreme for anyone with anything to say: it included a number of crying children, illicit parrots and mynah birds.

It was now the turn of his eyes to take offence. This room, so light, so airy, so nobly proportioned, had been utterly transformed by the invasion of the ladies. A narrow aisle led down the middle of the room to the first table, on which the two pretty Misses O'Hanlon had formed the habit of sleeping clasped in each other's arms; now they were sitting cross-legged on their bedding in chemises and petticoats playing some silly game which caused them every now and again to clasp their hands to their mouths, stifling mirthful shrieks. The aisle continued to the next table, which had only one occupant, old Mrs Hampton, the Padre's mother. She was very fat, short-sighted and almost helpless, unable to get off the table unaided. As the Collector entered she was sitting in her muddled bedding, peering unhappily around her as if marooned. On each side of the aisle charpoys or mattresses or both together had been set down higgledy-piggledy, in some cases partitioned off from their neighbours by sheets suspended from strings that ran from the wall to the chandeliers, or from one string to another. "Ah, the soft and milky rabble of womankind! How true!"

As he advanced down the aisle, not without difficulty because trunks, clothing, work-baskets and other possessions had overflowed into it from either side, a third of his senses was assaulted: this time his sense of smell ... Near the door there was a powerful smell of urine from unemptied chamber-pots which thankfully soon gave way to a feminine smell of lavender and rose water ... a scent which mingled with the smell of perspiration to irritate his senses. It made him conscious of the fact that many of the ladies were, when one thought about it, attractive young women, some of whom were only partly

clothed or not wearing stockings, or perhaps still altogether unclothed behind their flimsy, inadequate screens. He advanced
between them with a deliberately heavy and paternal step,
glimpsing an occasional movement of white skin which, because it was not clear what part of the body it might belong to
(and might, for all one could tell, belong to an intimate part),
he could not help feeling aroused by. He thought sternly:
"Really, they behave, here in their private territory, with as
little modesty and restraint as, in public, with sobriety."

"Mrs Rayne," he boomed with a severity born of this unwel-
come stimulation. "Could you please open the window? The
doctors have ordered them to be left open during the day to
guard against an epidemic from bad air and our cramped conditions." The authority of his tone silenced the chatter, but his
words produced some faint moans of protest and rebellion.
They were so hot already ! If the hot wind was allowed to
blow through the room it became intolerable. They could not
suffer it! "And a mouse ran over me last night!" cried Miss
Barlow, the daughter of the Salt Agent. "I felt its nasty,
scratchy little feet on my face."

"The *dhobi* has begun to charge an outrageous price, Mr
Hopkins," complained a sleepy voice from behind one of the
hanging sheets. "Can nothing be done to stop him?"

The Collector, suspecting that this was the voice of the passive, lovely, pregnant, perpetually weary Mrs Wright, widow
of a railway engineer, experienced another annoying twinge of
desire, and after listening to some further grievances relieved
his feelings by delivering an unusually stern homily.

The cause of the trouble among the ladies was, as he suspected, not simple but compound. Many of the ladies were
now having to look after themselves for the first time in their
lives. They had to fetch their own water from the well behind
the Residency when they wanted to wash. They had to light
fires for themselves (sometimes the old gentlemen from the
drawing-room helped them in this but they took such a long
time about it that the ladies found it almost easier to do it for
themselves) and to boil their own kettles for tea. The two
dhobis who had remained within the Residency enclave were
now beginning to profit by their loyalty and had been able to
treble their prices, it seemed, without diminishing their custom

... those ladies unable, or unwilling, to pay such prices were having to wash their own clothing, and perhaps that of their menfolk as well. And now combine all these painful, unaccustomed chores with the conditions in which they were having to live ... delicate creatures accustomed to punkahs and *khus tatties*, now exposed all day long to the hot wind which, incidentally, rendered the few punkahs still in motion quite useless! No wonder they were in such a poor frame of mind.

There were other grievances, however. One of the older ladies, Mrs Rogers, had been turned out of the private room she had been sharing with her husband to make way for a lady expecting her confinement, and she was very cross indeed at finding herself in the middle of what she did not hesitate to call, echoing the Collector's own thoughts, "a rabble". The ladies in the billiard room had divided themselves into groups according to the ranks of husbands or fathers. Mrs Rogers, who was the wife of a judge, found herself unable to join any of the groups because of her elevated rank, and so she was in danger of starving to death immediately, for to make things easier rations were issued collectively, a fact which had undoubtedly hastened this social stratification. The Collector had to address Mrs Rogers personally and in the hearing of the other ladies on the subject of the "unusual circumstances" which required certain sacrifices ... but he knew very well that Mrs Rogers, having established at least symbolically her superior social position, would be only too glad now to join more lowly ladies. For up to now the deference to which she was entitled, but which she had found difficulty in exacting, had been a dreadful weight in these "unusual circumstances" for poor Mrs Rogers to carry.

But all was not harmony even within these groups for in the most lowly of them the Collector had to settle one of the most serious problems of all; this was caused by the fact that the spoiled Mrs Lacy, who although not yet nineteen was already a widow (her husband having been killed at Captainganj), had a Portuguese maid. A row had developed because Mrs Lacy had felt justified in keeping her maid occupied exclusively with her own comfort, while the other ladies believed that the girl's services should be shared. The Collector found Mrs Lacy in tears, the ladies round her looking sulky, and the Portuguese

167

girl looking distressed to be the cause of so much strife. The Collector was not troubled by the democratic notion that in the "unusual circumstances" the Portuguese girl might have enough on her hands simply looking after herself; he solved the problem by a judicious division of the girl's labours. She should do certain things for the group in common, certain things for Mrs Lacy alone. Mrs Lacy dried her red eyes, satisfied that her honour at least had been vindicated.

Lucy Hughes provided a problem which the Collector was unable to solve. She was ostracized even by the members of the lowest group, in fact, by everyone except Louise. The *charpoy* on which she had spread her bedding had been pushed to the very end of the room, beneath the oven blast of the open window. It was the only bed that had any space around it, for even Louise's bed, which was next to hers, stood at a small, but eloquent distance.

All the younger women except Lucy had crowded round him closely to hear him speak; Lucy sat alone on her bed, hugging her knees plaintively. She seemed to be close to tears and the Collector felt sorry for her ... but he had so many other matters to think of. To make things more difficult his earlier stirrings of sensuality returned as he looked around the circle of young women who had come so close to him. Their flushed, rice-powdered faces gazed up at him trustingly, even provocatively ... he felt that he had a power over them, even the most virtuous of them, for no other reason than that he was a man (any man in his position would have had this same power). He thought: "Crowding them together like this has a strange effect on them ... it seems to excite their feminine nature."

Pleased with this scientific observation, he allowed himself for a moment to enjoy the sexual aura of which he was the centre and which was so strong that he could somehow feel, without actually having to touch them, the softness of these feminine bodies, clothed only in soft muslin or cotton and unprotected by the stays and spine-pads habitually worn even by the youngest of them outside the privacy of this room. But all too soon his conscience was awakened by the looks of disapproval cast in his direction by some of the older ladies, who had thought it improper to crowd close to him. So far his sense of touch had been exercised only in imagination but at this moment a round shot struck the outside wall in an adjoining room a few yards away. The sudden noise caused two of these young bodies to cling to him for a moment ... and he could not restrain his large hands from comforting them. By the window a shower of brick dust slowly descended on Lucy's lonely head and she began to cry.

Now it was time for him to unwrap the parcel he had brought with him, which contained a large quantity of flour, suet and jam from his private Residency store. This was to be divided equally between the groups, so that each could make a roly-poly pudding. He watched in wonder the excitement that this announcement provoked, the eagerness with which the younger ladies set about dividing it up, laughing like children and clapping their hands in anticipation. "It's true," he mused, "they're just like children."

Sometimes they exasperated him with their vulnerability, their pettiness. But they lived such sheltered, useless lives, even their children were given to *ayahs* to look after. What could one expect of them? At the best of times they had so little to occupy their hands and minds. And now, during the siege, it was worse; whatever tendencies had already existed in the characters of those who made up the garrison, the siege had exaggerated (this was another pleasing scientific observation which he must remember to pass on to the Magistrate). "They wait all day for their husbands to come. They have no resources of their own."

His mission accomplished, he turned to leave. But his sense of taste, which had so far escaped the assault on the other four, was now confronted with a hastily brewed cup of tea in a child's christening mug (for lack of china) and a rock bun. He drank the tea and nibbled a little of the bun, but asked permission to save the rest to sustain him as he made his daily round. He took it with him, wrapped in a piece of paper, with the secret intention of giving it to the Doctor's mongrel, poor Towser's friend and rival of yester-year, if he met him during the day.

He slowly descended the stairs, no longer noticing the landslide of furniture, boxes, curios, antlers, rowing oars and other trophies, but thinking: "Women are weak, we shall always

169

have to take care of them, just as we shall always have to take care of the natives; no doubt, there are exceptions ... women of character like Miss Nightingale, but not unfortunately like Carrie or Eliza or Margaret ... Even a hundred years from now ..." the Collector feebly tried to imagine 1957 ... "It will still be the same. They are made of a softer substance. They arouse our desire, but they are not our equals."

As he went out on to the portico and down the steps the sunlight once again smote him painfully, like a solid substance. Above, at the bedroom window he knew that Eliza and Margaret would be weakly waiting with the brass telescope which they used throughout the livelong day to watch over him lest any harm should befall him as he made his leisurely progress round the defences.

Later in the morning the Collector found himself reclining in a mass of paper documents on the floor of the vernacular record room in the company of the Magistrate and of Fleury, who had been permitted a temporary absence from his post as no attack seemed imminent. A strange contentment had settled over the Collector, perhaps because his senses, usually kept under lock and key, had enjoyed their unaccustomed exercise that morning, perhaps because he was most comfortably supported by the documents. There were salt reports bound in red tape under each elbow; a voluminous, but extraordinarily comfortable correspondence with a local landowner concerning the Permanent Settlement cradled his back at just the right angle, and opium statistics, rising to a mound beneath his knees and cushioning the rest of his body, filled him with a sense of ease verging on narcosis. From outside, a few yards away, came the regular discharge of cannons and mortars; but inside, such was the thickness of the paper padding, one felt very safe indeed. True, daylight appeared in places where holes had been made by round shot in the brickwork, but even that could be looked on as an advantage for it provided ventilation and prevented pockets of bad air forming; elsewhere it had become necessary to burn camphor and brown paper.

The Collector had been discoursing in an objective way on the perplexing question of why, after a hundred years of beneficial rule in Bengal, the natives should have taken it into their heads to return to the anarchy of their ancestors. One or two mistakes, however serious, made by the military in their handling of religious matters, were surely no reason for rejecting a superior culture as a whole. It was as if, after the improving rule of the Romans, the Britons had decided to paint themselves with woad again. "After all, we're not ogres, even though we don't marry among the natives or adopt their customs."

"I must take issue with the expression 'superior culture'," said Fleury; but neither of the older men paid any attention to him.

"The great majority of natives have yet to see the first sign of our superior culture," said the Magistrate. "If they're lucky they may have seen some red-faced youth from Haileybury or Addiscombe riding by once or twice in their lives."

("I say, 'superior culture' is a very doubtful proposition, but I think . . .")

"Come, come, Tom, think of the system of justice that the Company has brought to India. Even if there were nothing else . . ."

"This justice is a fiction! In the Krishnapur district we have two magistrates for almost a million people. There are many districts where it's worse."

("Look here, what I think . . .")

"Things are not yet perfect, of course," sighed the Collector. "All the same, I should go so far as to say that in the long run a superior civilization such as ours is irresistible. By combining our advances in science and in morality we have so obviously found the best way of doing things. Truth cannot be resisted! Er, that's to say, not successfully," the Collector added as a round shot struck the corner of the roof and toppled one of the pillars of the verandah.

"But what I think is this," declared Fleury when the rubble had ceased to fall, determined at last to get his word in. "It's wrong to talk of a 'superior civilization' because there isn't such a thing. *All* civilization is bad. It mars the noble and natural instincts of the heart. Civilization is decadence!"

"What rubbish!"

"I have seldom heard such gibberish," agreed the Collector, chortling as he got to his feet. "By the way, what on earth are you dressed like that for?"

Somewhat taken aback by the speed with which his theories had been dismissed, Fleury could not at first think what the Collector was talking about. All the same, he was indeed rather oddly dressed in a blue velvet smoking jacket and tasselled smoking cap. He had brought them out with him, assuming that in India, as in England, gentlemen wore such garments while smoking in order to protect their clothes and hair from a smell offensive to the ladies. It had turned out that in India no one took the trouble ... one of the many ways, alas, in which Indian society failed to live up to the rigorous standards set at home. With the shortage of clothes becoming acute Harry had found himself unable to replace his ripped tunic, so Fleury had generously given him the "Tweedside", which he had taken a fancy to and which, in any case, Fleury had been finding oppressively warm ... not that the smoking jacket was much cooler. As for the tasselled cap, he had improved it by attaching a flannel flap to the back to protect his neck from the sun, and a visor to the front, fashioned from the black cardboard binding of a book of sermons lent him by the Padre. The title of this book, inscribed in gothic letters of gold, glinted like braid as he accompanied the Collector out into the sunlight.

By contrast with the comfort of a few moments earlier the Collector suffered a painful return to reality as he stepped out into the glare. Worries, temporarily forgotten, assailed him once more ... still no sign of a relieving force! The dwindling garrison ... almost every day now someone was killed. The health of the garrison was beginning to deteriorate from the poor diet and lack of vegetables. Slight wounds became serious ... from serious wounds death was inevitable. He stood, blinking, outside the Cutcherry for a moment, appalled, unable to decided where to go next. But then, remembering that his daughters were very likely observing his dismay through the telescope and were perhaps even concluding that he had just been shot, he grasped Fleury by the arm and steered him towards the Residency; he needed someone's company to nerve himself for his daily visit to the hospital. Besides, he might take the opportunity to counter the demoralizing effect of the Magistrate's words on the young man's mind.

He began to say something about the principles behind a civilization being more important than the question of whether they were actually realized in a concrete manner . . . He had a firm grip on the arm of his audience, too, which is usually helpful when you have an argument to put across. But he found himself finishing what he had to say rather lamely, partly because Fleury was sulking over the rapid rejection of his own theories and refused to agree with him, partly because they were both chased into the lee of the hospital by an enemy rocket which careered down at them in wild loops out of the sky and, for an awful moment, seemed to be chasing them personally. Fortunately, it did not explode for it landed quite close to them, burying its cone-shaped iron head in the earth no more than ten yards away. Fleury indignantly began to prise it out of the earth with his sabre which was, perhaps, rather rash of him since smoke was still pouring from the vents in its case even if the fuse on its base appeared to be extinct. It was a six-pound Congreve rocket, one of many which had dived wildly into the enclave.

"One of the advantages of our civilization," said Fleury. But the Collector failed to grasp even this simple irony and observed mildly: "One of these days I'm afraid their rocketeers may hit something, if only by accident."

He continued to stand irresolutely beside the smoking rocket, thinking: "If we lose any more men we won't be able to man the defences adequately. Then we'll be in a pickle." At this moment Dr Dunstaple saw them through the window and sent a message out to ask Fleury if he would mind fetching half a dozen bottles of mustard from the Commissariat; he had another suspected case of cholera to deal with. Fleury hurried away and, after a short struggle with himself, the Collector made up his mind to enter the hospital.

The hospital had first been established in the Residency library, but this had proved too small and so it had been moved into the row of storehouses and stables immediately behind the Residency; this row of sheds had been roughly divided into two wards, one under the care of each doctor. Between the two wards what had, in happier days, been the saddle-room had been converted into an operating theatre where, surrounded by a mass of harness and saddlery, the two doctors united (at least, in principle) to perform amputations. Untidy stacks of *bhoosa* cattle feed piled up in the corners of the wards were another reminder that their former occupants had been quadrupeds and now provided a convenient refuge for rats and other vermin.

The door to Dr Dunstaple's ward stood open and even before the Collector had reached it the stench of putrefaction and chloroform had advanced to greet him. He moved forward, however, with an expression of good cheer on his face, while flies tried to crowd on to his smiling lips and eyes and swarmed thirstily on to his sweating forehead. At the far end of the ward he glimpsed the Padre kneeling in prayer beside a supine figure. As he passed into the acute stench rising from the nearest bed he clenched his fists in his pockets and prayed: "Please God, if I'm to die may I be killed outright and not have to lie in this infernal place!"

Dr Dunstaple, still waiting for Fleury to return with the bottles of mustard, had seen the Collector and came bustling forward, saying in a loud, exasperated tone: "Heaven knows what experiment that damn fella's up to now! Whatever it is, I wash my hands of it!"

The Collector gave him a worried look. In the few days since the siege had begun a disturbing change had come over the Doctor. In normal times the Collector found this fat little man endearing and slightly ridiculous. His arms and legs looked too short for his round body; his energy made you want to laugh. But recently his plump, good-humoured face had set into lines of bad temper and bitterness. His rosy complexion had taken on a deeper, unhealthy flush, and although clearly exhausted, he was, nevertheless, in a constant state of frenetic activity and fuss, talking now of one thing, now of another. There was something very harrowing about the way the Doctor passed from one subject to another without logical connection, yet what disturbed the Collector even more was the fact that he so often returned to the same topic: ... that of Dr McNab. Of course, he had always enjoyed making fun of McNab, retailing stories about drastic remedies for simple ailments and that sort

174

of thing. Alas, the Doctor had become increasingly convinced that McNab was experimenting, was ignoring his medical training to follow fanciful notions of his own.

Dr Dunstaple had begun to talk about the patient beside whose bed, a soiled straw mattress on a *charpoy*, the Collector found himself standing; the man was a Eurasian of very pale skin and dark eyes which feverishly swept the room. He was suffering, explained the Doctor in a rapid, overbearing tone as if expecting the Collector to disagree with him, from severe laceration, the result of a shrapnel burst, of the soft parts of the right hand; the thumb was partially detached near the upper end of the metacarpal bone. Though the lips of the wound were retracted and gaping there was no haemorrhage and it seemed possible that the deep arteries had escaped injury . . .

"Was that unreasonable to suppose?" demanded the Doctor suddenly. The Collector, who had been listening uncomfortably to these explanations, shook his head, but only slightly, not wanting to give the impression that he was passing judgement either one way or the other. At the same time he had become aware that another patient, an English private soldier who had escaped from Captainganj only to be wounded at Cutter's battery during the attack of the first of June, and who was strapped down to a *charpoy* near where the Padre was kneeling, had begun to sing, loudly and monotonously, as if to keep up his spirits. His song finished he immediately began it again, and so loudly as almost to drown the Doctor's vehement medical commentary:

"I'm ax'd for a song and 'mong soldiers 'tis plain,
I'd best sing a battle, a siege or campaign.
Of victories to choose from we Britons have store,
And need but go back to eight*een* fifty-four."

"A compress, dipped in cold water, placed on the palm after the edges of the wound had been evenly approximated and two or three interrupted sutures applied . . . then strapped, bandaged . . ."

"The Czar of all Russia, a potentate grand,
Would help the poor Sultan to manage his land;

But Britannia stept in, in her lady-like way,
To side with the weakest and fight for fair play."

"Stop that noise!" roared the Doctor. "Look here, Mr Hopkins, after twenty-four hours the integuments of the palm were flaccid and discoloured ... Imagine how I felt! If you put any pressure on the wound a thin, sanious fluid with bubbles of gas escaped, causing considerable pain ..."

"On Alma's steep banks, and on Inkermann's plain,
At famed Balaklava, the foe tried in vain
To wrest off the laurels that Britons long bore
But always got whopped in eighteen fifty-four ..."

"Then," said the Doctor, gripping the Collector's arm for he had stepped back, dizzy from the heat and smell, not to mention the noise (for, in addition to this desperate chanting there were groans and cries of men calling for attention), "the thumb was dark and cold and insensible. Another twelve hours and the dark hue of mortification had already spread over half the palm ... the thumb and two fingers were already cold, livid and without sensation ..."

"It's true at a distance they fought very well
With round shot and grape shot and rocket and shell
But when our lads closed and bayonets got play
They didn't quite like it and so ... ran away!"

"The pulse was small and frequent, the smell from the mortifying parts was particularly offensive, Mr Hopkins. I now advised amputation of the forearm, close to the carpal end ... *Silence!* I *had* thought that it would be enough to remove part of the hand only, but this was out of the question ... Ah, this wasn't good enough for McNab! He said gangrene must follow ... d'you hear? So for forty-eight hours it was left wrapped in a linseed poultice. This was not my idea. I knew the whole hand must come off in the end and that there would be no gangrene of the stump ... Here, sir, you can see for yourself the way the flaps are uniting in healthy granulations. D'you think that was McNab's linseed poultice? Had we waited a moment longer the man would have sunk completely!"

"No, no," broke in the Collector hurriedly. "Please don't

undo the dressing. I shall see it when you're discharged fit," he added brightly to the patient who paid no attention to him whatsoever; the man's eyes continued to roam about feverishly.

The Doctor tried to detain him for further explanations but the Collector forced him aside, unable to spend another moment by this bedside. He strode to the nearest window and looked out, clumsily knocking over a pitcher of water as he did so. It emptied itself in slow gulps on to the earthen floor by his feet. Beyond the deep shadow in which the horses of the Sikh cavalry stamped and thrashed in a frenzy of irritation from the flies which attacked them, he thought he could perceive a splash of colour from the few surviving roses beneath the shade of the wickerwork screens. He gazed at them greedily.

Then Fleury came into view, carrying the bottles of mustard and looking excited. Seeing the Collector at the window he called: "Mrs Scott has been taken ill."

The Collector immediately put his finger to his lips and shook his head vigorously, pointing towards the next ward, to indicate that Fleury should inform McNab. Fleury, however, simply stopped in his tracks and stared at the Collector in astonishment, unable to comprehend why the most important personage in the garrison should suddenly resort to this baffling pantomime. He came closer and the Collector, concluding that Fleury was a dimwit (a conclusion supported, moreover, by his peculiar ideas on civilization) said in an undertone: "Tell Dr McNab. Dunstaple already has too much to do. He must be spared. Here, give me those." And he took the bottles of mustard through the window, thinking: "What a time the poor mite has chosen to come into the world!"

The Doctor seemed surprised at first to be presented with the mustard and looked so irritated that the Collector wondered whether there had not been some mistake. But then the Doctor remembered, he had a case of cholera ... it was almost certainly cholera, though sometimes when the men first reported sick it was hard to know from their symptoms whether they were suffering from cholera or from bilious remittent fever.

Cholera. The Collector could see Dr Dunstaple's anger swelling, as if himself infected by the mere sound of the three syllables. And the Collector dreaded what was to come, for the subject of cholera invariably acted like a stimulant on the already overwrought Doctor. Cholera, evidently, had been the cause of the dispute between him and McNab which had brought about an unfortunate rift between the two doctors. Now he began, once again, to speak with a terrible eloquence about the iniquities of McNab's "experimental" treatments and quackery cures. Suddenly, he seized the Collector's wrist and dragged him across the ward to a mattress on which, pale as milk beneath a cloud of flies, a gaunt man lay shivering, stark naked.

"He's now in the consecutive fever ... How d'you think I cured this man? How d'you think I saved his life?"

The Collector offered no suggestions so the Doctor explained that he had used the best treatment known to medical science, the way he had been taught as a student, the treatment which, for want of a specific, every physician worthy of the name accorded his cholera patients ... calomel, opium and poultices, together with brandy as a stimulant. Every half hour he gave pills of calomel (half a grain), opium and capsicum (of each one-eighth of a grain). Calomel, the Collector probably didn't know, was an admirable aperient for cleansing the upper intestinal canal of the morbid cholera poison. At the same time, to relieve the cramps he had applied flannels wrung out of hot water and sprinkled with chloroform or turpentine to the feet, legs, stomach and chest, and even to the hands and arms. Then he had replaced them with flannels spread with mustard as his dispensers were now doing ... At this point the Doctor tried to pull the Collector to yet another bed, where a Eurasian orderly was spreading mustard thickly with a knife on the chest and stomach of yet another tossing, groaning figure. But the Collector could stand no more and, shaking himself free, made for the door with the Doctor in pursuit.

The Doctor was grinning now and wanted to show the Collector a piece of paper. The Collector allowed himself to be halted as soon as he had inhaled a draught of fresh air. He stared in dismay at the unnaturally bright flush of the Doctor's features, at the parody of good humour they wore, remembering many happier times when the good humour had been real.

"I copied it from the quack's medical diary ... With his permission, of course. He's always making notes. No doubt he thinks he will make an impression with them. Read it. It concerns a cholera case . . . He wrote it, I believe, in Muttra about three years ago. Go on. Read it . . ." And he winked encouragingly at the Collector.

The Collector took the paper with reluctance and read:

"She has almost no pulse.
Body as cold as that of a corpse.
Breath unbelievably cold, like that
from the door of an ice-cavern.
She has persistent cramps and vomits
constantly a thin, gruel-like fluid
without odour.
Her face has taken on a terribly cadav-
erous aspect, sunken eyes, starting
bones, worse than that of a corpse.
Opening a vein it is hard to get any
blood . . . what there is, is of a dark,
treacly aspect . . ."

The Collector looked up, puzzled. "Why d'you show me this?"

"That was his wife!" cried the Doctor triumphantly. "Don't you see, he takes notes all the time. Nothing will stop him . . . Even his wife! Nothing!"

Again, as the Collector put on his pith helmet and gave the brim a twitch, came the monotonous, desperate chanting he had heard before.

"Now, now my brave boys, that the Russian is shamed
Beat, bothered, and bowed down and peace is proclaimed,
Let's drink to our Queen, may she never want store,
Of heroes like those of eight*een* fifty-four."

14

From the beginning of the siege the Union Jack had floated from the highest point of the Residency roof and had constantly drawn the fire of the sepoy sharpshooters. Passing into the shadow of the Residency on his way to Cutter's battery, the Collector looked up and saw that the flag was once again in difficulties. The halyards had been severed and great splinters of wood had been struck off the shaft so that it looked as if a strong wind might well bring it down altogether. On one occasion, indeed, the staff had been completely shattered and a great cheer had gone up from the sepoys ... but as soon as darkness permitted, another staff and new halyards had been erected in its place. The flag was crucial to the morale of the garrison; it reminded one that one was fighting for something more important than one's own skin; that's what it reminded the Collector of, anyway. And somewhere up there, too, in the most perilous position of all within the enclave, there was an officer crouching all day behind the low brick wall of the tower, watching the movements of the sepoys with a telescope.

While the Collector's eyes had been lifted to the sky a loathsome creature had approached him along the ground; it was the hideous pariah dog, looking for Fleury. Since the Collector had last set eyes on the animal a ricocheting musket ball had taken off part of its rat-like tail, which now terminated in a repulsive running sore. The Collector launched a kick at it and it hopped away yelping.

As the Collector raised his eyes again for a last, inspirational glance at the flag before moving on, a dreadful smell of putrefaction was borne to his nostrils and he thought: "I must have something done about that tonight before we have an epidemic." This smell was no longer coming from the bodies of men and horses rotting outside the ramparts as it had done for the first few days; these, thank Heaven, had now been cleaned by the kites, vultures and jackals; it came from the dead horses and artillery bullocks that lay scattered over the Residency lawns and gardens, hit by the random shot and shells that unceasingly poured into the compound. But there was also a powerful and atrocious smell from behind the wall he had built to shield the croquet court, which lay between the Residency and Dunstaple's house. Here it was that Mr Rayne, aided by Eurasians from the opium agency, conducted the slaughter and butchery of the Commissariat sheep, commandeered at the outbreak of the mutiny from the Krishnapur Mutton Club on the Collector's instructions.

The smell, which was so atrocious that the butchers had to work with cloths tied over their noses, came from rejected offal which they were in the habit of throwing over the wall in the hope that the vultures would deal with it. But the truth was that the scavengers of the district, both birds and animals, were already thoroughly bloated from the results of the first attack ... the birds were so heavy with meat that they could hardly launch themselves into the air, the jackals could hardly drag themselves back to their lairs. And so, out of the garrison's sight, but not out of range of their noses, a mountain of corruption had steadily built up. Combined with the animals scattered on the lawns, the smells from the hospital and from the privies, and from the human beings living in too close contact with insufficient water for frequent bathing, an olfactory background, silent but terrible, was unrolling itself behind the siege.

The back wall of Dr Dunstaple's house, which like the Residency was built of wafer-like red bricks, had been amazingly pocked by the shot which dashed against it; hardly a square foot of smooth surface remained now to be seen. In some places round shot had smashed through one wall after another so that if you had been unwise enough to raise your head to the appropriate angle you could have followed their passage through a series of rooms. After one such journey, the Collector had been told, a shot had finally burst through the wall into the Doctor's drawing-room on the other side of the building, scattering candlesticks and dropping them to roll along the carpet, right up to where Mrs Dunstaple and a group of disobedient ladies playing truant from the suffocating air of the cellar were cowering under the piano. From these larger holes in the wall Enfield rifles bristled and occasionally orange flowers blossomed from their muzzles; the wall in the room behind them had been painted black so that no movement could be seen against them.

From the house a shallow trench had been dug out towards the crescent of earthworks behind which the cannons had been placed. Here, too, there was a pit about fourteen feet deep with a ladder against the side, down which the Collector now stiffly climbed. Lieutenant Cutter was standing at the bottom with his finger to his lips.

"Are they mining?"

"Yes. We're digging a listening gallery." Cutter described in a whisper what was happening: at the head of the gallery a man sat and worked with a short-handled pick or crowbar to loosen the earth; just behind him sat another man with an empty wine case to fill up with the loose earth; when full, this was drawn back by a rope.

The sepoys here were very close and it was thought inevitable that sooner or later they would begin mining, given the number of men at their disposal. For several nights the Collector had stayed up until dawn reading his military manuals by the light of an oil-lamp in his study to instruct himself in the art of military mining; only Cutter of the officers, two Cornish privates from Captainganj, and one or two Sikhs, had had any experience of mining before. What an advantage that knowledge can be stored in books! The knowledge lies there like hermetically sealed provisions waiting for the day when you may need a meal. Surely what the Collector was doing as he pored over his military manuals, was proving the superiority of the European way of doing things, of European culture itself. This was a culture so flexible that whatever he needed was there in a book at his elbow. An ordinary sort of man, he could, with the help of an oil-lamp, turn himself into a great military engineer, a bishop, an explorer or a General overnight, if the fancy took him. As the Collector pored over his manuals, from time to time rubbing his tired eyes, he knew that he was using science and progress to help him out of his difficulties and he was pleased. The inventions on his desk, the carriage which supplied its own track and the effervescent drinking vessel, watched him in silent admiration as he worked.

182

The Collector had learned that there are two cardinal rules of defensive mining ... One is that your branch galleries (whose purpose is for listening to the approaching enemy miners) should run *obliquely* forward in order not to present their sides to the action of enemy mines ... The other is that the distance between the ends of the branch galleries should be such that the enemy cannot burrow between them unheard (a distance which varies with the nature of the soil but which can be roughly taken as twenty yards).

The trouble with these cardinal rules, though wonderful in their way, was that they required a great deal of digging. No doubt they would have served perfectly if there had been enough men in the garrison to dig listening galleries in the approved manner, reaching towards the enemy like the spread fingers of a hand. But Cutter lacked men. The best he and the Collector had been able to devise was a single lateral tunnel, slightly crescent-shaped to follow the contour of the ramparts, and which more resembled the hook of a man whose hand had been amputated.

The Collector, at the head of the gallery, strained his ears despondently for the scrape of the sepoy picks, but the only sound that came to them was the ghostly echo of a phrase of Vauban he had read: *Place assiégée, place prise!* For the Collector knew the truth of the matter: the sepoys did not even have to resort to mining. By using their artillery to make a breach in the defences and then digging a properly directed series of saps to approach it, they would be able to take the Residency in a matter of days. It was a commonplace of siege-craft that there was no way of countering such a methodical attack except by making sorties to harass the enemy and destroy his works ... But where could he find the men to make sorties without hopelessly denuding the ramparts in several places?

Meanwhile Cutter, in a whisper, was explaining that he wanted to run an offensive gallery under the enemy lines and explode a mine of his own to breach their defences. With a sudden attack they might succeed in spiking or capturing the Sepoy cannons, in particular the eighteen-pounder which was slowly but surely reducing Dr Dunstaple's house to rubble. The Collector hesitated to agree to this ... There was another difficulty: the shortage of powder. Anything less than, say, two hundred pounds of powder at a depth of twelve feet underground would be insufficient to make the required breach. Yet with two hundred pounds of powder you could fire a cannon a hundred times! And the slightest error of length or direction would mean that all this valuable powder would be thrown away fruitlessly.

"Very well," he said at length, "but make sure it does what it's supposed to."

Later, as he walked away, he recalled a work by another French military engineer, Cormontaingne, who had described in his imaginary *Journal of the Attack of a Fortress* the inevitable progress of a siege through its various stages up to the thirty-fifth day, ending with the words: "It is now time to surrender." That, at least, was one option not open to the Collector.

The Collector, conscious of himself gently floating in the blue prism of his daughters' telescope like a snake in a bottle of alcohol, now had to cross the most dangerous piece of ground within the enclave. He strode out firmly, pulling down the peak of his pith helmet and lowering his head as if walking into a blizzard. It was here on this lawn, green and well-watered during the magnificent Indian winter, that he had been host to many enjoyable garden parties. Over there, beneath that group of now shattered eucalyptus trees, had stood the band of one of the infantry regiments. Once he had looked out from the upper verandah of the Residency as the bandsmen were assembling; it was evening and somehow the deep scarlet of their uniforms against the dark green of the grass had stained his mind with a serious joy . . . so that even now, in spite of everything, those two colours, scarlet and dark green, still seemed to him the indelible colours of the rightness of the world, and of his place in it. Looking towards the river as he skirted a shell crater, across a parched brown desert dotted with festering animals, he had to make an effort of imagination to perceive that this was indeed the same place where he and his guests had sat drinking tea.

From his pocket the Collector produced the last of his clean, white handkerchieves (soon he, too, would be in the power of the *dhobi* who had been terrorizing the ladies with his new prices) and held it to his nose while he considered a new and disagreeable problem. By now so many gentlemen had been killed that a large quantity of stores and other belongings had been collected. What he had to decide was whether to allow them to be auctioned, as they would have been in normal times, or to confiscate them for the good of the community. Ultimately, it seemed to him, the question boiled down to this: was it right that only those who had money to buy these provisions in the event of a famine should survive? The Magistrate was not the ideal person to ask for his view on such a matter. As the Collector had feared he had been unable to restrain his sarcasm.

"In the outside world people perish or survive depending on whether they have money, so why should they not here?"

"This is a different situation," the Collector had replied, scowling. "We must all help each other and depend on each other."

"And must we not outside?"

"People have more resources in normal times."

"Yet many perish even so, simply because they lack money."

The Collector's sigh was muffled by the handkerchief as he reached the fiercely humming rib-cage, head and flanks of a horse which had collapsed there with the saddle still strapped ludicrously to what was now only a rim of bones. Further on there was the carcase of a water buffalo, its eyes seething, its head and long neck looking as if they had literally been run into the ground. The Collector was fond of water buffaloes, which he found to have a friendly and apologetic air, but he could not think why there should have been one on his lawn.

By the time he had paid a visit to the banqueting hall the light was beginning to fade; on his way back, the Collector removed his pith helmet to air his scalp. It was his belief, based as yet on no scientific evidence, that lack of air to the scalp caused premature baldness; for this reason he had taken a particular interest in the hat shown at the Great Exhibition which had had a special ventilation valve in the crown; moreover, when the present troubles had started he had been considering the most delicate and interesting experiment to evaluate this suspicion and which would have involved hiring natives in large numbers to keep their heads covered and submit to certain statistical investigations.

At the thought of statistics, the Collector, walking through the chaotic Residency garden, felt his heart quicken with joy ... For what were statistics but the ordering of a chaotic universe? Statistics were the leg-irons to be clapped on the *thugs* of ignorance and superstition which strangled Truth in lonely byways. Nothing was able to resist statistics, not even Death itself, for the Collector, armed with statistics, could pick up Death, sniff it, dissect it, pour acid on it, or see if it was soluble. The Collector knew, for example, that in London during the second quarter of 1855 among 3,870 men of the age of 20 and upwards who had succumbed, there had been 2 peers of the realm, 82 civil servants, 25 policemen, 209 officers, soldiers and pensioners, 103 members of the learned professions including 9 clergymen, 4 barristers, 23 solicitors, 3 physicians, 12 surgeons, 43 men of letters, men of science or artists, and twelve eating- and coffee-house keepers ... and so much more the Collector knew. He knew that out of 20,257 tailors 108 had passed to a better world; that 139 shoemakers had gone to their reward out of 26,639 ... and that was still only a fraction of what the Collector could have told you about Death. If mankind was ever to climb up out of its present uncertainties, disputations and self-doubtings, it would only be on such a ladder of objective facts.

Suddenly, a shadow swooped at him out of a thin grove of peepul trees he was passing through. He raised a hand to defend himself as something tried to claw and bite him, then swooped away again. In the twilight he saw two green pebbles gazing down at him from beneath a sailor cap. It was the pet monkey he had seen before in the shadow of the Church; the animal had managed to bite and tear itself free of its jacket but the sailor hat had defied all its efforts. Again and again, in a frenzy of irritation it had clutched at that hat on which was written *HMS John Company* ... but it had remained in place. The string beneath its jaw was too strong.

Near the trees the Collector could see some dogs slumbering beside a well used by gardeners in normal times for the complicated system of irrigation which brought water to the Resi-

dency flower beds. He could recognize certain of these dogs
from having seen them in the station bobbery pack on their
way to hunt jackals with noisy, carefree young officers; they
included mongrels and terriers of many shapes and sizes but
also dogs of purer breed . . . setters and spaniels, among them
Chloë, and even one or two lap-dogs. What a sad spectacle
they made! The faithful creatures were daily sinking into a
more desperate state. While jackals and pariah dogs grew fat,
they grew thin; their soft and luxurious upbringing had not
fitted them for this harsh reality. If they dared approach the
carcase of a horse or bullock, or the fuming mountain of offal
beside the croquet wall, orange eyes, bristling hair and snap-
ping teeth would drive them away.

It was dark by the time the Collector's tour was over and the
night was brilliantly starlit. Tonight, as always, in the darkness
around the enclave he could see bonfires burning. Were they
signals? Nobody knew. But every night they reappeared. Other,
more distant bonfires could be seen from the roof, burning
mysteriously by themselves out there on the empty plain
where in normal times there was nothing but darkness.

During the daytime it had become the custom for a vast
crowd of onlookers to assemble on the hill-slope above the
melon beds to witness the destruction of the Residency. They
came from all over the district, as to a fair or festival; there
was music and dancing; beyond the noise of the guns the garrison could hear the incessant sighing of native instruments, of
flutes and sitars accompanied by finger-drums; there were merchants and vendors of food and drink, nuts, sherbets and sugar-
cane . . . sometimes a caprice of the wind would torment the
garrison with a spicy smell of cooking chicken as a relief from
the relentless smell of putrefaction (at intervals the Collector
would stop and curse himself for having so ignorantly ordered
the offal to be jettisoned to windward); in addition there were
the *ryots* from the indigo plantations and those from the opium
fields in bullock-carts or on foot, there were the peasants from
the villages, the travelling holy men, the cargoes of veiled
Mohammedan women, the crowds from the Krishnapur bazaars
and even one or two elephants carrying local zemindars, surrounded like Renaissance princes with liveried retainers. This
cheerful and multifarious crowd assembled every day beneath

awnings, tents and umbrellas to watch the *feringhees* fighting for their lives. At first the Collector had found this crowd of spectators a bitter humiliation, but now he seldom gave it a thought. He had issued orders that no powder was to be wasted on dispersing them, even though they were well within range.

The Collector still had one more call to make; this was to a shed with open, barred windows which formed the very last of the long row of stables, now converted into the hospital. It was here, in the days when life in Krishnapur had been on a grander scale, that a former Resident, anxious to emulate the local rajahs, had kept a pair of tigers. Now, where once the tigers had lived, Hari strode endlessly back and forth behind the bars, while the Prime Minister, sitting on a pile of straw, followed his movements with expressionless eyes.

Hari had been moved here "for the good of the community", causing the Collector another severe inflammation of conscience. It had been noticed that the one part of the enclave which the sepoys had been careful to avoid hitting with their cannons was precisely the spot where Hari was quartered. Word of his whereabouts had no doubt filtered out to the sepoy lines by way of the native servants who continued to defect one by one as the plight of the garrison became more desperate. Once this unfortunate discovery had been made, the Collector found himself morally obliged (it was his duty) to make use of it. So Hari had been turned out of the relative comfort and safety of the Residency and lodged in the tiger house which conveniently happened to be adjacent to the hospital.

Hari had not taken well to this change. Watching him as the days went by, the guilty Collector had noticed signs of physical and moral decline. His fat cheeks, always pale, had taken on a greyish tinge. He had complained, first that he could not eat, then that the food he was given was not fit for a human being . . . It was true that the food was not very good, but what could one expect during a siege? And food was not the only trouble. Always inclined to petulance, Hari had now taken on a permanent look of discontent.

"You should go outside, visit people, talk with them, perhaps even do a spot of fighting," the Collector had counselled him. increasingly disturbed by the change which was taking place in Hari's character. Hari had been so full of enthusiasm, so interested in every new and progressive idea. And now he was so listless!

"You give permission to going outside camp, perhaps?"

"Well, no, not outside the ramparts, of course."

"Ha!"

"But you must occupy yourself. You can't remain here in this room for ever. Who knows how long the siege will go on?"

"Correct! You keep me prisoner but you pretend to yourself that you do not keeping prisoner myself and Prime Minister. You want me to kill for British perhaps my own little brothers and sisters who plead with me for lives, raising little hands very piteously? I will not do it, Mr Hopkin, I will rather die than do it, I can assure you. It is no good. You torture me first. I still not killing little brother and sister."

"Oh, I say, look here . . . no one is asking you to kill your brother and sister. You mustn't exaggerate."

"Yes, you asking me to killing brother and sister and you asking Prime Minister to sticking with bayonet his very old widow mother lady!"

"Oh, what rubbish!"

"Oh, what rubbish, you say, but I knowing very different. All is not well that end well if I killing little babies for Queen, I assure you. I die rather than do that. Prime Minister also, to my way of thinking!"

The Prime Minister, sitting on his heap of straw, his eyes as expressionless as ever, had shown no sign of being partial either to killing babies or not killing them, or to anything whatsoever.

"If only the poor lad could have brought someone a bit more stimulating as a companion," the Collector had thought miserably. "He's pining away for lack of something to occupy his mind."

Once again the Collector had to take out his handkerchief and hold it to his nose, this time because he was passing the open doors and windows of the hospital. He could not shut his ears, though, to the cries and groans; he even believed he could hear the monotonous chanting of the Crimean veteran as he hurried by, but he already had enough to think about with

189

Hari. As he approached the tiger house he braced himself for the inevitable reproaches. But today, for some reason, Hari's interest in the world seemed to have revived.

As usual he was striding up and down behind the bars while the Prime Minister sat passively on his heap of straw. There was a significant change, however. Hari was looking excited, indeed feverishly so ... but something else had changed, too, and for a while the Collector could not think what it was. Then it came to him: the Prime Minister's head was bare. It was not simply that he had removed his French military cap, he had removed his hair as well. His skull was shaved and oiled, and it gleamed in the lamplight. For some reason it was covered by a hair net with a large mesh.

The Collector assumed that this shaving of the Prime Minister's skull had some religious significance; he knew that Hindus are always shaving their heads for one reason or another; but then he noticed that Hari's eyes kept returning to the gleaming cranium as to a work of art. Looking a little closer, he noticed that what he had taken for the strings of a net were, in fact, ritual lines drawn in ink on the Prime Minister's scalp.

"I become devotee of Frenloudji!" exclaimed Hari.

"Frenloudji?"

"Frenla-ji! Correct? Science of head!"

"Oh, phrenology! I see what you mean!"

"Correct! Let me explain you about phrenology ... Most interesting science and exceedingly useful for getting the measure of your man ... I have got measure of Prime Minister without least difficulties. You see, head is furnished with vast apparatus of mental organ and each organs extend from the gentleman's medulla oblongata, or top of spinal marrow, to surface of brain or cerebellum. Every gentleman possess all organ to greater or lesser degree. Let us say, he possess big organ of Wit, if he say very amusing things then organ of Wit is very big and powerful and we see large bump on right and left of forehead here ..." and Hari pointed to a spot somewhat above each of the Prime Minister's eyebrows.

"This organ is very big in Mr F. Rabelais and Mr J. Swift. In Prime Minister not so big. In you, Mr Hopkin, not so big. In me, not so big." The Prime Minister fingered his sacred thread but offered no comment.

"The man who discovered this science, Dr Gall of Vienna, remove many skulls from people he had known in life. He found brain which is covered by dura mater ..." (Hari pronounced this with relief, as if it were the name of an Indian dish) "has same shape as skull having during life. So that's why we see bump or no bump on Prime Minister's head."

"I see," said the Collector, who felt that his understanding of phrenology might be vulnerable to any further explanations from Hari.

"There are certain parts at base of brain, in middle and posterior regions, size of which cannot be discover during life and whose function therefore remain unknown. But some bumps we seen even though in difficult position. You see, for example ... *Amativeness* ..." Hari snatched up a book lent him by the Magistrate, and read: "Amativeness. The cerebellum is the organ of this propensity, and it is situated between the mastoid processes on each side ... and so on and so forth ... The size is indicated during life by the thickness of the neck at these parts. The faculty gives rise to the sexual feeling. In newborn children the cerebellum is the least developed of all the cerebral parts. It is to the brain as one to twenty and in adults as one to six. The organ attains its full size from the age of eighteen to twenty-six. It is less in females, in general, than in males. In old age it frequently diminishes."

Hari put the book down and beckoned the Collector to come and examine the Prime Minister.

"Amativeness is not very powerful organ in Prime Minister. In me, very powerful. In Father it is fearfully, fearfully powerful so that all other organ wither away, I'm thinking ..." Hari laughed heartily and then suddenly clutched his organ of Wit.

"Well, I must be on my way, Hari," said the Collector sadly. How distressed he felt to see this young man's open mind tainted by the Magistrate! But before Hari allowed him to leave he insisted on staring indiscreetly for a long time at the back of the Collector's neck and even prodding it with a muttered, "Excuse liberty, please." His only verdict, however, was a cough and modestly lowered eyes.

As he was returning to the Residency he thought he heard a voice calling from the far side of the hospital, beyond the churchyard wall. He went to investigate and saw the faint silhouette of the Padre, digging wearily with a spade and muttering to himself as he worked. Beside the path the Collector dimly perceived three long forms sewn up in bedding.

"Padre, is there no one to help you?"

But the Padre made no reply, perhaps had not even heard. He went on digging and muttering to himself. The Collector could just hear his words: "... Man that is born of woman hath but a short time to live. He cometh up, and is cut down, like a flower; he fleeth as it were a shadow, and never continueth in one stay ..."

The Collector spoke to him again, but still the Padre paid no attention. So in the end the Collector took the spade himself and made the Padre lie down on the path beside the corpses.

Then, for an hour or more the Collector dug steadily by himself. At first he thought: "This is easy. The working classes make a lot of fuss about nothing." But he had never used a spade in his life before and soon his hands became blistered and painful. He was invaded by a great sadness, then. The sadness emanated from the three silent figures sewn up in bedding and he thought again of his death statistics, but was not comforted ... And as he dug, he wept. He saw Hari's animated face, and numberless dead men, and the hatred on the faces of the sepoys ... and it suddenly seemed to him that he could see clearly the basis of all conflict and misery, something mysterious which grows in men at the same time as hair and teeth and brains and which reveals its presence by the utter and atrocious inflexibility of all human habits and beliefs, even including his own. Presently, he heard the Padre's voice whispering over the bodies in the darkness: "They shall hunger no more, neither thirst any more; neither shall the sun light on them, nor any heat. For the Lamb which is in the midst of the throne shall feed them, and shall lead them unto living fountains of waters: and God shall wipe away all tears from their eyes." When the Collector had finished digging two of the graves he helped the Padre carry the bodies over and bury them, and then set to work on the third grave. By the time a fatigue party came out of the darkness to relieve him he had composed himself again, which was just as well in the circumstances, for no garrison is encouraged by the sight of its commander in tears.

Now at last the Collector's long day was over. A lamp was burning in his study and in the glass of the bookcases he saw his own image, shadowy in detail, wearing an already rather tattered morning coat, the face also in shadow, anonymous, the face of a man like other men, who in a few years would be lost to history, whose personality would be no more individual than this shadowy reflection in the glass. "How alike we all are, really ... There's so little difference between one man and another when one comes to think of it."

As he moved to turn out the lamp before going upstairs he thought how normal everything still was here. It might have been any evening of the years he had spent in Krishnapur. Only his ragged coat, his boots soiled from digging graves, his poorly trimmed whiskers, and his exhausted appearance would have given one to suspect that there was anything amiss. That and the sound of gunfire from the compound.

On his way upstairs he passed Miriam in the hall and without particularly meaning to he put his arm around her. She was on her hands and knees when this happened, searching the floor with a candle for some pearls she had dropped when the string she was wearing had broken; in spite of their increasingly ragged appearance it had become the habit for the ladies to wear all the jewellery they possessed for safe-keeping. They should have been quite easy to find but some had rolled away into the forest of dusty, carved legs of tables and chairs which here comprised the lumber of "possessions". When the Collector touched her she did not faint or seem offended; she returned the pressure quite firmly and then sat back on her heels, brushing a lock of hair out of her eyes with her knuckles because her hands were dirty. She looked at him for a long time but did not say anything. After a while she went on looking for her pearls and he went on his way upstairs. He did not know what had made him do that. It had been discouragement more than anything. At that moment he had been feeling the need for some kind of comfort ... perhaps any kind would have done ... a good bottle of claret, for example, instead. Still, Mrs Lang was a sensible woman and he did not think she would mind. "Funny creatures, women, all the same," he mused. "One never knows quite what goes on in their minds."

Later, while he was drinking tea at the table in his bedroom with three young subalterns from Captainganj a succession of musket balls came through the window, attracted by the oil-lamp . . . one, two, three, and then a fourth, one after another. The officers dived smartly under the table, leaving the Collector to drink his tea alone. After a while they re-emerged smiling sheepishly, deeply impressed by the Collector's sang-froid. Realizing that he had forgotten to sweeten his tea, the Collector dipped a teaspoon into the sugar-bowl. But then he found that he was unable to keep the sugar on the spoon: as quickly as he scooped it up, it danced off again. It was clear that he would never get it from the sugar-bowl to his cup without scattering it over the table, so in the end he was obliged to push the sugar away and drink his tea unsweetened. Luckily, none of the officers had noticed.

That night, as soon as he closed his eyes the bed on which he lay began to spin round and round; within a few seconds, it seemed, he had been drawn down into a sleep where shattering events raged back and forth over his unconscious mind. Gradually, however, they receded and he fell into a more calm, profound sleep . . . but not so profound that he could not hear, though at a great distance, the heart-rending screams of Mrs Scott giving birth a few rooms away on the next floor. Once, he suddenly started up in bed, thinking: "The poor mite! What a world to be born into!" but perhaps that was merely part of a long, sad, ineffably sad dream he had before dawn.

But as it turned out, the baby was not born alive and Mrs Scott herself, in spite of everything that was done to save her, sank rapidly and died before morning. In the first light Dr McNab, who had not slept at all, sat at a table by the window in the room where Mrs Scott had died (which formed part of the flagstaff tower), writing in his notebook the brief details of what had happened. He wrote: "Caesarean section. Felt head of child, which had come low down, suddenly recede; symptoms of ruptured uterus followed . . . The foetus could easily be felt through the abdominal walls and was apparently quite loose, while it could not be reached by the vagina; it was evident that the uterus had given way. The patient not yet in a very collapsed state, but declining rapidly. Proceeded to remove the foetus by gastrotomy ... an incision about six inches in breadth was made in the median line between the umbilicus and pubes; the foetus was easily reached and, as expected was found loose in the peritoneal cavity; it was removed (dead) together with the whole of the cord and the placenta; not much haemhorrage occurred, nor was much blood found in the abdomen. Stimulants, opiates etc. were liberally employed afterwards, but in spite of them the woman sank, and died in about three hours ..."

Dr McNab paused for a moment in his writing and turned round in his chair to stare at the bed, which was now empty for Mrs Scott, sewn in her bedding, had been carried to the Church where she would lie until darkness came and it was safe to bury her. He frowned thoughtfully, as if trying to concentrate, then he went on writing.

In this room where throughout the night the most terrible shrieks of pain had echoed, there was now no sound to break the silence except the scratching of Dr McNab's pen-nib as he wrote and an occasional clink of china as he dipped it into the inkwell. Outside, the gunfire continued steadily.

15

It had been planned that on Tuesday, 7 July, Cutter should spring his mine beneath the sepoy positions; Harry and Fleury had been selected to join the sortie that was to coincide with this event. Tuesday also happened to be Fleury's birthday, and he was sentimental about birthdays, particularly his own; at the same time he affected to regard them as events of no importance.

Your sister, as a rule, can be relied on to remember when your birthday is; but when on the Monday evening Miriam and several other ladies and gentlemen gathered on the Residency verandah to sing hymns before retiring to bed Fleury could see no sign of awareness on his sister's face that an unusual event was soon to occur. She sang away unconcernedly, with great feeling: "O God our help in ages past . . ." She had a beautiful voice and normally Fleury loved to hear her singing; but this evening he suspected that she was putting it on for the Collector's benefit. The Collector, although not singing himself (for he had no voice), was leaning against the louvred wooden shutters in the semi-darkness, listening. Many members of the garrison were becoming a little perturbed about the Collector. His face had taken on a more haggard look and he was sometimes heard to be muttering to himself . . . once or twice he had even been heard laughing to himself as he walked about; it was an uncomfortable laugh, and if he saw you looking at him he would stop immediately; his face would become stern and expressionless once more inside its cat-like ruff of whiskers. There was no reason to make too much of this, however . . . a man has to be allowed a few personal idiosyncrasies, after all, and the Collector had done a splendid job so far. All the same, the Collector was in complete command of the garrison and everything that happened in the enclave happened at his behest. The siege, in a manner of speaking, was *his idea*. It would be unfortunate, to put it mildly, if now or at some later stage he should collapse when so much depended on him. So no wonder that people had begun to watch him rather uneasily. Mind you, he was probably still as sound as a bell. And it could hardly be a bad thing that he had come to listen to the singing of hymns. It was a pity that his face could not be seen more clearly in the shadows.

Miriam stood in the light of the lamp. Her face had grown pink, her eyes shone, and her breast heaved. She had never sung so thrillingly before.

"Yes," thought Fleury, "she's going at it hammer and tongs for *his* benefit!" Full of self-pity he made his way back to his lonely *charpoy* in the banqueting-hall.

The following morning he and Harry waited tensely with their horses in the shelter of Dr Dunstaple's house for the signal that Cutter was ready to spring his mine. The sortie was to be led by Lieutenant Peterson. A number of other gentlemen were also there, including Mr Ronald Rose, one of the railway engineers, Mr Simmons, the skin of whose face had now been totally flayed by the sun, and the Schleissner brothers, Claude and Michael, both ensigns from Captainganj.

"I say, I've just remembered, it's my birthday today," Fleury remarked casually to Harry, and then scowled at his blunder; he had not meant to tell anyone, then he had blurted it out.

"Many happy returns," said Harry, rather absentmindedly. He would have shown more interest but in a few moments, whirling his sabre, he would be riding for the enemy lines. Beside this crimson thought Fleury's birthday seemed anaemic.

Fleury clenched his teeth morosely, thinking: "Cutter is taking a devilish long time with his mine."

As a matter of fact, Fleury had something else on his mind beside his birthday. Recently he had been employing his idle hours (for a siege can be very dull to a man of culture) in a deep and thorough investigation of the military arts. Like the Collector he believed that nothing need be outside the scope of the man of intelligence. And so he had made a rapid, sceptical reading of the Collector's authorities, Vauban and so forth, groaning derisively to Harry over their lack of imagination, errors of logic, and sluggish mental processes. The only idea which had caused him any enthusiasm he had found in Carnot, who had attempted to prove mathematically that by using a thirteen-inch mortar to discharge six hundred iron balls at a time any besieging force could be rapidly wiped out.

For three or four days he had pestered the Collector with offers of advice, but then his enthusiasm for Carnot's idea had lapsed in favour of one of his own. This was a design for a new weapon which would, he believed, create a revolution in the cavalry charge. Now, the great difficulty in the cavalry charge, as Fleury saw it, is that you very often have to deal with two of the enemy at once, with the result that while you are cutting the head off one of your assailants his companion is doing the same for you. The weapon which Fleury had designed and made for himself in order to overcome this difficulty resembled a giant pitchfork with prongs roughly at a distance of a man's outstretched arms; it also had a wide tail, like that of a magnified bishop's crozier which, reversed, could be used for dragging people off horses; on the shaft, for psychological reasons, there fluttered a small Union Jack. His only problem was to find a place to attach the weapon to his saddle. For the time being the prongs of the instrument (which he had christened the Fleury Cavalry Eradicator) sprouted over his horse's head like a pair of weird antlers. Well, would it work or not? He would soon find out. Meanwhile, what on earth was Cutter up to?

The Collector, too, was waiting impatiently. So much depended on the success of this operation. He had been standing in the pit beside the battery for the past few minutes, since Cutter had disappeared along the shaft; at the Collector's side two Sikhs were working a primitive bellows attached to improvised pipes of canvas, pumping air to the head of the shaft. Up there somewhere, at a place which he estimated would be directly beneath the enemy position, Cutter had picked a small chamber in the side of the gallery wall in which to stow the charge, the intention being to increase the force of the explosion by keeping it out of the direct line of the gallery. Boxes of powder had been dragged up to him. He had stowed them and set the fuse of powder-hose; now he was tamping, that is to say, filling up the head of the gallery to prevent the charge blowing back down it; this, too, had to be done with care for if he disturbed the fuse and it failed to function the tamping would have to be unpicked again, a dangerous business; to add to the difficulty he had to work in complete darkness without so much as a candle, for fear of the powder exploding too soon.

At last Cutter crawled out of the gallery; he looked exhausted and in need of fresh air. He was ready now to spring the mine, was the attacking force ready? Yes. He lit a candle and ducked back into the gallery; in order to save powder he had not brought the fuse right back to the shaft; this powder-hose fuse had been extemporized from a tube of linen sewn by the ladies; it was immensely long and about an inch in diameter, and had provided the ladies with a task which had occupied their fingers for many hours; filled with powder it would burn at ten to twenty feet a second, so Cutter had no time to loiter in the gallery after he had touched it off.

The Collector raised his hand to give the signal for cannons and rifles to fire as Cutter touched off the fuse and sprinted back down the gallery. A storm of gunfire broke out. Cutter just reached the shaft in time to see the cavalry squadron (accompanied by Fleury on what looked like a reindeer) springing over the rampart and spurring for the enemy lines; then there was a great explosion and he was pelted with earth and pebbles from the mouth of the gallery.

To Fleury it seemed that the yellow earth was erupting before him scattering dark objects which might have been sepoys. It was as yet impossible to see in the dust cloud whether the enemy defences had been breached. Ahead of him Lieutenant Peterson flourished his sabre shouting soundlessly and then held it out stiff and straight in front of him over his horse's straining head. He vanished into the curtain of yellow dust followed by two Sikhs, then by Harry, then by the rest of the squadron including Fleury himself. In the yellow fog sepoys were wandering stunned and defenceless; everywhere the riders cut them down. In front of Fleury two *sowars* hesitated, uncertain whether to spur forward and do battle or to turn tail; behind him Mr Rose lifted his sabre to split the skull of a staggering infantryman. The two *sowars* continued to vacillate in front of Fleury; he unshipped the Cavalry Eradicator. His victims were ideally positioned, he would never have a better chance! Uttering a peculiar but scientific warcry (he had calculated that maximum discouragement to the enemy would be caused by a mixture of gutturals and sibilants) he drove forward with all his might.

The *sowars* each stared in amazement at the wicked, glistening point heading straight for his heart; they exchanged a
glance of despair ... but by a miracle the two steel prongs came
to a trembling halt an inch from their hearts. They looked
along the shaft to where Fleury, his eyes bulging, his face red
with exertion, tried to drive the points those extra inches
which would put them to death. Then, by a common accord,
they turned their horses and bolted. Behind Fleury, Mr Rose,
his brawny arms just beginning the downward swing that
would split the sepoy's skull, had found himself suddenly whis-
ked out of his saddle and was now struggling like a gaffed salmon
on the end of the Eradicator. By the time he had freed himself,
cursing, his victim also had vanished. Indeed, all the sepoys
had vanished by now or were lying dead or mortally wounded.

"Come on! The guns!"

Throwing down the Eradicator (which he now realized had
certain flaws of design) Fleury followed Harry through the
choking yellow fog. Lieutenant Peterson was already labouring
with two Sikhs to limber up a six-pounder to bring back to
their lines; Mr Ford and an indigo planter were working to
silence the dreaded eighteen-pounder.

"Spike the twelve-pounder!" shouted Harry and handed
Fleury a six-inch nail. Fleury took the nail but shouted back:
"Alright but where's the spike?"

"The nail, you fool! Hammer it into the vent and then
break it off."

Nobody likes to be called a fool ... even less a person of
Fleury's intelligence ... Least of all, a person of Fleury's intelligence by a person of Harry's. And how was Fleury to know
that spiking guns did not mean what it said (and what any
normally intelligent person would have thought it meant:
namely, hammering a large spike into the muzzle) but something quite different? Decidedly, Harry was letting his military training go to his head, but he had already hurried away
to hammer nails into other guns, so Fleury, too, set to work
and made rather a good job, he thought, of spiking the twelve-
pounder.

The six-pounder and a howitzer were dragged away by Sikhs
towards the Residency ramparts. Lieutenant Peterson shouted
the order to retreat; the yellow fog had now cleared to a light,

sparkling mist and the sepoys were re-grouping to launch a counter-attack. Now only Lieutenant Peterson himself lingered. He had found one of the sepoy ammunition stores, had quickly scattered a train of powder to it, and was now attempting to fire it. At last, he succeeded, swung himself into the saddle and was away. His horse cleared the sepoy rampart and sped like an arrow after his men across the open ground. Suddenly they saw him hit. He slid out of the saddle and bounced in the dust. Without hesitation both Harry and Fleury turned their horses and spurred back to where he lay. Fleury rode on to catch the reins of the Lieutenant's horse while Harry tried to lift him from the ground. Then together they struggled to get him into the saddle, but again he was hit. They felt his body shudder as another ball struck him in the back and they were obliged to give up the attempt. At this moment there was a great flash and an explosion rang around the plain. Harry and Fleury knelt beside Peterson and shook hands with him for the last time, and as they did so the pallor of death came over his face. Fleury struggled for a moment to remove the locket from around his neck to bring back to his wife, but it was too securely fastened. Then they were both in the saddle once more and riding for the safety of the Residency rampart. They sailed over it at last, accompanied by a volley of musket balls.

16

In spite of his difficulties with the Eradicator Fleury came very well out of this attack. He and Harry had both behaved with great bravery in full view of everyone. The ladies in the billiard room, who had been reciting the litany throughout the attack, were chattering with excitement and could talk of little else. Perhaps, if one takes the long view, this gallant action might be seen as a solstice in Fleury's life, for from now on as the days went by he grew steadily less responsive to beauty and steadily more bluff, good-natured and interested in physical things. So pleased was he, so busily engaged in modest assurances that anyone would have done the same in his place, that when at dusk he paid his usual evening visit to the Residency and found Miriam, Louise, Harry and Lucy (whom they had felt sorry for) waiting to lead him to a special celebration, his birthday had gone completely out of his mind. And it was a splendid affair, for Lucy, who was good at that sort of thing, had succeeded in begging a cup of sugar from one of the gentlemen working at the Commissariat . . . and this sugar, which none of them had tasted for days, made them as festive as if it had been champagne. They had saved some flour and some suet, too, and Miriam had bought a bottle of port wine from someone, and so they had made something which was not exactly a birthday cake, but more a birthday pudding, with "Happy Birthday, Dobbin!" written on top in pieces of broken sugar biscuit (Fleury's brow darkened for a moment at "Dobbin" but evidently Miriam had forgotten) and the whole thing thoroughly soaked in port wine. Of course, the rest of the port wine they drank to Fleury's health. As for Fleury, his eyes kept hurrying back to Louise to see if she were as happy as he was. How lovely she looked, and how gentle!

Louise was as happy as he was, almost. The only thing that slightly diminished her pleasure was the knowledge that she had an unsightly red spot on her forehead and another one, perhaps even a boil, coming up on her neck. In addition, she had been out in the sun without her bonnet, which she had given to a wounded Sikh, and her face had a much pinker look than she considered becoming.

But she was glad that the pudding was a success. It was she who had had to make it because Miriam had turned out to be hopelessly impractical when it had come to the point, the way capable, intelligent people often are when it comes to cooking and making things. And she was glad, too, that Fleury had turned out not to be a coward . . . of course, she had not expected that he *would*, but all the same, you could never tell and Fleury in some ways was so unusual . . . He had such interesting ideas, for one thing, and he knew everything. She could not think of anything he did not know and it was even a bit embarrassing to see how much more he knew than even the Padre, or the Magistrate, or her father, or even than the Collector. She sometimes thought him a little tactless and that he should sometimes pretend to be a bit more stupid so as not to make older people feel inferior. Perhaps that was why she had not liked him so much at first, and had thought him conceited. But now she thought him wonderful, and so personable, even though one had to admit that he smelled rather strong . . . but then they all did; it was so hard to keep yourself clean without the bearers to help. She herself had begun to smell rather disagreeable. She regretted this but without soap all her efforts to render herself odourless had proved vain . . . her only comfort was that she smelled less than many of the other ladies of her own class and, of course, than *all* those of the classes beneath her. It was the view of the billiard room that the artillery women could no longer be approached. But she was worried about that spot on her forehead and afraid that Fleury might start seeing her as she really was, and so she kept raising her hand to her forehead, as if in thought.

There was, however, a greater anxiety in Louise's life than either her smell or her spots. She was concerned for her father, Dr Dunstaple. As the days went by he became more and more liable to fits of rage. Nowadays he could hardly open his mouth without abusing Dr McNab, whom he had taken to calling "the Gravedigger". Louise had remonstrated with him but the Doctor was not in the habit of allowing his children to advise him on his conduct, least of all his daughters. He had flown into a rage, insinuating that she was "in league" with McNab. The Doctor had his fit of rage in his own drawing-room, in full hearing of the ladies cowering in the cellar below (as much in fear of his wrath as of the round shot which were slowly knocking the house to pieces around them). Mrs Dunstaple cowered there, too. She had never been able to do anything with her husband when he was angry, never, she sobbed.

So poor Louise, who loved her father very dearly, could only turn to Harry for help. But Harry listened to her in frank disbelief. Girls had a habit, he knew, of distressing themselves over things which did not exist. It was something to do with their wombs, so a fellow-officer had once told him. No doubt Louise was suffering from this womb-anxiety, then. He explained that if Father had started calling McNab "the Gravedigger" it was only from a robust sense of professional rivalry and nothing to worry about. Besides, McNab probably deserved it from all one heard.

Louise longed to confide in someone; above all, she longed to confide in Fleury; he would at least take her seriously; he would show concern. The trouble was that he would almost certainly be unable to refrain from some ill-advised action, such as taking her father's arm as if they were equals and giving him a condescending lecture. That was unthinkable. She must conceal her worries from Fleury.

In the end it was to Miriam that she had told them, thinking: "Miriam is mature and sensible. She'll know what to do." And so she had approached Miriam, though diffidently because one has a natural reluctance to discuss family matters with those outside the family. Miriam had given her a sensible opinion to the effect that the obvious person to ask for advice was a doctor, hence Dr McNab himself! Who could be better? Louise had had misgivings about this at first. But it was certain that her father needed a doctor's attention and that Dr McNab, who had suffered all his colleague's slanders without a murmur, deserved an apology.

Dr McNab, his eyebrows raised considerately, had listened to what Louise had to say. "Aye, you must get him to rest, Miss Dunstaple. The poor man is overworked."

"But how?"

"I wish I could tell you but I cannot. He'll not take advice from me." Then, seeing Louise's distress, he added: "But perhaps we shall think of a way."

Louise's grief and anxiety did not prevent her noticing that, in common with certain of the other gentlemen, Dr McNab appeared to show an interest in Miriam. He treated her with a decorous gallantry, as if her presence beside him in a patched and mended dress of grey cotton, stockingless, hands rough from washing her own clothes and hair full of dust, had been that of a lady in the most elegant drawing-room. When his eyes rested on her face an expression of good humour and sympathy replaced his habitually sad and grave demeanour. Louise had often noticed how thrilling it is to see a smile on the face of someone who does not often smile, particularly someone as grave as Dr McNab. She could not help saying to Miriam after this interview: "I think you have made another conquest among the gentlemen."

"Oh, surely not," said Miriam, laughing. "I don't think I have made a single one. Besides, I have often noticed that the gentlemen only have eyes for you, my dear, and although men are not usually the most intelligent of creatures, this time for once they are right, because you are the prettiest girl in India. I can assure you that if I wanted to make conquests I should take care not to appear in your company."

"You only say that because you're kind, but you know that it really isn't true. What gentleman in the world would not prefer your company to that of an empty-headed creature like me?"

"You must ask my brother that question," said Miriam smiling and taking Louise's arm to put an end to this unctuous exchange. "Let me tell you a secret. We shall both find, if we survive this dreadful siege, gentlemen who think each of us uniquely wonderful and who would not give a farthing for the other. Why? Who knows why? Because that's the way of the world, that's why." And with this comment, which was further proof to Louise of Miriam's superiority and good sense, the subject had been closed.

Now, although she was glad that the birthday pudding was a success, Louise found herself with yet another cause for family distress: the attention that Harry was paying to Lucy. Anyone who knew him less well than his sister might not have noticed how his manner had changed. How gruff he had become, how paternal, how full of authority!

"You'd better sit here, Lucy, where you can serve out the pudding and see that that young beggar Fleury doesn't get too much, ha ha, even though it is his birthday." And Harry had indicated a place on the floor beside himself. The party, as it happened, was taking place on the carpet of the Residency drawing-room, in the lee of a shattered grand piano; additional protection to their flanks was offered by the gorse bruiser which had been moved from the dining-room, a marble statue of Cupid sharpening his arrows on a stone ("How appropriate," thought Louise grimly, "for poor, innocent Harry"), a colossal statue of the Queen in zinc, and a display case of lightning conductors for ships (as used in HM Navy); all of these objects had once graced the Crystal Palace.

"You sit there, Lou, and, Miriam, you sit there," Harry was proceeding commandingly. "That's right, everyone. That's the spirit."

Astonished by how insufferable her brother had suddenly become, Louise could not help thinking that Miriam, who was older and in every way more mature than Harry, must object to being ordered about by him ... but she did not seem to; she seemed perfectly content to be given orders. Yet nobody seemed more content than Lucy. "Shall I do this? Shall I do that? Is that the right way?" she kept asking Harry, turning to him meltingly for more gruff instructions than could possibly be required. Although Louise was still glad that she had saved Lucy's life by sending that letter to the *dak* bungalow she could not help feeling that she had been rather taken advantage of ... If you save someone's life you do not expect them to start promptly making mincemeat of your innocent brother's affections with melting glances and flashings of pretty smiles. Not that Louise would normally have minded a pretty girl like Lucy capturing Harry's heart ... to have their hearts besieged and captured was, after all, at least one of the things that men were there for.

What Louise could not forget, however, was that Lucy had been dishonoured. This lovely and quite innocent-looking girl

206

who was sitting there with them now cheerfully eating pudding had allowed, perhaps even encouraged, certain things to be done to her by a man; she had perhaps allowed her clothes to be fumbled with and disarranged . . . she might even perhaps, for all Louise knew, have been seen naked by him. The thought of Lucy's delightfully shaped body, of which she herself had inadvertently glimpsed intimate parts in the billiard room (for Lucy was careless where modesty was concerned), exposed to the eyes of a gentleman, was very distressing to Louise. She was ready to be friendly and forgiving to Lucy, and she was ready to believe that the sin had been less Lucy's than that of her seducer . . . but she could not believe it a good thing that Harry should become infatuated with her. That a man (let us not call him a gentleman) should have been permitted to view that sacred collection of bulges, gaps, tufts of hair and rounded fleshy slopes which, as clear as the tossing arms of the semaphore on Diamond Head, signalled their own message: "Womanhood"; on this, apply cosmetics of exonerating circumstances though you might, Louise could only put an ugly complexion, for it added up to the betrayal of her sex.

But now it was time for Fleury's birthday present to be handed to him and, once again, although the idea had been Miriam's, the hard work had had to be done by Louise. With the Collector's permission they had cut the cloth off the billiard tables and made him a coat of Lincoln green together with a cap of the same material, garnished with a turquoise peacock's feather.

"I say, he looks as if he has just come from Sherwood Forest," cried Harry gruffly in his new insufferable manner. "Ho there, Locksley! Ha, ha!"

"Oh shut up, Dunstaple!" said Fleury, delighted with his new coat and secretly pleased to be compared with Robin Hood. He put the coat on and turned slowly in front of the ladies, exclaiming: "What a splendid fit it is!" and indeed it was a good fit, even though one arm seemed to be rather longer than the other ("That's so he can fire his long-bow the more easily, ha, ha!" cried Harry obnoxiously, causing Lucy to swoon with laughter). "Thank heaven it fits, anyway," thought Louise sadly. For some reason, she had no idea why, she suddenly felt close to tears. With one hand to her forehead, as if she were "thinking" again, she used the other one to give her collar a little tug to make sure no one could see her new boil, the one on her neck.

At this moment the Collector happened to pass through the drawing-room and seeing Miriam sitting with her brother and the young Dunstaples and Miss Hughes, could not help thinking how she still looked only a girl herself, even though she had been a widow for three years or more. They invited him to taste the birthday pudding, which he did, pronouncing it excellent and thinking: "What charming young people they are, to be sure. Why cannot every man and woman in India be so delightful to talk to?"

An expression of warmth had softened the Collector's features as he knelt beside the group of young people to sample their pudding, but Miriam watching his face closely, saw the shadow return as he stood up. Perhaps it was the endless worry of the siege: he was always anxious, she knew, as dusk was falling, particularly at the beginning of a moonless night when the sepoys might make a surprise attack. Would there be a moon tonight? She could not remember.

But the Collector was still following his earlier thoughts and wondering how it could ever be that the hundred and fifty million people living in India could ever have the social advantages that made young people like the Fleurys and the Dunstaples so delightful, so confident, and so charming.

He left the young people and strode wearily through the hall, muttering to himself aloud: "Surely it's impossible under any system of government or social economy?" The Collector frowned. A number of people lying on bedding in the hall among the lumber of "possessions" were watching him uneasily; perhaps they had seen him talking to himself. But again he thought: "Can it be that the Indian population will ever enjoy the wealth and ease of the better classes?" This was the melancholy question which had invited the shadow back over the Collector's countenance and which, presently, pursued him out into the pitch-dark compound to watch the construction of a new line of defence and to assist in the nightly digging of graves.

17

The Padre had become harder and more cunning in the service of the Lord; otherwise it is doubtful whether he would have survived the first weeks of the siege. Nobody had worked harder than the Padre; he had done his best. But he was only one man, surrounded by sinners and himself a sinner, born of Adam.

As silk-worms secrete silk, so human beings secrete sin. There is a normal quantity of sin which, for their everlasting punishment, any community of erring humans cannot help spinning in the course of their lives. But what puzzled the Padre was the nature of the particular divine grievance for which they were now suffering such an extreme punishment. What could it be? He had asked himself this question many times as the days had crawled by. And now, suddenly, as he began to dig the first of the evening's graves, illumination came to him. In the eye of his mind, whose blindness had been cured, the Padre again saw Fleury sitting among the children at Sunday school and shaking his head as if he did not believe in the Atonement. He paused in the act of digging, a heap of dusty soil on his spade. It could not be anything else. Their troubles had begun soon after the arrival of Fleury in Krishnapur.

He heard a footstep in the darkness. For a moment he thought that it must be Fleury himself, guided like a ram into a thicket. But it was the Collector carrying a spade. He had come to lend a hand.

"Three again tonight?"

"Alas!"

The Collector tried to remember who had died during the preceding night and day. One of these would be Peterson whose remains had been retrieved after dark; although only a few hours had passed the pariah dogs and vultures had already cleaned away the soft parts of Peterson's face and the flesh from his arms, leaving only the hands; these hands on the end of his outstretched, skeletal arms, had the appearance of gloves and lent the corpse an air of ghastly masquerade. Another of the bodies would be that of Jackson, the soldier who had been singing the song about the Crimea in order to keep his spirits up in the hospital. Day by day his bursts of singing had become more infrequent until at last they had been silenced altogether. Jackson had spent his last days lying with flies fighting over his staring eyes in the middle of the stench and horror of the hospital. The Collector had tried to speak to him but had got no reply. He was not sorry that Jackson was dead at last. The other shrouded corpse was that of Mr Donnelly, an indigo farmer and a Roman Catholic, who had died of a heart attack.

"We only need to dig two, Padre. Father O'Hara will be here presently to dig the other one in his own plot."

The Padre paid no attention; he was digging energetically. The Collector could see of him only the faint glimmer of his face and hands as he worked; his long clerical habit had rendered the rest of him invisible in the thick darkness.

"By the way, do we know which one *is* Donnelly?"

But the Padre remained engrossed in his own thoughts. His puny arms had become as strong again as when he had been a rowing-man at Brasenose; now the Collector, whose own hands had roughened like those of a member of the labouring classes, had to struggle to keep up with him.

"That could be a bit of a problem," mused the Collector.

"I believe, Mr Hopkins," said the Padre presently, "though as yet I have found no direct evidence of it, that there may be German rationalism at work within our midst. I hope I am mistaken."

"Ah?" The Collector's tired mind resisted the prospect of becoming excited over a possible invasion by German rationalism.

"Perhaps you are not aware of how the Church is ravaged in Germany, Mr Hopkins. In the universities there I have heard that unbelief is rife. Men who style themselves scholars do not hesitate to lead the young astray by directing them to study the Bible as if it were the work of man and not the revelation of God. It is said that a certain Herr de Wette denies that the first five books of the Bible were written by Moses and maintains that they were written at a period long after his death."

"Oh, the Germans, you know ..." The Collector with a shovelful of earth dismissed the Germans. But this attempt to soothe the Padre and render further theological exchanges unnecessary did not succeed.

"True, compared with the simple, healthy British mind the German mind is sickly and delights to feed on such morbid fantasies. But still, we must not forget how quickly unsound ideas can spread, particularly among the young and impressionable. They spread among the young like cholera! The German Church has no discipline; for its ministers it requires no adherence to the Thirty-nine Articles or to the Prayer Book. In Germany a clergyman can believe and teach whatever he wants, a disgraceful state of affairs. I hear there is a man called Schleiermacher who does not subscribe to many of the fundamental teachings of Christianity such as the Fall and the Atonement, but who is yet allowed to call himself a minister of the Prussian Church!"

"I don't think we in England need be anxious ..." began the Collector, but the Padre cut him short, waving his spade in the darkness.

"Rationalism! A vain belief in the power of the reason to investigate religious matters. Ah, Mr Hopkins, the abuse of man's power of reason is the curse of our day."

The Collector remained mute. He did not believe this last remark to be true. But he saw no prospect of the Padre listening sympathetically to his reservations and considered it fruitless to antagonize him.

"I say, you don't happen to know which of these bodies is Donnelly's, do you?" he asked again, indicating the three shrouded mounds of darkness lying beside the path.

"As we read in the Book of Isaiah: 'Thy wisdom and thy knowledge, it hath perverted thee'!"

"Well, of course, there are some ways in which no doubt ..." mumbled the Collector. At the same time he realized with a shock how much his own faith in the Church's authority, or in the Christian view of the world in which he had hitherto lived his life, had diminished since he had last inpected them. From the farmyard in which his certitudes perched like fat chickens, every night of the siege, one or two were carried off in the jaws of rationalism and despair.

Another footstep sounded in the darkness. The Padre paused, leaning on his spade, his eyes feverishly searching for the identity of the newcomer. This time he knew it must be Fleury, guided to an appointment with him so that his heretical notions might be extirpated. The Collector noticed that while he himself was scarcely ankle deep in the grave he was digging, the Padre had already lowered himself to the level of his knees, for while the Padre argued, he dug.

Meanwhile, the burly form of Father O'Hara had loomed out of the shadows. He had a spade over his shoulder. "Glory be to God!" he muttered as he tripped over something in the darkness. "Did ye ever see such a dark? I've no mind for this at all at all. Are ye there, Mr Hopkins, sor?"

"Just at your side, Father O'Hara. Mind you don't fall into the . . . ah . . . Here, let me give you a hand up."

"Now then, show me the lads and I'll be after taking mine to his eternal rest, God help him."

"Hm, Padre? Perhaps you could tell Father O'Hara which is Mr Donnelly?"

The Padre knelt on the path beside the three dark forms and peered at them uncertainly in the dim light afforded by the stars. After a pause for consideration he said: "Mr Donnelly is the one at the end."

"What! This little lad Jim Donnelly, is it? Not at all, not at all. He's no more Jim Donnelly than I am meself. This big lad here'll be your man."

"The small one is Donnelly," declared the Padre in a tone of conviction.

"Not at all. Sure, I've known him all me life."

"I fear you are mistaken."

"Indeed I am not! That big man over there is Donnelly if I ever saw him . . . He's the very image."

"Father O'Hara," broke in the Collector with authority. "Both you and the Padre are mistaken. I happen to know that the man in the middle is Donnelly. Now kindly take him away and bury him in the appropriate place and with the appropriate rites."

"But, Mr Hopkins . . ."

"Which lad is it?"

"This medium-sized corpse is the one you require."

"Should we not open up the stitching to make sure?"

"Certainly not. The middle one is Donnelly without a doubt. Now take him away." And the Collector returned to his digging. The matter was settled.

"Well, come along then, if you're Jim Donnelly and we'll put you in the earth," declared Father O'Hara shouldering the medium-sized corpse. He hesitated for a moment as if waiting for a possible disclaimer from the shrouded figure on his back, then, as none came, he staggered away with it into the darkness. They could hear him bumping into gravestones and blessing himself and muttering for some time as he groped his way towards his own plot.

So rapidly was the Padre now digging that to the weary Collector it seemed that he must be visibly sinking into the ground. The Collector, too, set to work in a more determined fashion, thinking with a mixture of virtue and self-pity: "I'm tired but it's my duty. It's right that a leader should bury with his own hands his followers and comrades." All the same, he was rather put out when the Padre dropped his spade for a moment to drag the shorter of the two remaining corpses over to measure against his half-dug trench. "He might at least have chosen the bigger one since he's dug twice as much of his grave as I have."

"Can I be of any assistance?" asked a voice at the Collector's side, causing him to jump violently for he had heard nothing and now a luminous green wraith appeared to be trembling at his elbow. But it was only Fleury. He had stopped by on his way back to the banqueting hall for the night's watch, still full of the energy generated by his love for Louise.

"Is that Mr Fleury?" came the Padre's voice.

"Yes."

A gargle of joy came from where the Padre was digging. Misinterpreting the reason for it the Collector said firmly: "He's taking over my spade for a while, Padre," and went to sit down on a nearby tombstone.

For a few moments there was no sound but the scrape of the spades in the earth; then, gentle as a dove, cunning as a serpent, came the Padre's voice. "I hear, Mr Fleury, that in Germany there is much discussion of the origin of the Bible . . ."

"Oh, is there?" Fleury's mind was still lovingly reviewing

the birthday party which had just taken place; he was trying to remember all the charming and intelligent remarks he had just made in Louise's presence; he had done rather well, he thought ... "I wonder what she thought when I said such-and-such and everyone laughed? I wonder what she thought when Harry was telling everyone about us spiking the guns? I wonder ..."

"Yes," went on the Padre, making a superhuman effort to maintain his conversational tone. "It is being studied as if it were not a sacred text, by the method of philological and linguistic investigation."

"Oh yes, I think I may have heard something along those lines."

Louise, Fleury had noticed, had a way, while seated of shifting her position slightly with a thoughtful look. There was something so feminine about it.

"A great variety of opinion has been advanced," continued the Padre impartially, breaking into a sweat. "Now people think one thing, now another."

"You mean like 'the dancing clergy' ... Some people think it's alright for them to do so, some don't?"

"I suppose the question of the 'dancing clergy' might be so considered," agreed the Padre mildly, but thinking: 'Surely the Devil is putting words on this young man's tongue!' "But I was thinking more of another much-debated question ... whether the Bible is literally true or not?"

The Padre had uttered these final words as casually as his exhausted state and impassioned convictions would allow. He had stopped digging. In his excitement he had dug one end of the grave to a tremendous depth, the other hardly at all, so that the body lying beside it would have to be buried at a peculiar angle ... But he was not thinking of this, he was waiting for Fleury's reply.

"Will the Padre never cease from these inquisitions?" wondered the Collector irritably. "Haven't we enough to worry about already?" He still felt displeased because the Padre had so selfishly snatched the smaller body.

The Padre was waiting for Fleury to reveal the thoughts in his mind about the Bible, but Fleury was having trouble seeing them against the radiance shed by Louise. What was it that he was supposed to be thinking about? Oh yes, the Bible, literally true or not?

"Frankly," he said in a mature and condescending way, "I tend to agree with Coleridge that it doesn't particularly matter ..."

"Not *matter*!"

"... that the important thing about the Bible is not that it tells us that Moses did this or that ... he may or may not have, for all I know, but I don't think it's important whether these German wallahs manage to prove it one way or another ... in other words not whether it's literally true, but whether ..." Fleury's voice took on a more solemn note, "... whether it's *morally* true, whether it appeals to and satisfies our inner spiritual needs. That, if I may say so, is the important question." After a moment he added, more condescendingly than ever: "I dare say our positions differ a trifle, eh, Padre?" This additional comment was designed to put an end to the argument ... his thoughts wanted to hasten back to the consideration of Louise.

"The Bible is the word of God, Mr Fleury," exclaimed the Padre gesturing in the darkness with his spade. "How will you interpret the spirit precisely, man? How will you say it is this and not that? Every man will set to work subjecting the Bible to his own limited intelligence and end up floundering in apostasy. You will have men like this misguided Schleiermacher who pick and choose among the doctrines of the Church and who decide, puffed up by confidence in their own powers of reason, that the Fall is not a moral teaching or that the Atonement is distasteful to them."

"But if it seems clear that certain parts of the Bible are not, hm, moral according to our latest nineteenth-century conceptions of morality ..."

"Fallen man is not able to understand the purposes of God," interrupted the Padre, who had thrown away his spade and was trying to ram the small, shrouded corpse into the hole he had dug in such a way that the feet would not stick up into the air. "Human conceptions of morality must be fallible like all human ideas!"

"The letter killeth, the Spirit giveth life, all the same, if you see what I mean," quoted Fleury feebly. He found himself unable to match the Padre's positive assertions with anything better than vague equivocations. Nevertheless, like all intellectual young men he disliked coming off worst in an argument, whatever the subject. He fell into a sullen silence as the Padre continued to harangue him, and looked around to see if the Collector would be thinking of relieving him soon. But the Collector had left his tombstone and melted deeper into the darkness.

"You cannot escape the fact," said Fleury, returning to the attack, "that our century has developed a morality higher and finer than anything the world has known before, based on the *spirit* of the New Testament, ignoring the letter of the Old Testament. The nineteenth century has witnessed a refinement of morality unknown to the antique world!"

"Thy wisdom and thy knowledge, it hath perverted thee!"

The Padre's words echoed after the Collector as he retreated through the darkness and he thought: "Young Fleury is perfectly right ... How arid the eighteenth century was in comparison to our own. They did their best, no doubt, but they were *at best* only a preparation for our own century. How barren in taste they were, how lacking in feeling! What a poor conception of Man, what fruitless ratiocination! Everything which they approached so ineffectually, we have brought to culmination. The poor fellows had no conception how far Art, Science, Respectability, and Political Economy could be taken. Where they hesitated and blundered we have gone forward ... Ah!" He stumbled. A round shot, skipping through the darkness, landed in the mud wall of the churchyard, showering him with pebbles.

Somehow the shock of this narrow escape had a sobering effect on him and his confidence drained away, and with it his satisfaction with his own epoch. He thought again of those hundred and fifty million people living in cruel poverty in India alone ... Would Science and Political Economy ever be powerful enough to give them a life of ease and respectability? He no longer believed that they would. If they did, it would not be in his own century but in some future era. This notion of the superiority of the nineteenth century which he had just

216

been enjoying had depended on beliefs he no longer held, but which had just now been itching, like amputated limbs which he could feel although they no longer existed.

The round shot had also served to remind him of the new line of defence, the need for which was becoming daily more desperate. And so he turned towards the Residency to see how the new fortifications were progressing. Alas, the Collector knew that Machiavelli, another member of his staff of nocturnal counsellors, would not have wanted him to construct this second line of defence. It was the opinion of that cynical man that if a possiblity of retreat existed, the defenders would use it, and thus bring about their own defeat. But there was nothing the Collector could do about that . . . Sooner or later he would have to reduce the perimeter of the enclave. Even at the beginning of the siege the ramparts had been too sparsely manned. Now, with two or three men dying every day and sometimes more, the interval between each rifle grew daily larger, and only the inability of the sepoys to concert an attack with all their disparate forces had allowed the defences to remain intact.

"Besides, Machiavelli was not speaking of Englishmen, but Italians . . . A very different matter."

At first, the Collector had considered a new line which would form a loop around the Residency, the Church, and the banqueting hall, but he knew that the labour of digging an adequate trench and rampart over such a distance must now be beyond the strength of his garrison, who were obliged to fight during the day and dig at night. He had considered leaving the banqueting hall outside, but he soon realized that this was out of the question; it dominated the Residency . . . even if demolished its ruins would still command the Residency from an impregnable position. And yet the banqueting hall itself could not be defended for more than a few days because it lacked water. But he knew that there must be a solution to his problem and presently, by exercising his powers of observation and reason, he found it.

Among the many inventions in his possession there was an American velocipede. He had never found very much use for it in the past. At the time it had been designed no satisfactory system of pedals had yet been devised and he himself was no longer supple enough to propel it by one foot on the ground, as its inventor had intended. Once or twice, it was true, he had had an eager young assistant magistrate speeding erratically across the lawns on it to the amusement of the ladies and the astonishment of the bearers. But two wheels, he had been obliged to reflect, or even, come to that, a dozen wheels, would never match for speed and convenience the four legs of the horse. Now, however, this machine suddenly rolled out of oblivion into his mind as the very design required for his new system of defence ... One large wheel, to include the residency and the churchyard (whose ready-made wall could be incorporated), and a smaller wheel around the banqueting hall. All that was needed was a double sap (a single trench with a rampart on both sides) to join the two wheels.

This system had many advantages. The banqueting hall would act as a barbican to the Residency, protecting one entire hemisphere from a direct attack, the Residency doing the same for the weaker hemisphere of the banqueting hall. If the garrison continued to dwindle, the survivors could be progressively drawn back from the connecting trench into each wheel without necessarily weakening the whole structure. If the worst came to the worst, one wheel could even be abandoned altogether.

When he had paid a visit to Ford, the railway engineer whom he had put in charge of the execution of this elegant idea, and had surveyed the progress of the night's digging, he turned away again into the darkness. Although exhausted, he dreaded the prospect of returning to his empty room to sleep. Once or twice, ignoring the anxiety of his daughters he had not returned to his own bed but slept instead cradled in the documents in the Cutcherry. He had come to love roaming about the enclave in the darkness; the darkness brought relief from the overcrowding of the Residency which disgusted him, from the danger of crossing open spaces, from the hot wind and, above all, from the eyes of the garrison which were continually searching his face for signs of weakness or despair.

Now the night had grown darker, increasing his sense of freedom. A low bank of cloud had spread across the Eastern horizon and was slowly mounting over the entire firmament, concealing the stars. A breathless silence prevailed and the heat had grown more intense. It seemed to him, too, though he could not be sure, that low on the Eastern horizon there was a glimmer of lightning ... but perhaps it was musket fire or simply the flickering of those mysterious bonfires which nightly burned on the empty plain. "If it rains it will give us more time, and that's what we most need ... Time to go as far as our food and powder will take us. After all, it's not as if we have to hold this place for the rest of our lives ... But why has there been no word of a relieving force?"

As he passed near the churchyard again he heard the sound of the Padre's voice. The Padre's energies, as singleminded as a pack of hounds, were relentlessly running down the one or two heretical notions owned by Fleury which, dodging here and there like tired foxes, had still managed to elude them. Before lighting the lamp in his empty room the Collector crossed to the verandah and stood outside for a moment, watching the bank of cloud cover the shrinking patch of starlit sky to the west.

"We look on past ages with condescension, as a mere pre-paration for *us* ... but what if we're only an after-glow of *them?*"

He lit the oil-lamp on the table beside a dish of *dal* and a chapati which his daughters had left for his supper; his shat-tered bedroom slowly materialized out of the darkness, the splintered woodwork, the broken furniture, the wallpaper hanging in shreds from the shrapnel-pocked walls; this once beautiful, complacent, happy, elegant room was like a physical manifestation of his own grieving mind.

Part Three

18

The Collector had half expected the rains to begin during the
night, but when he awoke the sky was cloudless once more;
he could sense, however, that they would not be long coming.
Already the burning winds had ceased to blow during the day;
the air had lost its crisp dryness and consequently the heat
seemed more oppressive than ever. Clouds gathered again in
the course of the next two days, but after an hour or two they
would disperse. From the roof of the banqueting hall he could
see that the river, which had been almost dry until now, had
swollen greatly, it continued to rise during the night until by the
following morning it had submerged the melon beds. This sudden rise of the river was familiar to the Collector; he knew
that it was not due to a fall of rain in the district but to the
melting of the snows in the high Himalaya. Usually it heralded
rains even so, but this year the river gradually subsided once
more. Clouds gathered several times but only to disperse again.

Among the disasters which multiplied in the enclave during
these last days before the monsoon none came as a more severe
blow than the death of Lieutenant Cutter. He had become a
hero for the garrison, for English and native defenders alike.
Many tears were shed, particularly by the younger ladies,
while the Padre made his eloquent funeral oration after the
mid-day service on Sunday the 12 July in the Residency cellars.

"Providence has denied his country the privilege of decking
his youthful brow with the chaplets which belong to the sons
of victory and of fame, but his deeds can never die. The pages
of history will record and rehearse them far and wide, and
every Englishman, whether in his island home or a wanderer on
some foreign shore, will relate with admiration what George
Foxlett Cutter did at the siege of Krishnapur!"

By this time the manner of Cutter's death was known
throughout the camp and somehow it appeared disconcertingly

trivial for a man who had so often exposed himself to such great danger. It had happened at the rampart by Dr Dunstaple's house where Cutter had just shot a sepoy the moment before and seen him fall; at the same instant he had caught sight of another sepoy levelling his musket and had said to the Sikh beside him: "See that man aiming at me, take him down." But the words had hardly passed his lips when the shot struck him. He had been on one knee, but had risen to "attention" and then fallen, expiring without a word or groan, or any valedictory comments whatsoever.

"I had no idea the poor fellow was called 'Foxlett', had you?" Fleury asked Harry. He had to struggle to convince himself that Cutter's heroic stature was not a tiny bit reduced by this peculiar name.

In the meantime the steady trickle of deaths from wounds and sickness continued. A growing despondency prevailed. A rumour spread through the camp that a relieving force from Dinapur had been cut to pieces on the way to Krishnapur. It was said that a massacre had followed the surrender of General Wheeler at Cawnpore and that delicate English girls had been stripped naked and dragged through the streets of Delhi.

Another disaster was the death of little Mary Porter, a child already orphaned by the mutiny. Mary had been playing with some other children in the stable yard and had suddenly fainted. The other children had called Fleury, who was passing. He had picked her up half-conscious, and while he carried her to the hospital she had clung to him with a pitiful force. It is a terrible thing to be clung to by a sick child if you are not used to it; Fleury was very shaken by the power of the protective instinct which was suddenly aroused in him, although to no avail, for there was nothing he could do. She was suffering from sunstroke and she died within a short time. Dr Dunstaple, under whose care she succumbed, was also strongly affected by her death. This was surprising when you consider that these days Death was the genial Doctor's constant drinking-companion. Perhaps he had glimpsed in Mary something of his own daughter, Fanny. Whatever the reason, the effect was terrible. He seemed to go out of his mind completely, raving about every imaginable topic from the Calcutta races to Dr McNab's diabolical treatment of cholera. The Collector ordered him to bed and both wards of the hospital were taken over by Dr McNab; but not for long. After a day or two of confinement in a darkened room he returned to the hospital and took over his ward again. No sooner was he back amongst his own patients than he set about exchanging the dressings applied by Dr McNab, even though they were in most cases identical to his own. When the Collector mentioned this to Dr McNab he shook his head and said: "Aye, the poor man has a way to go yet before he'll be sound"

Before the Collector continued about his business, Dr McNab asked him to come over to the window for a moment. He wanted to examine the Collector's right eye which had become red and rather swollen. The Collector himself had paid no attention to it, assuming it to be one of the many trivial ailments from which the garrison, deprived of adequate fresh food, was now suffering.

"It's inflamed, Mr Hopkins. Is it painful?"

"Not very."

McNab offered no further comment so the Collector went on his way.

The sight which greeted him now in the tiger house was a pitiful one. Hari no longer paced nervously up and down; he lay sprawled on a pile of dirty straw, his eyes extinct. Around him lay scattered the festering remains of half a dozen meals. There was a powerful stench of urine also, as if he no longer went outside to perform his natural functions. He had turned grey, as Indians do when they are unhappy. His eyes were very bloodshot, like small balls of scarlet in his dark countenance, and his cheeks, of which the Collector had always admired the plumpness and the polish, were now hollow and covered with a dark, wispy down. Half buried in the dirty straw, beside a bone crawling with flies, lay the phrenology book, undisturbed since the Collector's last visit.

The Prime Minister was singing softly to himself when the Collector came in and continued to do so all the time he was there. It was a religious song and a joyful one, the Prime Minister's eyes sparkled. But they sparkled not outwardly but inwardly, for the deity which was causing him such intense satisfaction was inside himself. The Collector was astonished by how little the Prime Minister had changed during his month of captivity. He looked exactly the same except for his hair, which Hari had shaved off for his experiments and which had now grown into a furry black stubble through which the numbered segments of his skull could still be faintly perceived. The siege had simply made no impression on him whatsoever.

Looking at the Prime Minister the Collector was overcome by a feeling of helplessness. He realized that there was a whole way of life of the people in India which he would never get to know and which was totally indifferent to him and his concerns. "The Company could pack up here tomorrow and this fellow would never notice ... And not only him ... The British could leave and half India wouldn't notice us leaving just as they didn't notice us arriving. All our reforms of administration might be reforms on the moon for all it has to do with them." The Collector was humbled and depressed by this thought. He noticed that Hari was watching him with dull eyes.

"Hari, I've decided to let you go home. I suggest that you leave here before it grows dark so that the sepoys don't shoot you by mistake."

A shudder, as from a slight cough, passed through Hari's inanimate frame, but there was no other response. Hari continued to stare at him dully. At length, after some preliminary champing of his lips during which the Collector caught a glimpse of a white-coated tongue, Hari spoke.

"Mr Hopkin, it is cruel to torture with words. You do better to hang me from mango tree without more ado about nothing."

"Hari, how could you think such a thing?" cried the Collector, shocked. "This is no game. You're free to leave here and go home today. Look here, I know that I've treated you badly ... But you must believe that I kept you here not because I wanted to, but because I believed it my duty to those whom God (or, well, the Company anyway) has placed in my care. Perhaps it was a mistake ... perhaps keeping you here has done no good ... I don't know whether it has made any difference, but now we're obliged to abandon some of our defences and it's certain that your presence can no longer help

226

us. You'll be in great danger if you stay. You must forgive me, Hari, for keeping you here. This was wrong of me, I acknowledge it."

"You acknowledge, Mr Hopkin, you acknowledge! But you ruin health. I die of starvation and disease. I die of musket fire and you acknowledge."

"Please, Hari, you must not think badly of me. You must put yourself in my position. Besides, I'm not well myself . . . indeed, I'm most definitely sick," added the Collector succumbing to a sudden wave of self-pity for it was true, he did not feel in the least well. His right eye, which he had hardly noticed until Dr McNab had looked at it a little while earlier, had begun to throb painfully, and at the same time he felt feverish and nauseated, though perhaps it was only on account of the fetid atmosphere and the stench of urine.

"You must go now, Hari, and take the Prime Minister with you."

Every moment the Collector became more unwell. All the same, he found it pleasant to watch Hari reviving like a thirsty plant which has just been watered. Hari had already got to his feet and little by little was becoming animated again.

"When you're ready, go to the Cutcherry and tell the Magistrate. He'll stop firing while you go across to the sepoy lines. I must ask you not to tell them of our condition, however. Goodbye, Hari." The Collector had a feeling that even if he survived the siege he would never see Hari again. But before he had reached the door Hari had called to him, following him to the door.

· Collector Sahib, though I do not forgive bad treatment from *Sircar* and from British Collector Sahib, I do not wish to cause personal grievance to my good friend, Mr Hopkin. I like to make to Mr Hopkin as private citizen a small gift of Frenloudji book, which is the only object in my possession and to give him handshake for last time. Correct!"

"Thank you, Hari," said the Collector, and tears came to his eyes, causing the right one to throb more painfully than ever.

A little later from his bedroom, where he had retired for a rest, he watched through his daughters' brass telescope as the

227

grey shadow of what had once been the sleek and lively Hari moved slowly over to the sepoy lines with, as usual, the Prime Minister dodging along behind him.

"I hope he doesn't tell them what a state we're in, all the same."

19

Now that the time had come for the depleted garrison to shrink back inside the new fortifications, accommodation had to be found for the ladies displaced from Dr Dunstaple's house. Volunteers from the billiard room were needed to move to the banqueting hall so that the new ladies, many of whom were elderly, might be installed in their places in comparative comfort. It was when he was on his way to the billiard room to ask for these volunteers that the Collector suddenly felt faint. The Padre, who was passing, helped him to his bedroom and offered to call one of the doctors.

"No, it's nothing. Just the heat," muttered the Collector, dreading lest he be taken to the hospital. "Send me the Magistrate."

When the Magistrate duly appeared the Collector, lying feverishly on his bed, asked him to take command of the garrison for a few hours. He explained what had to be done. The retreat must be carefully conducted so that it did not turn into a rout. He cursed himself inwardly for this sudden indisposition, which had come at the worst possible moment. Still, the Magistrate was a competent man. As an afterthought, he explained about the ladies who must volunteer for the banqueting hall.

But although they were terrified of the Magistrate, who in more peaceful times had so often savaged their verses, the ladies in the billiard room stoutly refused to volunteer for the banqueting hall, which they wrongly believed to be more dangerous than the Residency . . . except for Lucy, who was generally acknowledged to have nothing to live for anyway. As for Louise and Miriam, they had decided they must stay in the Residency in order to lend their assistance at the hospital, where the dispensers and orderlies could no longer cope. In the end, since there were no volunteers, the Magistrate was obliged to send the Eurasian women, half a dozen of whom had been quietly living in the Residency pantry and had spread their bedding on the pantry shelves. There were eight ladies to be accommodated. He still had to find room for two more, so he decided to banish the two foolish, pretty O'Hanlons from their billiard-table, sensing that they would make least fuss.

From the window of his room the Collector watched the final preparations being made for the hazardous withdrawal from his original "mud walls" to the new fortifications. Magnified as much by his fever as by the brass telescope to his eye, he saw Hookum Singh, a giant Sikh capable of carrying a barrel of powder on his back, stagger after Harry Dunstaple, emptying the powder in piles at the corners of the Cutcherry building and around pillars and supports. At the same time, a similar operation out of the field of his lens, was being performed at what was left of Dr Dunstaple's house. Fleury, Ford, Burlton, and half a dozen Sikhs, were digging a series of *fougasses* (holes dug slant-wise in the ground and filled with a charge of powder and stones), again with the intention of preventing the sepoys from converting their retreat into a rout. So far all the preparations had been made as discreetly as possible, under cover of darkness, but now the moment he most dreaded was approaching, the moment when the sepoys would realize that a retreat was taking place and would launch their attack. The Collector's hands trembled so badly that he had to rest the telescope on the shattered window sill. His face throbbed and his eyeball was seared by the white glare through which the dark figures of the men were moving about their work.

Shortly before five o'clock the sepoy cavalry made an attack near the Cutcherry but fortunately the men had not yet left their positions at the rampart. The attack was repulsed. The Collector watched this brief engagement in the dazzling circle of crystal but could no longer understand it. He saw a *sowar* hit as he spurred towards the Residency. He saw the man's limbs, tightly clenched as he drove his horse towards the Cutcherry guns, suddenly relax as if something inside him had snapped. Then he slithered out of sight into the dust.

Soon he could no longer bear to apply the scorching lens to his right eye and was obliged to hold it to his left, which he did more clumsily than ever. It trembled uncomprehendingly over Harry Dunstaple running towards the ramparts waving a sabre and shouting orders, with the bulging pockets of his Tweedside lounging jacket swinging about his knees ... over Ford, carefully laying a train back to the wall of the church-yard from one of the *fougasses* that had been dug . . . over the Sikhs staggering here and there with loads of small stones to shovel into another *fougasse* not yet completed ... over the green Fleury having a rest in the shade of a tamarind beside the Church wall ... and finally over the pariah dog, looking to-wards Fleury with admiration but from a respectful distance (for Fleury continued to reject its advances). The Collector, his mind too feverish to recollect for more than a moment what all this activity was about, became absorbed in the con-templation of this pariah dog. Its mouth was open, its lips drawn back, and it appeared to be grinning. From the thin, wretched creature it had been at the beginning of the siege it had become quite fat, for recently it had succeeded in eating two small lap-dogs which had unwisely fallen asleep in its pre-sence. Now it was ready for another meal and was keeping a hopeful eye on the battlefield in case some appetizing English-man or sepoy should fall conveniently near ... but most of all it would like to eat Fleury, such was the power of its love for this handsome, green-clad young man; it uttered a groan of ecstasy at the thought and a needle of saliva, dripping from its jaws, sparkled in the Collector's telescope.

The Collector, of course, was aware only of a loathsome, sinister, and rather fat dog ... How he wished this animal were a fluffy spaniel! How delightful that would be! Tea on the lawn, spaniels at one's heels, scarlet and dark green . . . the colours of the rightness of the world and of his place in it! Even in his fever the Collector's amputated hopes and beliefs continued to itch.

But now the men were sprinting back from the ramparts. They were plunging for the shelter of the churchyard wall as a typhoon of musket fire swept the defences, kicking dust into a mist around the ankles of the retreating men. Some fell and were dragged on by their comrades, others had to crawl as best they could, their heads barely emerging from the puffs of dust, across the open space between the Cutcherry and the church-yard wall. On the top of this wall stood Harry Dunstaple, shouting and waving his sabre as if conducting an orchestra, shouting for the men to hasten, for the Cutcherry must be blown up before the charging enemy could reach it and disturb the train.

"Let us have tea on the lawn again!" shouted the Collector from the window, but no one paid any attention to him. His swollen, inflamed face had become unbearable now; he could neither touch it, nor refrain from touching it.

There was a flash through the haze of dust as Ford knelt to fire the train. Already the first squadrons of sepoy cavalry were swooping over the abandoned ramparts and racing for the Cutcherry to kick away just a few inches of that thin trickle of grey powder before it burnt its way home. The Collector's telescope had wandered, however, to the slope above the melon beds where the densely crowded onlookers were shouting, cheering, and waving banners in a frenzy of excitement. "How happy they are!" thought the Collector, in spite of the pain. "It is good that the natives should be happy for surely that is ultimately what we, the Company, are in India to procure ..." But by misfortune his telescope had now wandered back again and was trained on the Cutcherry at the very moment that it exploded with a flash that burnt itself so deeply into the Collector's brain that he reeled, as if struck in the eye by a musket ball ... And then there was nothing but smoke, dust, debris, and a crash which dropped a picture from the wall behind him. But at the next instant from the other side of the Residency echoed another, even greater, explosion ... and that was the last of Dr Dunstaple's house.

The Collector was both clutching at his face and trying not to clutch at it. Yet he must somehow tear the pain out with his hands or he knew that it would kill him. A cheer rang out from the natives assembled above the melon beds; it could be heard even over the boom of cannons and rattle of musketry. He had dropped his telescope; for a few moments he groped on the floor beside the window, but he no longer needed the telescope; he could see perfectly well without it. For a moment, as he looked out of the window, his mind became clear again and he thought: "My God, the sepoys are attacking. I must tell someone. I must warn the men." He could see the sepoy infantry advancing in hordes across the open ground from the direction of the cantonment. The cavalry had already ridden

232

through the pall of dust and smoke that hung over the demolished Cutcherry and now they were ready to hurl themselves at the garrison, hastily assembled behind the churchyard wall. Less than a hundred yards from the wall they swerved and re-grouped for a charge as the infantry swarmed up behind them.

The Collector had become calm again. The reason was that his pain, although it was still there was no longer a part of him. His pain, a round, red, throbbing presence, sat beside him at the window enjoying the spectacle. Since Pain was paying no attention to him, he decided that he might without impropriety ignore Pain. He and Pain together watched a scene which reminded the Collector of the beach. How pleasant it is to sit on the cliffs of Dover and watch the waves rolling in. You can see them beginning so far out . . . you see them slowly grow as they come nearer and nearer to the shore, rise and then thrash themselves against the beach. Some of them vanish inexplicably. Others turn themselves into giants. As the sepoys, sensing that their chance had now come to abolish the *feringhees* from the face of the earth, massed for a great assault, the Collector could see that this time a giant wave was coming.

"This should be a splendid show," he murmured, and Pain nodded his agreement. The spectators from the melon beds howled with enthusiasm, threw things into the air, and hugged each other from sheer excitement as the charge began. For some reason it began in a thick snowstorm of large white flakes.

Now, as the cries of the spectators rose to a crescendo, they were joined by the familiar stomach-turning howl of the charging sepoys, which added an undertow of dread to the Collector's pleasure. Below him, Fleury raced along outside the churchyard wall under the bayonets of the galloping sepoys, touching off the trains to the *fougasses*. Abruptly, in front of the charging sepoys, who were already bewildered by the densely whirling white flakes, the ground erupted. Volleys of stones blew out of the earth.

Simultaneously cannons fired canister into their midst. The wave toppled, thrashed and boiled against the ground, but hardly advanced another step up the beach.

The sepoy officers shouted at their men and tried to rally

them. This was the time to charge on, while the cannons were being re-loaded. Victory was theirs if only they would press on *now*! But the men were blinded and confused by the snowstorm. They could see neither their officers nor the *feringhees* ... Then came a sudden, dreadful volley from their left flank, from the wheel of the banqueting hall. A few more seconds of hesitation and all was lost. The cannons were re-loaded. Another deadly volley of canister and scarcely a man was left on his feet and capable of charging even had he wanted to do so. It was all over. Thanks to that providential snowstorm the attack had been repulsed. The survivors scrambled back to the sepoy lines pursued by a vengeful squadron of Sikh cavalry.

The Collector had been unable to see the latter part of this action, which had taken place in thick yellow dust and smoke (the snow having mysteriously ceased). But even if there had been no dust, smoke or snow, he would still have been unable to see it, because he was now lying on the floor beside the window, having fallen off his chair. Pain had come to stretch out beside him. Unseen by either Pain or the Collector, the fat pariah dog in the shade of the tamarind was whining and jumping up and down with excitement at the prospect of a square meal or two, when all the fuss was over.

Fleury, exhausted and still quaking from his gallant dash beneath the sepoys' glistening bayonets, had slumped down with his back to the new rampart. He picked one of the snowflakes off the parapet and began to read it, but it was not very interesting ... just a salt report from some sub-district or other. He threw it away and pulled out the Bible, which he had stuffed superstitiously into his shirt to protect his ribs ... He had heard so many stories of musket balls lodging in Bibles, not of course that he *really* believed them, but all the same ... What he wanted to do now was to find some immoral passages with which to confront the Padre, thereby proving to him that this book could not possibly be the word of God (unadulterated, anyway). Now where was it that God commanded the Israelites to massacre the people of Canaan? That would do quite nicely for a start. The Padre (or God) would have trouble wriggling out of that one.

Meanwhile, the Magistrate had ordered the native pensioners

to collect up the vernacular records and documents which lay in shallow drifts in the new trenches . . . all that now remained of the experimental greenhouse in which he had observed the progress and ubiquity of the Company's stupidity. More papers lay scattered thickly over the ground between the churchyard wall and the rubble of the Cutcherry but they could not be collected because musket fire once more swept the open spaces. The Magistrate did not mind. He had no love for documents. And these had certainly proved more useful than most.

20

Such was the emotion caused by the attack that it was some time before any of the defenders recalled that the Collector had not been feeling well and wondered what had become of him. There was the binding of wounds and examining of bruises to be considered, and the saying of prayers and sewing-up in bedding of those whose lives had been forfeit ... and above all there was a great deal of talking to be done, for, as the Magistrate scientifically observed, nothing unusual can happen among human beings without generating an immense, compensating volume of chatter.

Fleury, as it happened, wanted to borrow a book and finding the door open took a few respectful steps towards where the Collector was sitting ... which was on the floor, for some reason. The light was poor in the Collector's bedroom and Fleury might not have noticed how red and swollen his face was, had the Collector not presently fallen sideways, rapping his head on the floor. Immediately all became clear to Fleury and he drew back with horror, thinking: "Cholera!" Then he raced away to find a doctor.

But when Fleury breathlessly informed Dr McNab of his diagnosis McNab did not seem to take it very seriously. He said to Miriam, who was helping him dress the wounds of those hurt in the recent engagement: "The poor Collector has erysipelas. I feared as much when I saw him this morning."

Miriam knew that people can die of erysipelas and when she saw what a state the Collector was in, rolling on the floor in delirium, his face red and swollen, she received an unpleasant shock. Fleury was quite wrong in thinking that Miriam had been nourishing amorous ambitions as far as the Collector was concerned; on the contrary, throughout the siege she had taken great pains not to allow her feelings to attach themselves to any individual man. Once in her life already she had become attached to someone and had allowed herself to be swept down with him in his lonely vortex into the silent depths where nothing moves but drowned sailors coughing sea-weed; only Miriam herself knew how much it had cost her to ascend again from that fascinating, ghostly world towards light and life. She knew that if she were whirled down again it would be for the last time. But there was yet another reason: Miriam was tired of womanhood. She wanted simply to experience life as an anonymous human being of flesh and blood. She was tired of having to adjust to other people's ideas of what a woman should be. And nothing condemned a woman so swiftly to womanhood as grappling with a man. All the same, she was shocked to think that the Collector might not survive.

"It is not yet too severe," said McNab, "but it can spread quickly. We must give him nourishment for it's a very lowering, debilitating disease. I'll ask you to prepare beef tea and arrowroot, Mrs Lang. Your brother perhaps will not mind fetching them from the Commissariat. And a bottle of brandy, too."

While Fleury hurried away for the stores Dr McNab wrote down the details of the Collector's illness . . . Subject to rigors and vomiting, redness and swelling of the face, pulse 86, respirations 30.

"Why d'you write down everything in that book?" demanded Miriam sharply, irritated by the Doc'or's methodical habits. She had a vision of McNab calmly recording the manner of the Collector's death, the way he had already recorded so many in the last weeks. He ignored her question ("because I'm a woman", thought Miriam) but smiled soothingly and said: "Will you look after him for me, Mrs Lang? I shall ask one of the other ladies to help you if need be. Miss Dunstaple perhaps. If he needs an aperient we must give him something which is not too irritating to the alimentary canal, such as castor oil. Above all, we must be careful not to exhaust him further. The poison of erysipelas is exceedingly depressing in its action. Our first object must be to antagonize the poison and at the same time uphold his powers."

The Collector started up with a groan, glaring wildly at Miriam, who could hardly bear to look at his red, bloated face.

"And we must keep him calm, as best we can. In addition to the beef tea and arrowroot, as much as he will take, we'll give him half an ounce of brandy every two hours, and twenty drops of laudanum every four." At the door McNab paused and said with a smile: "I'm sure he'll rally with such a fine young woman to care for him."

With that he took his leave, sighing enigmatically.

As night fell, although the Collector became quieter (no doubt thanks to the laudanum), he remained delirious. The heat was extraordinarily oppressive. No breath of air stirred the Collector's mosquito net. Miriam sat wearily by the window, feeling the perspiration soaking her neck and breast and the hollow of her back, leaking steadily from her armpits and from between her legs, and causing her underclothes to stick to her stomach and thighs. From time to time she crossed the room, soaked a flannel in the tepid water of a basin, and pressed it gently against the Collector's swollen face. At ten o'clock she gave him beef tea and brandy. But he scarcely seemed to notice any of these ministrations. He gulped down what he was given but continued muttering urgently to himself. His daughters, Eliza and Margaret, came to gaze dutifully at their stricken father. They, too, had taken to helping in the hospital and Miriam could read on their pale, shocked faces some of the terrible sights they had seen; after a little while she sent them away to bed.

Time passed, perhaps an hour, before there was a knock on the door and Louise came in, bringing Miriam a cup of tea. It seemed at first glance that Louise was wearing a turban; she had saved her day's ration of flour and had made a poultice of it for a boil which had erupted on her temple; her other boils seemed to be growing slightly better. Miriam, too, had a painful inflammation on her shoulder which she thought would turn into a boil; indeed, so many of the garrison now suffered from them that Louise had ceased to feel ashamed. Still, she would gaze in wonder at Fleury's clear, though dirty, countenance and wonder why he did not get any.

"It's stifling. Let us sit by the window."

"My dear, you must be tired. Let me sit up and watch over Mr Hopkins while you have a rest."

"No, my dear, you are just as tired as I am, and I shall rest presently in the dressing-room where I have made up a bed for myself. If I leave the door open I shall be able to hear him if his condition worsens."

To hear these "my dears" being so liberally dispensed you might have thought that the two girls had become bosom friends. And true enough, in the last few days they had grown much closer to each other. They had so many anxieties and sorrows to share. They had both loved poor little Mary Porter who had died of sunstroke. Fleury, too, continued to grieve for her and was now composing a poem in which her little ghost came tripping along the ramparts sniffing flowers, unperturbed by the flying cannon balls (it was not a very good poem). The fact was that both young women shared an unspoken anxiety for Fleury's safety and though Louise had not yet confided her feelings for him to Miriam, she really did not need to do so for these feelings were plain enough already. Louise now greatly regretted having made Fleury the green coat, which she feared made him too conspicuous ... and it was a fact that the sepoy sharpshooters could seldom resist trying to hit this brilliant green target. Out of bravado Fleury dismissed these fears as groundless, but he was secretly rather alarmed. Love, pride, and foolishness combined to make him keep on wearing the green coat, however.

"My dear, in a moment I shall have to call one of the bearers to assist Mr Hopkins with his natural functions in case it should be necessary."

Perhaps it was too dark for Miriam to notice how Louise was taken aback by this remark, how she blushed. Even though she had got to know Miriam so well during the siege she was still often taken aback by her boldness. In some respects, she could not help thinking, Miriam was just like a man the way she said things ... sometimes even worse. What on earth would people think if Miriam started talking of a gentleman's natural functions in front of the wedding guests when she and Fleury got married; in some ways the prospect of such a solecism seemed more terrible to Louise than the possiblity of one or both of them not surviving the siege. Still, that was Miriam all over. There was so much about her that Louise admired, she could only suspend judgement on the rest.

But Miriam had noticed the slight intake of breath; she had

239

been perfectly aware that Louise might be shocked by her words but she had spoken them anyway, partly because she felt too weary not to say what she meant, partly because, though she liked Louise, she sometimes found her sweetness and prudish innocence rather cloying and it gratified her to offend them.

"There seem to be more fires than ever on the hill tonight," said Louise brightly, hoping to divert Miriam from any further discussion of the Collector's natural functions. "How they shouted during the attack this afternoon!"

"I expect they thought they would be down here in a moment to indulge in carnal conversation with us and to murder us," replied Miriam rather cruelly, becoming blunter than ever. But this time Louise did not betray any signs of dismay. She was made of a strong enough fibre to cope with ideas to which she had already become accustomed, like murder and rape; it was novelty that she found hard to accept.

"And everywhere he is in chains!" cried the Collector urgently in his delirium, causing both young ladies to turn anxiously towards his bed ... but it was nothing, merely a passing fancy in his overheated brain. He continued to gabble away under his breath and the ladies returned to their gossip.

"To be fair, however, it must be said that the natives on the hill also applauded the firmness and resolve which the gentlemen displayed in our defence. Although, of course, it goes without saying another outcome would have pleased them better."

"How bright those fires shine in the darkness! How terrible to think that the men around them wish us ill!" sighed Louise. She tried to recall her life before the siege and the heads of young officers turning to look at her at the Calcutta race-course. Her mother had been so excited at the attention paid to her, almost as if it had not been Louise but she herself who was attracting the attention of the young gentlemen. As for Louise, strolling beneath the shade of her white silk parasol, she had remained so cool and chaste that she had scarcely deigned to notice that young men were admiring her. And yet, of course, she *had* noticed; the darkness once again hid the colour that rose to her cheeks at the recollection of the airs she had put on during those visits to the race-course. She had been so young and ignorant then; the most important thing in life had been the number of young men who were anxious to dance the opening quadrille with her. Her beauty had been something which had filled even herself with wonder; sometimes in the privacy of her own room she would gaze at some part of herself, at a hand, say, or a breast, and the perfection of its shape would fill her with joy, as if it were not a part of herself but some natural object of beauty. *"Eheu, fugaces!"* she thought and almost said, but was not quite sure how to pronounce it.

"Miriam," she said instead, "I cannot tell you how worried I am for Harry. He is so young and innocent; although he pretends to be a man he is still only a schoolboy. And now he is in such danger! I have tried to talk to him but he will not listen."

"But, my dear, there is no way that danger may be avoided whilst this dreadful siege lasts."

("The letter killeth, the spirit giveth life!" exclaimed the Collector fervently).

"Alas, it's not physical danger that I fear for him ... or rather, I fear that too, but since we are all in God's hands I trust that He will not forsake us . . . no, it's another danger that I fear for him. My dear, you cannot have failed to see how Lucy is leading him on. Think what unhappy circumstances would attend his career if he should now be trapped by a penniless girl without family whose reputation is known throughout India."

Miriam was silent. To worry that your brother might make an unfortunate marriage when at any moment he might be killed was something she found difficult to understand. But in a sense, too, she knew that Louise was not wrong to worry about Harry committing such a blunder, for Harry, moving in the social circles in which he *would* move, if he survived the siege, to the day of his death, would almost certainly suffer the inconveniences of having such a wife, would regret his marriage, and perhaps in due course would come to believe that his life had been ruined. He would be bound by the social fetters of Lucy's unsuitability simply because he too would believe in them.

"I don't think you should worry. Harry will probably get over his affection for Lucy once we return to a normal life again. And in any case, what Lucy may have done was surely not so dreadful and will be soon forgotten. A moment of foolishness with a man in one's youth, Louise dear, is more common even among the better classes than you might think. Lucy is much to be pitied. Let us worry about her future when the siege is over."

"But now she has gone to live in the banqueting hall where she will be able to use her . . ." Louise was going to say "feminine wiles" but hesitated, afraid that Miriam might find this ridiculous, and uncertain, in any case, exactly what "feminine wiles" might amount to. ". . . where she will be able to see Harry all the time," she corrected herself.

"With so many people under the same roof, my dear, Harry will be in no danger."

Presently, in the silence that followed these remarks, the two young women heard the sound of distant guns . . . more distant, it seemed, than the sepoy cannons which had been firing intermittently throughout their conversation; this sound echoed from across the dark rim of the plain. "Could it be the guns of a relief force?" Miriam was wondering as the first fat drops of rain splashed on the verandah.

"Rain! It's come at last!"

Almost immediately the first breath of cooler air reached them. The rain steadily increased in force, blotting out the fires on the hill above the melon beds, increasing the darkness until they could make out nothing in the compound below, and driving them back from the streaming verandah. Soon it had become a continuous deluge as if countless buckets of black ink were being emptied from the sky above them.

"In a moment it will be time to give Mr Hopkins another half ounce of brandy, poor man," sighed Miriam. The excitement of this first fall of rain had filled her with a desire that things should be different, that she should be happy again.

For the rest of the night the rain cascaded from the verandah roof, but the Collector paid no heed to it . . . he continued to mutter urgently to himself, thrashing weakly, possessed with the vehemence of a strange inner life where no one could reach him. The lamp beside his bed threw a faint glow over his swollen, passionate, tormented face.

21

On the following day Dr McNab made an incision in the Collector's right eyelid and a small quantity of pus escaped. Disturbed, the Doctor examined the rest of the Collector's body with care to see if there were any further local formations of pus gathering beneath the skin. There was a danger that the blood would become poisoned by pus or by some other morbid agent which would render death by pyaemia inevitable. The Collector's delirium still continued and he was undoubtedly becoming weaker; because of these continuing symptoms McNab now substituted bark, chloric aether, and ammonia in effervescence for the laudanum and asked Miriam to increase the brandy to half an ounce every hour. Although he did not say so it was evident that he still regarded the Collector's condition as serious; the one hopeful sign was that his pulse had become fuller and less frequent. Convinced that he was going to die, his brood of terrified, velvet-clad children came to his bedside and stood there, the eldest holding the youngest, dutifully watching the thrashings of their parent, until Miriam packed them off.

For the moment the sepoys had stopped firing and an eerie hush had settled over the Residency. A night and a day of intermittent rainstorms followed. From the roof it could be seen that the sepoys had remained in their positions and were building themselves shelters. The garrison conjectured that the sepoys' powder had been soaked by the downpour ... there was even wild talk of breaking out of the enclave and escaping to safety. But, alas, there was no sense in this. Even if they succeeded in breaking through the sepoy lines, where would they go? Where did safety lie on that vast, hostile plain? The silence continued, broken only by the shrieking and quarrelling of crows and parakeets. And now gaily plumed water birds began to appear on the rapidly swelling river. The birds had a new and shiny look; in India only the animals and the people look starved, ragged, and exhausted.

The heat, which had declined a little at the coming of the rains, grew more oppressive than ever. At night a clamour of frogs and crickets arose and this diabolical piping served to string nerves which were already humming tight a little tighter. The connecting trench was constantly full of water now, and because the firing-step was in danger of crumbling there was no alternative for someone who wanted to visit the other wheel but to wade through water and mud. The coming of the rains brought no physical relief to the besieged but in one respect it made things worse; the smell from the decaying offal and from the corpses of men and animals became intolerable and hung constantly, undisturbed by wind, as a foul miasma over the fortifications. While the lull in the firing persisted, the Magistrate ordered earth to be thrown over the rotting mountain of offal in order to cover it like the crust of a pie. But as soon as the next downpour came the crust was soaked, vile gas bubbles would belch forth from it and infect the surrounding air. The ladies in the billiard room kept a small fire of smashed furniture smouldering by the window and occasionally burned camphor in an attempt to palliate this tormenting odour.

But besides the lull in firing the rains did bring one advantage; the spectators were driven away from the hill above the melon beds. No longer did the garrison feel that their sufferings were taking place for the amusement of the crowd. But gradually even so, a new fatalism took hold of everyone. Some of those who did not possess a faith in God which was proof against all adversities now saw that the great hope of a relief force reaching them, which had so far buoyed them up, was an illusory one; even if a relief now came, in many different ways it would be too late . . . and not only because so many of the garrison were already dead; India itself was now a different place; the fiction of happy natives being led forward along the road to civilization could no longer be sustained. Perhaps this was in the Collector's mind as he lay there, silent and motionless now that the fever had left him and he was beginning to recover. By the end of the third day his delirium had diminished, by the fifth day it had gone entirely and the redness and swelling of his face had also begun to disappear. Dr McNab now ordered the stimulants to be decreased gradually from day to day, meat and beer from the stores being substituted for the brandy and beef tea. At last, he was convalescent.

The illness had aged him. He lay still for hour after hour, naked beneath a sheet because of the heat and humidity, the mosquito net cast aside for air, too exhausted even to lift an arm to drive away the mosquitoes which constantly settled on his face. Miriam or one of the older children of the garrison who could no longer play outside since the shrinking of the perimeter sat constantly at his bedside to fan him and to defend him against the mosquitoes. He said nothing. He seemed too exhausted even to speak or move his eyes.

Miriam, too, was very tired. Her body itched constantly and salt crystals from the drying of perspiration clung to the hair of her armpits and rimed her skin. Life no longer seemed real to her. As the hours fled by she was sometimes unable to remember whether it was night or day. In a dream, which was not a dream, she was called away to assist Dr McNab perform an amputation on a Sikh whose arm had been shattered by shrapnel. The man was too weak for chloroform and had to be held by two of the dispensers, yet he did not utter a groan throughout the operation. Afterwards she found herself back at the Collector's bedside in the same churning confusion of day and night.

"What's that noise? Is that the sepoys?"

"Frogs." Miriam could hardly believe that he had spoken at last.

"Then it must have rained at last."

"It's been raining for a week."

When at last he was able to throw aside his damp sheet and make his way to the window the panorama he had last seen on the day of the sepoy attack had been transformed. The glaring desert had turned a brilliant green. Foliage sprouted everywhere. Even the lawns had been restored, like emerald carpets unrolled before his eyes; sunblasted trees which might have been thought dead had miraculously clothed themselves with leaves. Only the new trench leading to the banqueting hall cut a brown gash through the green, but even there green mus-

taches were perhaps beginning to cover the lips of the parapets
... the Collector hoped they were: he did not want the ramparts to be washed away.

Presently Miriam entered the room and found him, half
dressed, sitting on his bed with his head resting wearily against
the pillows.

"Now that I've recovered we must think of your reputation,
Mrs Lang."

"After all this, Mr Hopkins, do you think that reputations
still matter?"

"If they don't matter, then nothing does. We must obey the
rules."

"Like your precious hive of bees at the Exhibition? I'm glad
you still believe in them."

"It's hard to learn new tricks," said the Collector smiling
doubtfully, "especially when you reach my age. Have you any
idea where my boots are, Mrs Lang?"

"Under the bed. But I don't think that Dr McNab would be
pleased to see you getting up so soon."

"I must."

"Because of the bees?" And Miriam shook her head, half
smiling, half concerned.

The Collector sat for a long time contemplating his boots
which, because of the dampness, had become covered in green
mould. His shoes, his books, his leather trunks and saddlery
would similarly be covered in green mould and would remain
so now until the end of the rainy season. The Collector wondered whether the garrison, too, would become covered in
green mould.

He saw his reflection in the mirror as he was adjusting his
collar; not only had his side-whiskers grown while he had been
ill, there was also a growth of beard on his chin. He was shocked
to see that this beard, unlike his hair and whiskers which were
dark brown in colour, was sprouting with an atheistical tint of
ginger, only a little darker than the whiskers of the free-thinking Magistrate. Later, seated dizzily at the desk in his study,
he reached for a piece of paper to write some orders for the
defence of the banqueting hall. But the paper was so damp that
his pen merely furrowed it, as if he were writing on a slab of
butter.

22

Now, as always at the beginning of the rainy season, dense black clouds began to roll in over the Residency from the direction of the river, advancing slowly, not more than a few feet above the ground and masking completely whatever lay in their path. These black clouds were formed of insects called cockchafers, or "flying bugs", as the English called them; they were black as pitch and quite harmless, but with a sickening odour which they lent to anything they touched. When the cockchafers arrived, Lucy, the O'Hanlon sisters, Harry, Fleury, Mohammed and Ram were all seated around a little fire in the middle of the floor of the banqueting hall not too far from the baronial fireplace which had unfortunately become impossible to reach through the stacks of "possessions"; this fire had been cleverly made by Lucy herself out of bits and pieces of smashed furniture; a large "gothic" chair of oak, which Lucy's lovely but not very powerful muscles had been unable to get the better of, lay on its side with one leg in the fire while the kettle hung from the leg above it, an ingenious idea of Lucy's own. Lucy had just made tea and was boiling the kettle again for another cup; by now supplies of milk and sugar were exhausted and tea had to be drunk without either. Harry was a little worried to see the water supply diminishing so rapidly but was pleased that Lucy was enjoying herself. She had gone through rather a bad patch since she had come to live in the banqueting hall. Once or twice, when Harry and Fleury had had to leave her to her own devices for a few moments in order to fight off the sepoys, she had become very upset and had made little attempt to conceal the fact.

Not long ago she had begun to talk of life not being worth living again and she had demanded that Harry should tell her, once and for all, why it *was* worth living. She did not seem to mind that she was distressing poor Harry by such questions. She had said that, in the circumstances and since he could do nothing but mumble, she would probably kill herself. She was so hungry ... so tired and hot. When the rations were yet again reduced, that was really the last straw. No, she did *not* want some of Harry's handful of flour and *dal*! She wanted a decent meal with vegetables and meat.

Harry and Fleury conferred about this problem and decided that they would club together and see if they could afford to buy some hermetically sealed provisions when there was an auction, though with the prices that food fetched now in private barter they were not very hopeful. Fleury and Harry were becoming dreadfully hungry, too, but Lucy and the O'Hanlons must come first, of course. They had approached Barlow to see if he would be prepared to contribute, but Barlow had made it clear that he would not.

"The Eurasian women are managing alright so why can't Miss Hughes?"

The answer, as far as Lucy was concerned, was that she was a more fragile flower altogether, but if that was not obvious to Barlow there was no use in trying to explain it to him. The young men were very indignant with Barlow. Their indignation acted on Lucy like a tonic and she cheered up considerably.

A little while ago, Lucy had commanded her favourites to come and have tea. Her favourites included Ram and all the Europeans except Barlow and Vokins. Vokins, branded indelibly as one of the servants, had not even been considered for an invitation. She had also decided to invite Louise and Miriam, whom she wanted to impress with her domestic abilities, but only after a struggle in which she was torn between the pleasure of impressing them and the displeasure of having two more women and thereby disturbing what she considered to be a favourable balance of the sexes. They seemed to have been delayed, however.

Her guests might have preferred to drink their tea on the verandah outside, since at that moment it was not raining. Inside, it was so hot and humid, and the smoke, which was supposed to vanish towards the great baronial chimney, hung in the air instead and stung your eyes. But Lucy's invitations were not open to negotiation, and none of her favourites had thought it wise to refuse. So now, although her guests had really had

enough tea and would rather have been somewhere else, everyone was showing signs of impatience for another cup. But just
as the kettle was coming to the boil a black cloud billowed in
through one of the open windows and enveloped the entire tea
party.

Fleury had not finished his first cup when this happened. As
he raised it to his lips he saw that it was brimming with
drowned black insects. Both his arms were covered in seething
black sleeves, a moment later and his face was covered with insects, too, and they were pouring down the front of his shirt. He
opened his mouth to protest and insects promptly filled that
too. Spluttering and spitting and brushing at himself he dashed
to a clearer part of the hall.

The cloud of cockchafers presently thinned a little, but everything round about lay under drifts of glistening black snow.
The fire had been doused under a great, smoking heap of insects; the human beings shook themselves like dogs to rid themselves of the sickening creatures, which were showing, for some
reason, perhaps because she was wearing a white muslin dress,
a particular desire to land on Lucy.

Poor Lucy! Her nerves had already been in a bad enough
state. She leapt to her feet with a cry which was instantly
stifled by a mouthful of insects. She beat at her face, her bosom,
her stomach, her hips, with hands which looked as if they
were dripping with damson jam. Her hair was crawling with
insects; they clung to her eyebrows and eyelashes, were sucked
into her nostrils and swarmed into the crevices and cornices of
her ears, into all the narrow loops and whorls, they poured in a
dark river down the back of her dress between her shoulder-
blades and down the front between her breasts. No wonder the
poor girl found herself tearing away her clothes with frenzied
fingers as she felt them pullulating beneath her chemise; this
was no time to worry about modesty. Her muslin dress, her
petticoats, chemise and underlinen were all discarded in a trice
and there she stood, stark naked but as black and glistening as
an African slave-girl. How those flying bugs loved Lucy's white
skin! Hardly had her damson-dripping fingers scooped a long
white furrow from her thigh to her breast before the blackness would swirl back over it. Then she gave up trying to scrape

them away and stood there weakly, motionless with horror. As you looked at her more and more insects swarmed on to her; then, as the weight grew too much for the insects underneath to cling to her smooth skin, great black cakes of them flaked away and fell fizzing to the ground. While Fleury and Harry exchanged a glance of shock and bewilderment at the unfortunate turn the tea party had suddenly taken, an effervescent mass detached itself from one of her breasts, which was revealed to be the shape of a plump carp, then from one of her diamond knee-caps, then an ebony avalanche thundered from her spine down over her buttocks, then from some other part of her. But hardly had a white part been exposed before blackness covered it again. This coming and going of black and white was just fast enough to give a faint, flickering image of Lucy's delightful nakedness and all of a sudden gave Fleury an idea. Could one have a series of daguerrotypes which would give the impression of movement? "I must invent the 'moving daguerrotype' later on when I have a moment to spare," he told himself, but an instant later this important idea had gone out of his mind, for this was an emergency.

Lucy was wavering. Any moment now she would faint. But they could hardly dash forward and seize her with their bare hands. Or could they? Would it be considered permissible in the circumstances? But while they hesitated and debated, Lucy's strength ebbed away and she fell in a swoon, putting to death a hundred thousand insects beneath her lovely body. Harry looked round desperately for the O'Hanlons to assist him, but the O'Hanlons had fainted at the very outset and had been dragged clear by Ram, who was now trying to fan them back to consciousness with a copy of the *Illustrated London News*. There was nothing for it but for the two young men themselves to go to Lucy's aid so, clearing their minds of any impure notions, they darted forward and seized her humming body, one by the shoulders, the other by the knees. Then they carried her to a part of the banqueting hall where the flying bugs were no longer ankle deep. But now they were faced with another predicament, how to remove the insects from her body?

250

It was Fleury who, remembering how he had made a visor for his smoking cap, found the solution by whipping his Bible out of his shirt and tearing the boards off. He gave one of these sacred boards to Harry and took the other one himself. Then, using the boards as if they were giant razor blades, he and Harry began to shave the black foam of insects off Lucy's skin. It did not take them very long to get the hang of it, scraping carefully with the blade at an angle of forty-five degrees and pausing from time to time in order to wipe it clean. When they had done her back, they turned her over and set to work on her front.

Her body, both young men were interested to discover, was remarkably like the statues of young women they had seen . . . like, for instance, the Collector's plaster cast of *Andromeda Exposed to the Monster*, though, of course, without any chains. Indeed, Fleury felt quite like a sculptor as he worked away and he thought that it must feel something like this to carve an object of beauty out of the primeval rock. He became quite carried away as with dexterous strokes he carved a particularly exquisite right breast and set to work on the delicate fluting of the ribs. The only significant difference between Lucy and a statue was that Lucy had pubic hair; this caused them a bit of a surprise at first. It was not something that had ever occurred to them as possible, likely, or even, desirable.

"D'you think this is *supposed* to be here?" asked Harry, who had spent a moment or two scraping at it ineffectually with his board. Because the hair, too, was black it was hard to be sure that it was not simply matted and dried insects.

"That's odd," said Fleury, peering at it with interest; he had never seen anything like it on a statue. "Better leave it, anyway, for the time being. We can always come back to it later when we've done the rest."

But at that moment there was a noise behind them and both young men turned at once. There stood Louise, Miriam, and the Padre, gazing at them with horror.

"Harry!"

"Dobbin!"

The Padre was unable to find any word at all; his eyes had

come to rest on the golden letters "Holy Bible" on the back of Fleury's razor blade.

"You couldn't have come at a better time," said Fleury cheerfully. "Harry and I were just wondering how we were going to get her clothes on again."

23

"Forasmuch as it hath pleased Almighty God of his goodness to give you safe deliverance, and to preserve you in the great danger of childbirth; you shall therefore give hearty thanks unto God . . ."

At the beginning of August when the heat, humidity and despair reached their zenith in the Residency, when all eyes searched the Collector's face for the signs of collapse which they knew to be imminent, two babies were born. One of them died almost immediately; its little body was dressed in a clean nightdress and linen cap and its arms were folded on its breast; then it was taken at night to be buried. Burial was a risky business now since the churchyard was constantly swept by fire, and for adults it had been abandoned. Mature Christians were dragged to the more distant of the two wells in the Residency yard and, without discrimination between the finer points of their creeds, thrown in. No doubt the infant would have followed the adults down the well, too, had not the Padre offered to take the risk of burying it. He could not bear the thought of it being thrown down the well, however dangerous the alternative. It was too like throwing rubbish away.

By some miracle the other infant, a girl born to Mrs Wright, the widow of a railway engineer who had been killed at the rampart some weeks earlier, survived. Mrs Wright was the sleepy young woman whom the Collector had found so desirable on the occasion of his visit to the billiard room. What was it that had attracted him? Perhaps it was her soft, drawling voice or the fact that, no matter how interesting the topic of your conversation, you would inevitably see her smothering amiable yawns as you talked; you would see the muscles of her jaw tighten and the tears start from her eyes as she tried to repress them. The Collector, for some reason, was attracted to ladies who were overpowered by the fumes of sleep in his presence, but not everybody enjoyed it as much as he did. The

Magistrate, for example, when told that Mrs Wright had been taken ill, showed no interest whatsoever, and when further informed, a little later, that she had given birth, observed dryly: "I'm surprised that she had the energy." This remark naturally made everyone furious. How typical of the Magistrate! The man was odious. No wonder he was so universally detested.

The garrison was extraordinarily affected by Mrs Wright's baby. Even gentlemen who did not normally display interest in babies sent anxiously to enquire about its progress. And it seemed perfectly natural, given the circumstances, that the child should be named "Hope", though nobody knew whose idea it had been originally . . . probably not Mrs Wright's, however, for though in every respect resembling a Madonna, she was finding it more difficult than ever to stay alert. Only that drear atheist and free-thinker, the Magistrate, was seen raising a sardonic eyebrow at this name.

Now the time had come for Mrs Wright to be churched and the baby christened; every member of the garrison who was not occupied at the ramparts had assembled in the rubble-strewn yard of the Residency to hear the service, for it was no longer safe to hold a service in the ruined Church. A table which the Collector strongly suspected was his favourite Louis XVI had been brought out of the Residency drawing-room and covered with a clean white cloth to serve as an altar table.

"The snares of death compassed me round about, and the pains of hell gat hold upon me." The Padre's voice reading the 116th Psalm echoed between the walls of the hospital and those of the Residency. The Collector listened from the Residency verandah, his head uncovered, but seated because he still felt too weak to stand for long. Between the ranks of bared heads (one or another of which would occasionally turn to take a quick glance of inspection at his own face) he could just make out the graceful figure of Mrs Wright herself, kneeling on a hassock in front of the table. Beyond her, there were more ranks of bared heads, this time facing the Collector; their eyes, too, scanned him greedily, looking for fissures . . . and further away still, two or three faces of sick or wounded men watched from the open windows of the hospital. How haggard and bereft of hope they looked! The Collector shuddered at the thought that he might have had to endure his own illness within those walls.

'The Lord preserveth the simple," came the Padre's voice, quite aptly, it seemed to the Collector for he considered himself to be a simple man. "I was in misery and he helped me."

His eyes came to rest on the tear-stained face of Mrs Bennett, whose baby had so recently died, and he suffered a pang of pity for her. How terrible it must be for her to attend this service for Mrs Wright whose baby had survived . . . and while the Padre was speaking the Collector accompanied his words with a silent, sympathetic prayer for Mrs Bennett: "O God, whose ways are hidden and thy works most wonderful, who makest nothing in vain, and lovest all that thou hast made, Comfort this thy servant whose heart is sore smitten and oppressed . . ." but the rest of the prayer was no longer in his mind, stolen no doubt by the foxes of despair that continued to raid his beliefs . . . in any case, it faded into a mournful reverie in which he sought an explanation for the death of Mrs Bennett's child. The Collector felt no confidence at all that her child had not been made in vain.

The lovely Mrs Wright, still on her knees, stirred sleepily and the Collector saw her profile mirrored in a pool of rain-water beside her.

"O Lord, save this woman thy servant."

The Collector's moving lips silently accompanied the response. "Who putteth her trust in thee."

"Be thou to her a strong tower."

"From the face of the enemy."

"Lord, hear our prayer."

"And let our cry come unto thee."

The Collector had pulled a grey handkerchief from his pocket to mop his brow and was gazing at it with pleasure, thinking again that he was a simple man at heart. The reason for his pleasure, as well as for the handkerchief's greyness, was that he had washed it himself . . . and really he had done just as good a job as the *dhobi* had been doing for the most extravagant prices. He had not washed merely a handkerchief either . . . his underclothes, too, had a grey look, and so did his shirt, whose grey cuffs peeped from beneath the dirty, tattered sleeves of his morning coat. He had done it all himself and without soap. Miriam had offered to do it for him, and so had Eliza and Margaret, and he could, of course, easily have given it to the *dhobi* in spite of his inflated prices. But it was the principle of the thing that mattered. He wanted to help those who were ashamed to be seen washing their own clothes but could not afford the *dhobi*'s new prices . . . While quite capable of overlooking more serious misfortunes, the Collector was sensitive to such cases of threatened dignity. And so, to the *dhobi*'s astonishment and terror, the Collector had suddenly materialized beside him at the water-trough. For a while he had stood there at his side studying how he worked, how he soaked the garments and slapped them rhythmically against the smooth stone slabs. Then he had set to work himself, though rather clumsily, he was still weak from his illness. Soon the slapping of his own clothes had counterpointed the rhythmic slapping of the *dhobi*'s.

The news that the Collector had been seen doing his own laundry caused a mild sensation at first and was interpreted as the long-awaited collapse, particularly by those members of the garrison who had once belonged to the "bolting" party. But then the other faction, the shattered remains of the erstwhile "confident" party, had argued rather differently . . . far from being a sign of collapse it was, in fact, a sign of the Collector's *resolve*, his determination not to submit to oppression, to fight back, in other words. Soon he was joined by other Europeans and henceforth it became a common sight to see one or other of the ladies or gentlemen of the "confident" party slapping away at the trough where once the *dhobi* had slapped (for on the day after the Collector's appearance the *dhobi* had vanished from the enclave, either because he considered it too dangerous to remain any longer now that the commander of the garrison had assumed the caste of *dhobi* or, more likely, because he resented the competition). But perhaps the general, median view that was held by the garrison of this strange behaviour of the Collector was that it signified nothing more than his eccentricity.

"Yes, I'm a simple man. I don't believe in standing on ceremony," the Collector congratulated himself piously. "But then, what else could I be when I look like a scarecrow and smell like a fox?" How ragged all these devout figures looked!

One would have thought it was the congregation of a work-house. Louise Dunstaple, who had once been so fair, now looked like some consumptive Irish girl you might find walking the London streets; in spite of the angry red spots on her pale brow she no longer wore the poultice of flour ... the temptation had been too much for her and she had eaten it. To make things worse the women had now discovered lice in their hair. He had visited the billiard room that morning and his nerves had been set on edge by the distressing scenes he had witnessed. Yet the sobbing of the unfortunate women who had found lice in their hair had been easier to endure than the malicious pleasure of those who had found none. Why in such wretched circumstances, faced by such great dangers, did they still prosecute these petty feuds? The Collector had flown into a rage. In tones that had reduced the cannon outside the window to an occasional discreet cough he had lectured them on their duties to each other. They must help each other through these difficult times. If one of them found lice it must be a tragedy for all of them ... they must comb each other's hair, help each other when they were sick, live as a community, in short.

They had listened meekly, shamed by his anger and, like children, trying to think of ways to please him; but once he had left the billiard room he knew that the feuds would start once more to germinate.

"Perhaps it is our fault that we keep them so much in idleness? Perhaps we should educate them more in the ways of the world? Perhaps it is us who have made them what they are?"

But the Collector was no better at suspecting himself of faults than of virtues. "But no. It's their nature. Even a fine woman like Miriam is often malicious to the others of her sex." And he remembered with satisfaction, because it proved that he was not at fault, that Miriam and Louise had both approached him with some wild tale about Miss Hughes leading their brothers into debauchery and sensuality. Simply because the poor girl had happened to faint while not fully clothed! Ridiculous! He had been a little surprised that Miriam should surrender to this sort of jealousy, but perhaps he was not altogether displeased, because he found it feminine ... in an attractive woman even faults and weaknesses are endearing.

"Besides, Miss Hughes is made for sensual love as surely as the heron is made for catching fish. It's absurd to expect a heron to behave like a blackbird!"

Now the churching was over and it was time for the baptism to begin. The Collector was obliged to lift his heavy frame out of the chair on the verandah and advance to stand by the altar table, for he was to be godfather to the child. Meanwhile, the Padre had disappeared into the Residency for a moment. He came back carrying something draped in a table-cloth which, like a conjuror, he placed on the table.

As the Padre began the baptism the cannons fired almost in unison from the other side of the hospital and a faint stirring of breeze brought with it the brimstone smell of burnt powder. The infant, cradled in Miriam's arms, began to cry, but so feebly that its noise made hardly any impression on the expanse of open air. Miriam was smiling down at it while it squirmed and stretched, screwing up its tiny face and fists with the effort it was making. The Collector's mind wandered again as he thought of the baptism of his own children . . . how long ago it now seemed that the eldest had been baptized! Soon their own children would be born and he himself would become superfluous, an old man sitting in the chimney corner whom no one thought it worth their while to consult. He frowned at this suspected future injustice, but the next moment he remembered the siege and the fact that there was every chance that he would not live to suffer the humiliations of old age, and his thoughts promptly took a different line: "After so many hardships, how sad to be deprived of the tranquil evening of one's life!"

The Collector's face had assumed an alert expression, for the Padre was now addressing the godparents; but his still wandering mind was harrowed by the thought of the gentle, pious Mr Bradley of the Post Office department who, only the day before, had been deprived of the evening of *his* life, and the afternoon as well, come to that. By a singular misfortune Mr Bradley had been shot through the chest at the rampart when only the Magistrate was near at hand. And so the poor man had been obliged to die in as Christian a manner as possible in the arms of the atheistical Magistrate who had, of course, listened without the least sympathy to Mr Bradley's last pious ejaculations, impatiently muttering: "Yes, yes, to be sure, don't worry about it," as poor Mr Bradley, looking up into that last, glaring, free-thinking, diabolical, ginger sunset of the Magistrate's whiskers, commended his soul to God. "Don't worry. They'll certainly let *you* in after this performance," the Magistrate had said ironically as Mr Bradley made one or two more last-minute arrangements with Saint Peter for the opening of the celestial gates. Ah, what a terrible man he was, the Magistrate !

"Dost thou," the Padre asked the Collector, "In the name of this child, renounce the devil and all his works, the vain pomp and glory of the world, with all covetous desires of the same, and the carnal desires of the flesh, so that thou wilt not follow, nor be led by them?"

"I renounce them all," said the Collector, not very firmly, it was thought. Again the cannons fired, this time in succession. A vast bank of black cloud was mounting over the eastern horizon and advancing rapidly to bring the next downpour.

"O merciful God, grant that the old Adam in this child may be so buried, that the new man may be raised up in her. Amen, Grant that all carnal affections may die in her, and that all things belonging to the Spirit may live and grow in her. Amen."

"Hurry up or we'll all be soaked," the Collector exhorted the Padre silently. And then his thoughts wandered again and he began to worry about the speed with which the vegetation was growing around the ramparts. The grass, the creepers, the shrubs, the plants of every kind grew thicker every day, and the thicker they grew, the better cover they provided for the sepoys to advance undetected on the ramparts, but for some terrible reason, on the ramparts themselves nothing would grow.

The black cloud was right above them now and some of the congregation had begun to stir uneasily in expectation of the downpour, wondering whether the Padre would manage to get through the service before it fell. But even as he at last turned and, more like a conjuror than ever, whipped the cloth from the object on the table, which turned out to be a sauce-pan containing water scooped from the shattered font, the first heavy drops began to drum on the altar table; and while the Padre was saying: "Hope Mary Ellen, I baptize thee In the name of the Father and of the Son, and of the Holy Ghost, Amen," the Collector, forgetting that he had only just renounced an interest in the vain pomp and glory of the world, thought crossly: "That won't do the Louis XVI table any good at all."

24

Now in the banqueting hall another pleasant tea-party was taking place, even though tea itself was in such short supply that there was really only hot water to drink.

"Another cup, Mr Willoughby?" asked Lucy who, as hostess, was behaving impeccably. A wonderful change had come over her since the episode with the cockchafers. It was as if they had served to draw some morbid agent from her blood, as if they had been a great black and damson poultice to draw off her petulant humours and leave her as placid as a Madonna. Sometimes, of course, she would still get cross with her favourites, but only when their behaviour fell below an acceptable standard, when they refused invitations and that sort of thing. But who would think of refusing Lucy's invitations, providing as they did the last vestige of a social occasion within the enclave? Evidently not even the Magistrate, for there he was, drinking his cup of hot water with enjoyment and gazing in fascination at his hostess.

It had not been a good day for the Magistrate. He had come to the banqueting hall in order to have a look at the river from the roof; the river had risen and widened so much that the entire countryside seemed to be sliding past and one felt as if one were standing on the deck of a ship. From the roof of the banqueting hall the *sal* trees on the distant bank might have been the masts of other ships. The Magistrate knew, alas, what would be happening when this great volume of water reached the depression made by the giant's footprint a few miles away ... The embankments which he had vainly tried to have reinforced by the *zemindars* would now be brimming and beginning to overflow ... within a few hours the country around the embankments would be flooded and ignorance, stupidity and superstition would have triumphed once more as they have triumphed again and again in human affairs since time began! With a bitter sigh the Magistrate returned his thoughts to Lucy.

Lucy herself said she remembered nothing of the dreadful cockchafer affair. She could recall seeing the first black insect flying towards her and then she must have fainted. The next thing she had known, Louise and Miriam were wrapping her unclothed person in a clean towel while, not far away, the Padre was discussing religious matters with Harry and Fleury. Louise and Miriam had been doing their work with set faces and compressed lips but that was doubtless because of the smell of the insects which was frightful. True, they had behaved coldly to her afterwards but that was probably because they were envious of the success of her tea parties, to which she did not always feel obliged to invite them ... But why *should* she always invite them? She hated having nothing but women around her. Why did they not give tea parties for their own men (if they were able to find any)?

"Can I top you up, Mr Willoughby?" asked Lucy in the most polished social manner that anyone could desire, and soon the Magistrate was drinking his third cup of hot water, and still gazing at her in fascination, or to be more precise, at the back of her neck, which was the part of her which most interested him. Lucy was quite pleased by the Magistrate's interest and was considering making him one of her favourites.

The Magistrate had long been interested in Lucy but not because Cupid had at last managed to lodge an arrow in his stony heart. Alas, it was for a less creditable reason ... it was because he wanted, though for the loftiest scientific purposes, to take advantage of her. Until now the Magistrate had been in the position of a scientist who has made a discovery which he knows to be true but is unable to prove. For years it had been evident to him that the phrenological system was sound and he had been tormented by his inability to demonstrate it to people who, like the Collector, were inclined to scoff. But now, at last, in Lucy he had a person ideally suited to his purposes ... a person who was subject to a very powerful propensity. Lucy was Amative. Nobody could deny Lucy's Amativeness. Not only had she a history of past Amativeness (the fact that she was a "fallen woman" and so forth), but anyone who looked at her could see Amativeness written all over her. She positively glowed with it. Nobody, no scientist anyway, would or could deny that Lucy had this propensity to an extraordinary degree, of this the Magistrate was sure. So all that remained for him to do was to demonstrate that Lucy's organ of Amativeness was extraordinarily well developed. He was in no doubt but that this was the case. But for the moment, as ill-luck would have it, he was unable to verify it. The trouble was that the organ was in a rather awkward situation at the base of the skull, below the inion (that is, the external occipital protuberance), a part of the body which, in most ladies, Nature has thoughtfully cloaked with a fine growth of hair. The Magistrate licked his lips and took a swig of hot water. He did not know quite what to do about this.

Now you can tell how well developed an organ is in two ways: either by seeing how big it is, or by feeling the heat it generates. As a matter of interest, this very organ of Amativeness was first brought to the attention of its discoverer, Professor Gall, when he noticed its unusual heat in a hysterical widow. But for the Magistrate one way presented as many difficulties as the other. For the very reason that he could not lift Lucy's dark tresses and have a look, he could not slip his hand on to her neck. To a person more interested in the advance of science he might perhaps have tried to explain what he was after, but with Lucy he perceived that this would not be a success. What was he to do? He could think of nothing but disguising himself and rushing her on a dark night. He would need only the briefest of feels. Full of hot water, he belched dejectedly.

As he rose to take his leave the Magistrate thought again of the stupidity of the *zemindars* who had refused to reinforce the embankments; near him, in the lumber of possessions, was an oil painting of a stag at bay: that was just how he felt himself ... Reason being savaged by a pack of petty stupidities which, because of their number, would in the end bring him down. His ginger-clad lips parted and he belched again, more dejectedly than ever.

A few miles away, however, a handful of confident *zemindars* were standing on the embankment with the water almost licking their sandals. There were a number of Brahmin priests there too, and a man holding a black goat. Everyone was chuckling nostalgically at the thought of the Magistrate, who was very likely dead by now. One of them asked another if he remembered how the Magistrate Sahib had tried to make them strengthen the embankments and this caused such merriment that one of the landowners almost fell into the water. In due course the black goat was sacrificed with the appropriate ceremonies to appease the river and nobody was in the least surprised when, little by little, the river began to fall. By the following morning, aided by another black goat for good measure, it had dropped several inches and the worst was over.

Although the level of the river had begun to drop, there was no corresponding decrease in the rain that continued to pour out of the skies. If anything, it grew worse. And heavy rain, at this period of the siege, was something that the garrison could have well done without. The truth was that as the days went by and the heavy rain showed no sign of slackening for very long it became clear that something very frightening had begun to happen. The earthen ramparts which had been hastily thrown up to give substance to the Collector's revised plan of fortification were steadily melting away beneath the drumming rain. The fortifications were vanishing before the garrison's startled eyes!

Something clearly had to be done, and done quickly, for the ramparts were not diminishing at a steady rate ... the longer the rain lasted, the more quickly the ramparts melted. Where a week ago a man could stand up to his full height behind them without being seen, now he had to stoop; tomorrow, perhaps, he would have to get down on his hands and knees. Action must be taken immediately. All eyes followed the Collector as he strode about the enclave grimacing and muttering to himself.

When the garrison had begun to give up hope that he would act, he at last did something. Even though members of the erstwhile "bolting" party had declared him incapable of any further action and took a gloomy view in general of his morale, he somehow mustered his last resources and confounded their gloomy forecast by leading out a party of Sikhs and native pensioners to shovel under the downpour. The "confident" party were all the more delighted because even they had come to entertain one or two small doubts. But the Collector, always inclined to be moody and difficult, had taken on a persecuted look again. As the garrison watched him from the shelter of the verandah they could tell that the rain was having a bad effect on him; he clearly did not like the way it beat on his head and shoulders raising a fine spray; nor did he seem partial to the way it poured down the neck of his shirt and coursed down his trouser legs. He was seen to cast frequent despairing glances at the sky, at the melting rampart, and, indeed, in every conceivable direction; despairing glances were aimed positively everywhere.

The rain had also altered his appearance. His once magnificent ruff of side-whiskers had been slicked down against his cheeks like wet fur and his ears had flattened apprehensively against his head. Only his beard continued to grow these days, for he had given up shaving; a bad sign. The longer his beard grew the more ginger it became; another bad sign. No longer did he lecture people on the splendours of the Exhibition or on the advance of civilization. Civilization might be standing rock still, or even going backwards, for all the Collector seemed to care these days. It was clearly all up with the Collector. But still, he stayed out there shovelling, confounding the pessimists . . . even though his task was clearly hopeless. You dug up a spadeful of earth, but by the time you threw it on the rampart it was nothing but muddy water.

In due course, however, the Collector had to give up the idea of shovelling under these conditions. The rain was too heavy. He issued an order that all the able-bodied men in the garrison should turn out with shovels during the rare intervals between the downpours. From then on, by day and night, the garrison laboured to keep that shield of earth between themselves and the sepoys. The Collector had the remaining wooden shutters stripped off the Residency windows and dug into the mud of the ramparts to prevent them melting. But to no avail . . . they continued to wash away in streams of yellow-brown water.

Why would nothing grow on the ramparts? Everywhere else the ground was held solid under the rain by the vast grip of the vegetation which had so rapidly sprung up. But on the ramparts nothing appeared; when the Collector tried transplanting weeds, bushes, vegetation of every kind, within a few hours everything had wilted.

In desperation then he ordered certain solid objects in the Residency to be carried out to arrest that dreadful bleeding away of earth. The furniture was the first to go. He strode about the Residency and the banqueting hall, followed by those men who were still strong enough to lift heavy objects. Every now and again, without a word, he would point at some object, a chair perhaps, or a sideboard or a marquetry table which had graced some Krishnapur drawing-room, and his henchmen would dart forward seize it, and carry it away. Can you imagine how the owner of a fine chesterfield sofa must have felt to see it thus frogmarched away to its doom under the lashing rain? At this stage the Collector seemed to be sparing only occupied beds and *charpoys*, his own desk and chair, and the Louis XVI table from the drawing-room. Disputes arose. More than one unwary member of the garrison found that his bed had vanished while he had been defending the rampart against a sepoy assault. Sometimes a person would arrive just as the divan on which he had been sleeping was dragged away.

Sofas and tables, beds, chests, dressers and hatstands were thrown on to, or upended along, the ramparts, but still their strange haemophilia continued. Now the Collector's finger was pointing at other objects, including even those belonging to himself. Statues were pointed at and the shattered grand piano from the drawing-room in the hope that they might help, if only a little, to shore up the weakest banks of soil. For the Collector knew that he had to have earth as a cushion against the enemy cannons; brickwork or masonry splinters or cracks, wood is useless; only earth is capable of gulping down cannon balls without distress. But still it continued to wash away, around the edges of tables, between the legs and fingers of statues. After each fresh deluge only the skeleton of solid objects, the irregular vertebrae of furniture, trunks, packing-cases and other miscellaneous objects, was left standing over the swamp. Even the trench behind the rampart would be brimming with oozing earth.

When the supply of heavy furniture, and of the more ponderous artistic objects, had been exhausted, there began the rape of "the possessions" which had so long encumbered the Residency and the banqueting hall. Very often the last journeys of these beloved objects were accomplished to the tune of distressing protests, or of heart-rendring pleas for clemency. You would have thought that there was no one better fitted in the world to understand these pleas than the Collector. He, at least, was qualified to perceive the beauty and value of "the possessions". Yet he accompanied their tumbrils without a word, his eyes blank and bloodshot, his fur slicked down, his ears still flattened against his skull.

But although a great deal of solid matter had soon accumulated on one or other side of the ramparts and sometimes on both, it had little or no effect. It was like trying to shore up a wall of quicksand. The Collector resorted to even more desperate remedies. He had the banisters ripped off the staircase, for example, but that did no good either. So in the end he took to pointing at the last and most precious of "the possessions" ... tiger-skins, bookcases full of elevating and instructional volumes, embroidered samplers, teasets of bone china, humidors and candlesticks, mounted elephants' feet, and rowing-oars with names of college eights inscribed in gilt paint; the ladies were instructed to improvise sandbags out of linen sheets and pillowslips and fine lace tablecloths. In this last period of devastation even the gorse bruiser and the rest of the Collector's inventions met their doom.

So impassive and peculiar had the Collector become, so obviously on the verge, everyone thought so (you would have thought so yourself if you had seen him at this time), of giving up the ghost, that his face was scrutinized more closely than ever for any trace of remorse as the gorse bruiser was carried out. But by not so much as a flicker of an eyebrow did he betray his emotion. In the matter of these smaller "possessions", you might have thought that he would have let you get away with the things which you could not possibly do without, a set of fish-knives, for example, which had been a wedding present, or a sketch of the Himalayas as seen from Darjeeling. But the Collector remained quite implacable. It was almost as if he enjoyed what he was doing.

Soon the Residency and the banqueting hall were virtually stripped. How naked the drawing-room and the dining-room seemed. Beneath the chandeliers only the Louis XVI table, the Queen in zinc (for patriotic reasons), a few objects in electrometal such as *Fame scattering petals on Shakespeare's tomb* with the heads of certain men of letters, and a few stuffed birds in the rubble of plaster and brickwork brought down by the sepoy cannons, remained. I think that perhaps the snake in alcohol was left too. And only then, at long last, when almost everything was gone, did the terrible rain relent just enough for the ramparts to stop their melting.

While the ramparts had been melting, the jungle beyond them had been growing steadily thicker. The officer posted on the tower beneath the flagstaff could now, because of the foliage, scarcely detect an enemy sortie even during the brief periods of moonlight. When the rain was falling and the sky was overcast the number of men on watch at night had had to be doubled, men already exhausted by lack of food and the interminable restoration of the ramparts. One thing was clear: it was as important to clear away the vegetation close to the ramparts as it was to maintain the ramparts themselves. There was already enough cover for a large number of sepoys to approach very close to the enclave without being detected.

Was enough being done about the vegetation? Indeed, was anything at all being done? This was the question, an understandable one in the circumstances, that the garrison soon began to ask. Any moment now they expected that the Collector would make up his mind to do something about it. But he did not seem to be in any hurry. What he was expected to do exactly, nobody quite knew. The vegetation clearly could not be burned off. It was too wet for that. As for cutting it away, it was obvious that to wander about on the other side of the rampart was to invite certain death. The only idea that seemed feasible was for the Collector to put on the rusty suit of armour which stood in the banqueting hall and to go out there with a scythe. But when this idea was mentioned to him he said nothing. He showed no enthusiasm. It was plain that he was in no hurry to execute it.

In the end it was Harry Dunstaple who approached him with a really sensible idea. They must fire chain shot. If chain shot were capable of removing a ship's rigging it should do the same for the jungle.

"We haven't got any," said the Collector.

"We have some chains. There's a pile of them in the stables. We could cut them into lengths if we had a file.'

"Have we a file? Yes, so we have."

The Collector remembered that he not only had a file but a fine British one at that. He went upstairs to his shattered bedroom to fetch it for Harry. He had often wished for an opportunity to try out this splendid tool in peaceful days gone by. But the Resident even of a relatively unimportant station like Krishnapur cannot really allow himself to file things, even surreptitiously. The natives would quickly lose their respect for the Company if he did.

This file, or one identical to it, had emerged the victor of a curious contest at the Exhibition between Turtons' English Files and a French company which manufactured another brand of file. Even though Turtons' had selected their file indiscriminately from stock to do battle with the French champion, even though the French company had brought over a special engineer to manipulate their product while Turtons' had picked a man at random from the Sappers and Miners at the Exhibition, the French file had been humiliated. Two pieces of steel had been fixed in vices and the two men had set to work on them simultaneously. What a cheer had gone up as the Englishman with Turtons' file had filed the steel down to the vice before the Frenchman was one third the way through! As he stood by the glass cabinet in his bedroom where the file had reclined on a couch of red velvet since the Exhibition recuperating from its victory, the Collector remembered, with amazement and disgust at his petty chauvinism, how pleased he had been by this trivial affair. He was frowning as he took the victor downstairs to Harry.

"Where shall I start the operation, Mr Hopkins?" Harry wanted to know.

Several people were standing nearby when the Collector made his reply to this reasonable question. They all heard clearly what he said, difficult though they found it to believe. He said: "Please yourself."

Even Harry, who was not unaccustomed to the caprices of superiors, could not help looking astonished.

"Please yourself," repeated the Collector in a flat tone. "I'm going to bed. If you have any questions ask the Magistrate."

One or two of the bystanders, filled with dread, knowing already that the catastrophe had occurred but unable to prevent themselves verifying the fact, discreetly consulted their time-pieces. It was as they thought. The time was not yet noon.

25

While the Collector went off to bed in the middle of the day, Harry made a round of the Residency wheel accompanied by the giant Sikh, Hookum Singh, festooned in lengths of chain. Soon the chain was singing out through the foliage, cutting empty avenues through the greenery. The garrison kept an eye on the Collector's bedroom, expecting to see his face appear for an inspection of Harry's work. Although worried by the expense in powder Harry continued to open one green avenue after another, but the Collector's window remained empty.

As one day followed another the garrison could not help wondering what was going on behind the Collector's closed door. Very likely he was simply lying on his bed in a state of dejection and, perhaps, of remorse for his massacre of "the possessions" which was now generally thought not to have been necessary. They pictured him lying abandoned to the grip of despair. He was believed to sleep a good deal and to groan occasionally. On one occasion the door to his bedroom was left open and if you had passed along the corridor you could have caught a glimpse of the Collector, slumped on his bed, haggard and ginger-whiskered, the very picture of despair. The siege was being left to pursue its course without the participation of its principal author, the begetter of "mud walls" and cunning fortifications. No wonder that people grew despondent.

The garrison, in spite of everything and without the assistance of the Collector, continued to labour between one downpour and the next to prevent their walls of mud from oozing back into the plain from which they had been dug, but the number of men available to wield a shovel had suddenly begun to decrease alarmingly. This was not because of the enemy fire, which was less frequent now than it had ever been, for evidently the sepoys had decided to bide their time until the end of the rains. It was because an epidemic of cholera, with black banners fluttering, was advancing in solemn, deadly procession through the streets of the enclave.

In the hospital the constant retching of the cholera patients made breathing a torment; the air was alive with flies which crawled over your face and beneath your shirt, covered the food of those who were able to eat, and floated in their tea. The Padre found that they even sometimes flew into his throat while he was reading or praying with a dying man. By the last week of August the mortal sickness in the wards had become so general that he could no longer hope to pray individually with the dying. The best he could do was to take up a central position in the ward, using a chair for a hassock, and to make a general supplication for all the patients collectively. Afterwards, he would read aloud from the Bible, but with difficulty because the letters on the page seemed to crawl before his eyes like flies, and sometimes *were* flies. Once, in a moment of despair, he snapped his Bible shut and squashed them to a paste.

It was in these unpromising circumstances that the great cholera controversy, which had been smouldering for some time, at last burst into flame. The rift between the two doctors had grown steadily wider as the siege progressed. It had become clear to the garrison that not only did the doctors sometimes apply different remedies to the same illness, in certain cases these remedies were diametrically opposed to each other. So what was a sick man to do? As cholera began its measured advance through the garrison people instructed their friends privately as to which doctor they should be carried to in case of illness.

Certain people, perhaps because they were friendly with one doctor but held a higher opinion of the professional ability of the other, took to carrying cards in their pockets which gave the relevant instructions in case they should find themselves too far gone to claim the doctor they wanted. Sometimes, too, there was evidence on these cards of the conflicts which were raging in the minds of the garrison. You might read: "In case of cholera please carry the bearer of this card to Dr Dunstaple" ... the name of Dr McNab being carefully scratched out and that of Dr Dunstaple substituted. And you might even find the names of both doctors scratched out and substituted more than

272

once, such was the atmosphere of indecision which gripped the enclave.

Of the two doctors it was undoubtedly Dr Dunstaple who had the largest number of adherents; he had been the civil surgeon in Krishnapur for some years and was known to everyone as a kindly and paternal man. In more peaceful times he had assisted many of the ladies of the cantonment in childbirth. Besides, he was what they felt a doctor ought to be: a family man, with authority and good humour. After all, when you are ill, or when someone whom you love is ill, what you most want is someone to take the responsibility. Dr Dunstaple was very good at doing this.

By contrast, though Dr McNab also possessed authority and combined it with a calm and dignified manner, he seemed to lack Dr Dunstaple's good humour. He seldom smiled. He seemed to take a pessimistic view of your complaint, whatever it was. No doubt this was only his manner. Scots very often appear bleak in the eyes of the English. But the garrison, distressed by the revelation that Dr McNab had actually written a description in his diary of his own wife's death by cholera, feared that in the case of Dr McNab even the caricature of a Scot might be mild in comparison with the truth; they could think of few less tantalizing prospects than that their deaths should become medical statistics. On the other hand, nobody could have failed to notice that Dr Dunstaple was in a state approaching nervous collapse. His denunciations and his shouting made even his staunchest admirers wonder sometimes whether it might not be better to change their allegiance to the calmer Dr McNab. But, of course, there was still no getting round the fact that Dr Dunstaple was the more experienced, and hence the more reliable, of the two.

It was after the evening service in the vast cellar beneath the Residency that Dr Dunstaple suddenly chose to speak his mind. Hardly had the Padre finished saying the *Nunc Dimittis* when the Doctor, who had been kneeling innocently in the front row, sprang to his feet. While skirts were still rustling and prayer-books being closed, he shouted: "Cholera!" Silence fell immediately, a silence only made more absolute by the sound of a distant cannon and by the gurgling of rainwater. This was the word that every member of the garrison most dreaded.

"Ladies and gentlemen, I need not tell you how we are ravaged by this disease in Krishnapur! Many have already departed by way of this terrible illness, no doubt others will follow before our present travail is over. That is the will of God. But it is surely *not* the will of God that a gentleman who has come here to practise medicine ... I cannot dignify him with the name of 'physician' . . . should send to their doom many poor souls who might, with the proper treatment, recover!"

"Father!" exclaimed Louise in dismay.

Some of the tattered congregation turned their heads to right and left, searching for Dr McNab; others, though merely ragged skeletons these days, were required by their good breeding to remain facing to the front with expressions of indifference. Dr McNab was quickly located, half sitting and half leaning on a stone ledge at the back. The thoughtful look on his face did not change under Dr Dunstaple's abuse, but he frowned slightly and stood up a little straighter, evidently waiting to hear what else Dr Dunstaple had to say.

"I don't pretend that medical science has yet found a method of treating cholera that's quite satisfactory, I don't say there isn't room for improvement, ladies and gentlemen ... but what I *do* say is that it's the duty of a member of the medical profession to use the *best available treatment* known and accepted by his fellow physicians! It's his duty. A licence to practise medicine isn't a licence to perform whatever hare-brained experiments may come into his head."

"Dr Dunstaple, please!" protested the Magistrate, who was one of the few cantonment-dwellers who had never experienced any affection for Dr Dunstaple. "I must ask you to withdraw these abusive remarks which are clearly aimed at your colleague. Whatever the rights and wrongs of the matter medically speaking you've no right at all to impugn the motives of a dedicated member of our community."

"It's no time for niceties of etiquette when there are lives at stake, Willoughby. I challenge Dr McNab to justify his so-called remedies which fly in the face of all that's known about the pathology of this disease."

"Father!" cried Louise again, and burst into tears.

274

"I'm perfectly willing to discuss the pathology of cholera with Dr Dunstaple," said Dr McNab in a mild and gloomy manner, "but I doubt if there's anything to be gained by doing so publicly and in front of those who may tomorrow become our patients."

"See! He tries to avoid the issue. Sir, there is everything to be gained from exposing a charlatan."

The Magistrate's eye moved from one doctor to the other over the passive rows of tattered skeletons and he forgot for a moment that he was as thin and ragged as they were. What chance was there of this little community, riddled with prejudice and of limited intelligence, being able to discriminate between the strength of one argument and the strength of another? They would inevitably support the man who shouted loudest. But what better opportunity could there be of examining the fate of those seeds of reason that might be cast on the stony ground of the communal intelligence?"

"Dr Dunstaple, you will hardly make any progress if you continue to abuse Dr McNab in this way. If you insist on a public debate then I suggest you give us your views in a more suitable manner."

"Certainly," said Dr Dunstaple. His face was flushed, his eyes glinting with excitement; he seemed to be having difficulty breathing, too, and he spoke so rapidly that he slurred his words. "But first ladies and gentlemen, you should know that Dr McNab holds the discredited belief that you catch cholera by drinking ... more precisely, that in cholera the morbific matter is taken into the alimentary canal causing diarrhoea, that the poison is at the same time reproduced in the intestines and passes out with the discharges, and that by these so-called 'rice-water' discharges becoming mingled with the drinking-water of others the disease is communicated from one person to another continually multiplying itself as it goes. I think that Dr McNab would not disagree with that."

"I'm grateful to you for such an accurate statement of my beliefs." Could it be that McNab was actually smiling? Probably not, but there had certainly been a tremor at each corner of his mouth.

"Let me now read to you the conclusion of Dr Baly in his *Report on Epidemic Cholera*, drawn up at the desire of the

Royal College of Physicians and published in 1854. Dr Baly finds *the only theory satisfactorily supported by evidence* is that 'which regards the cause of cholera as a matter increasing by some process, whether chemical or organic, in impure or damp air' ... I repeat, 'in impure or damp air'." Dr Dunstaple paused triumphantly for a moment to allow the significance of this to seep in.

Many supporters of Dr McNab exchanged glances of dismay at the words they had just heard. They had not realized that Dr Dunstaple had the support of the Royal College of Physicians ... and felt distinctly aggrieved that they had not been told that such an august body disagreed with their own man. Two or three of Dr McNab's supporters wasted no time in surreptitiously slipping their cards of emergency instructions from their pockets, crossing out the name McNab, and substituting that of his rival, before settling back to watch their new champion in the lists. The Magistrate noted this with satisfaction. How much more easily they were swayed by prestige than by arguments!

Meanwhile Dr Dunstaple was continuing to disprove Dr McNab's drinking-water theories.

"Ladies and gentlemen, the fact that cholera is conveyed in the atmosphere is amply supported by the epidemic in Newcastle in 1853 when it became clear that during the months of September and October an invisible cholera cloud was suspended over the town. Few persons living in Newcastle during this period escaped without suffering some of the symptoms that are inescapably associated with cholera, if not the disease itself. They suffered from pains in the head or indescribable sensations of uneasiness in the bowels. Furthermore, the fact of strangers coming into Newcastle from a distance in perfect health ... and not having had any contact with cholera cases ... being then suddenly seized with premonitory symptoms, and speedily passing into collapse, *proves* that it was the result of atmospheric infection."

"What a fool! It proves nothing of the sort," thought the Magistrate, stroking his cinnamon whiskers with excitement that bordered on ecstasy.

However, Dr Dunstaple had now adopted a less ranting and more scientific tone which the audience could not help but find impressive. Some of his oldest friends, who for years had been accustomed to seeing him, fat and genial, as the leading light of a pig-sticking expedition, were astonished to hear him now holding forth like a veritable Newton or Faraday and discussing the latest discoveries in medicine as fluently as if they were entries in the Bengal Club Cup or the Planters' Handicap. One or two of his supporters turned to direct malicious glances at Dr McNab, who was still leaning calmly against the ledge and listening attentively to what his prosecutor had to say. Louise, too, had dried her tears. Her father was not doing too badly and perhaps, after all, he might be right about McNab.

"When you inhale the poison of cholera it kills or impairs the functions of the ganglionic nerves which line the air-cells of the lungs ... hence, the vital chemistry of the lungs is suspended; neither caloric nor vital electricity is evolved ... hence, the coldness which is so typical of cholera. The blood continues to be black and carbonated ... the treacly aspect of the blood in cholera is well known ... and in due course the heart becomes asphyxiated. This is the true and basic pathology of cholera. The disease is, however, attended by secondary symptoms, the well known purging and vomiting which, because they are so dramatic, have frequently been taken by the inept as indicating the primary seat of the infection ... I need hardly add that this is the view held by Dr McNab."

Once again, heads turned in McNab's direction and the Magistrate's sharp eyes were able to detect a number of veiled smiles and smothered chuckles. McNab was frowning now, poor man, and looking worried as well he might with Dr Dunstaple, transformed into Sir Isaac Newton, mounting such an impressive attack. But Dr Dunstaple had now moved on to the treatment.

"What must it consist of? We must think of restoring the animal heat which has been lost and we must consider means of counter-irritating the disease ... Hence, a warm bath, perhaps, and a blister to the spine. To relieve the pains in the head we might order leeches to the temples. An accepted method of counter-irritation in cholera is with sinapisms applied to the epigastrium ... or, if I must interpret these learned expressions for the benefit of my distinguished colleague, with mustard-plasters to the pit of the stomach ..."

There was subdued laughter at this sally. But the Doctor held up his hand genially and added: "As for medicine, brandy to support the system and pills composed of calomel, half a grain, opium and capsicum, of each one-eighth of a grain, are considered usual. I could continue to talk about this disease indefinitely but to what purpose? I believe I have made my point. Now let Dr McNab justify his curious treatments, or lack of them, if he can."

Dr McNab was silent for such a long time that even those of his supporters who had remained steadfast throughout Dr Dunstaple's persuasive arguments and had not yet crossed his name from their emergency cards, began to fear that perhaps he had nothing to say. It surely could not be that McNab was confounded, utterly at a loss, for surely almost anyone could string a few medical terms together (enough to convince the survivors of Krishnapur if not the Royal College of Physicians) and save face. But still the silence continued. McNab's head was lowered and he seemed to be pondering in a lugubrious sort of way. His lips even moved a little, as if he were giving himself a consultation. At length, with a sigh and in a conversational tone which did not match Dr Dunstaple's oratory for effect, he observed: "Dr Dunstaple is quite wrong to suggest that there is an accepted treatment for cholera. The medical journals still present a variety of possible remedies, many of which sound most desperate and bizarre . . . missionaries report from China that they have been cured by having needles stuck into their bellies and arms, yet this is not thought too strange to mention . . . and almost every variety of chemical substance has been proposed at one time or another, all of which is a sure sign that our profession remains baffled by this disease."

"Needles stuck in people's bellies to cure cholera, whatever next!" the audience appeared to be thinking. And the Magistrate, watching like a stoat, could see by the alarm on their faces that they were assigning this treatment to Dr McNab for no other reason than that he had happened to mention it. Here, in a test-tube before his very eyes, ignorance and prejudice were breeding like infusoria.

"In the greater number of epidemic diseases," McNab went on, "the morbid poison appears to enter the blood in some way, and after multiplying during a period of so-called incuba-

278

tion, it affects the whole system. Such is undoubtedly the case in smallpox, measles, scarlet fever and the various kinds of continued fever ... but it must be remarked that in these diseases the illness always begins with general symptoms, such as headache, rigors, fever and lassitude ... while particular symptoms only appear afterwards. Cholera, on the other hand, begins with an effusion of fluid into the alimentary canal, without any previous illness whatsoever. Indeed, after this fluid has begun to flow away as a copious diarrhoea the patient often feels so little indisposed that he cannot persuade himself that anything serious is the matter."

"Irrelevant!" muttered Dr Dunstaple loudly but McNab paid no attention and continued calmly.

"The symptoms which follow this affection of the alimentary canal are exactly what one would expect. If you analyse the blood of someone with cholera you'll find that the watery fluid effused into the stomach and bowels isn't replaced by absorption. The experiments of Dr O'Shaughnessy and others during the cholera of 1831–2 show that the amount of water in the blood was very much diminished in proportion to the solid constituents, as also were the salts ... Well, the basis of my treatment of cholera is quite simply to try to restore the fluid and salts which have been lost from the blood, by injecting solutions of carbonate of soda or phosphate of soda into the blood vessels. Does that sound unreasonable? I don't believe so. At the same time I try to combat the morbid action by using antiseptic agents such as sulphur, hyposulphite of soda, creosote or camphor at the seat of the disease ... that's to say, in the alimentary canal ..."

"How eminently full of reason!" thought the Magistrate. "It will be too much for them, the dolts!"

"It's often been regretted by physicians that calomel and other medicines aren't absorbed in cholera ... but this regret is needless, in my opinion, as they don't need to be absorbed. If calomel is given in cholera it should obviously not be in pills, as Dr Dunstaple suggests, but as a powder for the sake of better diffusion."

To say that the audience had found Dr McNab's discourse dull would not be entirely accurate; they had found it soothing, certainly, and perhaps monotonous. Many of those present

279

had found it hard to pick up the thread of what he was saying and instead had thought with a shiver: "Needles driven into your belly! Good heavens!" But Dr McNab had at least one attentive listener and that was Dr Dunstaple.

"Dr McNab has omitted to mention certain post mortem appearances which refute his view of cholera and support mine," cried Dr Dunstaple waving his arms violently in his excitement and making thrusting gestures as if about to spear a particularly fine pig. "He hasn't mentioned the distended state of the pulmonary arteries and the right cavities of the heart. Nor has he mentioned the breathlessness suffered by the patient after he has inhaled the cholera poison!"

Dr McNab shrugged negligently and said: "These symptoms are obviously the result of the diminished volume of the blood . . . Its thickened and tarry condition impedes its passage through the pulmonary capillaries and the pulmonary circulation in general. This is also the cause of the coldness found in cholera."

"Pure reason!" barked the Magistrate, unable to contain himself a moment longer.

"Nonsense!" roared Dr Dunstaple and started forward as if he meant to make a physical assault on Dr McNab. He was halted in his tracks, however, by a shout from the Padre.

"Gentlemen! Remember that you are in the presence of the altar. I must ask you to stop this quarrelling instantly, or to continue it in another place." Furious, Dr Dunstaple now seemed on the point of turning on the Padre and mowing the wiry cleric down with his fists, but by this time Louise and Mrs Dunstaple had hastened to his side and now they dragged him away, hushing him desperately.

26

It was only to be expected that sooner or later the Collector's sense of duty would reassert itself. Sure enough, within a day or two of this regrettable difference of opinion between the two physicians word went round the garrison that he had been seen up and about again. On the first day of his reappearance he contented himself with walking about, avoiding people's eyes, or shovelling at the still melting ramparts like a man with a crime to expiate. But on the following day he had shaved the red stubble from his chin, was wearing a cleaner shirt, and was once more beginning to adopt a stern and overbearing expression. The Magistrate continued to give the orders which regulated the defence of the enclave, but in a subdued tone, as if referring them to the final authority of the Collector, should he wish to exercise it. It was not until the auction, however, on the third day, that it became clear that the roof of the Collector's collapsed will had once more been shored up with the stoutest timbers.

Food within the enclave had become so critically short by now that it was evident to the Magistrate that anything edible must now be used. So many people had died during the siege either from wounds or illness that a considerable quantity of private stores had accumulated. Their distribution could wait no longer. The Magistrate was in a position to order the confiscation of this food for the good of the community, to order that it should be equally divided among the survivors. But the relatives of the dead, when they heard what was afoot, raised a storm of protest and demanded that their rights to the stores should be respected. The Magistrate hesitated, stroking those terrible, radical, flaring whiskers of his . . . since he had shouted himself hoarse as a young man in 1832 he had been devoted to the radical cause, a supporter of Chartism, of factory reform, and of every other progressive notion which crossed his path. Now at last he had an opportunity to *act*, not merely to argue.

Would he dare to grasp this chance and order the abolition of property within the community?

The Magistrate, standing in hesitation on the verandah, was illuminated by a rare shaft of watery sunlight for a moment and his whiskers flared more brilliantly than ever ... but then the sun moved on, extinguishing them. He realized now that his belief in people was no longer alive ... he no longer loved the poor as a revolutionary must love them. People were stupid. The poor were just as stupid as the rich; he had only contempt for both of them. His interest in humanity now was stone dead, and probably had been for some time. He no longer believed that it was possible to struggle against the cruel forces of capitalist wealth. Nor did he particularly care. He had given up in despair.

"Yes, we'll hold an auction," he muttered. "That's the easiest thing."

At the time appointed for the auction the poor and the thrifty were left to man the ramparts; everyone else crowded into the hall of the Residency which was considered to be the most suitable place for the proceedings. The goods to be sold had been piled up on the stairs where once "the possessions" had been piled; bottles of jam and honey, heaps of hermetically sealed provisions, bottles of wine, cakes of chocolate pliable with the heat, tins of biscuits and even a few mouldy hams had been stacked against the splintered stumps which were all that now remained of the banisters Fleury had found so elegant the first evening he had entered the Residency.

With an effort the Collector removed his eyes from the food and looked at the crowd assembled to bid for it. How starved they looked! Only Rayne, standing on the stairs with his fingers idly drumming on the lid of a tin of Scottish short-bread, still looked as sleek as he had before the siege. Was this because Rayne had been in charge of the Commissariat? Behind Rayne stood his two servants, Ant and Monkey, as thin as their master was fat; their job was to deliver the food to those who bid successfully for it.

But just as the auction was about to begin there was a commotion amongst the knot of gentlemen who had gathered around the foot of the stairs. The stocky figure of Dr Dunstaple was seen thrusting his way towards the stairs. He looked nervous and excited. He said something to Rayne which the Collector could not hear; Rayne shook his head. They argued for a moment and Dr Dunstaple fell back dissatisfied. Using the butt of a pistol as a gavel Rayne began the auction.

The first lot to be put up was a tin of sugar biscuits and a jar of "mendy", a pomade of native origin for dyeing the hair black. Rayne started the bidding at a guinea and after some brisk competition among the gentlemen at the foot of the stairs it was knocked down to one of them for five guineas. Faces in the hall registered distress at this price as it became clear to many of those present that they would be unable to win anything with their limited resources. More tins of biscuits followed, then other foodstuffs. Then came a battle over a fine tooth-comb among the ladies who had lice in their hair; this ended at forty-five shillings amid tears and despair. A ham came next; after some frenzied bidding at the lower prices it climbed to thirteen guineas, then to fourteen where it seemed likely to stay until at the very last moment, a cautious male voice offered fifteen guineas.

"Vokins, what d'you need a ham for?"

Everyone was startled by the sound of the Collector's familiar, commanding tones, particularly Vokins. He mumbled unintelligibly and looked abashed. He had known it would be a mistake.

"And look here, man, how d'you think you're going to pay for it. You haven't a penny to your name."

Again Vokins mumbled. "Speak up, man!"

"It's not for me, sir."

"Then who is it for?"

"It's for Mr Rayne, sir."

All eyes turned towards Rayne, who smiled apologetically and said, yes, that he had asked Vokins to bid on his behalf as he himself would be conducting the auction and it would clearly be difficult for him to put in bids and be auctioneer at the same time.

"Who else has been making bids for Mr Rayne?" A number of gentlemen raised their hands uncertainly and a gasp of surprise went up from the assembly as it became evident that almost all the food had been bought on Rayne's behalf.

"D'you have enough money to pay for all these goods, Mr Rayne?"

"Not at the moment, sir, but I soon will have."

"You intend to sell them again?"

"Most of them, yes ... There should be no difficulty ... unless, of course," Rayne added with a smile, "the relief comes sooner than expected."

"Mr Rayne, d'you consider it honourable to profit from the distress of your comrades ... of the men, women and children with whom you are fighting for your life?"

"It's a question of fortune, Mr Hopkins. One has to make the best of a situation, after all. Besides, everyone else is bidding out of their next pay, just as I am. They can bid against me if they are prepared to risk it."

"Is everyone bidding out of future pay?"

Several gentlemen nodded and someone said: "Nobody has cash, of course. That was the only way to do it."

"Stand down, Mr Rayne."

Rayne shrugged and ceded his place to the Collector. The Collector looked down at the gaunt, upturned faces gathered at the foot of the stairs. They stared back at him with dull eyes. One or two of the men were smiling. The Magistrate was smiling, and so were Mr Rose and Mr Ford, and so were the Schleissner brothers. The smile spread to more and more people, then turned into a laugh. Everyone was laughing; it was a bitter, unpleasant laugh which the Collector recognized as the sound of despair. Hardly any of the men making these rash bids expected to live to pay for them. In their present mood people would think nothing of mortgaging themselves for years ahead in order to acquire some trifling luxury like a jar of brandied peaches or a few leaves of tobacco.

"Listen to me. It may seem to some of you that there's very little hope left for us in Krishnapur. But this is not so. With every passing day our chances of relief improve. D'you think that the Government in Calcutta is prepared to leave us to our fate? Consider the immense resources available to our nation, consider the British soldiers who must now be converging on the mutinous Indian plains from every part of the Empire. Just think! Nearly three months have passed ... by now a

DOLLAR
ACADEMY
LIBRARY

relieving force may be no more than a day's march away, and yet you're prepared to mortgage away your future lives as if they did not exist! At the very outside, relief can't be more than two weeks away. A mere few days are nothing when we've already survived so much!"

The Collector, surveying the crowd, felt a little hope begin to stir in the hungry and despairing bodies below him. After all, they seemed to be thinking, it was perfectly true, relief should not be much longer in arriving.

"I don't believe that this is the time for us to profit from each other's misery so I hereby cancel all sales of food which have taken place this afternoon. The food will be handed over to the Commissariat and distributed either among the garrison as a whole, or among the sick, depending on its nature. The Commissariat will henceforth be administered by Mr Simmons, and Mr Rayne will take up his duties at the ramparts; his bearers, however, will remain to assist in the Commissariat. Let me say finally, that it's my intention that we should all starve together, or all survive together."

Once again there was silence. People looked at each other in astonishment. Then a man at the back of the hall began to clap, and someone else joined in. Soon the clapping became fierce applause. Such was the enthusiasm that you might have thought that the Collector had just sung an aria.

But hardly had the applause for the Collector died down when two hands reached up and dragged him down the stairs by his braces and into the crowd.

"I expect they're anxious to chair me around the hall," thought the Collector triumphantly. His success had come as a complete surprise to him. However, nobody seemed anxious to chair him round the hall, or anywhere. Indeed, they seemed to have forgotten about him altogether, for the hands which had grasped his braces to drag him off his podium had belonged to Dr Dunstaple. No sooner had he freed the platform of the Collector's superfluous presence than the Doctor sprang into his place and held up his hand for silence. The Collector had already perceived that all was not well with the Doctor. While speaking he had been aware of the Doctor's red, exasperated features grimacing in the first rank at the foot of the stairs; he had seemed nervously excited, anxious, impatient that the auction should be over. "Disgraceful!" he had muttered. "We could all be dead." But now the Doctor had begun to speak.

"Ladies and gentlemen, Dr McNab still hasn't offered any evidence to support his strange methods which amount, it seems, to pumping water into cholera victims. Nor has he provided any evidence to support his belief that cholera is spread in drinking water. Now, ladies and gentlemen, shouldn't we give him his opportunity?" And Dr Dunstaple laughed, though in a rather chilling manner.

As before in the cellar, all eyes turned to McNab who, once again, happened to be leaning against a wall at the back. On this occasion, however, his calm appeared to have been ruffled by Dr Dunstaple's words and he replied with a note of impatience in his voice: "If any evidence were needed it would be enough to see what happens when a weak saline solution is injected into the veins of a patient in the condition of collapse. His shrunken skin becomes filled out and loses its coldness and pallor. His face assumes a natural look . . . he's able to sit up and breathe more normally and for a time seems well . . . My dear Dr Dunstaple, perhaps you could explain to us why, if the symptoms are caused, as you seem to believe, by damage to the lungs or by a poison circulating in the blood and depressing the action of the heart . . . why it's possible that these symptoms should thus be suspended by an injection of warm water holding a little salt in solution?"

Dr McNab had asked this question with a smile. But the smile only irritated Dr Dunstaple and he bellowed: "Rubbish! Let Dr McNab give his reasons for saying that cholera is spread by the drinking of infected water!" He paused a moment to let his words sink in, and then added: "Perhaps he'll explain away the case, reported *officially* to the Royal College of Physicians, of a dispenser who accidentally swallowed some of the so-called 'rice-water' matter voided by a patient in a state of collapse from cholera . . . *but who suffered no ill-effects whatsoever!*"

"No, I can't explain that," replied McNab, who had now recovered his composure and was speaking in his usual calm tone. "Any more than I can explain why cholera should have always attacked those of our soldiers who had recently arrived in the Crimea in preference to those who had been there for some time . . . Or why, as has been suggested, Jews should be immune to cholera, and many other things about this mysterious disease."

Ah, it had been a mistake to mention Jews. The Magistrate could see people thinking: "Jews! Whatever next!"

"How d'you explain its high incidence in places known to be malodorous?"

"It should be obvious that in the crowded habitations of the poor, who live, cook, eat, and sleep in the same apartment and pay little regard to the washing of hands, the evacuations of cholera victims which are almost colourless and without odour can be passed from one person to another. It has often been noted that the disease is rarely contracted by medical, clerical or other visitors who don't eat and drink in the sickroom. And consider how severely the mining districts were affected in each of the epidemics in Britain. The pits are without privies and the excrement of the workmen lies about everywhere so that the hands are liable to be soiled by it. The pitmen remain underground for eight or nine hours at a time and invariably take food down with them into the pits and eat it with unwashed hands and without a knife and fork. The result is that any case of cholera in the pits has an unusually favourable situation in which to spread."

"Gentlemen," interrupted the Collector, "it's clear that the difference between you is a deeply felt and scientific one which none of us here are qualified for adjudicating . . . To an impartial observer it seems that there's something to be said on either side . . ." The Collector hesitated. "Let us therefore be content, until the . . . er . . . march of science has freed us from doubt, to take precautions against either eventuality. Let us take care, on the advice of Dr Dunstaple, to ventilate our rooms, our clothes and our persons as best we can lest cholera be present in an invisible poisonous miasma. And at the same time let us take care with washing and cleanliness and other precautions to see that we don't ingest the morbid agent in any liquid or solid form. As for the treatment of those unfortunate enough to contract the disease, let them choose whichever approach seems to them the most expressive of reason."

The Collector fell silent, hoping that these words might bring the meeting to an end without leaving too great a schism between the two factions. But Dr Dunstaple's bitterness was too great to be satisfied with this armistice.

"Dr McNab still hasn't granted my request for evidence that cholera is spread by drinking water. Does he expect us to be convinced by his words about the prevalence of cholera in the pits? Ha! He's forgotten to mention, by some slip of the memory, the one fact about the pits which is known to everyone . . . the impurity of the air breathed by the pitmen! Moreover, I should warn those present of the risks they expose themselves to under McNab's treatment . . . which is, however, not a treatment at all, but a waste of time. Let him who is prepared, should McNab decide on another experiment, to have needles driven into his stomach, allow himself to be treated by this charlatan. I believe I've done my duty in making this plain."

"I shall also give a warning to those present, to the effect that, in my view, nothing could be worse for the treatment of cholera than the warm baths, mustard-plasters and compresses recommended by Dr Dunstaple, which can only further reduce the water content of the blood . . . No medicine could be more dangerous in cholera collapse than opium, and calomel in the form of a pill is utterly useless."

"Thank you, Dr McNab," put in the Collector hurriedly, but McNab paid no attention to him.

"As for the evidence that cholera is spread in drinking-water, there is, as Dr Dunstaple should be well aware, a considerable amount of evidence to support this view. I'll mention one small part of it only . . . evidence collected as a result of the epidemics of 1853 and 1854 by Dr Snow and which concerns the southern districts of London. These districts, with the exception of Greenwich and part of Lewisham and Rotherhithe, are supplied with water by two water companies, one called the Lambeth Company, and the other the Southwark and Vauxhall Company. Throughout the greater part of these districts the supply of water is intimately mixed, the pipes of both companies going down all the streets and into almost all the courts and alleys. At one time the two water companies were in active competition and any person paying the rates, whether landlord or tenant, could change his water company as easily as his butcher or baker ... and although this state of things has long since ceased, and the companies have come to an arrangement so that the people cannot now change their supply, all the same, the result of their earlier competition remains. Here and there one may find a row of houses all having the same supply, but very often two adjacent houses are supplied differently. And there's no difference in the circumstances of the people supplied by the two companies ... each company supplies rich and poor alike.

"Now in 1849 both companies supplied virtually the same water ... the Lambeth Company got theirs from the Thames close to the Hungerford Bridge; the Southwark and Vauxhall Company got theirs at Battersea-fields. Each kind of water contained the sewage of London and was supplied with very little attempt at purification. In 1849 the cholera epidemic was almost equally severe in the districts supplied by each company.

"Between the epidemic of 1849 and that of 1853 the Lambeth Company removed their works from Hungerford Bridge to Thames Ditton, beyond the influence of the tide and out of reach of London's sewage. During the epidemic of 1854 Dr Snow uncovered the following facts ... out of 134 deaths from cholera during the first four weeks, 115 of the fatal cases occurred in houses supplied by the Southwark and Vauxhall Company, only 14 in that of the Lambeth Company's houses, and the remainder in houses that got their water from pump wells or direct from the river. Remember, this was in districts where houses standing next to each other very often had a different water supply,"

"Pure reason!" ejaculated the Magistrate. "It will be too much for them. Ha! Ha!" If anything was destined to distract the assembly from an objective consideration of rival arguments it was this strange, almost mad, outburst from the Magistrate. Dr McNab continued, however: "During the epidemic as a whole which lasted ten weeks there were 2,443 deaths in houses supplied by Southwark and Vauxhall as against 313 in those supplied by the Lambeth Company. Admittedly the former supplied twice as many houses as the latter ... but if the fatal cases of cholera during the entire epidemic are taken in proportion to the houses supplied, it will be seen that there

were 610 deaths out of 10,000 houses supplied by the Southwark and Vauxhall Company, whereas there were only 119 out
of 10,000 supplied by the Lambeth Company. I challenge Dr
Dunstaple to deny in the face of this evidence that cholera is
not spread by drinking water!"

The effect of Dr McNab's arguments was by no means as
overwhelming as might be supposed; with the best will in the
world and in ideal circumstances it is next to impossible to
escape cerebral indigestion as someone quotes comparative
figures as fluently as Dr McNab had just been doing. The
audience, their minds gone blank, stared craftily at Dr McNab
wondering whether this was a conjuring trick in which he took
advantage of their stupidity. Very likely it was. The audience,
too, was painfully hungry and yet in the presence of food
which was not apparently destined for their stomachs; this
made them feel weak and peevish. The heat, too, was atrocious; the air in the hall was stagnant and the audience stinking.
Every time you took a breath of that foul air you could not
help imagining the cholera poison gnawing at your lungs. Even
Fleury, who was perfectly conscious of the force of McNab's
arguments, nevertheless gave a visceral assent to those of Dr
Dunstaple.

What would have happened if Dr Dunstaple had replied to
Dr McNab's challenge it is hard to say. He had taken a seat
on the stairs while McNab was speaking. As he finished, however, he sprang to his feet, his face working with rage, his
complexion tinged with lavender. He opened his mouth to
speak but his words were drowned by a volley of musket fire
nearby and the crash of a round shot which brought down a
shower of plaster on the heads of his audience.

"Stand to arms!" came a cry from outside, and immediately
everyone began to disperse in pandemonium (and more than
one tin of food was accidentally grabbed up in the confusion).
The Doctor was left to wave his arms and shout; he could not
be heard above the din. However, he had one final argument,
more crushing than any he had yet delivered, and for this he
needed no words. From his alpaca coat he whipped a medicine
bottle of colourless fluid, flourished it significantly at Dr McNab
and drank it all off. What was in the bottle that he had thus
publicly drained to the last drop? The Doctor himself did not

say. Yet it did not require much imagination to see that it could only be one thing: the so-called "rice-water" fluid from a cholera patient, which Dr McNab claimed was so deadly. Against this argument Dr McNab's tiresome statistics could not hope to compete.

27

At first, there had been great enthusiasm over the Collector's decision to suppress the rights of property in the food that was to have been auctioned and to give a share to everybody. But this enthusiasm swiftly evaporated and soon it became difficult to find anyone who was satisfied with it, let alone enthusiastic. A share for everybody would mean less than half a mouthful ... and if "everybody" meant natives as well, the amount you received would hardly be worth opening your jaws for. The food in question had, of course, belonged to the dead; but now the living who still possessed their own meagre stores began to fear for their safety. Prices had already quadrupled during the siege; now a frenzy of economic activity took place in which more than one lady gave a handful of pearls for a bottle of honey or a box of dates. This was regarded by many of the erstwhile "bolting" party as the twilight of reason before the Collector's increasingly communistic inclinations demanded that you give up not only your stores, but perhaps your spare clothes, and, who knows? maybe even your wife as well. Others, conscious that they were eating the equivalent of a diamond brooch or a sapphire pendant, sat down to a last giddy meal, eating before the Collector could get his hands on it, all at once, what they had hoarded for weeks. Exasperated by this foolishness, the Collector told Mr Simmons to distribute the extra food with the rations as quickly as possible.

"The rations?"

"The normal daily rations of the food in the Commissariat." The Collector looked at Mr Simmons as if he were being obtuse.

"There's no food left in the Commissariat ... None to speak of, anyway."

The Collector went with Mr Simmons to have a look. What he had said was quite true; there was almost nothing left. There remained a little grain and rice in the Church, but in the vestry there was nothing. So again the rations had to be reduced. Since there was no meat left now, the ration from now on until the supplies were exhausted would consist of one handful of either rice or *dal* and one of flour per person, the men being given a more generous helping than the women and children. The Collector estimated that at this rate they might carry on for another two or three weeks. Then it would all be over.

It was not only food that was running short; the Collector was shocked to see how little powder and shot remained ... the mine, the *fougasses*, and the firing of chain shot to clear the foliage had seriously depleted what he had considered an ample provision of powder; if used sparingly it might last for two weeks, but the shot was almost exhausted. Of ready-made balled cartridge there remained only two full boxes and one half full. As for cannon balls, canister, and so forth ... The Collector scowled disagreeably.

Towards evening Fleury was leaning against the rampart at the banqueting hall staring dully out over the foliage, occupied in vague thoughts about food and reviewing in his mind various outstanding meals he had eaten in the course of his existence. What a fool he had been to waste so much time being "poetic" and not eating. He uttered a groan of anguish. On the cantonment and river sides of the banqueting hall there had been no firing of chain shot to clear the jungle: this was partly to save powder, partly because the banqueting hall was, anyway, higher than the surrounding land and thus more difficult to surprise; there were also natural clearings to be seen here and there where the ground was too stony for a thick growth. From the edge of one of these clearings Chloë suddenly flushed a sepoy.

Although he had not recognized her immediately Fleury had noticed Chloë a moment earlier as she came trotting into the clearing; since he had last set eyes on her Chloë's golden curls had grown foul and matted and in places mange had already begun to remove them; a cloud of flies followed her and every few yards she stopped to scratch. Abruptly she noticed that a man was hiding in the under-growth and some recollection of the carefree days of her life before the siege must have stirred in her. Instead of taking to her heels, as any sensible pariah dog would have done, she advanced wagging her tail to sniff at him. For a few seconds the sepoy tried discreetly to shoo her away, hoping to be able to continue unobserved his stealthy creeping through the jungle. But Chloë, still under the influence of distant memory, thought that he was playing a game with her and wagged her tail even harder. Infuriated, the sepoy sprang out of his hiding and flourished his sabre with the clear intention of butchering this loathsome *feringhee* dog. Again and again he swiped at Chloë, but she remained convinced that this was a game and every time her friend approached she darted away and went to sit somewhere else in the clearing, her tail brushing the ground frantically.

Fleury urgently pointed out the sepoy to Ram; he had left his own rifle inside the hall. He watched in agony as Ram, with the deliberate movements of long service and old age, tore the cartridge, emptied the powder into the muzzle, and took his ramrod to drive down the rest of the cartridge.

Having finished loading, Ram stopped to scratch the back of his head, which was rather itchy, and then his elbow, which had been bitten by a mosquito some days earlier but which still itched occasionally. All this time Fleury gazed speechless and appalled as the sepoy sped back and forth in the clearing like a trout in a restaurant tank. Ram was now raising his gun as calmly as the waiter who dips his net into the tank . . . ah, but Ram had paused again, this time to cough and to smooth back his white mustaches which had been somewhat disarranged by the gust of air from his cough . . . then he took aim at the gliding sepoy, there was a sudden wild foaming and thrashing of water, and the sepoy lay gasping on the turf. A final electric spasm shook his frame, and then he lay still.

Fleury turned away, sickened, for Chloë had wasted no time in bounding forward to eat away the sepoy's face. He told Ram to kill her as well and hurried away to take refuge in the banqueting hall and try to erase from his mind the scene he had just witnessed. Presently, as he sat by himself in a remote corner of the banqueting hall, he noticed on the wall beside him an ascending column of white ants; as they reached the ceiling they spread their wings and slowly drifted down in a delicate living veil. Once they reached the ground they shook their wings violently, until they fell off. Then the white, wingless creatures crawled away.

"How strange it is," mused Fleury, feeling the futility of everything yet at the same time enjoying the feeling, "that these millions of wings, with all their wonderful machinery of nerves and muscles, should be made to serve the purpose of a single flight. How sad it is to behold how little importance life has for nature, these myriads of creatures called into being only to be immediately destroyed." And he sat for a long time in a melancholy reverie as the ants continued to drift down, thinking of the futility of all endeavour. When at last he came to his senses, rather ashamed of his lapse into sensitivity, the floor around him was thickly carpeted with tiny discarded wings, as if with the residue of his own aerial poetic thoughts.

Fleury had been expecting that Louise would pay him a visit before she retired to bed. While indulging his melancholy thoughts he had taken care to position himself in a nobly pensive attitude, with the candle at his side lending a glistening aureole to his dark profile. But in due course the candle coughed, spat, and went out, and there was no sign of Louise. Later in the evening a rumour spread that Dr Dunstaple had cholera. Harry immediately hurried away to the Residency, very agitated. Fleury would have liked to have gone, too, but both he and Harry could not go at the same time; someone had to stay behind to fight off the sepoys.

A little before midnight Miriam, who had been unable to sleep, came over to see him and tell him the news. Shortly after supper the poor Doctor had been seized with the tell-tale purging and vomiting. For the sake of privacy he had been carried, not to his own ward in the hospital, but to the tiger house next door where Hari and the Prime Minister had been incarcerated. As people bustled around him the Doctor had harangued them frantically with all the strength that was left to him. "It was only water in that medicine bottle I drank from!" he had protested again and again. "On no account let that charlatan near me!"

While his strength was ebbing he had hurriedly given instructions for his treatment to his daughter and the native dispenser from his ward. A hip-bath was dragged into the tiger house and fires built outside to heat water. The unfortunate Doctor had been immersed and then lifted out, as he had instructed, for a blister to be applied to his spine. Dr McNab had come to the door of his ward for a few moments to watch the heating of the bath-water; then with a sigh and a shake of his head he had retired inside again.

By this time poor Dr Dunstaple had voided a great deal of "rice-water" fluid and was seized by perpetual, agonizing cramps. He was delirious, too, and his breathing was laboured. He was clearly sinking fast. Finally, unable to bear it any longer Louise had gone to find Dr McNab. The trouble was this: although the native dispenser had applied Dr Dunstaple's treatments on numerous occasions under his direction, he was overcome by stage-fright at the prospect of applying them to the Doctor Sahib himself. His hands trembled and he constantly looked to Louise for advice and support. As for Mrs Dunstaple, she was so distraught that she no longer knew what she was doing and had been taken away, given a composing draught surreptitiously obtained from Dr McNab, and put to bed on her shelf in the pantry.

"I can only treat Dr Dunstaple as I would treat any of my patients and I fear that your father would not agree to my methods. But if you want I shall attend him."

Louise hesitated. Her father was now so sunk in his illness, so delirious, that he was barely conscious.

"Treat him as you think best, Doctor, but please hurry."

Within a few moments of Dr McNab's saline injections Dr Dunstaple had begun to revive. Louise was astonished by the sudden improvement; she could feel the warmth returning to her father's limbs and see his breathing becoming easier every moment. It had been like a miracle. But as Dr Dunstaple's brain cleared he had demanded to know why there was no mustard-plaster on his stomach. Dr McNab had thoughtfully retired as his patient was regaining consciousness, for fear of irritating him. Meanwhile, Dr Dunstaple was gradually coming to realize that other things were missing. Where were the calomel pills and opium and brandy? Why were there no hot compresses on his limbs? Louise tried to soothe him and persuade him to drink the antiseptic draught which McNab had given her. But he had demanded to know what it was, and finally poor Louise had been obliged to explain what had happened. He had sunk so low that she had been obliged to approach Dr McNab for his help.

"Miserable girl! D'you want to kill me? Bring back the mustard-plasters instantly! Bring brandy and the other medicaments I ordered. Hot compresses and be quick about it or else I'm doomed!"

Such was the Doctor's rage, so accustomed was Louise to obedience, that she could not prevent herself from hurrying to execute his orders. By this time Harry was there too, saying: "Look here, we don't want that McNab fellow putting his oar in. Father seems to be treating himself well enough without help from him."

Alas, soon the Doctor began to sink again. Miriam, unable to endure this harrowing sight a moment longer had fled from the tiger house.

Fleury was beside himself with distress, but more for Louise's sake than for the Doctor's (he had privately come to consider his prospective father-in-law as an opionated old fool). He begged Miriam to hurry back and find out how the old man was faring under his own treatment. But no sooner had Miriam gone than Harry suddenly returned looking more cheerful than one might have expected. He told Fleury that his father had once again sunk very low ... almost to death's door. Again McNab had been summoned and again he had insisted on clearing away the mustard-plasters and compresses. Again he had injected a saline solution into the Doctor's blood vessels. And again, wonderful to relate, the Doctor had made an astonishing recovery.

But hardly had Harry finished imparting this encouraging news when Miriam returned, her face showing deep concern. Harry must go at once to help Louise. Apparently there had been yet another terrible scene when the old Doctor, his wits once more restored by salt and water, had discovered that he had again been disobeyed. Dr McNab, too, had been angry: "Every time I revive him he abuses me! How much longer am I supposed to put up with this?" Dr Dunstaple, in any case, had settled the matter by clearing everyone out of the tiger house except for the unfortunate dispenser, who was ordered to adhere to the Dunstaple treatment until death, if necessary, and to lock the door against everyone else.

Fleury and Miriam waited in silent depression for further news, but none came. Presently they went out on to the verandah where it was cooler. The sky was sprinkled with stars. Soon the rainy season would be over, Fleury thought, and the sepoys would once again be able to dig mines and to launch concerted attacks. Counter-mining would be impossible given their shortage of powder; at best they might be able to break into the enemy mines and fight it out hand-to-hand. But would they even have the strength to dig counter-mines? It was not an encouraging prospect.

"Listen to the jackals."

Somewhere not far away, surrounded by jungle, Chloë and the sepoy lay side by side and rotted, or were eaten by the specialist animals of the night.

Towards morning they heard that Dr Dunstaple had died, inconclusively, of a heart attack.

The curious thing about Dr Dunstaple's death was that although the harrowing circumstances which had attended it were well known throughout the camp, it was not generally considered that, by dying, the Doctor had lost his argument with McNab. After all, it was maintained, who was to say that the Dunstaple treatment was not just beginning to work each time as McNab began to apply *his* treatment? The Doctor's subsequent relapse might well have been because of Dr McNab's interference. Above all, Dr McNab was discredited by the fact that he had "stuck needles" into Dr Dunstaple. It made little difference that these needles had been for injections and not for some sinister Chinese purpose. Besides, McNab was a Jew. He'd said so himself.

"I never believed such stupidity could exist," the Collector said to McNab, for whom he had come to entertain a great respect.

"Och, they're confused. They'll learn in time."

But still the notion that Dr Dunstaple had been right somehow persisted, independent of thought or reason, as insubstantial as the supposed "invisible cholera cloud" itself which Dr Dunstaple believed had once hung over Newcastle. But McNab continued as he always had, grave and rather lugubrious, knowing that given time, the "cholera cloud" would move on, too, and that his own view would come to be accepted ... but this would only happen imperceptibly and not, perhaps, like a cloud passing, but more in the way that sediment settles in a glass of muddy water.

Part Four

Part Four

28

At the end of August the rains stopped as suddenly as if taps had been turned off. September was considered by the English community even under normal conditions to be the most unhealthy month of the year; while the hot sun resumed its office of drying out the pools of water which had collected on the sodden earth, fever-bearing mists and miasmas hung everywhere. Clouds of flies and mosquitoes pursued every living creature.

Hardly had the rains stopped when the spectators began to return to the slope above the melon beds, coming in greater numbers than ever before. No doubt this was because the weather was much better, now that September was under way; it was cooler and the spectators could stroll in the sunshine without needing the shade of umbrellas. Some of the wealthier natives brought picnic hampers in the European manner, and their servants would unroll splendid carpets on the green sward; while their banquets were spread out on the carpets they could watch what was going on through telescopes and opera-glasses which they had had the foresight to bring with them . . . though what they saw, as they swept the ramparts of the Residency and banqueting hall can hardly have looked very impressive to them: just a few ragged, boil-covered skeletons crouching behind mud walls. But they settled down, anyway, with satisfaction amid the bustle of the fairground, like gentlemen returning to their seats in the theatre after the interval. It did not look as if this last act would take very long.

The garrison, too, had taken to watching the spectators through telescopes, above all to see what they were eating. The more weak-willed of the defenders very often spent more time watching the native princes eating their banquets than they did watching the enemy lines. Food had become an obsession with everyone; even the children talked and schemed about it constantly; even the Padre, at this period, could hardly fall asleep without dreaming that ravens were coming to feed him ... but alas, no sooner did these winged waiters arrive with nourishment than he would wake up again. But in spite of everything perhaps it was just as well that none of the things they could see ... none of the plump fish or chickens being toasted on skewers, none of the creamy breads, chapatis, nan, and parathas, none of the richly bubbling curries and glistening mounds of rice, which the skeletons' scarlet rimmed eyes could see in their lenses and at which they glared for hour after hour ... that none of these things were available, for in their starved and debilitated condition it was very likely that a heavy curry would have killed them as dead as a cannon ball.

Desperate remedies were resorted to in the search for food. Any piece of rotten meat that could still be found in the enclave was slipped over an improvised fish hook, attached to a rope and hurled over the parapet in the vain hope of catching a jackal or a pariah dog that might swallow it. Mr Worseley, the engineer, shot a thousand sparrows and made a curry out of them, which all who tasted it proclaimed excellent, but which aroused the Collector's fury because of the waste of powder and shot. The men at the ramparts had often tried in vain to tempt one of the stray artillery bullocks near enough to capture it, but at long last, towards the end of the first week of September, an old horse was captured at the banqueting hall and put to death. The meat was distributed as rations, the head, bones and entrails used for soup, and the hide cut into strips for the children to suck. For a day and a night the feasting on the horse filled everyone in the enclave with a dreadful exultation, but gradually it died down as the garrison came to realize that one horse was hardly enough to stay their hunger for more than a few hours. This meal of horse might be compared to the draught of air that a drowning man who has fought his way to the surface manages to inhale before being whirled down into the depths again. After the besieged had licked the corners of their mouths and sucked their fingers clean one by one, the cold ocean of hunger closed over their heads again with scarcely a ripple to be seen.

On September 10th, which was Louise's birthday, Fleury bartered his gold cufflinks, a silver snuff-box, and a pair of shoes with Rayne in exchange for two lumps of sugar. He ground the sugar into a powder, mixed it with water and with his daily handful of flour, adding a little curry powder to give it a spicy taste: then he grilled the result on a flat stone beside the fire. He also bought a teaspoonful of tea from one of the artillery women for ten pounds, to be paid after the siege was over or, in case of death, by his executors to certain of her relations; to lend substance to this rather nebulous arrangement which at first only seemed to excite the suspicion of the woman selling the tea, Fleury had drawn up an elaborate letter which began impressively: "To Whomsoever May Find This Missive, I, George Fleury, Being Then Deceased," and which seemed to Fleury to give a certain legal solemnity to the transaction. Thus provisioned, he invited Louise to come to the banqueting hall to celebrate her birthday, though in a very quiet way, he assured her; he had not forgotten that she must still be suffering on account of her father, who had only recently taken his last dive down the well in the Residency yard in the wake of so many of his former patients.

Fleury's cakes had not turned out very well; in fact they had dried as hard as the stone they were baked on, and had to be chipped off it with a bayonet. But even so, Louise was so hungry that she stared at them with a fearful concentration, ignoring Fleury's polite conversation as he made the tea. Unfortunately, when the time came to devour the cakes, she found she had difficulty in eating hers because of its hardness. She tried exchanging it for Fleury's but that was just as hard. The trouble was that Louise, like a number of other members of the garrison, was suffering from scurvy; there had been several cases of partial blindness and of swollen heads, but the most common symptom, and the one which was troubling Louise, was the loosening of teeth. She felt that her teeth would come out altogether if she tried to bite Fleury's cake. Fleury was not sure that his own teeth were very sound either so they decided that the best thing to do was to suck the cakes and perhaps dip them in the tea to soften them. Besides, in one way it was an advantage that they were so hard, because they would last longer. But in spite of their hardness they seemed to vanish in no time. Louise looked at Fleury and felt so vulnerable that presently she began to cry.

"Oh I say, what's the matter?"

305

But Louise could not tell him. Apart from the fact that she believed her teeth to be on the point of falling out, she had not had her period for several weeks and was afraid that she was barren. She wanted desperately to confide in someone about this, but once again found it impossible to find anyone suitable . . . her mother was too distraught, her father was dead, and she could not bring herself to mention it to Miriam for fear of provoking some too blunt observations on the mysterious workings of a lady's insides. After a while, however, she forced herself to smile, and dried her eyes on one of Fleury's shirt sleeves that looked fairly clean. She promised herself that she could continue sobbing later on, after she had gone to bed in the billiard room. Sobbing there was so commonplace that nobody noticed any more.

29

It had become evident by now that the sepoys were preparing to make a major assault in order to bring about the end of the siege. From the observation post on the Residency roof Mr Ford reported that new contingents of sepoys were streaming into the enemy lines from every direction. It was impossible to be sure whether these were new recruits to the Krishnapur field, perhaps freed from the victorious siege of the *feringhees* somewhere else on the plain, or simply men who had deserted during the rains returning now to finish the job. Among the arriving troops, however, Mr Ford noticed several squadrons of lancers trailing the green flag of Islam; they looked much too well drilled and well equipped to be merely returning deserters. He also noticed several cannons being dragged into the sepoy camp by bullocks from the direction of the bridge of boats.

Mr Ford, as befitted an engineer, possessed a methodical nature; he made a careful scrutiny of the sepoy encampment and noted on an improvised map the location of various groups and regiments; he also came to deduce, by painstakingly observing the arrival and departure of ammunition carts, the position of the main sepoy magazine. This last piece of information was passed on to Harry Dunstaple, whose skill as a gunner was now celebrated throughout the enclave. But Harry was unable to use it. The magazine was out of his range.

On the afternoon of 12 September, a Saturday, Mr Ford sent an urgent message to the Collector ... He had become certain by watching the preparations in the sepoy camp that they would make a major assault within the next few hours. The Collector had independently arrived at the same conclusion by watching the slope above the melon beds where the number of spectators was beginning to increase rapidly.

"Is there no way we could hit their magazine? That would give us a few extra days."

"It's just out of range, Mr Hopkins. If we still had horses ..."

The Collector smiled wanly. "If we still had horses we could eat them."

Towards evening the Collector gave the order for everyone who could be spared from the ramparts to assemble in the hall, he wanted to say a few words to the garrison.

"I suppose he's going to tell us that gentlemen now abed in England will be sorry that they're not here," remarked the Magistrate, but nobody was amused by this loathsome display of cynicism and the Magistrate was left to chortle grimly by himself, his soul pickled in vinegar.

"We've a lot of work to do tonight," said the Collector when everyone had assembled in the hall. "It's almost certain that the enemy will attack the Residency from the north, very likely at dawn tomorrow. We shall do our best, of course, to hold the Residency against them, but the chances are that we are now too few to be able to do so ... For this reason all the wounded, the ladies, and the children must be taken to the banqueting hall tonight, together with water, powder, cloth, and indeed every single object that might come to our assistance. Provided we take enough water with us there's no reason why we shouldn't be able to hold out for a considerable time in the banqueting hall, which is in a far better situation for defence ... and let me remind you that with every passing day, relief comes nearer ... perhaps as much as twenty miles nearer with every day's march ... You must believe me when I tell you that they're out there on the plain somewhere and coming towards us. I know they are. Another week and we are saved.

"There's just one other matter which I mention only to set your minds at rest ... We've decided to conserve sufficient powder in the banqueting hall to blow ourselves up if the worst comes to the worst. I think we're all agreed that it's better for us to die honourably together in this way than to risk a worse fate at the hands of the enemy." A tremor went through the Collector's audience at these words. Vokins, in particular, could not see how this announcement was supposed to set his mind at rest. His enthusiasm was in no way aroused by the prospect of being blown up honourably with the ladies and gents. Indeed, the more he thought about it, the less appetite he found he had for it. Still, he thought with a shudder, perhaps it was better than falling into the hands of those negroes out there!

When he had finished speaking the Collector hesitated for a moment on the stairs, looking down at the tired and gaunt faces below him. Earlier he had heard that a young clerk from the Post Office had shot himself while lying in bed ... he had left a young widow, to whom he had been married in Calcutta during the previous cold season; this act of despair had moved him more than any other of the many deaths he had witnessed since the beginning of the siege; it was perhaps the fact that the young man had been lying in bed when he had shot himself that the Collector found so sad. Such hopelessness! It was terrifying. "It was my fault. I should have been able to give him something to hope for," he thought with a sigh, as he descended the half dozen stairs and went to kneel beside Miriam on the stone flags.

"The Lord our God is one Lord: them that serve other gods, God shall judge."

"Lord have mercy upon us," muttered the congregation of skeletons.

"Idolaters and all them that worship God's creatures, God shall judge."

"Amen. Lord have mercy upon us."

"The Lord's day is holy; them that profane it, God shall judge."

The Collectors lips moved but his mind had already wandered away, besieged by practical questions ... how would they manage for privies with so many people in the banqueting hall, assuming that they were driven out of the Residency? Would there be enough water? He must try and have a moment alone with each of his children before tomorrow morning. It was his duty. Besides, he might have no other chance to tell them that he loved them; Miriam, too. He had grown fond of her in the last few days. He would have liked to have put a hand on her shoulder now to comfort her. But even as this thought entered his mind the Padre's voice came promptly to reprimand him: "Adulterers and fornicators and all unclean persons, God shall judge."

"Amen. Lord have mercy upon us," said the Collector

heavily, making it sound more like a command than a supplication. But would it not have been better, he mused, to have left the banqueting hall and defended the Residency where there was a well? No, not so . . . he had taken the right decision. The Residency was vulnerable. Even if shot to pieces the commanding position of the banqueting hall would still make it defensible. And how were the sepoys faring? They must know by now whether a relief force was coming near. Perhaps that was why they were determined to attack now without further delay? What a shame it all is, even so! What a waste of all the good work that has been done in India! Still, there must be some way of destroying their magazine.

"Covetous persons and extortioners and them that grind the faces of the poor, God shall judge."

"Amen. Lord have mercy upon us, and lay not these sins to our charge."

The Padre had asked the Collector if he might preach a sermon. The Collector had agreed provided that it was brief, for there remained so much to be done before morning. As text the Padre had chosen: "I see that all things come to an end, but thy commandment is exceeding broad." The Padre had become very weak since the end of the rains. His face had grown so thin that as he spoke you could plainly see the elaborate machinery of his jaw setting to work with all its strings, sockets and pulleys. Those at the back of the gathering now had to ask each other in whispers what the text had been, for they had been unable to hear it.

Once again the Padre urged his listeners to repent because now the most dangerous time of all was at hand, and he repeated the words he had read earlier: "His fan is in his hand, and he will purge his floor, and gather his wheat into the barn; but he will burn the chaff with unquenchable fire." He urged the garrison to trust in God, and referred to David and Goliath, to Israel triumphing over that mighty host by the seashore, to Daniel in the den of lions. Then he fell silent for a little while, as if in meditation.

When he next spoke it was to ask the forgiveness of anyone present whom he had unwittingly wronged during his ministry in Krishnapur. Then, having asked the congregation to pray for him, he paused again . . . and this time it was evident that

310

it was physical weakness that obliged him to rest. Once he had recovered a little strength he ended his address with a quotation from Archbishop Leighton: " 'How small a commotion, small in its beginning, may prove the overturning of the greatest kingdom! But the believer is heir to a kingdom that cannot be shaken ... He who trusts in God looks death out of countenance; and over him the second death shall have no power, ...' "

The gathering dispersed. The Collector went upstairs for his pistols. One of these, the Colt Patent Repeating Pistol, he had been in the habit of using throughout the siege and it was now stuck uncomfortably in the cummerbund he wore round his waist; he was anxious that the others should not fall into the hands of the sepoys if the Residency were lost. They lay in a glass case in his dressing-room, displayed, like Turtons' file, on a cushion of faded red velvet with the shadow of a pistol in darker red where until recently the Colt had been. This case of pistols was the last and longest-surviving of the Collector's many treasures from the Exhibition, and really, he thought, with the possible exception of the velocipede which had inspired the trace of fortifications, the only one to have been of any use; most of the others, of course, were now immovably set in the dried mud ramparts and could only have been recovered with a pick. The Collector selected just two more of these pistols, a small and reliable five-barrelled pistol by Lefaucheux of Paris, which he wanted to load and give to Miriam, and the English revolving pistol by Adams, which had caused such a stir at Woolwich by its lightness and by the rapidity with which it could be loaded and fired (up to ten times a minute had been claimed for it). The rest of the pistols he bundled into a towel and gave to one of his daughters to carry to the banqueting hall.

Before going down to the northern ramparts where the brunt of the attack was expected to fall, he took a last look round the room and saw Hari's phrenology book lying on the floor. He picked it up and opened it at random. It opened at "Hope." "This organ is situated on each side of that of Veneration, and extends under part of the frontal and part of the parietal bones. It inspires with gay, fascinating, and delightful emotions, painting futurity as fair and smiling as the regions of primeval bliss. When too energetic and predominant, it disposes to

Credulity, and in mercantile men, leads to rash and inconsiderate speculation. When the organ is very deficient, and that of *Cautiousness* large, a gloomy despondency is apt to invade the mind."

Chuckling, the Collector went downstairs. On his way he spotted a large black beetle on the stairs; he caught it between finger and thumb and took it out with him to the ramparts. There he generously offered it to the Magistrate, who was busy carrying cartridges to the firing-step. The Magistrate hesitated.

"No thanks," he said, though with a note of envy in his voice.

The Collector popped it into his mouth, let himself savour the sensation of it wriggling on his tongue for a moment, then crunched it with as much pleasure as if it had been a chocolate truffle.

30

Just before dawn the sound of a voice singing came over the darkened expanse of what had once been the Residency compound from the direction of what had once been the Cutcherry. It was a beautiful sound. It had a strange and thrilling resonance, as if the singer were standing in a large room or a courtyard built of stone in one of the ancient palaces left by the Mogul emperors further to the west. But, of course, there was no palace, nor even a large room, unless the Cutcherry cellar had somehow survived. It could only be some quality in the stillness of the air which made the voice carry so beautifully. Fleury asked Ram what the song was.

"It is the name of God, Sahib," said Ram respectfully. As the old pensioner listened to the song, which was now accompanied by the ringing of bells, Fleury saw an expression of tender devotion come over his lined face, and he, too, thought, as the Collector had thought some weeks earlier in the tiger house, what a lot of Indian life was unavailable to the Englishman who came equipped with his own religion and habits. But of course, this was no time to start worrying about that sort of thing.

Instead, Fleury looked to his armament, which was impressive; it included a sabre, unbearably sharp, a couple of wavy-bladed daggers from Malaya, and another, Indian, dagger like one of those that Hari had shown him, with two blades and a handle for the whole fist, like that of a hand-saw. Lastly he had picked an immense, fifteen-barrelled pistol out of the pile rejected by the Collector. This pistol was so heavy that he could not, of course, stick it in his belt; it was all he could do to lift it with both hands. But he had been so enthusiastic about it that he had willingly gone through the laborious loading of its honeycomb of barrels, one after another, and now it was ready to wreak destruction. He already saw fifteen sepoys stretched on the ground and himself standing over them with this weapon smoking in his hand . . . or rather, in both hands.

As the sky slowly brightened and they waited, Fleury thought of how he and Harry had waited for the first attack of all at the beginning of June. How long ago that seemed! He remembered how innocently they had discussed which natives they would blow to smithereens and which they would grant a reprieve to. Now they were too weak to discuss anything.

In spite of his physical weakness Harry was busy. The balustrade beside him looked like the shelves of a hosiery shop: dozens of pairs of silk stockings hung from it or lay in piles on the flagstones beside the brass six-pounder. If you had lifted the dresses of the Krishnapur ladies on that morning of the last assault, you would have found them correspondingly bare-legged, for it was they who had donated their stockings to help solve Harry's difficulty with his brass cannon ... Because, incredible though it may seem, he had fired so many round shot in the course of the siege that the muzzle had been hammered into an ellipse. Such was the distortion that the muzzle would no longer accept round shot; nor would it have accepted canister had not Harry had the idea of tapping the canisters and using silk stockings to contain the iron balls. Beside the brass six-pounder there stood another six-pounder, this one of iron with a longer chase. This cannon, too, had been fired a great deal and although its muzzle had shown no distortion Harry had an uneasy feeling that it might soon be about to burst.

The Collector had gone up to join Ford on the roof because he wanted to be in a position from which he could give the order to retreat at the right moment; in his own mind there was no doubt but that he would have to give it sooner or later. But the cannons on the north-facing ramparts had an essential function if the garrison was to survive the morning; these cannons must break the impetus of the first enemy attack. It was now just light enough on the roof for him to see to load his pistols. He sat cross-legged in the native fashion beside the parapet and listened to the flag stirring restlessly in the light airs above him. Scowling with concentration he began to load the six chambers of his Colt Patent Repeating Pistol with the lead which dragged down one pocket of his scarecrow's morning coat. One by one he filled each chamber with powder and then, without wadding or patch, placed a soft lead ball on its mouth and pulled the long lever beneath the barrel; this lever moved the rammer which forced the lead down into the chamber and sealed it so completely, the Collector had been assured that the powder would still fire even if you immersed your arm completely in water. When he had finished, and the Adams, too, had been loaded, the Collector settled down calmly to wait for the attack. He felt very weak, however, and every so often he retched convulsively, though without vomiting for he had consumed nothing except a little water in the past twenty-four hours. He was inclined to feel giddy, too, and was obliged to support himself against the parapet in order to steady his troubled vision.

The Collector had expected that the attack would begin with the howling warcry he had come to dread, but for once it did not; out of the thin ground mist that lingered in a slight dip in between the churchyard wall and the ruins of the Cutcherry the shapes of men began to appear. Then he heard, faintly but distinctly, the jingle of a bridle. He stood up shakily, then shouted: "Stand to! Prepare to fire!" From the roof his voice echoed over the sleeping plain like that of the muezzin. When they heard it the sepoys threw back their heads and uttered a howl so piercing, so harrowing that every window in the Residency must have dissolved if they had not been already broken. With that, bayonets glistening, they began to charge, converging from every angle of the hemisphere; before they had advanced a dozen yards squadrons of lancers had overtaken them racing for the ramparts.

The Collector waited until he estimated their distance at two hundred yards and shouted: "Fire!" This was at the limit of the effective range of canister but he could afford to wait no longer; his men were so weak, their movements so sluggish that they would need every extra second if they were to re-load and fire another charge before the enemy reached the ramparts. As half a dozen cannons flashed simultaneously at the ramparts, gaps appeared in the ranks of charging men and horses thrashed to the ground ... But the Collector could see that he had given the order to fire too soon. Not enough damage had been done ... It was like watching leaves floating on a swiftly flowing river; every now and then one of the leaves would be arrested against a submerged rock while the great mass of them flowed by even faster on each side. And he could see that the distance was in any case too short: his cannons would never be able to re-load in time. He ought to have waited to fire one really effective salvo at close range. The enemy *sowars* were already on top of the ramparts.

"Spike the guns!" he shouted, but no one could possibly have heard him. Half the men were already straggling back into the Residency building or into the hospital in order to form a new position while the remainder did their best to hold off the sepoys who were already swarming over the ramparts. Some of the sepoys were shot or cut down as they struggled to get over "the possessions" which stuck out jaggedly here and there; a *sowar* pitched headless from his horse on to a silted-up velvet chaise longue; a warrior from Oudh dived head first in a glittering shower through a case of tropical birds while a comrade at his elbow died spreadeagled on the mud-frozen wheels of the gorse bruiser. But this did not delay the charge for more than an instant. More sepoys poured forward over the bodies of their fellows and a number of the defenders who had lingered too long hammering nails into the vents of the cannons were cut down as they tried to make their way back to the shelter of the buildings; many more would have perished had not a small rescuing party which included Rayne, Fleury, half a dozen Sikhs and a couple of Eurasian clerks, wielding sabres and bayonets, surged forward in a sudden counter-attack to surround their companions and drag them back. Fleury, of course, had no business being there at all, but Harry had sent him to the Residency with a message and while passing by he had found the defence so desperately hard pressed that he had forgotten all about Harry. Now he was whirling his sabre in a novel manner, invented by himself to give optimum performance in hand-to-hand combat, and which suggested the sails of a windmill. He had discovered, however, that it was very exhausting but at the same time, once started, felt that it would be unwise to stop, even for a moment. For the moment the sepoys, perplexed by his behaviour, were keeping well out of his way until they could think of some way of dealing with him.

"Get under cover!" yelled the Collector from the roof, not that anyone could possibly hear him. He and Ford had a cannon on the roof loaded with everything that they had been able to lay their hands on: stones, penknives, pieces of lightning-conductor, chains, nails, the embossed silver cutlery from the dining-room, and even some ivory false teeth, picked up by Ford who had seen them gleaming in the undergrowth; but the greater part of the improvised canister was filled with fragments of marble chipped from "The Spirit of Science Conquers Ignorance and Prejudice". Naturally they were anxious to fire this destructive load before it was too late; the angle of the chase was depressed to such an extent that they were afraid that in spite of the wadding the contents of their canister might dribble out . . . already a fountain of glass marbles commandeered from the children had cascaded about the ears of the defenders.

By this time the last of the garrison had fought their way back into the buildings and were trying to defend doors and windows against a swarm of sepoys. The Collector nodded to Ford who was standing by with the portfire. Ford touched it to the vent. There was a flash and a deep roar, followed by utter silence . . . a silence so profound that the Collector was convinced that he could hear two parakeets quarrelling in a tamarind fifty yards away. He peered over the parapet. Below nothing was moving, but there appeared to be a carpet of dead bodies. But then he realized that many of these bodies were indeed moving, but not very much. A sepoy here was trying to remove a silver fork from one of his lungs, another had received a piece of lightning-conductor in his kidneys. A sepoy with a green turban had had his spine shattered by "The Spirit of Science"; others had been struck down by teaspoons, by fish-knives, by marbles; an unfortunate *subadar* had been plucked from this world by the silver sugar-tongs embedded in his brain. A heart-breaking wail now rose from those who had not been killed outright.

"How terrible!" said the Collector to Ford. "I mean, I had no idea that anything like that would happen."

But Ford's only reply was to clutch his ribs and stagger towards the parapet. He had toppled over before the Collector had time to catch his heels.

But already a fresh wave of sepoys was pouring over the ramparts and bounding forward to the attack over that rubbery carpet of bodies. The Collector knew it was time he hurried downstairs . . . he had expected that something like this would happen, but not so quickly. He had not reckoned with the fact that the second charge of canister could not be fired. Just as he was leaving the roof there was a crack which stung his eardrums and the flagpole, struck near the base by a round shot, came down on top of him dealing him a painful blow on the shoulder. He found himself struggling on his back with the stifling presence of the flag wrapped round him like a shroud; the strange thing was that as he weakly continued to struggle (for the staff lay across his legs, pinning him down, and the lanyards had somehow trussed his elbows to his sides), he recognized the sensation immediately: this was a nightmare he had had on the night they had taken refuge in the Residency, and repeatedly since then throughout the siege; when the Collector, cursing, had at last fought his way out of the flag, it was such a relief to escape from his nightmare that he felt he did not mind so much about the sepoys.

Downstairs, the Sikhs, the Magistrate, Rayne, a couple of young ensigns, and a motley collection of indigo planters and Eurasians, were engaged in a desperate fight to keep the sepoys out of the building; but already they were being driven back from doors and windows. The Collector had fortunately laid a plan to meet this contingency. He had ordered the men at the north-facing ramparts and at the churchyard wall to fight their way back through the Residency from room to room towards the hall, from where a dash could be made for the head of the connecting-trench; once safely inside the trench the north-facing cannons of the banqueting hall, firing over their heads, could give them covering fire to complete their withdrawal. But it was essential that the various rooms of the Residency through which they were retreating should be defended and relinquished in concert, so that they should not find themselves outflanked. So the Collector had arranged that the giant Sikh, Hookum Singh, should be at his side in the most central part of the Residency ready to wield the Church bell which had been toppled from its tower earlier in the siege and which only he was strong enough to lift. Beside the door of each room a supply of ready-loaded firearms had been laid; every available weapon from the Enfield rifles of those killed earlier in the siege to native flintlocks and the countless sporting guns which had been such a feature of "the possessions", had been pressed into service. It was the Collector's hope that thus even a few men would be able to keep up a heavy fire.

The Residency itself would be lost: the Collector had never been in doubt about that. The important question was *how* it was lost ... for, at all costs, the momentum of the attack must be broken. He had come to think of the attack as a living creature which derived its nourishment from the speed of its progress. Delay it, and its vitality would ebb. Halt it for a few minutes and it would die altogether. Until now its speed had been so great that it had grown into a ravening monster, capable not only of swallowing the Residency, but of gulping down the banqueting hall as well.

The Collector had posted all the men he could spare on the upper, north-facing verandah. From this vantage point they were to keep up a steady rifle fire on the sepoys advancing over the open ground until they heard the first ringing of the Church bell. In addition they had two camel guns, small cannons which could be mounted on saddles and fired from the backs of camels; for the circumstances these had been mounted on the back of a plush sofa which had been recovered from the rampart where it had served during the rains. Fleury, unaware of the Collector's plans for a graduated retreat because he was not supposed to be in the Residency anyway, had dashed upstairs carrying the fifteen-barrelled pistol with which he was hoping to do battle from the upper storeys. In the first room he looked into, the window space had already been commandeered by two native pensioners and an indigo planter; in the next room he was just in time to see the camel guns fired ... the sofa recoiled on its protesting castors and the men serving the guns set to work to re-load. He hurried down the corridor to the music-room. That should do fine. As he entered, he heard the pealing of a bell reverberating through the building above the din of battle, and he paused a moment, wondering what on earth it could be. But never mind ... no time to worry about things like that. He hefted the pistol towards the window, laid it on the sill, cocked it, put a percussion cap beneath the hammer, directed it at some sepoys trotting below, and pulled the trigger, confident that a sepoy would throw up his arms and sink to the ground. There was a crack, but no sepoy dropped dead; the percussion cap had fired but not the pistol. Fleury uttered a curse and started to examine it, for the life of him he could not see what was the matter. Soon he was absorbed in the workings of the pistol, which was designed according to principles that were new to him. He would not be surprised to find that by using his intelligence he could add one or two significant improvements to this design. Again the great bell rang out. What on earth could it be? The next time it rang he was so absorbed in the problem of getting the pistol to work that he did not notice it; nor the next time either. Or the one after that.

Downstairs, the Collector was becoming desperate. He had just heard the banqueting hall cannons fire, which must mean that the sepoys were attempting an attack from the flank; he hoped that their attack had not succeeded because he and his men had more than they could cope with already. It was not that his plan of fighting from room to room was not working ... on the contrary, it was working to perfection: every room they retired from was crammed with dead and dying sepoys. The only trouble was this: the sepoys kept on bravely coming forward, while he and his men kept on retreating. Against such an onslaught there was nothing much else he could do. They had fought their way backwards through pantries and brushing-rooms and knife rooms, past the European servants' staircase, past the European butler's room, the nurseries, the nursery dining-room, and the *ayah's* rooms, until in the dining-room he knew he would have to make a stand. But the dining-room was too spacious: there the sepoys could use their numbers for a devastating bayonet charge. So, once again, he had to give the signal to Hookum Singh. The giant Sikh's muscles bunched, the veins stood out on his throat and temples, his eyes bulged, and somehow he heaved the great iron bell into the air and swung it back and forth three times, making the walls sing and tremble, before silencing it again on the pulsing floor. Then he dragged it away to the drawing-room. The door into the drawing-room must be defended, no matter what happened ... Otherwise, so quick had been the retreat through the Residency, the men fighting their way back from the hospital and across the yard would find them-selves outflanked and unable to reach the connecting trench. So the Collector and Hookum Singh and half a dozen others prepared themselves to defend the drawing-room door, if necessary with bayonets as well as firearms.

Upstairs, Fleury had taken the pistol to pieces (as far as it could be taken to pieces which did not seem to be very far) and put it together again. He did not believe himself to be any the wiser as regards the reason for it not firing, but he thought he might as well try again.

"I say, you don't happen to know how this blessed thing works, do you?" he asked the person who had just come into the music-room. But he did not wait for a reply before throwing himself to one side as a sabre whistled down and buried itself deep in the brickwork of the window-sill where he had been sitting. Somehow a burly sepoy had found his way into the music-room; this man's only ambition appeared to be to cut Fleury in pieces. Luckily, the blade of the sabre had snapped off and remained embedded in the wall, giving Fleury time to aim the pistol and pull the trigger. But this time there was only a disappointing click; not even the percussion cap fired. Never mind, Fleury had plenty of other weapons. He was now trying to drag one of the wavy-bladed Malayan daggers out of his belt, which was actually a cummerbund; he was having difficulty, though, because the corrugated edges had got caught in his shirt. Well, forget about his dagger, where was his sabre? His sabre, unfortunately, was on the other side of the sepoy (it was a good thing he had not noticed it because it was so sharp that he would have been able to slice Fleury in two without even pressing). Fleury had no time to draw his final weapon, the two-bladed Indian dagger, for his adversary, it turned out, was no less impressively armed than he was himself and he was already flourishing a spare sabre which he had been carrying for just such an emergency.

In desperation Fleury leapt for the chandelier, with the intention of swinging on it and kicking the sepoy in the face. But the chandelier declined to bear his weight and instead of swinging, he merely sat down heavily on the floor in a hail of diamonds and plaster. But as the sepoy lunged forward to put an end to the struggle he stumbled, blinded by the dust and plaster from the ceiling, and fetched up choking on the floor beside Fleury. Fleury again rolled away, tugging at first one dagger, then the other. But both of them refused to yield. His opponent was clumsily getting to his feet as Fleury snatched a violin from a rack of worm-eaten instruments (the survivors of an attempt by the Collector to start a symphony orchestra in the cantonment), snapped it over his knee and leapt on to the sepoy's back, at the same time whipping the violin strings tightly round the sepoy's neck and dragging on them like reins.

The sepoy was a large and powerful man, Fleury had been weakened by the siege; the sepoy had led a hard life of physical combat, Fleury had led the life of a poet, cultivating his sensibilities rather than his muscles and grappling only with sonnets and suchlike . . . But Fleury knew that his life depended on not being shaken off and so he clung on with all his might, his legs gripping the sepoy's waist as tight as a corset, his hands dragging on the two broken pieces of violin. The sepoy staggered off, clutching at the violin strings, out of the music room and down the corridor with Fleury still on his back. He tried to batter his rider against the wall, scrape him off against a fragment of the banisters, but still Fleury held on. They galloped up and down the corridor, blundering into walls and against doors, but still Fleury held on. The man's face had turned black, his eyes were bulging, and at last he crashed to the ground, with such force that he almost shook Fleury off . . . but Fleury remained dragging on the violin until he was certain the sepoy was dead. Then he returned, quaking, to the music-room to collect his sabre. But he was shaking so badly that he had to sit down and have a rest. "Thank heaven for that violin," he thought. "Still, I'd better not stay long with the sepoys attacking . . ." He thought he had better leave the pistol where it was; it was much too heavy to carry around if it was not going to work. He had scarcely made this decision when he looked up. The sepoy was standing there again.

Was he a spectre returning to haunt Fleury? No, unfortunately he was not. The sepoy was no phantasm . . . on the contrary, he looked more consistent than ever. He even had red welts around his throat where the violin strings had been choking him. Moreover, he was chuckling and making humorous observations to Fleury in Hindustani, his eyes gleaming as black as anthracite, pointing at his neck occasionally and shaking his head, as if over an unusually successful jest. Fleury made a dash for his sabre, but the sepoy was much nearer to it

322

and picked it up, making as if to hand it to Fleury, and chuckling more loudly than ever. Fleury faltered backwards as the sepoy advanced, still making as if to offer him the sabre. Fleury tripped over something and sat down on the floor while the sepoy worked his shoulders a little to loosen himself up for a swipe. Fleury thought of jumping out of the window, but it was too high . . . besides, a thousand sepoys were waiting below. The object he had tripped over was the pistol; it was so heavy that it was all he could do to raise it. But when he pulled the trigger, it fired. Indeed, not just one barrel fired, but all fifteen; they were not supposed to, but that was what happened. He found himself confronted now by a midriff and a pair of legs; the wall behind the legs was draped in scarlet. The top half of the sepoy had vanished. So it seemed to Fleury in his excitement, anyway.

The Collector and half a dozen Sikhs were still managing to hold the door into the drawing-room, but only just, They had first closed the door itself, but within seconds it was bristling like a porcupine with glittering bayonets . . . within a few more seconds it had been hacked and splintered to pieces by these bayonets, and now it no longer existed. But while it was being chopped down the Collector and his men had emptied their guns into the hacking sepoys, and the door had become tightly jammed with the dead, many of whom still had bayonets wedged in their lifeless hands. Behind them their live comrades were shoving to force the pile of bodies through into the drawing-room to free the doorway; meanwhile the Collector and the Sikhs were shoving with all their might to hold the bodies in place, although their efforts were hindered by the protruding bayonets. The Collector and Hookum Singh had their backs to this wall of flesh, with bayonets sprouting from between their legs and under their armpits; they were shoving and shoving, and they in turn were being shoved by the other Sikhs, who were struggling to keep them in place. But inch by inch they were being driven back. The Collector found he could hardly breathe in the middle of this appalling sandwich; a few inches from his nose the face of a dead sepoy grinned at him with sparkling teeth; the Collector had the odd sensation that the man's eyes were watching his efforts with amusement. He turned his own eyes away and tried not to think about it. But he was still so close that he could smell the perfume of patchouli on the corpse's mustache.

Slowly but surely the mass of bodies was yielding . . . soon it would be forced out into the drawing-room like the cork out of a bottle of champagne. When they could hold it no longer the Collector shouted the order to retire to the next door: that which led from the drawing-room to the hall and where, several weeks earlier, the Collector had been lurking as he tried to make up his mind to attend the meeting of the Krishnapur Poetry Society. Behind that door would be yet another stack of loaded firearms ready to deal with the next assault. All this time Mr Rayne on one side of the staircase and Mr Worseley on the other, each with half a dozen men, should have been fighting their way back to converge with his own party in the hall. For a few moments, to give Hookum Singh time to get to the hall and ring the bell for the last time, the Collector held the toppling pile of bodies by himself, then he sped across the drawing-room after the Sikhs, his boots crunching broken glass from the cases of stuffed animals; the Sikhs had bare feet, however, and did not crunch it so loudly. Together they barely had time to take up a position at the far door, seize a loaded gun, drop to one knee, and aim as, with a final heave, the bulging mass of bodies exploded into the room, followed by the living.

"Fire!" shouted the Collector, and another morbid volley took effect. "Front rank, bayonets: Second rank, change guns, prepare to fire!"

Again there was a sharp skirmish at the door. Soon the bodies began to pile up here, too, and yet again the Collector and his men had to put their shoulders to the carnal barricade to prevent it from being ejected into the hall; and yet again, as if in a dream, the Collector found his face an inch from that of an amused sepoy and thought: "It surely can't be the same man!" for from this corpse's mustache there was also a scent of patchouli. But the Collector had no time to worry about the locomotion of corpses; this doorway had to be held until the defenders on the other side of the staircase had made good their retreat. A barricade of flagstones prised up from the floor had been erected for a final stand and the Collector, snatching a moment to look back towards it, was dismayed to see that the other party was already behind it, thus leaving himself and his men exposed on the flank. He bellowed at the Sikhs to retreat and as they stumbled back under a cross-fire from the other side of the hall, two of them fell dead and another mortally wounded. Once again there was a flurry of bodies from the doorway they had been defending and another charge. It was now time for the Collector to play his last card.

All this time he had been keeping a reserve force waiting in the library. This "veteran assault force" (as he called it) was composed of the only men left from the cantonment community whom he had not yet made use of, the few elderly gentlemen who had managed to survive the rigours of the siege. Their joints were swollen with rheumatism, their eyes were dimmed with years, to a man they were short of breath and their hands trembled; one old gentleman believed himself to be again taking part in the French wars, another that he was encamped before Sebastopol. But never mind, though their blue-veined old hands might be trembling their fingers could still pull a trigger. It was this force which the Collector now threw into the engagement, though he had to shout the order more than once as their leader, Judge Adams, was rather deaf. From the library they staggered forth with a querulous shout of "Yah, Boney!" Shotguns and sporting rifles went off in their hands. The hall chandelier crashed to the ground and shot sprayed in every direction. For a moment, until the old men had been dragged back to the barricade, all was chaos. The veteran assault force had not been a success.

Again the Collector heard the crash of cannons from the banqueting hall. If they were to escape back through the trench they would have to move quickly; any moment now the sepoys would have crossed the yard from the hospital and outflanked them. At this moment, as if to give substance to the Collector's fears, the Magistrate and two planters came running back along the outside of the Residency wall from the direction of the hospital.

"Where are the others?"

"Dead."

"Get back to the banqueting hall with the old men." The Collector had an unpleasant feeling that unless something unexpected happened he and the Sikhs would find themselves cut off . . . But just then something did happen.

Ever since Ford had pointed out the location of the sepoy magazine Harry had been unable to get it out of his mind. He had even fired a round shot in its direction with the long iron six-pounder at the normal maximum elevation, that is to say, five degrees; the brass six-pounder, of course, no longer consented to swallow round shot. The shot, as he had expected, had fallen short by somewhere between three and four hundred yards.

The difficulty was this: he wanted to increase the elevation to creep forward over those last 300 yards (he did not dare exceed the two-pound charge) but, as every gunner knows, increasing the elevation beyond five degrees can be a risky business; it is not the great number of rounds that destroys a cannon but the high elevation at which it is fired. A gun which at any elevation from point blank to five degrees could stand two hundred rounds without a strain, at thirty degrees would almost certainly burst before fifty rounds had been fired. And this iron six-pounder had already fired heaven only knew how many rounds before coming into Harry's hands at the banqueting hall. But when Fleury came back at last and told him how they were faring in the Residency, Harry knew he would have to take the risk.

The banqueting hall was now filled with ladies and children, refugees from the Residency. Before dawn Harry had set them to work collecting up any combustible material they could find; pieces of shattered furniture, empty ammunition cases, even books. Then, assisted by Ram and Mohammed, he had built a crude furnace of bricks on the verandah in which to heat up the shot. Now his heart was thumping as he turned the elevating screw past five degrees. Until he reached five degrees he had found that it turned easily, through long use . . . but now it became stiff and awkward. Yet Harry continued to turn.

When at last he was satisfied with the elevation he supervised the loading; a dry wad over the cartridge and then a damp one. Then he ordered Ram to serve out the reddest shot he could find in the furnace, watched it loaded and, motioning the pensioners back, himself took the portfire and touched it to the vent. There was a crash. The cannon did not burst. A small, glowing disc swam calmly through the clear morning air trailing sparks. It climbed steeply for some moments and then hung, apparently motionless, like a miniature sun above the sepoy encampment. It dipped swiftly then towards the magazine and smashed through the flimsy, improvised roof. The flash that followed seemed to come not just from the magazine itself but from the whole width of the horizon. The trees on every side of the magazine bent away from it and were stripped of their leaves. A moment later the men who watched it explode from the verandah felt their ragged clothes begin to flap and flutter in the blast. The noise that came with it was heard fifty miles away.

The Collector did not know how the magazine had been blown up but he did not stop to wonder. While the sepoys hesitated, afraid that they were being attacked in the rear, he and the few surviving Sikhs made a dash for the trench and safety.

31

On 17 September, a Thursday, at about ten o'clock in the morning, the Collector found himself in conversation with the Padre. The Collector sat on an oak throne which had been chipped out of the mud rampart for fuel, but had not yet been used, though it had lost one of its front legs. The throne, whose gothic spires rose high above the Collector's head, had been placed on a wooden dais at one end of the banqueting hall. Because of the missing front leg, the Collector had to sit well back and to one side; even so, he sometimes forgot about it and, waving an arm for emphasis, narrowly avoided plunging to the floor; this could have caused him a severe injury since the floor was some way below. The Collector had sat a good deal in this chair over the past few days and it had come to affect his habits of thought. He had found that since the chair discouraged emphasis, it also discouraged strong convictions. It had once even gone so far as to empty him on to the floor for voicing an intolerant opinion on the Jesuits. So now he was gradually coming to see that there were several sides to every question.

For the moment, however, the Collector's mind was idly considering the question of food. It was on just such a dais as this above the feudal retainers, he supposed, that the Saxon thanes would have sat down to trenchers of roasted wild duck and suckling pig. He was numbed by the thought of this imaginary food and could hardly keep his mind on what the Padre was saying. What was it? Oh yes, he was recanting on the Exhibition which, for some reason he had taken to calling "The World's Vanity Fair".

It was true. A terrible knowledge had been swelling slowly in the Padre's mind, like a sweet, poisonous fruit, which for a long time he had not dared to taste. He had committed a grave error in lending his approval, together with that of the Church he represented, to the Exhibition. The Collector had shown such enthusiasm for its hollow wonders that he himself had been tempted and misled; he had allowed his own small stirrings of doubt, which he recognized now to have been stirrings of conscience, to be smothered. Besides, there had been so much in the Exhibition that might be clearly seen as innocuous, if not actually beneficial to God's cause. The Floating Church for Seamen was not the only example ... there were inventions that might also serve God: the pews for the use of the deaf, for example, which could be connected to the pulpit with gutta-percha pipes.

The Padre was very weak now, and could only move from place to place if someone helped him. But he knew that he had one more duty to perform before he allowed himself to succumb to his craving for rest. He must persuade the Collector of his error and make him realize that his veneration for this Vanity Fair of materialism was misplaced. But the Collector refused to pay attention for very long. He would murmur: "Hm, I see, I see," with a distant look in his eye, as if he were hardly listening. Then he would stride away.

This striding away would not have mattered if the Padre had been able to keep up with him ... but the Padre could not move unaided. Sometimes he would have to wait for an hour or more before he could find someone to carry him to the Collector's side. Then, likely as not, he would hardly have had a chance to open his mouth before the Collector would be off again. But the Padre did not give up easily. Besides, the banqueting hall was small and the Collector could not get far. Sometimes, nevertheless, he had to muzzle his temper. He had to muzzle it now, for example, as the Collector suddenly bounded out of his three-legged chair and away. It had taken so long ... it had taken two young ensigns, a native pensioner and a Eurasian clerk to lift him up to this platform, and now he would have to get himself down again! What increased his anger (which the chemistry of his soul swiftly transmuted into love for the Collector) was the fact that no able-bodied person seemed to be looking in his direction. He might remain up here indefinitely without anyone noticing his feeble signals!

As it happened, the Collector would not have minded agreeing with the Padre about the Exhibition. He had come to entertain serious doubts about it himself. He, too, suffered from an occasional enlightening vision which came to him from the dim past and which he must have suppressed at the time ... The extraordinary array of chains and fetters, manacles and shackles exhibited by Birmingham for export to America's slave states, for instance ... Why had he not thought more about such exhibits? Well, he had never pretended that science and industry were good *in themselves*, of course ... they still had to be used correctly. All the same, he should have thought a great deal more about what lay behind the exhibits. Feelings, the Collector now suspected, were just as important as ideas, though young Fleury no longer appeared to think so for he had given up talking of civilization as a "beneficial disease"; he had discovered the manly pleasures to be found in inventing things, in making things work, in getting results, in cause and effect. In short, he had identified himself at last with the spirit of the times. "All our actions and intentions are futile unless animated by warmth of feeling. Without love everything is a desert. Even Justice, Science, and Respectability." The Collector was careful to embrace this conviction in a moderate manner, lest he be tipped out of the chair in which he was no longer sitting.

He had nothing left now from the Exhibition. He had thrown his pistols away since he had no more soft lead balls to use in them. He sighed regretfully as he picked his way slowly through the tattered refugees camped here and there on the floor, wondering what had become of his Louis XVI table. Beauty, of course, and Art, also needed warmth of feeling, there was no getting away from it ... and, in passing, he allowed himself to feel a cautious contempt for the greedy merchants of England for whom the Exhibition had been an apotheosis.

The Collector's eye came to rest on the corner where Miriam lay; she was too weak to help Dr McNab now, but although she could no longer be of any service to the ailing figures who lay nearby, she had refused to let the Collector move her mattress up to the dais where the air was better and where cholera clouds would be less likely to hang (if such things existed, which of course they had been proved not to by Dr McNab, but all the same ...). Not that the air was very bad anywhere now since most of the roof had been removed by round shot and considerable holes had been made in the walls. At night, indeed, it became quite chilly and a fire had to be built in the centre of the hall. It was Louise who usually attended to Miriam, bringing her a ration of water and helping her nearer the fire at night. The Collector's chivalry was aroused by Miriam's weakness, for the heart of a gentleman still beat beneath his ragged morning-coat; besides, he found her an attractive young woman in spite of everything, for she could still smile as sweetly as ever. "Can I do anything for you?" he asked her, thinking absently: "She has a mind of her own."

"I'm perfectly alright. You must consider your other responsibilities," said Miriam, proving it yet again. She smiled, rejecting his chivalry.

"Ah, duty!" sighed the Collector. "Mind you, where would we be without it?"

Of all the ladies who had survived both shot and cholera (for the dreaded disease had taken its toll of the billiard room as of other parts of the garrison) none now displayed greater fortitude than Louise. Although she had come to dislike Dr McNab, believing him to have been indirectly responsible for her father's death, she remained constantly at his side, helping him to care for the sick and wounded. From this pale and anaemic-looking girl who had once thought only of turning the heads of young officers, and whom the Collector had considered insipid, he now saw a young woman of inflexible will-power emerging. He watched her as he passed the section of the hall reserved for the sick, the wounded, and the dying. Her cotton dress was rent almost from the armpit to the hem and as she leaned forward to bring a saucer of water to the lips of a wounded man, the Collector glimpsed three polished ribs and the shrunken globe of her breast; modesty was one of the many considerations which no longer troubled her. She stood up, mopping her brow with the back of a skeleton wrist. The Collector moved on, walking unsteadily. He went out for a few moments and stood on the steps between the Greek pillars, looking in the direction of the Residency for any sign of movement. But he could see none. These pillars, he could not help noticing, were dreadfully pocked and tattered by shot. He thought contemptuously: "So they weren't marble after all." He lingered for a moment sneering at the guilty red core that was revealed beneath the stucco of lime and sand. He hated pretence. But then, with a shrug, he went back inside: this was hardly the time for sneering at pillars.

At the far end of the hall a great pile of earth was growing steadily; here the Sikhs were trying to dig a well. They had run out of water the day before. In spite of their weariness and thirst they declined to drink the water which the Europeans had been using and which was stored in half a dozen hip-baths brought over from the Residency a week earlier (only one of which still contained any water). The Magistrate, nowadays a mere heap of bones decked with cinnamon whiskers, had summoned a little energy with which to pour scorn on the "death by superstition" which faced the brave Sikhs. The Sikhs, ignoring him, had been digging steadily for hours; now they were beginning to shovel up wet earth. The Collector sat on his heels by the edge of the pit and watched for a few minutes before continuing on his way.

Outside on the verandah the sun was shining with the crisp brilliance of the Indian winter. What a lovely day it was! In spite of everything the Collector felt his spirits lift as he sat down beside Lucy on a sheltered corner of the verandah and watched her making cartridges. Mingled with the brimstone smell of burned powder he fancied that he could smell the perfume of roses from the Residency garden, pruned this year by musket fire. Then the smell of warm grass came to join that of the roses and gunpowder and he fell asleep for a few moments, dreaming of cricket fields and meadows. When he awoke Lucy was still at his side and the position of the sun had hardly changed.

For the first three or four days after the Residency had been abandoned a number of the ladies had been employed in making cartridges; now, because of the shortage of lead for the moulds, the job had been left to Lucy, who had become extraordinarily skilful. She sat cross-legged, like a native in the bazaar, surrounded by her implements ... the knife and the straight edge for cutting the cartridge paper, the wooden mandrels for rolling the paper into shape, the powder flask, the two-and-a-half dram tin measures for measuring out the powder ... and finally, alas, the pot of grease, the cause of all the trouble. Lucy's grease, however, was a mixture of beeswax and rancid butter. A Hindu could have eaten a pound of it with pleasure.

The Collector watched with admiration as Lucy's deft fingers dipped a cartridge up to the shoulder in the grease and then set it neatly in a row with the others she had made. At intervals the defenders would come from one part or another of the ramparts to collect a supply of them; but for the moment the firing was slack. The sepoys must be well aware that the garrison's ammunition was all but finished. They could tell by what was being fired at them. They knew that in another day or two they would not even have to charge the ramparts; they would merely have to step over them and kill off the garrison as they pleased. But of course, by then the garrison would have blown itself up.

The Collector, in a remote and academic sort of way, was musing on this question of ammunition, considering whether there was anything left which still might be fired. But surely they had thought of everything. All the metal was gone, first the round objects, then the others. Now they were on to stones. Without a doubt the most effective missiles in this matter of improvised ammunition had been the heads of his electro-metal figures, removed from their bodies with the help of Turtons' indispensable file. And of the heads, perhaps not surprisingly, the most effective of all had been Shakespeare's; it had scythed its way through a whole astonished platoon of sepoys advancing in single file through the jungle. The Collector suspected that the Bard's success in this respect might have a great deal to do with the ballistic advantages stemming from his baldness. The head of Keats, for example, wildly festooned with metal locks which it had proved impossible to file smooth had flown very erratically indeed, killing only a fat money-lender and a camel standing at some distance from the field of action.

A few other metal objects had been fired, such as clocks and hair brushes ... but they had proved quite useless. Candlesticks filed into pieces and collected in ladies' stockings had served for canister for a while, but had been swiftly exhausted. Then a find had been made. Poor Father O'Hara had contracted cholera and died shortly after the withdrawal to the banqueting hall; when his body had been heaved over the ramparts for the jackals and pariah dogs (the only way that remained for disposing of the dead), a number of heavy metal beads, crosses, Saints and Virgins had been discovered in his effects. The Padre, consulted as to the propriety of firing them at the enemy, had given his opinion that they could perfectly well be fired and that they, or any other such popish or Tractarian objects, would very likely wreak terrible havoc. However, this did not seem to have been the case, particularly, except for the metal beads.

There was a small explosion at the ramparts several yards away, but it was nothing to worry about . . . only Harry trying to free the long, iron six-pounder in which the head of a French cynic, Voltaire, had become jammed . . . rather surprisingly, the Collector thought, a narrow, lozenge-shaped head like that; Harry had been unable to ram the head home to the cartridge and so, according to normal procedure, was obliged to destroy the charge by pouring water down the vent; followed by a small quantity of powder, also through the vent, to blow out his makeshift shot. Harry had worked as tirelessly as his sister for the last few days; now he sank down on to a stool beside his cannon out of sheer weakness, and began to weep at the thought of the wasted powder and the wasted water resulting from this misfortune. However, he had successfully blown Voltaire's head out of the bore of the six-pounder; it rolled over the rampart and landed among the skeletons, scattering the pariah dogs who were sunning themselves there while waiting for their next meal to be heaved over.

"The sepoys are very quiet," the Collector called to Harry conversationally to stop him weeping, because now Lucy was starting and he was afraid that she would spoil the powder by dropping tears into the flask.

"D'you think they're going to attack?"

"I expect so." Harry dried his eyes on a piece of wadding, annoyed with himself.

"There's one thing . . . the spectators have got tired of waiting, anyway."

The melon beds had been virtually deserted for the last two or three days. Only a lonely rajah or two was to be seen now, solitary figures surrounded by servants, watching through elaborate brass telescopes acquired at one or other of the Euro-

pean stores in Calcutta. At night there were no longer any bonfires to be seen, either on the hill or way out on the surrounding plain.

The Collector heard shuffling and heavy breathing and knew,
though the breathing was not the Padre's, that the Padre was
nevertheless approaching. He could have told this without turning to look; but he did turn, because he did not want to give the
Padre the impression that he was avoiding him. The Padre was
strung limply between the shoulders of a young ensign and of
an ancient pensioner, both of whom looked ill, worn out, and
exasperated. They laid the Padre down at the Collector's side
as instructed and arranged his limbs in a suitable position of
repose.

"There was something I forgot to mention to you earlier,"
said the Padre, who did not normally favour such a blunt
approach but felt that given the state of his health there might
not be any time to lose . . . This time he was determined to go
as straight as an arrow aimed at Saint Sebastian to the core of
the problem, as he saw it.

"I'm referring to a leading article which appeared in *The
Times* concerning the Exhibition and which I should like to
read you (by a fortunate chance I happen to have it on my
person). It goes as follows: 'So man is approaching a more
complete fulfilment of that great and sacred mission which he
has to perform in this world. His image being created in the
image of God, he has to discover the laws by which the
Almighty governs His creation; and, by making these laws his
standard of action, to conquer nature to his use, himself a
divine instrument.' Hm, I wonder did you hear that, Mr Hopkins, or should I read it again?"

"Thank you, Padre. I heard it perfectly and found it most
interesting."

"It seems to me, Mr Hopkins, that the doctrine of this passage has no foundation whatsoever in the word of God. If we
turn to the history of man's creation in the sacred volume, we
find that his mission was simply to dress and keep the garden of
Eden and to serve and obey his Creator . . . and that, so far
from having any mission to pry into the laws by which the
Almighty governs His creation, he was expressly forbidden to
do so. The only forbidden tree in the garden was the tree of

science and intellect. It is a remarkable fact, Mr Hopkins, that the argument used by the serpent to seduce Eve from her allegiance to her Creator is almost precisely that used by the Editor of *The Times*: 'Ye shall be as GODS, knowing good and evil' . . . that is, as wise as God Himself!"

The Collector's mind had wandered yet again, though he nodded intelligently from time to time, hoping thus to soothe the Padre. But his concentration was poor these days: he could hardly keep his mind on anything for more than a moment . . . and even when he heard what the Padre said it made no sense . . . "the Editor of *The Times* as wise as God Himself!" Really, what rubbish. As the Padre's feeble voice continued to denounce the Editor of *The Times* the Collector lifted his eyes to the sky where, as always, the kites and vultures were circling.

The Collector was fond of vultures and did not share the usual view of them as sinister and ominous creatures. By their diligent eating of carcases they had probably spared the garrison an epidemic or a pestilence, but that was not what the Collector liked about them . . . though clumsy on the ground, their flight was extraordinarily graceful. They climbed higher than any other birds, it seemed; they ascended into the limitless blue until they became lost to sight or mere specks, drifting round and round in a free flight in which their wings scarcely seemed to move. They more resembled fish than birds, gliding in gentle circles in a clear pool of infinite depth. The Collector would have liked to watch them all day. Their flight absorbed him completely. He thought of nothing while he watched them, he shed his own worries and experienced their freedom, no longer bound by his own dull, weak body.

He was obliged to return to earth, however, by signs of excitement at the ramparts, which doubtless heralded another attack . . . and by the Padre who had asked him a question and was waiting with signs of impatience for his reply.

"Well . . . " said the Collector cautiously, "of course it's a matter of opinion . . ." He had not heard the question but hoped that this reply would serve. The excitement was increasing and he looked anxiously towards the rampart, afraid that the attack might develop before he even saw what was happening. Alas, the Padre was evidently not satisfied. A look of despair, of righteous anger came over his face. Suddenly, to the Collector's astonishment, the Padre gripped him by the throat and shouted: "A matter of opinion! The Crystal Palace was built in the form of a *cathedral*! A cathedral of Beelzebub!"

"I say," said a voice a little distance away. "We've come to relieve you."

"A cathedral of Baal! A cathedral of Mammon!" The Collector, trying to prise the Padre's fingers from his throat and at the same time turn his head, was just able to see a pink young face with a blonde mustache surmounting a brilliant scarlet tunic. This man was peering winningly over the rampart.

"I say, d'you mind if we come in. We've come to relieve you."

The young man who had peered over the rampart to see this extraordinary collection of scarecrows was known to more than one of the garrison of Krishnapur, for he was none other than that Lieutenant Stapleton who had danced so often with Louise in Calcutta the previous cold season and who had been given a lock of blonde curls as a keepsake; he had made a point of wearing this lock of hair next to the rather wispy blonde hair that grew on his own chest. Louise had hardly been out of his thoughts for a moment during the past six weeks while the relieving force, under the command of General Sinclair, had been advancing circumspectly over the plains. It had not seemed possible to him that the fair creature could still be alive, for messages from native sources had indicated that Krishnapur had been invested since the beginning of June. And if she were dead, what had happened to her before dying did not bear thinking about (though he did think about it, all the same).

The men of the relieving force, which was a large one, handsomely equipped with field batteries, were not surprised to find Krishnapur deserted as they advanced in the direction of the iron bridge. The "pandies" usually decamped. As they marched through the empty streets, however, a little old man put himself in front of the marching column and led the way, beating a kettle-drum and pronouncing the restoration of the *Company Bahadur*.

When they reached the sepoy lines it was pretty obvious

that the mutineers had been there not long before; fires were still burning and private belongings lay scattered about. From the sepoy lines they could see that the Residency had been abandoned, but a tattered Union Jack still flew over the banqueting hall. They were not too late! Lieutenant Stapleton asked the General, who was his uncle, if he might ride over first, and the General obligingly agreed.

As he trotted his horse forward over the intervening space Lieutenant Stapleton noticed two giant white faces smiling at him with understanding and compassion. There was something about those faces, however, that made him uneasy and coming nearer he saw that they had been terribly pocked by round shot and musket fire, as if by a disfiguring disease. On the outside of the rampart there was an astonishing collection of white skeletons which he tried not to look at but which rattled unpleasantly as the jackals took to their heels at his approach. He could not help wondering why a rousing cheer had not gone up as soon as the garrison had spotted his red uniform. He understood it a little better when he saw what a state the survivors were in. They stared at him as you might stare at orange rats trying to get into bed with you. Lieutenant Stapleton suddenly realized with a shock of fear that he was lucky not to have been shot down by one of these tattered lunatics.

Gradually, though, as the rest of the column led by his uncle on a fine white horse arrived, the survivors who could walk came out of the banqueting hall and allowed themselves to be greeted by the relieving troops. The General could see that the garrison were having trouble adjusting themselves to the new state of things and so, to give them time, he called for iced sherry and soda to be served. The poor devils looked as though they could do with some refreshment. On second thoughts he also sent one of his aides to fetch blankets as well, for some of the ladies did not seem to be very decently attired and, although they did not look very enticing, he still did not want them to give his men ideas. He had never seen Englishmen get themselves into such a state before; they looked more like untouchables.

Lieutenant Stapleton had managed to recognize Louise without too much trouble, though her appearance had given him a bit of a surprise. It was when he went to embrace her, mur-

338

muring: "Don't worry, my dear, you're safe now," that he got a really severe shock . . . for she stank. Then, as he was trying to think of something to say to her (all the speeches he had prepared had somehow been predicated on the fact that, although in distress, she would be lovely, well dressed, and as sweet-smelling as he remembered her), an emaciated individual in a green jacket pushed his way rudely between them. This rude fellow in the green jacket had an advantage over Lieutenant Stapleton . . . he seemed able to get closer to Louise without discomfort than he could himself, no doubt because he stank worse than she did. The three young people stood in a rather hostile and malodorous silence waiting for something to happen. Lieutenant Stapleton was very conscious of the thick cloud of flies that buzzed round each of his companions.

"Well, we've relieved you, eh?" said the General to the Collector, trying to break the ice. "Nick of time, what." This Collector-wallah was a devilishly hard fellow to talk to, he was finding. He'd heard stories about him in Calcutta and half expected something of the sort. Mind you, he'd probably been through a sticky time. "Now, where's that sherry pawnee?"

Lucy, all this time, was still sitting on the verandah surrounded by her cartridge-making tools and weeping bitterly as she looked at the neat rows of cartridges she had made and which were no longer needed. She dried her eyes presently because she realized that the Magistrate was watching her from not far away. The Magistrate often watched her. He approached her now and sat beside her, saying: "Well, the relief has arrived after all." A rent in her dress, oddly similar in position though not as severe as the one in Louise's, permitted him to see her breasts which, sadly deflated by hunger, were no longer like plump carp (they were more like plaice or Dover sole). The Magistrate put a companionable hand on her shoulder and then, after a moment's hesitation, slipped it on to the back of her neck. Perhaps Lucy would have melted weakly into his bony arms had not an expression of dismay and incredulity come over his face. She promptly slapped him as hard as she could, which was not very hard. She did not know what the matter was but knew instinctively that this was the right thing to do. And it was just as well that she did so because Harry appeared at that moment, to lead her out for sherry and soda.

"How dare he, that despicable atheist!" cried Harry, both indignant with the Magistrate and gratified by Lucy's response. The Magistrate, mortified, had made himself scarce.

The Padre had wasted no time in equipping himself with fresh and healthy bearers and now had himself carried with exhilarating swiftness in a litter to where the Collector was standing with the General.

"Think of the American vacuum coffin guaranteed to preserve corpses from decomposing! Was that not against the word of God who decreed: 'Dust unto dust?' Think of the countless statues of unclothed young women. Think of the male statues which are even now being exposed at Sydenham without adequate covering and which may be viewed by innocent girls!"

The Collector sighed but said nothing. The General also could find no comment, but eyed the Padre nervously.

Quite suddenly, after they had refreshed themselves, the members of the garrison began to talk; soon they were babbling away garrulously to their deliverers, laughing, cheering and even singing. The General beamed; things were going much better now. But then, one by one, they began to topple over like skittles, and in no time the green, shot-scarred turf was littered with unconscious figures. The General shouted for litter-bearers and retired to his tent in a bad mood for a bath and a change of clothes. Even when allowances were made, the "heroes of Krishnapur", as he did not doubt they would soon be called, were a pretty rum lot. And he would have to pose for hours, holding a sword and perched on a trestle or wooden horse while some artist-wallah depicted "The Relief of Krishnapur"! He must remember to insist on being in the foreground, however; then it would not be so bad. With luck this wretched selection of "heroes" would be given the soft pedal ... an indistinct crowd of corpses and a few grateful faces, cannons and prancing horses would be best.

32

Crossing for the last time that stretch of dusty plain which lay between Krishnapur and the railhead, the Collector experienced more strongly than ever before the vastness of India; he realized then, because of the widening perspective, what a small affair the siege of Krishnapur had been, how unimportant, how devoid of significance. As they crept slowly forward over the plain his eyes searched for those tiny villages made of mud with their bamboo groves and their ponds; and though the plain was perfectly flat the villages were somehow hidden in its folds, blending with it. When they paused near one of these villages to rest the horses the Collector remained in the carriage and watched the men drawing water from the well, drawing it up in a huge leather bag with the help of their bullocks, and he knew that the same two men and two bullocks would do this every day until the end of their lives. And this was the last impression the Collector had of India. When he thought of India in later years he would always see these two men and two bullocks and the leather bag flooding out its water as it settled on the ground.

There is nothing much more to be said about the siege of Krishnapur. It is surprising how quickly the survivors returned to the civilized life they had been living before. Only sometimes in dreams the terrible days of the siege, which were like the dark foundation of the civilized life they had returned to, would return years later to visit them: then they would awake, terrified and sweating, to find themselves in white starched linen, in a comfortable bed, in peaceful England. And all would be well.

It may be said that, although he survived it, the siege nevertheless had a bad effect on the Collector. When he returned to England from Calcutta, which he did as soon as he was well enough to travel, he did not take up the glorious and interesting life that was waiting for him there, as one would have expected.

Instead, he resigned from Fine Arts committees, and antiquarian societies, and societies for reclaiming beggars and prostitutes; nor did his interest in crop rotation appear to have survived the siege. He took to pacing the streets of London, very often in the poorer areas, in all weathers, alone, seldom speaking to anyone but staring, staring as if he had never seen a poor person in his life before. As he grew older, however, he gave up walking and seldom stirred from his club in St James; there he could be seen reading newspapers, endlessly, indiscriminately, about great events and small in the order they appeared on the page. But he was never heard to say what he thought (if, indeed, he thought anything at all) about this vast amount of random detail he must have accumulated in his later years. He took to eating and drinking too much also, that most gentle of all the sins. He grew very portly as an old man and although by this time he had become something of a legend to the other members of his club ("The Hero of Krishnapur"), one might have thought that he himself had entirely forgotten about the siege.

But one day, in the late seventies, he and Fleury happened to come face to face in Pall Mall and, after a moment, succeeded in recognizing each other. Fleury, too, had grown stout and perhaps rather opinionated; he and Louise had a number of children whom Fleury was inclined to hector with his views, showing extreme displeasure if they disagreed with him. The two men fell into step together; the old gentleman's pace, however, was a little too slow for Fleury who kept having to master an impulse to stride on firmly, as was his custom. Conversation was more difficult than one might have expected. They exchanged some fragments of personal news. Fleury told the Collector that his brother-in-law, General Dunstaple, who had married Miss Hughes that was, still lived in India and was currently, according to their most recent mail, shooting tigers in Nepal. His own sister, Miriam, the Collector probably did not know, had subsequently married Dr McNab and they, too, had remained in India.

"Ah yes, McNab," said the Collector thoughtfully. "He was the best of us all. The only one who knew what he was doing." He smiled, thinking of the invisible cholera cloud, and after a moment he added: "I was fond of your sister. I don't suppose I shall see her again."

Half anxious to be on his way, for he had an appointment with a young lady of passionate disposition, Fleury asked the Collector about his collection of sculpture and paintings. The Collector said that he had sold them long ago.

"Culture is a sham," he said simply. "It's a cosmetic painted on life by rich people to conceal its ugliness."

Fleury was taken aback by this remark. He himself had a large collection of artistic objects of which he was very proud.

"There, Mr Hopkins, I cannot agree with you," he declared loudly. "No, culture gives us an idea of a higher life to which we aspire. And *ideas*, too, are a part of culture . . . No one can say that ideas are a sham. Our progress depends on them . . . Think of their power. Ideas make us what we are. Our society is based on ideas . . ."

"Oh, ideas . . ." said the Collector dismissively.

But now Fleury really *had* to go. The old fellow walked so slowly and he himself was late already. And so Fleury raised his hat, shook hands, and hurried away. He was glad to have met the Collector again, but he had the uncomfortable feeling of many things left unsaid. Well, never mind . . . nobody has time to settle everything.

The years go by and the Collector undoubtedly felt, as many of us feel, that one uses up so many options, so much energy, simply in trying to find out what life is all about. And as for being able to do anything about it, well . . . It is hard to tell what he was thinking during this last conversation with Fleury when he said: "Oh, ideas . . ." After all, McNab had been right, had he not? The invisible cholera cloud had moved on. Perhaps he was thinking again of those two men and two bullocks drawing water from the well every day of their lives. Perhaps, by the very end of his life, in 1880, he had come to believe that a people, a nation, does not create itself according to its own best ideas, but is shaped by other forces, of which it has little knowledge.

Afterword

The reality of the Indian Mutiny constantly defies imagination. Those familiar with the history of the time will recognize countless details in this novel of actual events taken from the mass of diaries, letters and memoirs written by eyewitnesses, in some cases with the words of the witness only slightly modified; certain of my characters also had their beginnings in this material. Among the writers whom I have cannibalized in this way are Maria Germon and the Rev. H. S. Polehampton of Lucknow, F. C. Scherer, and the admirable Mark Thornhill who was the Collector at Muttra at the time of the Mutiny. The verses admired by Mr Hopkins at the meeting of the Krishnapur Poetry Society are taken from an epic poem by Samuel Warren Esq celebrating the Great Exhibition, a work which had a great success in its day, though dismissed by one reviewer as "the ravings of a madman in the Crystal Palace".

Lastly, I am most grateful to Mrs Anthony Storr for letting me see family letters relating to the Mutiny, and to the historians, too numerous to mention individually, on whom I have relied for the facts of Victorian life to support my fiction. It has, however, been on my conscience since the first edition of this book that I have not specifically acknowledged my debt to Professor Owen Chadwick's work on the Victorian Church and to M. A. Crowther's *Religious Controversy of the Mid-Nineteenth Century*.